EDDIE'S BASTARD

EDDIE'S BASTARD

A NOVEL

WILLIAM KOWALSKI

HarperCollins*Publishers*

HarperCollins books may be purchased for educational, business, or sales promotional use. For information please write: Special Markets Department, HarperCollins Publishers Inc., 10 East 53rd Street, New York, NY 10022.

FIRST EDITION

Designed by Philip Mazzone

Library of Congress Cataloging-in-Publication Data

ISBN 0-06-019355-7

99 00 01 02 / 10 9 8 7 6 5 4 3 2 1

For
McKinley Patrick Miller
and
In Memory of Dale

ACKNOWLEDGMENTS

Although writing is essentially a solitary endeavor, no writer can accomplish a work of any magnitude without the support of those friends and family who believe in him and in what he is doing. Mary Ingram Waugh was the first person to read this story in its earliest form, and it was she who convinced me that it was worth finishing; without her encouragement, this book would most likely not exist. My father, Dr. William John Kowalski Jr., unquestioningly and unhesitatingly supported me while this novel was in the final phase of completion. At the same time, my mother, Kathleen Emily Siepel, generously provided me with a quiet place to work. My friend and mentor, W. S. "Jack" Kuniczak, himself a novelist of formidable talent and achievement, gave me the advice and encouragement I needed whenever I needed it, which was often. And Peter Nash, also a gifted writer and a selfless teacher, had the decency and kindness to point out in exactly the right way that the book was not actually done when I thought it was, that I needed to take a deep breath, collect my thoughts, and begin yet again—a lesson for which I will be forever in his debt.

The following people also helped me a great deal, whether they knew it or not: my brother, Patrick; my sister, Laura; Chris Maher; Heather Lovaglio; Dr. Ken Schiff, my first writing instructor and a good friend, and Marie, Rebecca, and Nick Schiff; Anita Iannello; Loretta Frankovitch; Lhasa de Sela; Bob and Laurie Martin; Annie and Ezra Nash; Paul Schmidt; Dave Beltran-del-Rio; Patricia Beltran-del-Rio; Bill Blais; Dr. Jorge Aigla; the entire Andrae family; Esther Woodruff; Anne Windom; Kevin Siepel; Tom Zimolzak; Tony, Anita, Emily, and Dante Stefanelli; Timothy March; Jonathan Cramer; John Hawkins; Father Hildebrand Greene; Jim Kerr; Chris Sarko Kerr; Jodi and Payton Kelly; Sandie Stefurak; and the indomitable Markus Greisshammer.

I will never have adequate words to thank my agent, Anne Hawkins of John Hawkins and Associates, whose tireless energy, patience, and devotion to her trade have been an example in many ways, and without whose vision I would not have been able to achieve this final step of publication.

I also wish to thank my editor at HarperCollins, Marjorie Braman, whose sweet nature and insightful comments were of invaluable help to me in the difficult process of revising this book, and whose confidence in me has been the source of renewed inspiration.

Finally, to all my teachers, friends, and family members who are not mentioned here by name—every one of you who has touched me has helped me on my way, and you will have my gratitude always.

Just as the mightiest oak topples without its roots,
so will a man without knowledge of his people come
crashing to earth, dreamless and unfulfilled.
We cannot hope to understand ourselves until we
know something of those who have come before us.

William A. Mann III
from the diary, c. 1885

I Am Born; Grandpa Discovers Me, and I Am Named; I Learn to Read; the Ghosts; I Encounter Annie Simpson

I arrived in this world the way most bastards do—by surprise. That's the only fact about myself that I knew at the beginning of my life. At the very beginning, of course, I knew nothing. Babies are born with minds as blank as brand-new notebooks, just waiting to be written in, and I was no exception. Later, as I grew older and learned things—as the pages of the notebook, so to speak, became filled up—I began to make certain connections, and thus I discovered that among children I was unusual. Where others had a mother, I had none; father, same; birth certificate, none; name, unknown. And as soon as I was old enough to understand that babies didn't just appear from midair, I understood that my arrival was not just a mystery to myself. It was a strange occurrence to everyone who knew me.

Nobody seemed to know where I was born, or exactly when, or to whom. Nor did anyone know where I was conceived. How, of course, was obvious. Contrary to my earliest notions, babies don't just appear, though in my case this seemed entirely possible. Somewhere, sometime, my father had sex with my mother, and here I am.

In the space for *mother*, then, there is nothing but a blank.

I know who my father is—or was, rather. He was Eddie Mann, Lieutenant, USAF (dec.). The *dec.* stands for *deceased*. At one time, I had my own suspicions of who my mother was, and so did everyone else who knew me. They were all vague and unprovable, however, and suspicions are best left to the tabloids, which I read sometimes while waiting in line at the supermarket.

I confess to a weakness for tabloids; they stimulate my imagination, get me to thinking that perhaps the impossible is not so far removed as we might think. My favorite articles are the ones about Bat Boy, half human child and half bat, which someone claims to have found in a cave somewhere in the South. I sympathize with Bat Boy, even though I don't believe in him. I imagine myself having lengthy conversations with him, teaching him how to play baseball, being his friend. Like me, his appearance was unexpected, and nobody seems to know quite what to do with him.

My imagination—the part of my mind that allows me to believe in Bat Boy—also stretches back to the time before I was born, and before. I see my mother, a pregnant young girl, panicked but with a strong conscience, and some desire to see me succeed in life. She gives birth to me in secret somewhere: a train station, a taxi, under a tree in the middle of the forest. Then, after I'm born, she—a princess, a faerie queen, Amelia Earhart—deposits me on the back steps of the ancestral Mann home in Mannville, New York, where my father had been born and raised—as had his father, and his father before him. This is where my imagination is relieved of duty and the facts take over. This part of the story really happened.

It was the third of August, 1970. My grandfather, the herbalist and failed entrepreneur Thomas Mann Junior (no relation to the writer of the same name), who lived alone and abandoned in the farmhouse, found me there. Like some character in a Dickens novel, I'd been wrapped in a blanket and placed inside a picnic basket. Many years later, I was to discover that Grandpa had saved the picnic basket, a deed for which I've always been profoundly grateful. For years, it was my greatest treasure. It was the one thing in the world I was sure my mother had touched.

It was just after dawn, and the day was Grandpa's birthday.

Grandpa celebrated his birthday the same way he celebrated every other day: he drank whiskey, sitting alone at the scarred and ancient kitchen table. He drank whiskey in the morning, drank it for his lunch, drank before dinner, and drank after dinner. Sometimes he didn't bother to eat dinner at all. Eating sobered him up, and that was unpleasant; he preferred to be drunk. But today there was something unusual going on, something to break the monotony of his drunkenness. It was my crying. Grandpa heard it dimly, out of the corner of his ear, as it were. It sounded familiar. It was a noise he'd heard before, but he couldn't quite place it.

"Chickens," he said to himself. I know he said this because later he was to tell me the whole story over and over again. There were no chickens left on our farm anymore and hadn't been for years, but sometimes he forgot this. Grandpa, when drunk, remembered better days, when chickens on the farm meant prosperity and things going right. In those days the farm was still operating, the crops were still growing, my father was still just a baby, the Ostriches had yet to wreak their havoc upon our future, and chickens roamed free. In Grandpa's sodden and inebriated mind, chickens meant hope, and they had to be protected.

So he interrupted his drinking. He stepped out the kitchen door to see if there were foxes in the chicken coop, which, though long deserted, still stood. Instead of foxes, however, he found me.

Years afterward, Grandpa told me he'd nearly stepped on me as he came out the door. The sudden roar of a military jet overhead had caused him to stop his foot in midair as he looked up. It saved my life.

"Thank God for that jet," Grandpa said, "or I would have squashed you like the little bug you were."

It was the year the polluted Cuyahoga River burst into flames and burned for three days. The nation, divided by Vietnam, was united in its horror at the alchemic spectacle of flaming water; the beginning of my life coincided with a growing awareness that the world was polluted and dying, and that it was our own fault. I've always considered that event an omen of my birth. A flaming river is a symbol, it seems, of something powerful. Rivers are time. They run and run, always forward, never backward, sometimes fast and sometimes slow, just like the steady stream of days that make up our lives. And fire is cleansing, fire is power. The Phoenix was born in fire. Prometheus stole fire from the gods. Fire has to happen. It clears forests of debris, and tiny new plants spring up afterward; eventually a new forest is born, and the fire is forgotten until it returns.

Flaming river. Power over time, time as catharsis. If we Manns had a family crest, that's what it would be.

Another omen of my coming was the appearance of the military jet. It was an F–4 Phantom, the same kind of fighter jet my father Eddie flew in Vietnam. There was no reason for it to be flying over a rural town in western New York that day, or any other day. In fact, there are no Air Force bases within a hundred miles of Mannville. There are some parts of the country where mysterious aircraft appear all the time, but Mannville isn't one of them.

Grandpa recognized it as an F–4 from the photo Eddie had sent home several months earlier. In that photo, which I still have, my father is standing in front of his plane, a hotshot, a pilot extraordinaire, already with two kills to his credit. He was just twenty-one years old. He's bare-chested and muscular, arms crossed, teeth bared in a dazzling smile. The hazy blueness of his eyes is noticeable even on black-and-white film.

There was no doubt in Grandpa's mind about whose son I was. I had the same eyes as my father, and Grandpa recognized them immediately. "All babies have blue eyes when they're born," he said later, as he was telling me the story of my arrival, "but most grow out of 'em. Mann eyes are always blue, come hell or high water. And they're not the same blue as other families. Take the Simpsons up the hill. They've got eyes like muddy water. Blue, but muddy, like there was some brown mixed in there. You can tell everything about a man by his eyes. There's not a member of our family that's lost a staring contest yet. As for those Simpsons—stay the hell away from them. Folks with eyes like that have got plenty to hide."

On that late summer morning in 1970, Grandpa stopped and stared at the spectacle of a baby in a basket on his own doorstep, completely astounded—"beard brushin' my boots," as he later put it, even though he didn't have a beard. He looked around suspiciously to see who might have left me there. Nobody was in sight. The property, though not as large as it had been before the Fiasco of the Ostriches, was still large, and it would have been easy for anyone to hide behind the many trees and bushes that were scattered throughout the vast yard. But there was no one. Off behind the garage, which had once been a fancy carriage house, there was a faint rustling of bushes, but that might have been the wind, or a dog, or anything. Grandpa chose not to think it was my mother, whoever she was, hiding and watching to make sure I was discovered before I perished of hunger. Some poor young girl had left me there, he was thinking; doubtless she had her reasons.

Already his mind was working, turning over various possibilities. Eddie had had a lot of girlfriends, and could have had lots more if he'd wanted them. The girls of Mannville fell for him like dominoes. No one could blame them. My father was irresistibly handsome.

Nor could Grandpa blame my father for getting someone pregnant; accidents happened. It was a simple matter of biology.

Grandpa decided he would not force her to identify herself. He ignored the rustling and focused on me instead. Scotch-taped to my basket was a note. On one side it said, in large printed letters: EDDIE'S BASTARD.

Well now, Grandpa thought—or told me he thought later—that's not a very nice way of putting it. He reconsidered flushing whoever she was out of the bushes. But the rustling had stopped. If my mother had ever been there, she was gone.

And that's pretty much how I've come to think of myself—Eddie's Bastard, plain and simple. It's not a very dignified title, but it's a title nonetheless, and I've learned to bear it, if not with pride, then at least without shame.

On the other side, in meticulous Palmer script, the note read:

July 15, 1970

1 gallon milk
1/4 lb. cheese
1/2 doz. apples
1 loaf bread

It was a receipt from Gruber's Grocery. Grandpa examined it carefully. He could show the note to Harold and Emily Gruber and ask if they remembered who had bought these items on the fifteenth of July.

That way he could find out who had left me on the steps.

"It was almost as if she *wanted* me to figure out who she was," Grandpa told me later. "Either that, or she wasn't very smart."

But he would do that later. At the moment, my wailing filled him with paternal tenderness and anxiety. He picked up the basket, brought me inside the house, and set me on the kitchen table, where he sat looking at me.

"Ahh, Eddie," he said, "if only you'd lived long enough to see him."

Then, Grandpa said, he began to cry, because my handsome and popular father had been shot down over the South China Sea three months earlier, and no parachute had been sighted.

We sat crying together, Grandpa and I, the last remnants of the once-great Mann family, I because I was hungry and Grandpa because he was sad. Then Grandpa dried his eyes, put me in the front seat of his Galaxie, and drove to the doctor's office in town.

The doctor's office wasn't really an office; it was the first floor of the doctor's house, and Doctor Connor was Grandpa's best—in fact, his only—friend. Doctor Connor looked up in surprise as Grandpa came marching through his front parlor with a screaming infant in a basket.

"Give 'im the once-over and see if he needs a tune-up," said Grandpa, who was always a mechanic at heart. "I aim to keep him."

"Where in the hell—?" asked the doctor, interrupting his own question by peering into the basket at me.

"I don't know for sure," said Grandpa. "But he's a Mann. You can see that a mile off."

"There's tests for that now, if you want me to run one," said Doctor Connor as he tickled the bottoms of my feet. My toes curled, and Doctor Connor smiled in satisfaction. "Might take a couple of weeks."

"I don't need any goddamn test to know my own flesh and blood," said Grandpa. "You just make sure everything's where it's supposed to be. I'll be right back. I got to go get some Formula One."

"Formula," Doctor Connor corrected him. "Formula One is a racing car."

"Right," said Grandpa. "Formula, then."

"Get diapers, too, if you aim to keep him," said Doctor Connor.

"I will, then," said Grandpa. He was still drunk but he was all business.

There had been no babies in the Mann home for over twenty years. There were tricks, secrets, inside information that one needed to know to raise a baby, and of the members of Grandpa's generation these secrets were known largely only by women. Grandpa had been a father in a time when men had nothing to do with the actual day-to-day business of raising children. Men didn't change diapers, warm bottles, or nurse babies. As a result, it was Grandpa's wife, and not Grandpa himself, who knew how to do all these things. Had she still been around, no doubt she would have taken over the business of raising me herself. But she—my grandmother—was no longer present to discuss it with; she'd simply disappeared one day when my father, Eddie, was still little, just after the Fiasco of the Ostriches, and Grandpa had never heard from her or of her again. He would have to do the best he could on his own.

Grandpa went to Gruber's and bought baby things, searching his memory for what else a growing boy might need besides formula and diapers, things even men knew about: there were safety pins, he recalled, and bottles, talcum powder, a rattle, strained food, several beginning reader's books, and a .22-caliber rifle. He found himself growing more excited by the minute, leaping ahead in years to when I would already be a young man. *He'll learn to shoot, to hunt, to read. I must open him a bank account*, he thought. *He must go to college.*

"Havin' a baby, Tom?" asked Harold Gruber as he rang up my grandfather's purchases.

"Already had one," said Grandpa. He suddenly changed his mind about showing Harold the receipt. He didn't want to know. Not just yet, anyway. And he didn't want people talking. "Grandson, actually."

"I didn't know Eddie had a baby," said Harold, raising an eyebrow.

"Neither did I," said Grandpa, "and I'll thank you to keep it under your hat, until I get things all straightened out."

Harold nodded and didn't say another word. Harold Gruber was a well-respected man; everyone trusted him. He heard all Mannville's gossip in his store on a daily basis, and he'd learned early the value of keeping his mouth shut and his ears open. He was also one of the few

Mannvillians—besides Doctor Connor—who hadn't made fun of Grandpa after the Fiasco of the Ostriches in 1946. It was because of this that Grandpa knew he wouldn't go blabbing my sudden arrival all over town. People already talked about him enough: crazy old hermit, up there in that old house. Drinks all day, talks to himself. Yells at kids when they wander through his yard. He didn't want to add to the problem.

Grandpa loaded his purchases into the Galaxie and went back to Doctor Connor's office. Together the two men warmed some formula on the kitchen stove, put it in a bottle, and watched apprehensively to see if I would take it. I did. Grandpa held me while Doctor Connor held the bottle.

"That settles it, I guess," said Grandpa. "He's a keeper."

"I don't want to intrude on your personal affairs," said Doctor Connor, "but how in the hell do you expect to raise a baby on your own in that house? You can't even take care of yourself!"

"What else can I do with him?" Grandpa said. "I can't give him to some agency or something. I couldn't sleep nights, knowing there was a baby Mann out there somewhere not knowing who he was."

"It's going to be tough, Tom," said Doctor Connor.

"I did it once before."

"When you had a wife."

"Well, I'm not getting another wife at my age. Besides, Connor. I don't mean to get corny, but he's the answer to my prayers."

"You've been praying for a *baby*?"

"No, you dingleberry, I haven't been praying for a baby. But I've been thinking. We're all gone now—all of us Manns. I'm the last one."

"I know," said Doctor Connor. "You tell me that every time I see you."

"Well, now I'm not the last one anymore."

"Now *he* is," said Doctor Connor, pointing to me. "So what?"

Connor was a practical, scientific man who saw through most human vanity right away. People, to him, were merely biological organisms. They all had breakable bones and soft, vulnerable internal organs, and things went wrong with them that needed to be fixed from time to time—it made no difference to him what their last name was. He himself was married but had never had children. When asked why there were no little Connors, he would say, "There's already almost a billion Chinese!" which was his way of explaining that the world was overpopulated as it was. He did not wish to contribute to the problem.

"I always thought it would be a damn shame if I was the last of the Manns," said Grandpa.

"Is that so important?"

"I got stories to tell him," said Grandpa. "I'm sick of talking to myself in that house. He needs to know everything."

"What are you going to name him?"

And Grandpa, as he told me later, answered immediately and without thinking, "Connor, meet William Amos Mann IV. But I'm going to call him Billy."

"Hello there, Billy," said Connor.

At this point, Grandpa told me, I spit up formula all over myself.

"Little fella can't even hold his liquor," said Grandpa.

He had the doctor refresh him on the major points of baby-raising while he cleaned me up. Then Grandpa put me back in the Galaxie and drove us back out to the old farmhouse.

The farmhouse in which I was to be raised wasn't really a farmhouse. It was more of a wood-and-brick mansion. A sweeping, curving driveway led up to it from the road, and the front porch, like those of the old Southern plantation manors, boasted two immense pillars, which flanked an oak door nearly eight feet high. Brass hitching posts, now covered with a patina of fine green, still stood at proud right angles to the ground just in front of the porch, though no horse had been hitched to them since before the Second World War. The farmhouse itself was three stories tall, not including the attic and basement. Each floor was a wilderness of bedrooms, closets, and parlors, some of which hadn't had a human occupant in fifty years. It was a huge, dilapidated, spooky place, and since I was a Mann, it was now mine.

The house had been built in 1868 by my great-great-grandfather, Willie Mann, and once it had been filled with Manns, but they were all dead now, and the house was empty except for Grandpa and me. I learned to walk in the kitchen. It was mostly bare except for a table and chairs, with a wood stove for heat, a single gas ring for cooking, and an icebox instead of a refrigerator. The floor, like all others in the house, was of local hardwood, shiny and smooth and cool. It's the first part of the house of which I have a clear memory:

I'm sprawled on my stomach, perhaps ten or eleven months old, and Grandpa is at the other end of the kitchen on his hands and knees. The floor is a gleaming expanse stretching away before me. I plant my hands on it and push myself up into a runner's crouch. Grandpa is shouting encouragement as though he's at a horse race and I'm the odds-on favorite. I work my way into a squat, and then, hanging onto a nearby chair for support, I'm standing. Grandpa erupts with joy. He picks me up and whirls me around. I remember the room spinning, and Grandpa's hat.

Grandpa always wore a battered tweed fedora set far back on his mostly bald head. His breath smelled of whiskey and his eyes crinkled when he smiled. When I was old enough to walk unaided, he took me on guided tours of the entire house, from basement to attic, and told me stories about every room. He knew the history of the house by rote and could recite the whole biography of every person who'd lived in it from 1868 onward. There was the master bedroom, in which three generations of Manns had been conceived. Each of the other bedrooms had been the residence of some Mann child or teenager or adult at one time or another; Grandpa knew stories about every one of them, and I heard these stories again and again until I myself had them memorized, and my ancestors were living, breathing entities who loomed as large in my memory as though they'd just left yesterday.

The only room that really interested me, however, was my father's. It was the one room in the house that Grandpa kept dusted and scrubbed. The walls were lined with pictures of Eddie in his Boy Scout uniform, his football uniform, and later in his Air Force uniform. I spent several hours a week in there, looking at his pictures, hoping that perhaps I would learn something of my father just by being there. All I gained, however, was the overwhelming sense that he was not home. The room, for me, was empty.

I was free to wander through the house at will. The other bedrooms were thick with dust but still made up, as though the occupants of the house had gotten up en masse one day and walked away. The

closets were full of moth-eaten clothing that hadn't been popular for
decades. I became particularly attached to a top hat that came down
over my eyes, and I carried a polished walking stick that had belonged
to my great-great-grandfather Willie, the builder of the house. His
monogram was engraved in the gold handle. They were the first letters I learned to recognize: W.A.M. III—William Amos Mann the
Third, founder of the present town of Mannville, at one time the rich-
est person in Erie County, and the man for whom I—William Amos
Mann IV—had been unofficially christened by Grandpa. With—as he
told me later—a drop of whiskey dabbed on my forehead, not in the
shape of a cross but the letter *M*.

"To hell with the church," Grandpa used to say. "Church never did
me any damn good at all. When it comes right down to it, boy, you got
your family and that's it. Jesus isn't going to come floating down out of
the sky and save your ass. You have to do it yourself. Or I will, for as
long as I'm alive."

The dank basement was lined with shelves and stocked with hundreds of Mason jars. Inside each jar was a solution of grain alcohol that
preserved a different kind of herb. I learned to read the handwritten
labels—henbane, feverwort, basil, wormwood, fennel. These amused
me, the wormwood because I thought it came from worms and the
henbane because chickens have always seemed to me an innately
humorous animal. The jars were dusty from disuse. Grandpa hadn't
practiced the art of herbal healing in many years. I wasn't allowed to
touch the jars, but I learned to read my first words from them. Pushing
my top hat back from my eyes, I would strain to read the labels on the
highest shelves. These jars were up high because they were the most
deadly. Hemlock was there, the plant that had brought death to
Socrates, and so was an herb that could make a woman abort her
unborn baby. Grandpa warned me repeatedly not even to think about
touching those in particular. Death was a thing that he kept in a Mason
jar, a real thing, too far away to help yourself to unless you were big.

In the evenings Grandpa sat in his rocking chair and I sat in his lap.
There was always a large glass of whiskey within comfortable reach,
and he breathed it on me as we read the paper together. These are the
smells of my childhood—whiskey, newsprint. We started by looking at
the photographs—in those days still of soldiers in the jungles of

Vietnam, Cambodia, and Laos—and Grandpa made me tell him a story about each one. I invented them as I went. They always had a common thread. They were always about my father.

"That's my daddy," I would say, pointing to the photograph of a complete stranger—a nineteen-year-old from Iowa, perhaps, trying to look brave for the photographer and clutching an M–16. "He's got a gun and a pet chicken named Fred. And he's coming in his plane tomorrow."

"Your daddy didn't have buck teeth like that," Grandpa would say. He couldn't bring himself to remind me that my father wasn't coming in his plane tomorrow, or ever. "Turn the page."

Then we would plod our way through sentences from the Associated Press, I reading them out loud and Grandpa correcting me. By the time I was six I could pronounce all the words in a three-para-graph article, though I understood few of them. I went around the house reading everything: detergent labels, whiskey bottles, instruc-tions on how to dismantle the Galaxie out in the old carriage house. I was, Grandpa said, a prodigy. There were two rooms on the second floor devoted to Grandpa's books, and I began to plow my way through them, following Grandpa around from room to room or out to the carriage house, reading them in a sportscaster's voice. He would pause—while banging together a rack of shelves or changing the Galaxie's oil filter—to correct my pronunciation and inflection or to define words for me. Despite his lack of education, there was nothing my grandfather didn't know, and he was determined that I should be even smarter and more well read than he. In this way my education began, long before I went to school.

Our only visitor in those days was Doctor Connor. He was a kind, soft-spoken man with large warm hands and white hair, and he arrived in a green Volkswagen every few weeks with his little black bag full of medical instruments and lollipops. After he had stuck a popsicle stick down my throat and made me cough twice while holding my balls, he would give me a cherry lollipop, my favorite, and he and Grandpa would sit down at the kitchen table with a bottle of whiskey between them. Sometimes I would read to the two of them from whatever book I was working on at the time—something from Steinbeck, or Livy's *Early History of Rome*, which for some reason was a favorite of mine when I was very young. Doctor Connor would sit and listen in open-mouthed bemusement as I read.

"Well, I guess he just skipped right over those books you bought him at Gruber's," he said once to Grandpa, and the two of them laughed as though enjoying an immensely funny private joke. I laughed too, which made them laugh harder because I didn't know what I was laughing at. I didn't know what I was reading, either, of course. But I liked the way the words sounded rolling off my tongue—my love affair with words had already begun. And it made me feel good to make them laugh. I listened as Grandpa and Doctor Connor sat and talked for hours, the level of whiskey in the bottle going steadily down, telling jokes and stories and sometimes arguing.

When they argued, their voices got louder and they banged the table with their fists. Sometimes, I knew, the subject of their arguments was me. Doctor Connor kept trying to convince Grandpa of something, and Grandpa would sit with his arms folded, shaking his head ceaselessly from side to side while Doctor Connor gesticulated and shouted and pleaded. I didn't know exactly what they were arguing about, so I listened from the living room with the hope of gleaning some clue.

"There's nothing they can teach him in school that I can't teach him at home," said Grandpa. "Just because of the ostriches, everyone thinks I'm an idiot."

"You're not an idiot," said Doctor Connor. "You're the most well-read man in the county. And Billy—he's incredible. I've never seen anything like it. But he needs to meet other children!"

"Time enough for that later," said Grandpa. "The world is full of people. He'll get his fill of them by and by."

"No he won't," said Doctor Connor. His voice was low and vehement now. "Not if you keep him locked up like this."

"He's not locked up," said Grandpa. "I'm not some lunatic like you read about in the paper."

"That's what people are saying."

"Let 'em! Let the bastards say whatever they want. I don't care!"

"Tom," said the doctor, "how long are you going to sit and stew over something that happened almost thirty years ago? Why can't you forget it and get on with things?"

"Why can't *they*?" Grandpa countered. That, as far as I could tell, was the end of the argument for that day. I was always relieved when they stopped yelling.

Aside from Doctor Connor and our occasional trips into town to buy necessities from Harold and Emily Gruber, we saw nothing of other people. Our nearest neighbors were half a mile away at the top of the hill. They were the Simpsons of the muddy blue eyes, and Grandpa never spoke of them without bitterness, so I learned not to ask what they were like. When we went into town in the Galaxie, I was permitted to talk with the Grubers and nobody else. "Walk tall," Grandpa instructed me. "Hold your head up and look straight in front of you. Remember you're a Mann, and we used to own this whole damn town and everything around it for a ten-mile radius."

The Grubers were a kindly old couple who always fussed over me. Mrs. Gruber smelled like perfume, and she used to pick me up and let me choose a piece of candy from the row of shining glass jars they kept—licorice, gobstoppers, chocolate kisses, peppermints, and lollipops of an infinitely greater variety than the ones Doctor Connor carried in his black bag. Grandpa tolerated this with a sort of injured pride.

"Just one, now," he warned me.

"Just one," Mrs. Gruber would echo, and then when Grandpa wasn't looking she would stuff my pockets with handfuls of whatever was closest. I thought she was an angel. She was the first woman with whom I fell in love. Grandpa always took the candy from me later, but he didn't throw it away; he kept it in a tin on top of the icebox and let me have it back—one piece at a time, so I wouldn't get sick.

But Grandpa's warnings about not speaking to anyone were unnecessary, because nobody ever spoke to us. We passed people on the street who must have known who we were, but they ignored Grandpa and he ignored them. Sometimes grown-ups would sneak a smile at me. Later, when I got to recognize certain faces, I would smile back. But this was always surreptitious, and if Grandpa saw me do it he would give my hand a quick tug to make me remember his instructions: Walk tall. Head up. Look straight. You're a Mann, damn it.

So I spent my time wandering the house and grounds, which were reduced from their former size of three thousand acres to one. That was big enough for me to be satisfied with. I climbed trees and built forts in the hedges that lined our little brook, talking to imaginary friends and conducting elaborate rituals to conjure up the spirit of my father.

Talking to ghosts was a pastime I had learned from Grandpa. He sat in his rocking chair and muttered to himself continually, sipping his whiskey and carrying on an endless dialogue with the ghosts who shambled through the empty house. Only he could see them, but we both knew they were there. It was a source of continual vexation to Grandpa that nothing in the house ever stayed where he had left it for longer than an hour. A hammer he'd placed on the workbench in the carriage house would go missing for three days and then turn up in the attic, standing on its head. Various sets of keys were often discovered hanging from the same bar in the same second-floor closet, the spread-able metal ring always somehow wrapped firmly around it so that Grandpa had to take the bar down to slide them off and hide them somewhere else. It was useless, of course. He was being toyed with, and he knew it. He even enjoyed it, for the most part. Only once did he ever lose patience with the forces at work in our home. One afternoon when Grandpa was preparing to fry me some baloney for lunch, he turned to reach for a spatula, and when he turned around again the frying pan was gone.

"Goddamn it!" he shouted. I was startled—I thought he was yelling at me. "I'm sick of this! Show a little care for your own family, why don't you!"

The frying pan fell to the floor with a clatter—from the counter behind him. "Petulant," Grandpa said, of the spirit who had been chastised. But his warning had struck a chord in some ghostly conscience; nothing more happened after that, at least nothing of which I was aware. This sudden show of respect convinced me that the ghost was somehow related to us. I thought of him as a sort of transparent cousin, one with whom I could have played if I chose. But ghosts bored me, with their despondency and their hints of the grave, and I didn't stay in the house much after that.

As my seventh year came to a close, I took to wandering farther and farther from the farmhouse. I spent entire days walking in the remnants of the forests that had once spread over the countryside like a race of giants. The trees existed now only in sparse patches of growth, cut down to make way for fields, which in turn gave way to mobile home parks and suburban neighborhoods. It was still possible to walk from the farmhouse to the shore of Lake Erie, half a mile away, without leaving the cover of the trees, but if I wished to avoid being seen by suburbanites I had to be stealthy. "Stay away from the white trash," Grandpa warned me continually. That was his term for every-one who wasn't a Mann. "They're living on what used to be our corn-fields." I made a game of it. I spied on pudgy white-legged fathers as they barbecued hot dogs and mowed their lawns, eavesdropped on the conversations of clattery-voiced women as they hung their laundry. I discovered the nearby Lake on my own, thinking, like a miniature Hudson or de Gama, that it was mine, and I went to it frequently to play on the sand and to torture minnows. I also took to spying on the Simpsons.

The hill on which the Simpson house sat was surrounded at its base by the original forest, and on one side the trees crept up the slope far enough to afford ample cover for my missions of espionage. I lay concealed behind their trunks and observed the goings-on of the Simpson family. I was deeply curious about them—Grandpa spoke of them with such contempt that I thought they must be fascinating, whoever they were and whatever they were about. As far as I could tell, they didn't do very much. Their house was dilapidated, in far worse repair than ours. The yard was strewn with the wreckage of old cars and other machinery. A few mangy chickens scratched in the balding grass, growled at occasionally by a large and ferocious dog of indeter-minate background who otherwise lay on the warped boards of the porch and stared at nothing. He wasn't much of a dog. He never detected me, and I never saw anybody pet him.

The Simpsons themselves appeared to be a tribe of corpulent and unmotivated Neanderthals whose sole pursuit was to watch television. That is, they sat in the living room and stared at what looked to me like a blue flickering light—we didn't have a television, and I'd never seen one before, so the light was a complete mystery to me. There were sev-eral girls, most of them teenagers. The father had an impressive belly that extended far over his belt. He was always home. The sight of him, which was rare, was terrifying. He had small beady eyes, a walrus mustache, and a flabby white body. His daughters mirrored him in appearance with stunning genetic accuracy, except for one of them.

She was a girl about my age. She had long pigtails that bounced between her shoulder blades as she ran—she was the only Simpson who did run as she went from place to place, simply because she wasn't fat like the rest of them. I watched her as she played on the porch. She had an imaginary life as vivid as mine, it seemed, for she spoke constantly to herself, as though she were surrounded by throngs of admirers. Sometimes she sang. I kept myself flattened among the fallen leaves behind the trees as she bounced around the yard, addressing the chickens in a clear, high voice. There would on occasion come a loud male rumble from the house, and the girl would stop what she was doing and trudge back onto the porch and inside, her spirit suddenly gone. After that, there would sometimes be crying, not just from her but from the other girls too—a chorus of wails, sometimes hysterical. So I knew her father was mean. I vowed solemnly to rescue the little girl when I was big enough. She became the object of my fantasy. I considered speaking to her from my observation post among the trees, but discretion, it seemed to me, would be rewarded in time with success. I had to wait until I was bigger. Then I would lock her father in his room and she would run away with me, and perhaps be my girlfriend. It seemed like a very good plan, and I worked it over in my head repeatedly until it had an infinite variety of plots and endings, all of which culminated in her release and unending gratitude, and sometimes kissing.

I knew better than to reveal my plan to Grandpa. He would have been livid with rage had he known I was considering contact with the Simpsons. So I explained it all to my father, with whom I held regular conversations in my fort along the brook at home. My father was fully in approval. He always wore his uniform, and whenever we met he would remove one of his medals and pin it on my chest. "I'm very proud of you, son," he said. Sometimes we would take a ride in his F–4. He let me fly it whenever I wanted because I was good. I piloted it around the yard, up over the Simpson house, and far out above the massive Lake, which sat always dreaming and impassive half a mile to the north. I shot down enemy planes by the score and flew low over people's houses. My father thought I was a genius and said he would help me in my plans to liberate the Simpson girl. I was a chip off the old block, he said. The apple didn't fall far from the tree. He wished he'd had more men like me in Vietnam.

Grandpa sat in his rocking chair in the darkened living room and drank and whispered to himself. Now that the ghost had stopped harassing him, it was only the diary he spoke of—a mysterious book to which he'd never referred before. Talking to Grandpa was like talking to someone who is speaking in their sleep. You could answer him or not, as you liked, and his responses might or might not make sense. I usually ignored him, but my interest was piqued by his mention of this diary. I attempted to draw him out.

"I ain't seen your diary in years," he might say suddenly. "I left it with someone else."

"Seen what?"

"You remember?" This was not addressed to me, I knew, but to some new and invisible presence, another ghost, but not a mischievous one. I had been aware of him for some time, but since he never threw things or hid things, I ignored him too. But now I answered Grandpa for him.

"Yeah, I remember," I said. "Now where is that old diary of mine?"

"Hanged if I know," said Grandpa. "It's got all the old stories in there. There was that time you went down to Buffalo with Frederic and joined up. It's all in there."

"Who's Frederic?"

"I hope you ain't mad. I had to leave it with him. We made a deal."

"Leave it with who?"

Grandpa said a name. It was not a regular American-sounding name, and I couldn't make any sense of it. He wouldn't repeat it.

"Wake up," I said. "I'm hungry."

Grandpa could rouse himself from his stupor when he chose, but I could tell that in general he was slowly surrendering his hold on the present in favor of some forgotten time when he hadn't been sad and the house was full of people. We were entirely alone now. Doctor Connor didn't visit anymore. The last time he'd come, there had been a tremendous argument, worse than any they'd ever had before, and Grandpa had cursed and thrown a whiskey bottle at him. Connor ducked just in time. The bottle exploded against the wall, and the shards of glass sat on the kitchen floor for days before I finally cleaned them up myself.

"What do you want to eat?" Grandpa asked me.

"Fried baloney," I said.

He got up slowly from the rocking chair. "Where you been these days?" he asked as he went into the kitchen.

"Playing," I said.

"By yourself?"

"Uh-huh."

I could hear him clattering around in the kitchen. He dropped the frying pan and groaned as he bent down to pick it up. I went and sat in his rocking chair. A half-empty glass of whiskey was on the table next to it. I took a tiny sip and immediately began choking. It burned like fire in my mouth. Tears came to my eyes and my nose started to run. So that was what he drank all the time: poison. Hot poison.

I could hear him mumbling over the sound of baloney sizzling in the pan. Gradually his mumbles gave way to soft sobs. He cried quietly to himself as he cooked my fried baloney. "Be sure to make enough for everybody," he said. "Never let anyone go hungry. Nobody leaves the Mann house hungry."

I sat in his rocking chair feeling the burn in my mouth start to fade. I hugged my knees to my chest and rocked back and forth as he cried to himself in the kitchen, trying to stifle it so I wouldn't hear. I hoped he would sober up by bedtime. It frightened me to lie awake at night and hear Grandpa wandering through the house, talking aloud to invisible presences and crying to himself as he did now. And I was ashamed of myself for being frightened. My father would never have been scared of anything. I hoped, at that moment, that he wasn't watching me.

2

Grandpa's War Story, as Told to Me by Himself

There'd been a time, long before my arrival in the world, when Grandpa wasn't yet a bitter and lonely recluse; when he wasn't a bottle-a-day drinker of Irish whiskey; when he was, in fact, a charming and pleasant young man, the apple of his mother's eye and Mannville's brightest star. This was before the Second World War. I heard much about the war growing up; we'd had many wars, we Americans, but to hear Grandpa tell it there was really only one war that mattered, and that was his war. All the others, from the Revolution to World War One, had been practice wars, a sort of warm-up for the real thing, and all the wars afterward, such as Vietnam and Korea, merely weak imitations of it. The Second World War, I learned from Grand+pa, grabbed hold of millions of lives like a leprous and inescapable fist. If it didn't snuff them out, it changed them forever. That was what wars did, of course. But few of them did it on the scale this particular war managed to achieve. That was what it did to Grandpa, more or less, and even almost forty years later it still occupied the greater part of his attention. I heard this story over and over

again until I had it memorized, and I can tell it almost without thinking, as though it had happened not to him but to me.

In 1943, when Grandpa was nineteen, he joined the Army and
became a regular infantryman. He did this over the protests of his
mother, Lily, who thought he ought to go to college instead. College,
however, held no interest for Grandpa. He was more interested in the
war. Most of the young men his age in Mannville had either already
gone to war or were about to go. The town was full of soldiers and
sailors strutting about in their fine new dress uniforms. In fact, it was
becoming impossible to get noticed by girls unless one was in uniform,
and getting noticed by girls, Grandpa admitted to me later, was his
only real concern at the time. The war was a fever that had swept
unchecked through the hearts and minds of Mannvillians, and nobody
had any time for those who weren't caught up in the same frenzy.
Grandpa burned to fight and to distinguish himself; perhaps, he
thought, if he was lucky, he would get wounded just badly enough to
develop an interesting limp, and he would be sent home to live out his
days in glory, like his grandfather Willie. Willie limped because there
was a Confederate musket ball in his leg. Everyone, from the Mayor
on down, worshipped him.

Lily Mann despaired. The infantry, she believed, was below the
station of the Manns, who were millionaires thrice over and whose
landholdings were of locally legendary proportions. She thought
Grandpa at least ought to have become a cavalryman; she hadn't yet
grasped the concept of mechanized warfare, which had already swept
over much of Europe and the Pacific like the shadow of a bloodthirsty
hawk. To ride, she pointed out, was much more dignified than walking. When Grandpa—who, of course, was not called Grandpa yet, but
Thomas Junior—explained to her that horses were useless against
tanks and fighter planes, she relented. But, Lily said, at least he could
go fight in the European Theatre, so he could imbibe some of the culture there.

"Ma," said the young Thomas Junior, "when they say *European
Theatre*, they're not talking about a fancy opera house. They're not
going to let me just wander around looking at museums all the time."
He was being sarcastic, of course. Lily knew very well what the phrase
European Theatre meant, and to remind her son of it she swatted him

on the top of his head, which, though he was only nineteen, was already balding.

"You might at least learn to speak a little French," she said. "French comes across so well in social circles."

"Nobody around here speaks French," said Thomas Junior. "Who would I speak it with?"

"You could speak it when you returned home and went to Harvard," said Lily icily.

Thomas Junior dropped the subject. Her mind was made up. He knew better than to argue directly with his mother. She was the toughest person he'd ever met, man or woman. In fact, he thought, sometimes she got her way so much because she was a woman. If a man spoke to people the way she did, he would have to back himself up with his fists. But women didn't have to fistfight. A shame, really, Thomas Junior thought. If his mother could fight as well as she could talk, she would have ended the war herself within the year.

Lily had been only sixteen when she married Thomas Junior's father, Thomas Senior. She was widowed a year later, when her husband died attempting to prove that it was possible to drive an automobile across Lake Erie, when frozen, all the way to Long Point, Ontario, Canada, a distance of roughly twenty miles. Theoretically this feat *is* possible, but Thomas Senior—my great-grandfather, Grandpa's father—picked the wrong night to do it. There was a raging snowstorm, which limited visibility to less than twenty yards. Also, he was drunk. Also, the Lake hadn't yet completely frozen over. But none of these factors seemed to deter him. We are daredevils, we Manns, every last one of us, and unconcerned with the laws of physics, which strictly prohibit the driving of automobiles on water. The inebriated Thomas Senior got in his brand-new Pierce-Arrow convertible, waved good-bye to a party of equally drunken friends on shore, and drove off gaily into the blizzard, never to be seen again.

Lily was pregnant with Thomas Junior at the time. She absorbed the news of her husband's death with characteristic stoicism; she was not seen to cry, either when she learned of his death or at his funeral. And as soon as her son was born and her lying-in period was over, she single-handedly took control of the Mann estate with a firmness and sense of purpose her frivolous husband had never possessed.

"Everything," Lily used to tell her son, "is a matter of life or death. So *live*."

Lily herself was born to a poor but fanatically respectable farming family in nearby Springville. She'd married Thomas Senior not because he was rich but because he was irresistible. He had charm, wit, good looks, and smiled all the time; parties generally didn't pick up speed until he arrived, and after he left they began to wind down. Lily had married him for love, not money, but she knew nevertheless that she was lucky to have married into such a fortune, and she was determined to keep her husband's farms and orchards and vineyards profitable or die in the process.

Thomas Senior's father, Willie, had retreated into his bedroom in a sort of self-imposed exile. He was old now, nearing death, or so he claimed, and he spent most of his time with his wounded leg propped up on a footstool, scribbling in his journal. Willie showed no interest in taking over operations again after his foolhardy son drove his Pierce-Arrow to the bottom of Lake Erie, an action that, incidentally, gave him no surprise. He'd always known his son was too giddy to be a businessman and perhaps even too foolish to live very long. Willie himself had announced his retirement from business affairs some years earlier, and in the same breath had politely requested that everyone leave him alone. Lily could, he said, run the whole show if she was so inclined. It made no difference to him whether she succeeded or went bankrupt. All he wanted to do was write in his journal, and he could do that in the poorhouse just as well as in his mansion.

Lily, being Lily, chose to take Willie at his word. She was barely eighteen years old, but her will was inexorable, her planning impeccable, her business instincts deadly accurate. In short, she was a success, and under Lily's strong hand the Manns became wealthier than they'd ever been since Willie Mann made them rich after his return from the Civil War. By the time Lily was only twenty, she was the reigning queen of Erie County, in social, economic, and even political circles. Sheriffs and council members found it difficult to maintain their office if they didn't have Lily Mann on their side. It was this strength of will that her son, Thomas, found himself confronted with now, and he followed the course of action he'd learned years ago to adopt when dealing with his mother: obey her.

The U.S. Army, however, had never heard of Lily Mann. After Thomas enlisted, he received orders to go to Buffalo, where he would board a bus for New York, a plane to San Francisco, and a transport to the Philippines, where he would do battle against the Japanese.

Lily was outraged. Much to Thomas's embarrassment, she placed a phone call to a certain senator's office in Albany. It was useless to fight, however. Although the senator was apologetic, he had the gall to suggest that there was nothing Lily could do; he compounded the insult by requesting a campaign contribution in the same breath. As an interesting footnote to history, and not entirely by coincidence, the senator's campaign for reelection was unsuccessful.

"The Japanese indeed!" Lily raged. "Who are the Japanese, anyway? Nobody I know has ever even *met* a Japanese!"

"They're small and yellow and they eat their own children," said Thomas, which was the popular perception of the Japanese at the time. "They're not really even human. Not like us. That's why we need to fight them. They're trying to take over the world."

Lily shuddered. Thomas was delighted. Over the next few days he filled her head with as much anti-Japanese propaganda as he could make up. Thomas himself was terrified of the Japanese, and his terror was worsened by his own lies, but he wanted his mother to think he was doing something magnificent. He would, of course, have preferred going to Europe. But he knew there was nothing he could do about it, and he was determined to make the best of a bad situation. Gradually Lily's attitude shifted, and then she was not only in favor of his going to the Pacific but actually bragged about it to her friends at parties and Red Cross fund-raisers. "My son is off to destroy the Yellow Menace," she said proudly. "The Mann family simply will not tolerate Japanese aggression, no matter where it takes place."

As rich as Lily became from selling food supplies to the Army, she gave almost all of her war profits back again in the form of donations to the Red Cross, her favorite charity, and also set up a fund for local women whose husbands had been killed in action and who had children to raise. She became even more of a celebrity than she had been before, and she became so proud of her son, off to the Philippines in just a few short weeks now, that she could barely speak of it in public without tears of joy. Thomas, though secretly afraid of being blown to *gooeyr syrupy*

bits by the Japanese, was proud of his mother too; she gave him the sort of courage to go on that he might otherwise have gotten from his daredevil father, had he still been alive. So it was with this mutual admiration in their hearts that Thomas kissed his mother farewell at the train station and boarded the seven-seventeen for Buffalo, an hour and a half away.

Thomas Junior was the second Mann to travel to Buffalo to be inducted into the Army. Eighty-two years earlier, his grandfather, William Amos Mann III, had walked barefoot from Mannville—which was then called Clare Town, after the Irish county that was the birthplace of most of its citizens—to join the Army of the Union and go down South to "whup Rebs," as he put it. Thomas had known his grandfather well. He was a stooped old man with a tremendous white beard. He'd walked with a polished stick of hickory topped with gold and engraved with his monogram—W.A.M III. He'd died only a few years earlier, at the remarkable age of ninety-five, still limping from a wound he'd received at the battle of Antietam. Willie had finally finished writing his diary, which everyone took to be an autobiography of sorts, and he gave it to Thomas in a ceremony utterly devoid of portent or majesty a short time before his death. He'd simply called him into his room one day, dug the diary out of an old trunk, and handed it to him, saying, in his gentle and diluted brogue, "Most of what I learnt in my life, lad, I tried to write down, so's the next fella could maybe make some sense out of things. Bein' as your father is gone to his reward, you're the next fella. This is for you."

Thomas had been only sixteen, the same age his grandfather had been when he marched down the road barefoot to go fight his own war, and he hadn't thought much of the incident at the time. He put the diary in a safe place and promptly forgot about it. But when he was packing his personal effects before going off to the Philippines, he suddenly remembered the diary, and dug it out again. It was a gift from one warrior to another, he thought grandiosely. He would read it on the train. No doubt it contained stirring accounts of hand-to-hand combat that would give him courage to face the enemy.

Thomas reached into his duffel bag now on the train and took out the diary. It was bound in cracked leather, the covers plain and unadorned. He opened it to the first page. The paper had aged surprisingly well; it was only slightly yellowed and still supple. On the inside of the front cover, in an unpracticed hand, his grandfather had written the following:

1866

This Is Willie Mann's book!

The first entry read:

May 21, 1866

> *My Naym is Willie Amos Mann I Learnt to Write from a Feller in the Army of the Union and I be Twenty One Yeres old the feller who learnt me to Write and Reed was a Scoolmaster. To-day tis hot and We half been Working at the Corn all day Hoing Wedes.*

Thomas put the diary away again. This was not glamorous war history. This was boring farmer talk. Besides, the churning in his stomach made it impossible for him to concentrate. Though he hadn't mentioned it to his mother, or to anyone else, he was desperately afraid, and though home was barely behind him, he was already lonely. More than anything he wished the war would end before he arrived in Buffalo. But he knew the chances of that were slim. So he sat on the train with his head against the window and his eyes shut, remembering home, until the train arrived in Buffalo and he disembarked, trembling, along with several other young men his age from various towns along the Mannville–Buffalo line. There a waiting sergeant lined them up on the platform and marched them off single file down the street to the induction center; and my grandfather walked into the open maw of the U.S. Army, never to return in quite the same form.

The real reason Thomas Junior had joined the Army—as opposed to the other branches of the military—was not one of which he was proud. He'd never flown in his life, and had no wish to do so, so anything to do with airplanes was out of the question. He'd grown up on Lake Erie, and so was familiar enough with water to know that drowning also terrified him; therefore, the Navy was also out. The Marines were too crazy—he didn't want to be among the first in any attack. He assumed that in the Army he would spend his time on the ground, a medium with which he was thoroughly familiar, with lots of other homesick and scared young men, and as long as he had at least one foot on the earth at all times, he thought being shot at was something he could tolerate with a modicum of manliness.

However, after being inducted in Buffalo, Thomas was placed in a large cargo plane, along with forty-nine of his fellow soldiers, and flown to San Francisco. He spent his first flight vomiting quietly behind a bulkhead. After basic training, which he handled well enough, he thought, because it took place on solid land, he was placed on a troop ship and sent to the Philippines. There was more vomiting. When he arrived in the Philippines, it appeared that there'd been a mistake; he hadn't been wanted in the Philippines after all, but in the Marianas. He was placed in another cargo plane and flown there.

By this time Thomas realized he was in the hands of dangerous idiots. He imagined a room full of generals somewhere, gleefully poring over charts and maps and plotting where to send him next. When he arrived in the Marianas, he reported for duty and was told that there'd been another mistake; he was supposed to be in the Philippines after all, and so he simply did an about-face on the runway and got back on the plane.

Not only was Thomas now airborne again, but he was flying high over an ocean that afforded plenty of opportunities for drowning, should they be shot down. When Thomas realized this, he resigned himself to death. He sat on his helmet, as he'd seen other soldiers do, to prevent any wayward shards of metal from doing damage to his nether parts in the event of an attack. Willie Mann's diary was wrapped in several layers of oilcloth and secured to his stomach by means of packing tape.

He was the only passenger on this particular flight. There was a pilot, a copilot, and a navigator, with whom he chatted from time to time. The navigator was a twenty-three-year-old engineering student from Kansas City who'd abandoned graduate school to join the Army

Air Force. He hunched over his charts, shouting above the roar of the plane's engines, reading coordinates aloud to Thomas to pass the time. They made no sense to him, but he was grateful for anything that would take his mind off the fact that he was flying, and over an ocean, no less.

Incredibly, the next thing that happened was precisely what Thomas had been fearing since he boarded the first plane in Buffalo: an attack by a Japanese fighter plane, the dreaded Zero. It came as a complete surprise to everyone. They were not in an area of heavy Japanese presence and no trouble had been expected. He noticed first that the pilot was shouting loudly enough to be heard in the back of the plane. Then the plane reared upward on its tail and began a straining, creaking climb upward. Thomas was sent tumbling into the tail. The copilot came scrambling back into the cargo area. He and the navigator shouted at each other for a moment, with much pointing at charts and gesticulating heavenward. It occurred to Thomas that if they were lost, it was because the navigator had been too busy talking to him, and therefore it was at least partly his fault.

The copilot went back to the cockpit. The plane completed its climb and promptly dove almost straight down, so that Thomas was sent flying into the tail again, this time floating wierdly, buoyed by G-forces. The navigator threw open a porthole near his table and unstrapped the machine gun that was fixed there. He pulled the trigger and swiveled his upper body back and forth. Shell casings spewed rapidly from the breech of the gun and littered the floor, and the reek of cordite filled the thin air. Through the porthole Thomas caught a glimpse of the underbelly of another plane, a small one with a gray body, as it zoomed past. It seemed ridiculously close. When they leveled out, the copilot came back into the cargo area.

"Put on your damn parachute!" he screamed. He helped Thomas struggle into the bulky backpack that contained his parachute.

"I've never used one of these before!" Thomas shouted.

"Hopefully you won't have to!" yelled the copilot. "But if we ditch, jump out that door"—he pointed to the great sliding cargo door, which Thomas doubted he could move by himself—"and pull this cord here!" He showed Thomas the rip cord and went back into the cockpit.

That was the last Thomas ever saw of him. There was a tremendous rattling just then, as though the plane was being showered with baseballs, and several ragged holes appeared in one wall of the plane and then in the wall opposite as Japanese bullets passed through with the velocity of tiny meteorites. At the same moment, smoke began issuing from the cockpit. Thomas felt a sickening lurch as the plane keeled over to one side and began heading downward again.

The navigator fired one last burst of the machine gun and ran to the cargo door. Together he and Thomas managed to push it open.

"Wait here!" shouted the navigator. He ran into the cockpit and came out again immediately, his face the color of milk.

"What about those guys?" my grandfather shouted.

"They're dead," said the navigator. He said it quietly—Thomas saw his lips move, but he didn't hear the words. He turned and looked out the cargo door, squinting against the fierce wind. Then he felt the navigator's hands on his back. Suddenly he was tumbling out the door and through open space. He felt frantically for the rip cord as he flipped over and over, occasionally catching a glimpse of the navigator falling above him. Finally he found it. His parachute opened with a tremendous yank, as though the hand of God had reached down and pulled on his underwear. He stopped tumbling. He looked up again to see if he could spot the navigator, but all that was visible was the underside of his own parachute. The bright Pacific sun shone through it, lighting up the silk exactly like a lampshade that Thomas remembered from one of the parlors at home.

He looked down. He was, he guessed, about a mile above the sea, which from this height looked like a wrinkled blue bedsheet. Not so very far off were a smattering of tiny islands; he tried to steer toward them but only succeeded in spilling air out of his parachute, making himself fall faster.

"I'm going to fucking die," he said.

Far below him he saw a minuscule splash as the cargo plane crashed into the sea. A sick feeling pervaded his body and he stifled the urge to vomit. Then from the corner of his eye he saw the navigator float past. He'd spotted the islands too, and was more adept at controlling his parachute than Thomas was, so that he was falling closer to them. There was about a quarter-mile of space between the two men. Thomas began to shout.

"Hey! HEY! Hey YOU!"

The navigator looked over. Ridiculously, he and Thomas waved at each other. Then the navigator realized Thomas's predicament and showed him, pantomiming furiously, how to control his fall. The ocean was growing alarmingly closer, but so were the islands. He wouldn't quite land on them, but he hoped fervently that he would fall close enough to swim for it. Thomas was a very good swimmer, perhaps because his fear of drowning was so keen; he'd never swum in very deep water, but he didn't think it would be different from swimming in shallow water, provided he could get his clothes off before they dragged him down. He began shedding as many articles of clothing as he could reach. His boots would be the hardest to lose once he was submerged, so after much straining and contorting, he managed to loosen them enough to kick them off. Next he pulled off his socks with his toes. He removed his belt from under the straps of his parachute harness; once he was in the ocean, he would have to struggle out of the straps themselves. It would be very difficult. Thomas took a deep breath and closed his eyes.

Calm down, he told himself. *The only way out of this is to remain calm.* He rehearsed in his mind the steps he would go through: unbuckle the chest straps, pull his arms out of the harness, and then his legs. He would have to hold his breath for a long time, but he thought he could do it if only he could avoid the panic trying to beat its way up through him. Then would come his clothes. If he could get out of his pants underwater, he thought he could make it.

He was only a thousand feet or so above the water now. The islands were still a good swim away, perhaps a mile. But he had swum that far many times before. He could do it. He was sure of it. He looked at the navigator again. He'd drifted closer to Thomas, and he was shouting something at him, something about "parks" or "barks," but Thomas ignored him. He had to focus. Concentration was of the utmost importance now.

When he hit the water, he pulled himself up into a ball. Then he went through the steps he had rehearsed in his mind. His parachute was designed to come off quickly, and he shed it exactly as planned. His pants, however, gave him a good deal of trouble. He sank several feet below the surface while he was trying to kick them off, and the panic came again, surging up from his belly through his throat. But he fought it off again. Finally he succeeded in getting out of them, and he pushed his way to the surface, where he took a deep gasping breath, removed his shirt, and began to tread water.

Immediately he saw the navigator's chute. He'd landed closer to the islands than Thomas, but not by much; in fact, the islands now looked impossibly far away. It was going to be a hell of a swim. Thomas struck out for the navigator. There was a slight swell, which bobbed him up and down like a cork; Thomas was grateful the waves weren't larger. For the first time in his life he tasted salt water. It tasted like blood, he thought. He swam slowly, pacing himself, forcing his breath to come regularly.

"Dear Mother," he said aloud. "I'm sorry to inform you that I died while swimming for my life in the ocean, where I landed due to Army incompetence. I have discovered that the U.S. Army is a far more dangerous enemy to me than the Japanese."

It took him forever to reach the navigator. When he got there, he found the man floating, his head protruding from the hole in the center of the parachute, which billowed around him like a massive baptismal gown.

"Get me the fuck out of this goddamn fucking thing," said the navigator. He was crying like a child. "I can barely move."

"Right," said Thomas. He began rolling up one side of the parachute until he reached the man's head. He slipped it over him and saw that the man was wearing a flotation jacket.

"They make us wear them," said the navigator, "thank God. I'd share it with you but I'd drown. I can't swim."

"I'll be fine," said Thomas. "I'm a good swimmer. Let's unstrap you."

"I can't *swim*," said the navigator again.

"Don't worry," said Thomas. "We'll leave the jacket on."

"*You* can swim," said the navigator. "Do you know how much money I'd give to be able to swim right now?"

"I'm guessing quite a lot," said Thomas. "Get out of that thing."

The navigator began to struggle with the straps of his harness. After several minutes he was free. He was still crying, ashamedly trying to stifle his sobs.

"Don't panic," said Thomas. "Hear me? Stop crying. If we panic we're done for. We have to make it to those islands."

"What's that on your stomach?" asked the navigator.

Thomas had forgotten about his grandfather's diary. He looked down. It was still there, safely secured around his middle.

"It's a book," he said.

There was a moment of awkward silence. Thomas thought of explaining why he had a waterproofed book taped to his stomach, but decided that could wait.

"I'm from Kansas City," said the navigator. "There's no damn water there. I should have joined the fucking infantry and gone to fucking Europe. Instead I'm in the fucking Air Force and I'm sitting in the water and we're going to be fucking eaten by fucking sharks!"

"No we're not," said Thomas. "Start swimming."

"Yes we are," said the navigator. "I saw them when I was falling. Big ones. Back there." He pointed over his shoulder out to the open sea.

A cold chill swept through Thomas. "Oh my Lord," he said. "Are you serious?" So *that* was what he'd been shouting as they fell.

"Yes," the navigator said simply. Then he looked up, holding one hand over his eyes to shield them from the sun. "Look," he said. "There's another parachute."

Thomas followed his gaze. There was indeed another parachute drifting gently above the islands, a falling cloudlet dislodged accidentally from its nest high above the world.

"Is it Tony? Is it Blake?" asked the navigator.

"It can't be," said Thomas, guessing he was talking about the pilot and copilot. "They're dead. You told me so."

"Oh my God," said the navigator. "It's the Jap. I must of got him! I shot his plane down!"

"Start swimming," said Thomas. "I'm going to go ahead of you. You'll be much slower than me but you won't sink. Just keep your breathing regular."

"Okay," said the navigator. He was smiling now. "I shot down a Jap plane!"

"I'll see you over there," said Thomas. "Just head for the closest one."

He began swimming with strong, even strokes.

"I'm Phillip Neuberg from Kansas City," the navigator called after him. "If I don't make it, will you write to my family?"

Thomas didn't answer, but he made a mental note of it. Phillip Neuberg of Kansas City requests a letter home in the event of his demise. Right. Got it. He couldn't waste any more time talking. He focused on his movements: kick, stroke, turn, breathe in, kick, stroke, exhale downward. He didn't look any more to see how far the islands were. He just swam. He heard the navigator's splashes grow farther and farther away behind him. He had been swimming for about fifteen minutes when the first shark hit.

The navigator let out a scream that pierced Thomas through to his soul. He forced himself to keep going. He couldn't afford to let himself turn and look; there was nothing he could do anyway. He swam faster, as fast as he could without spending himself too soon. There came another scream, then another, and then the screaming abruptly stopped.

Thomas swam as he had never swum before. *I will not by eaten by sharks*, he repeated in his head. *I refuse. I'm going to make it. They won't come after me. They don't like me. They like Phillip Neuberg from Kansas City. I am the fastest swimmer in the world. I'm the human torpedo. I'm going to make it to the island and I'm going to kill that fucking Jap who shot us down and put me in this mess and I'm going to get rescued and go home to Mannville and sit in the front parlor with the lampshade that looks like a parachute with the sun streaming through it, and I'm never going to leave it again except to get another beer or to go to the bathroom. Swim. Swim. Swim.*

And in his head, he composed another letter, this one beginning "Dear Mrs. Neuberg, My name is Thomas Mann—no relation to the writer—and I'm sorry to inform you that I was with your son Phillip when he . . . "

Thomas was flopped up on the beach by the surf like a sodden rag doll. He lay there for several minutes, just breathing. He thanked God that he'd been born on Lake Erie and not in Kansas. He had the feeling, at that moment, that his entire life had been spent in preparation for being shot down over the South Pacific and swimming to this island. He forgot about returning to Mannville. He forgot about the war. He forgot everything he knew except that he was alive, and that somehow he'd escaped the horrible fate of Phillip Neuberg of Kansas City, consumed by sharks.

Thomas took stock of himself. He was nineteen years old and completely naked, except for the diary wrapped in oilcloth and strapped with packing tape to his stomach. He was half-full of seawater, and he was lying on a beautiful white beach several thousand miles from Mannville. Somewhere on the island was a Japanese pilot, a sword-wielding, idol-worshipping, baby-eating lunatic. Thomas had no food and no gun. It might be that there was no fresh water on the island. It might be that there was nothing to eat either. The situation, to put it mildly, was grim.

His first thought, however, was for his penis. It was two or three o'clock in the afternoon, and the full brunt of the southern sun was blasting down on him like a thousand bonfires. The rest of him was tanned a deep nut brown from his last summer on the Lake, but from his waist to the tops of his thighs Thomas Junior was as pale as a missionary. His penis was completely unprepared for a frontal solar assault. He was afraid it would get sunburned. It was that thought, and no other, which motivated him to get up and look for shade. If not for that, he might have lain there forever, just breathing.

When he stood up, Grandpa told me later, he puked seawater. He must have swallowed gallons of it during his mad rush through the ocean. He took a few steps and puked seawater again.

"Sometimes I think I spent the whole damn war just throwing up," Grandpa told me later.

He decided it would be wiser to crawl from that point on, so he moved like a baby on his hands and knees, away from the gently rolling surf and into the line of bushes and palm trees. Once his manhood was safely shaded, he made himself a nest of leaves—huge leaves, bigger than any leaves he'd ever seen in his life—and went to sleep.

When he woke up, there was a small, dark-skinned man standing above him. The sun was almost down, and there was barely enough light to see by. The little man was silhouetted against the surf, which glowed a deep dark blue in the sunset, and the horizon, which was orange. Thomas shot to his feet. He and the little man stood there looking at each other. Neither of them moved.

"Japs are just like rattlesnakes," Grandpa said later. "They're just as afraid of you as you are of them."

Technically, Thomas knew, he was supposed to kill any Japanese he met. That was what war was about. Failing that, he was to take them prisoner. He'd spent the two years since the attack on Pearl Harbor working himself into a frenzy of hatred against the Japanese. There had been a time when he was quite capable of killing one. But standing here in front of this little man, Thomas realized that he didn't want to kill anybody, and he didn't know how to take someone prisoner. Besides, he had no weapon to threaten him with, and it seemed ridiculous to say, "You're my prisoner. Come with me." What was he to do with him? So they stood there looking at each other, until the sun went down and blue faded to bruise-purple and then soft black. A chill sea breeze began to blow across the island. Grandpa and the Japanese soldier began to shiver in unison.

Seeing this, realizing Japs got cold too, Thomas decided then and there to resign from the U.S. Army. The war was over for him. He was exhausted and nauseated and hungry, and when you came right down to it, the only reason he'd really wanted to go to the war was so girls would pay attention to him when he got back. Right at that moment, that seemed like the stupidest reason in the world.

There is an entry in Willie Mann's diary that addresses this very issue. I know about it because the diary is back in possession of the Manns again, after an absence of several decades, and I have it with me now. Like many of Willie's later entries, made when he was an old man reflecting on his long and strange life, it's concise, well written, and philosophical in nature—and by that time his grammar and spelling had greatly improved. Wrote Willie:

> *Men are fond of blaming their wars on women. Poor Helen suffers the blame for the siege of Troy, as if she asked to be kidnapped and then rescued. But it's not the fault of women that men go to war against each other. It's the fault of men for being warlike in the first place.*

"We need a fire," said Thomas. He pantomimed the rubbing together of two sticks. The Japanese pilot nodded, his Asian eyes—the first Thomas had ever seen—guarded but enthusiastic.

"That's a fine idea," said the pilot. "It's getting a little cold."

Thomas was flabbergasted. He stared openmouthed at the pilot.

The pilot cleared his throat uncomfortably after several moments. "I said, 'That's a fine idea,'" he repeated. He was wondering if my grandfather perhaps had a hearing problem.

"You're speaking English," said Thomas.

"Do you speak Japanese?" inquired the man.

Thomas shook his head. The pilot smiled. His white teeth glistened in the dusk.

"I didn't think so," he said triumphantly. "Therefore, I'm speaking English."

"Well, I'll be damned," said Thomas.

"I am Enzo Fujimora," said the pilot. "Harvard class of thirty-five."

"Well, I'll be damned," said Thomas again. "A Jap Harvard man."

"Exactly," said Enzo Fujimora, and he bowed slightly from the waist.

"My mother wanted me to go to Harvard," said Thomas. It sounded ridiculous, but that was all he could think of to say.

"Your mother has high aspirations for you," said Enzo Fujimora. "I hope someday you are able to attend. I liked it there very much. Shall we make a fire?"

That's the story of how my grandfather met the man who was to change the course of his life forever, as told to me by himself more times than I can remember, enough times so that I can recite it as I have here almost as if it really happened to me.

Enzo Fujimora was thirty years old. He was a schoolteacher, the son of a well-to-do family in Nagasaki, and he had a wife and two children—a boy aged three and another aged seven. When the atomic bomb was dropped on his hometown two years later, all three of them were wiped out in an instant. Enzo could not have known this ahead of time, of course, but Grandpa said later that he wouldn't have behaved a bit differently if he had. He was a devout Buddhist, and up to that point he was the most profound person Thomas had ever met.

He believed people should live every moment as if it were to be the last.

"That," said Enzo, "is the best way to avoid wasting time."

It was three long weeks before they were discovered. In that time, Enzo Fujimora and my grandfather became fast friends. They were both naturally amiable and outgoing, and they shared a distaste for war and in fact for violence in general. During their time together on that tiny South Pacific island, they told each other every detail they could remember of their lives, right up to the point where they had met in midair in their respective airplanes. Enzo had been separated from his squadron when he spotted the American cargo plane, and he had thought to cover himself in glory by shooting it down to avoid the disgrace of getting lost.

"It was a selfish action," he told Thomas. "I deeply apologize." And he bowed again. Thomas, who was a fast learner, bowed back.

There was a tiny pool of fresh water on the island, but it was not spring-fed and it was covered with a floating blanket of green scum. There was also very little food. Enzo had a pistol with six rounds of ammunition, and with it they managed to shoot two parrots. Other than those birds, which were musky in flavor and tough to chew, the only things they had to eat were some sort of tiny fruit, which gave them diarrhea, and a few herbs that grew near the spring.

Enzo recognized the herbs right away. As he told Grandpa, he was an herbalist as well as a pilot; the knowledge of herbs was a tradition in his family that went back several generations. What he really wanted more than anything was to return to Massachusetts someday and practice herbal medicine. He taught Grandpa the Japanese names for the plants they found. Perhaps because there was little else to do, Grandpa found himself interested. He rapidly mastered the names and various uses of wormwood, fennel, and henbane. Enzo, finding a willing student in my grandfather, went on to teach him everything he could remember in the three weeks they were together.

In return, Grandpa read aloud to him from the diary of Willie Mann. They were both hearing it for the first time, and far from being the monotonous account of farm life Grandpa had expected, it was fascinating. It got easier to read, too, as they progressed further, for Willie had gradually and on his own mastered the mechanics of spelling and grammar, until by the time he was forty or so his entries read with the smoothness and ease of Dickens or Proust—both of whose works Enzo had read. The slight Japanese pilot sat and listened, enthralled, for as long as Grandpa cared to read to him. When Thomas's voice grew tired, Enzo read it himself, silently, pondering over the truths contained therein like a Talmudic scholar.

One day their longed-for rescue took place. A single-engine American fighter plane flew overhead, attracted by the smoke from the signal fire they kept burning day and night on the beach. The next morning the silhouette of a ship appeared on the horizon; it rapidly grew closer. Thomas and Enzo watched in silent apprehension as it approached. Enzo, they both knew, was about to become a prisoner of war, and my grandfather was probably going to have to return to active duty. Neither of them were thrilled with the prospects their immediate futures seemed to hold, but it was better for both of them than being found by the Japanese. Grandpa had heard horror stories about how they treated American prisoners—although doubtless Enzo had heard the same stories about American treatment of Japanese prisoners—and Enzo certainly would have been in disgrace for having been lost and then shot down. Too, the pair were emaciated, dehydrated, sunburned, and so starved they were no longer hungry, and so rescue by either side was better than the certain death that otherwise would have been their lot.

"That Robinson Crusoe business is all a bunch of hooey," said Grandpa to me later. "We probably would have been dead within the week if they hadn't found us."

A flare went up from the ship as it anchored offshore. As a landing party made its way toward the island in a small skiff, Grandpa turned to Enzo impulsively.

"Here," he said, handing him the diary. "I want you to take this."

Enzo looked at him in bewilderment. "I cannot," he said. "This is the property of your ancestors."

"You can give it back someday," said Thomas. "I don't want you to keep it forever. But you seemed to get a lot more out of it than I did." He was thinking that Enzo would need something to keep his mind occupied while he was a prisoner. And the truth was that Thomas didn't want it. The diary contained many stories, fascinating stories, about his family. But it had also informed him of something he would rather not have known. In fact, he realized with a shudder, he was the only Mann to know the true story of his grandfather's Civil War experiences, the only Mann to know that Willie Mann was not a hero at all. That he had never been in battle. That it was not a Confederate musket ball that wounded him. That, in short, Willie did not deserve all the recognition and admiration that had been his all his adult life. Willie had given him the diary with the full knowledge that Thomas would find out the truth about him when he read it; Thomas thought this was an incredibly reckless act, and was wishing now that the old man hadn't given it to him at all.

Enzo, however, was touched by the gift. He knew nothing of Thomas's reaction to the diary; to him it was a wonderful story, one that inspired him and made him think. Thomas had said he must give it back "someday." In those days, *someday* was a brave and optimistic word to be using. One didn't know, in wartime, how many more days lay ahead. There was absolutely no guarantee that either of them would make it through the war alive.

"I will return it, if I live," said Enzo. "I swear it."

"I believe you," said Thomas.

The landing party made shore. Thomas, naked, saluted and reported Enzo, also naked, as his prisoner. Enzo was placed under guard and, once on board the ship, manacled and locked in the brig.

"That was the last I ever saw of him," said Grandpa to me, some thirty-five years later. "But he still has the diary. I made them let him keep it. And he's going to bring it back—I know he will. He was the most trustworthy fellow I ever knew, American or Jap or otherwise."

I first heard this story when I was about six years old, or rather that's the first time I remember hearing it. I'm sure I must have heard it before then. The first time Grandpa told it to me, I already knew the ending, so perhaps I'd been hearing it from the time I was born or even before, as if in my sleep. Grandpa used to talk me to sleep when I was little, his cracked bass voice soothing and lulling me as it rose and fell like those Pacific waves he'd swum through to reach safety. This was one of my favorite bedtime stories. I always felt the same thrill of security when he landed on the beach, just ahead of the sharks that had already consumed poor Phillip Neuberg of Kansas City. I could feel them nipping at my toes as I raced through the salt water, which felt to me in my imagination as warm and salty as blood, not cold and tasting of pond water like Lake Erie. I would shiver with excitement and pull my feet well clear of the end of the bed, so nothing could reach up from underneath it and grab me in the darkness.

One might think a story about Japanese fighter planes and sharks would give a young boy nightmares. I had nightmares aplenty, but they weren't about that. They were entirely different. It was only one nightmare, really, repeated over and over. In it, I'm not me. I'm a girl. I'm running through the woods, frightened beyond words, holding up my dress so I won't trip over it. There are men in uniform chasing me, soldiers, not from this country. They speak a different language and their uniforms are bright green with red trim. The woods are familiar to me. They're these woods, here, the woods of Mannville, but long before there were subdivisions and trailer parks. The forest is deep and menacing, with scarcely a shaft of sunlight penetrating the trees. I run like a wildcat, always just ahead of them. I can hear their puffing and blowing and their strange guttural shouts, the jangling of the equipment on their belts. And just when I think I've lost them, I trip over a root and fall flat on my face. The soldiers are upon me in an instant. They surround me in a circle. One of them draws his sword, holds it up high, and in one swoop, he cuts off my head.

The picture goes dark.

I always awake from this dream screaming. Grandpa comes when he hears me, more often than not. When he does he lies down next to me in my bed and throws one arm over me.

"Easy," he whispers. "Easy now, lad."

"They were chasing me," I whimper.

"I know," said Grandpa. "They chase me too. And you were her, weren't you? Not yourself, but a girl?"

I nod. I'm far too young to find it odd that Grandpa should know what my nightmare is about before I tell him. He's Grandpa; he knows everything.

"I have that dream too," said Grandpa. "We all had it, all of us Manns. We're supposed to."

"I hate it!"

"It's the price we pay," says Grandpa, "for our greatness." And he sighs, not a sigh of apprehension but one of deep contentment, because my having this dream is the final proof that I really am a Mann, more conclusive evidence than any DNA test ever would have been, and also it shows that we are not yet completely fallen. For as long as we pay the price, there must be something to be obtained from it, and we are not doomed after all. Perhaps, Grandpa is thinking, our greatness has only just begun.

When Grandpa returned to Mannville at the end of the war, he was given the elaborate sort of welcome that people have always reserved for their greatest heroes. His mother, Lily, had already spread the story of how he was shot down and survived on a desert island by his wits, omitting for the sake of Mann honor his friendship with Enzo Fujimora, and perhaps embellishing other details here and there. When he disembarked from the train, there was a crowd of four hundred people there to welcome him, many of whom were convinced that Thomas was an ace fighter pilot who had taken over the island himself by single-handedly slaughtering the hundreds of Japanese who occupied it. Several of them carried signs, saying WELCOME HOME, TOMMY BOY! and MANNVILLE SALUTES ITS HERO. It was December of 1945. Thomas had left as a nineteen-year-old boy and returned a grizzled twenty-two-year-old veteran. He'd finished out the war at a desk job, as he'd requested after his rescue, but nobody seemed to know that. He carried with him only his duffel bag and his memories of the screams of Phillip Neuberg, and he jumped down to the platform, kissed his mother (who was briefly and regally hysterical), shyly greeted the crowd, and went home to the family seat, the huge farmhouse on the north side of town.

Thomas himself had no delusions about his role in the war. He'd

only done what he had to do to survive, as had everyone else who'd
made it home, and he didn't consider himself any more of a hero than
the other boys from Mannville. Some of them had come home missing an arm or a leg, or with holes blown through their sanity, and some
of them hadn't come home at all. Thomas felt no pride, no heroism
when he thought of himself in comparison to these other wartime victims. But he found his mother greatly changed toward him. She worshipped his presence like a devoted servant. Lily had grown terribly
lonely during his absence, Thomas discovered, and she'd aged a good
deal more than the three chronological years he'd been gone; her hair
was mostly gray, though she was just over forty, and her heart was
beginning to fail. She'd barely managed to maintain her queenly
facade through the war. She'd been waiting for Thomas to come home
so that she could begin the gradual process of turning over the farm
and its various side industries to him, her only son; and that huge trust,
combined with the wide-eyed awe with which he was treated in town,
began to swell inside him, until he walked with a strut and affected a
fancy mustache, and didn't correct people when they accidentally
called him "Lieutenant." He never mentioned what he'd discovered
about his grandfather in his diary, of course; there was no reason to
upset his mother, and it had all happened so long ago that it didn't
matter anyway. He put those nagging doubts to rest by ignoring them.
And the diary was safe in Japan, where nobody in Mannville would
ever find it. That was the other reason he'd given the diary to Enzo.
He couldn't quite bring himself to destroy it. Better to send it far away.

Lily died of a heart attack in the early spring of 1946. Thomas,
married now to the young and lovely Ellen Hurley of Buffalo, was suddenly free to do whatever he wished with his money. His tastes, though
grand by Mannville standards, were not extravagant, and he was not
the type to waste money on useless luxuries. Instead, he acted upon a
plan that had been brewing in the back of his mind for some time.
Farming corn and vegetables had always seemed boring to him. He
was therefore going to liquidate his assets, import ostriches from
Australia, and begin an ostrich ranch. It couldn't fail, he told himself.
He was just the sort of far-thinking man who could pull it off. He was,
after all, a millionaire and a war hero, and nobody would dare contra-
dict him. In fact, he envisioned it as the start of a growing trend in

America. He'd eaten ostrich meat once while visiting Australia on leave and found it delicious. Mannvillians would soon follow his example, simply because he was who he was, and then he would have a hold on the ostrich market that would be unshakable. And he wouldn't do this on a small scale, either. All his land would be converted to ostrich ranching; all his attention would be focused on it.

Straightaway Thomas imported two thousand ostriches from Australia at phenomenal cost and hired seventy-five workmen to fence in the entire farm. Thomas and the rest of Mannville waited expectantly for the arrival of the birds. A week went by, then two weeks, then a month, then three. Then came a telegram; nearly half of the ostriches had died aboard ship en route to America. Of those that survived the trip, another half died promptly after their arrival, victims of various New World diseases to which they had no immunity.

The rest of the ostriches milled about disconsolately after their arrival in the huge area Thomas had ordered fenced. There they remained until they discovered the fences, which they promptly jumped over, never to be seen again. Thomas had told the workmen of his plan, but none of them had ever seen an ostrich before, and they had no idea of the true size or strength of one. Most of them had the vague impression that an ostrich was a very tall chicken. The fences were built accordingly, and the ostriches found them no serious obstacle to their freedom.

That was the end of that. After only three months, Thomas found himself almost bankrupt, and with not a single ostrich to show for it. What was worse, however, was that his reputation among the people of Mannville had plummeted. People in town laughed in his face. Outraged farmers barraged him with phone calls—rampaging ostriches were ruining their corn crops, and they shot them on sight. Ostrich sightings began to be reported in the neighboring towns of Springville, Angola, and Hamburg, and one even came from as far away as the tiny mountain town of Ashford Hollow, nearly sixty miles distant. The Mannville *Megaphone* carried weekly articles on the subject for the next year, with such headlines as MANNVILLE'S MANIACAL MILLIONAIRE MISSES MARK and GIANT CHICKENS INVADE NEW YORK! Finally, however, the whole affair came to be known as the Great Ostrich Fiasco of 1946. It is, I believe, still mentioned in history classes at Mannville

High School as an interesting and colorful piece of local legend.

Broke, depressed, and suddenly friendless, Thomas retired permanently to his farmhouse. My father, Eddie, was born in late 1947; soon after, Ellen Hurley, whose name I know only from reading the wedding announcement on microfilm in the Mannville Public Library, returned alone and forever to Buffalo, having discovered belatedly that her love had been for the Mann fortune and not for Thomas Mann himself. My grandfather never mentioned her name to me, and Eddie barely knew of her. All of Thomas's energy was focused on his son. It was only through Eddie, Grandpa knew, that the Mann name could begin its long and gradual ascension from the muck into which he had accidentally plunged it.

Everything had to be sold to pay off his debts. The three main Mann farms, including land and equipment, were publicly auctioned. The land was mostly purchased by developers eager to participate in the postwar frenzy of prosperity. Everywhere across the country, servicemen were returning home and reproducing at a fantastic rate. It was as if they were making up for lost time, time wasted in France and England and the Pacific and everywhere else the long and miserable war had been fought, time wasted in fighting when they should have been carousing in the sack with their wives. These servicemen had money now, and good jobs, and they demanded homes. Within four years, by 1950, the three thousand acres had been subdivided, parceled, built upon, and sold, and where once fruitful fields of wheat and corn and grapes had stretched impressively across the landscape, there were driveways with shiny new cars parked in them, women hanging laundry in backyards, and quiet streets filled with children on bicycles and scooters. A new town existed, and all because of a lousy idea my grandfather had that never came to fruition.

"This is all my goddamn fault," he told me, as he had told my father, waving at the same neighborhoods. "If I'd been born with a brain, none of these suburban dipshits would be here. Better yet, I should have been eaten by sharks instead of that poor Phillip Neuberg. I bet he would never have been so stupid as to invest in ostriches. He was an engineer. Engineers are smart."

My father entered kindergarten in 1952. His academic career from that moment on was brilliant, according to my grandfather. Like me, he could read phenomenally well at an early age, and as a result he skipped the first grade and was promoted to the second. In middle school he began playing football and baseball, as well as working a part-time job at Gruber's Grocery. "He was never home after he turned thirteen," said Grandpa, and he did not add that he didn't blame him. Who would want to stick around the dying remains of a once-great empire, as its once-great emperor sat glumly amid the ruins, sipping straight Irish whiskey, shunning all human contact?

Eddie also learned to fight: "Kids used to tease him, on account of his old man was the laughingstock of the town," Grandpa said. "So they would say things to him and he'd pound on 'em till they took it back. That business didn't last long. He was one of the strongest kids around, and after someone got a taste of him once, they usually didn't come back for more. Then he started getting noticed on the field. By the time he was in high school, everybody forgot who he came from. He was just Ready Eddie. His name was in the paper every week or so. Girls used to call here all the damn time and lose their nerve before they could say anything. God, he was something."

He was more than something; he was a Mann. His natural tendency toward greatness could hardly be suppressed by a mere lack of money. If anything, it made him shine more.

"We don't have any money," Grandpa would tell me. "We don't have any friends. We just have this house, and you have me. And I have you. But by God we still have more than any other family in this town, because we have Mann blood. And don't you ever forget it."

"I won't," I promised.

And I haven't, because it's my story too. Even though it didn't happen to me. If I am to tell my own account, the story of who I am, how I came to be, and where I'm going, then the other stories need to be told too. Not necessarily in order, of course, but where they fit. Time is a river, but sometimes rivers run in circles. They eddy, they create backwaters, little forgotten pockets of shoreline where things persist in an unchanged state, far removed from the frantic pace of the deeper middle. It's a good idea sometimes to allow yourself to drift into these spots, just floating and spinning, and forget about things for a while.

3

My Early Childhood Continued; the Kind of Man My Father Was; the Munchkins; Grandpa Has an Accident

My father's old bedroom was on the second floor of the farmhouse. It had one window facing north, toward the Lake, which was barely visible on clear days as a faint blue line just above the trees. His was the only uninhabited room that was kept up—it was far cleaner than the kitchen, for example, with its unwashed dishes, or the living room, littered with newspapers and whiskey glasses sticky with residue at the bottom. One wall of the bedroom was lined with shelf upon shelf of golden trophies, thirty-eight of them in all, polished and dusted and lined up neatly in order of height. They were all gold, not silver or bronze, because my father had never taken second place in anything in his life. He competed in cross-country running, the 100-meter dash, the 200-meter dash, discus throwing, javelin hurling, the breaststroke, shot put, and football. He excelled at everything, but football was his love.

Eddie became the first-string quarterback for the Mannville Meteorites when he was only fifteen years old, and he threw against boys three and four years older than himself. He danced without effort

from the clutches of behemoth farm boys from neighboring towns like
Springville and Angola, boys strong enough to grab a cow by her horns
and twist her head until she went mooing to her knees, and who wanted nothing more in their lives than to crush my father like a grape so
he would stop throwing touchdown pass after touchdown pass. The
Meteorites won four consecutive regional championships while my
father was throwing for them, and went to the state finals three times,
once returning victorious. On another wall were photographs: Eddie
in a boat holding a prize-winning walleye, Eddie in a three-point
stance wearing his helmet and jersey, Eddie throwing a javelin and
looking like Achilles on the beach at Troy, various blurry Achaeans in
the background shouting their approval. And finally, Eddie in his Air
Force uniform, an American flag stretched out gloriously behind him,
the white of the bars mimicking the brightness of his smile. This picture was taken about a year and a half before my birth. *Hey, son*, he
seemed to be saying to me, *war is great, flying is great, America is great,
everything is great. Isn't it fun to be a hero? Isn't it great to be a Mann?*

I stared at this particular photograph for hours, wishing mightily
that I could jump into it and join my father in representing everything
that was good about the world, and about America. Grandpa allowed
me into my father's room on the condition that I wouldn't mess anything up. Certain things on the desk had been left untouched since my
father placed them there. These were icons, religious relics that must
never be disturbed, since Eddie was the last to use them. As a result,
the desk was perhaps two or three centimeters thick with dust, a filthy
oasis of sentimentality in a desert of spotlessness. The items themselves were nothing of note: a pen, some paper clips, a copy of *A
Farewell to Arms*. Eddie had been a Hemingway fanatic. I was forbidden by my grandfather to read Hemingway, on the principle that it was
he who'd inspired my father to go to war in the first place. I found this
interdict enticing, but it would be several years before I picked up the
book and read it for myself. For now, it was enough to look at the
cover, the title barely visible under the dust, and know that the book
hadn't been moved since 1969, and that the last person to touch it had
been my own dad, and that perhaps the only way for me to keep his
ghost alive, to speak to him through the veil of death, was to venerate
these things as my grandfather did, to treat them as though they were

some sort of radio transmitters permanently tuned in to the frequency of the afterlife.

My father had been a daredevil, Grandpa told me proudly. He was convinced at an early age that he could fly; Grandpa still had the collection of plaster casts to prove it. They were kept in the basement, near the jars of herbs, permanent impressions of my father's various limbs taken at different ages, removed and saved after the bones healed. There were five of them—three legs and two arms. I inherited my father's madly suicidal tendencies, much to Grandpa's delight, although my courage—some might call it stupidity—took the form of high-speed stunts performed on the riding lawnmower, which interested me more than jumping off the carriage-house roof—my father's favorite routine. Grandpa had long since given up mowing the huge yard, and he'd removed the blade from the mower to make it safe for me to operate. It was a good thing he had. I was constantly practicing such tricks as standing on the hood while steering backward, or attempting a headstand on the seat while steering with my bare toes. Grandpa sat on the doghouse roof and roared his drunken approval. I fell off more times than I stayed on, especially in the higher gears, and several times the mower rolled over an arm or a leg, and once my whole body. Thanks to the foresight of Grandpa, however, I came through my childhood not only intact, but entirely unafraid of anything the physical world had to offer.

Sometimes in the afternoons we played Munchkins. This was great fun because it was bloody and murderous and frightening, and I never knew exactly what was going to happen. But it went mostly like this:

Grandpa sat on the roof of the old doghouse, unoccupied now by any dog, with a glass of whiskey nearby and his fedora pushed back on his head. I would stand next to him and he'd put his hand on my shoulder. We would be absolutely silent. My ears would ring with the vast depth of the quiet that had suddenly descended over the yard. I was attuned, coiled, ready. Suddenly there would come a rustle from the bushes.

"There they are," I whisper, pointing.

"Right!" Grandpa shouts. He sets down his whiskey and begins pulling imaginary things out of the doghouse, handing them to me.

"Dynamite?" he says.

"Check."

"Fuse?"

"Check."

"Plunger?"

"Check."

"You have all your equipment? Compass, pistol, flare gun, life jacket, inflatable raft, fishing rod?" Sometimes this game became confused in Grandpa's mind with his sojourn in the South Pacific, and he liked to make sure I had everything I needed in case I somehow ended up in the ocean.

"Check."

"Okay," he says. "Go plant your charge."

I would sneak off to whatever bush or tree or hedge the Munchkins were hiding in this time. The Munchkins were a band of horrible ferocious creatures who'd lived in our yard since the beginning of the world. They were small, about my height, and they had long fangs dripping with saliva and claws that could rip you in half. The men had beards reaching to their waists. The women ate human children whenever they could get them. It was imperative that they be wiped out so the world would be safe for kids again. Blowing up Munchkins was my terrifying duty, and I was proud to perform it. It was my responsibility as a hero, as the son of my father. I planted my charge in the bush, one hand on my pistol in case they should attack. Sometimes they did; the hand-to-hand combat that ensued was fierce, and I was often gravely wounded, but I always defeated them.

"How many are there?" Grandpa would shout from the doghouse.

"Eight hundred and eleven!"

"Jesus Christ! Report back to headquarters!"

I would race back to the doghouse.

"Ready on charge!"

"Right! Countdown!"

"Ten nine eight seven six five four three two one!"

"Kablammo!" shouted Grandpa, pressing down the plunger. The world would be shaken by a tremendous explosion. I'd be knocked to my feet, lie unconscious for a few moments, then return to where I'd set the charge to finish off any survivors or to take prisoners, depending on my mood toward them that day.

This was long before I'd ever watched a television; my stealthy reconnaissance of the Simpson home and their mysterious flashing box didn't count, since I hadn't come close enough yet to figure out what it was. The Munchkins were the first things in my life of which I was seriously afraid. I was twenty years old when I finally saw *The Wizard of Oz* and the creatures of my childhood nightmares were revealed to me for what they really were: a sham, a put-on, a master hustle pulled on me by unwitting Hollywood con men. Munchkins were not ferocious or terrible at all, although they were slightly unnerving. I was outraged. It would be many more years before Willie Mann's diary was restored to me, its rightful owner, and I would read the following entry, which, like so many of Willie's other entries, seemed addressed specifically to me:

> *There comes a time in every man's life when his worst fears are shown by the cold light of reason to be mere shadows cast by insignificant objects. When this time comes, one may either grow angry over it, or shrug one's shoulders and keep on. This is the true test of adulthood, for he who is resentful of the events which have shaped him has not yet assumed control of his own destiny.*

But in those days I knew nothing of adulthood or destiny or even of reason. I only knew that the Munchkins frightened me but that I loved to play the game over and over because it was a game Grandpa told me he'd played with my father, just the way he did with me; a man and a boy, utterly alone in the world, defying nature by pretending that what was real was not and what was not real was.

Between the nightmares of the strange foreign soldiers chasing me through the woods and the Munchkins who haunted the vast yard, I began to lose sleep. My entire world, which had previously been limited to the woods and the Lake and occasional spying trips to the Simpson home, had been invaded by powerful evil. It lurked everywhere, growing darker and more terrible by the day, until it became a feeling that came over me, a feeling with a personality of its own. It even had a name: the Dreaded Scarum.

I don't remember how or why I invented the name of the Scarum. Most likely I'd heard Grandpa say it once: "That'll scare 'em," he might have told me, of the Munchkins, or perhaps the Pittsburgh Steelers, whom Grandpa despised. The Scarum became fixed in my mind as the being who controlled all bad things. Not only did he cause them, he *liked* to cause them. It was his raison d'être. The Scarum was always on the lookout for a chance to scare me. I drew pictures of him: he was a great winged dog with the head of a lion, and at night he floated in the sky over the old farmhouse. Sometimes I could hear him breathing.

It was the Scarum who'd killed my father, not the Viet Cong. It was he also who'd caused Grandpa to be shot down by Enzo Fujimora; who'd made Grandpa lose all our money in the Fiasco of the Ostriches; who made Mr. Simpson shout at his children. They were his long and slippery hands that reached out from under my bed at night, scrabbling frantically at the covers to grab my feet and pull me under with him. I lay shivering every night in a tight ball under my blankets, too scared to sleep and too ashamed to call to Grandpa. The occasional bumps and squeaks and groans of the ghosts in our house hardly disturbed me at all anymore. They were, after all, my relatives, and I knew they wouldn't hurt me; it was Grandpa with whom they were upset. The Scarum was far worse than any ghost, and to make it worse, the ghosts themselves were powerless over him. They could only ring me in a protective circle, which they did each night in the form of tiny dancing lights; occasionally I could feel a warm hand on my cheek, when one or another of them would materialize long enough to give me a comforting pat. I would start out of half-sleep when I felt this, unsure if it had really been a ghost or if Grandpa had sneaked in just long enough to check on me. It didn't matter. I was watched over by my family, and it was they who carried me safely through the darkness of each night.

The winter of 1977 was a particularly bad one. Late that fall, before winter had even officially begun, there came a storm that encased everything in a solid inch of ice. The world as I knew it was once again transformed, this time into something beautiful. Trees, shrubs, power lines, the ancient brick oven next to the old carriage house, even the old farmhouse itself—everything was sealed in solid glass, arrested in the endless path of birth and decay and held still like a preserved animal to be examined. The Dreaded Scarum, whose presence still remained known only to myself, receded, as though this inexplicable phenomenon of nature merited a temporary truce. The sun, small and white and cold, glinted on everything with magnified vigor. The backyard became an acre of mirrors, upon which I could slide with incredible velocity.

With the retreat of the Scarum, I rediscovered my love of dangerous and stupid stunts. The sudden absence of friction from the world created new and fascinating possibilities. This was not the same sort of ice that formed on the surface of the Lake. That ice was rough and uneven, sometimes buckling into huge white mountains, the tombs of waves, it seemed, that had been caught and held there. That ice was also unpredictable. It looked solid enough, but it was precisely that illusion of solidity that had led Grandpa's own father to his death in 1912 when he tried to drive across it to Canada. This ice was smooth and pure, scoured unceasingly by the winds of the storm into absolute flawlessness, with not a smudge or a crack in it. By propping open the kitchen door and running from the far wall, I could get up enough speed to launch myself onto the ice and skim gracefully on my belly almost a hundred feet across the yard. It was like flying. The first time I did it I smacked my face and split my lower lip open, but I'd done that so many times already in my life it hardly seemed worth crying about. I flew again and again and again, until I was exhausted but too hysterical with delight to stop. Finally I decided that I would make one last run and then find Grandpa so he could fix me some lunch.

I hadn't seen Grandpa all morning, but that was nothing unusual. Sometimes several hours would pass without us encountering each other in the huge old house. When one of us needed to see the other on some matter of importance, we rang the old iron dinner triangle that hung outside the kitchen door. After my last slide I would ring for Grandpa, who would appear and say, "Fried baloney all right?" It was what he always said. It was what we always ate, and it was always all right.

I never completed my last slide. Instead I ran smack into Grandpa, who was coming up the back stairs to ring the triangle himself. *He'd* been wondering where *I* was, and was coming to ask me if fried baloney would, once again, be all right.

We collided just as I parted company with the last inch of runway.

I heard the air go out of him in a soft, surprised "Hooo!" as my head drove into his elderly abdomen. He was propelled backward as though shot point-blank with a howitzer. We landed together, me on top of him, safely cushioned by his comfortable stomach. He, however, had nothing to cushion him except an inch of ice. I heard and felt a mighty crack somewhere deep inside his body, and he gave such an anguished and horrified scream that I knew the Scarum hadn't been gone after all; he'd only been lurking, waiting for my defenses to drop in the false lull of terror.

"Oh, shit," I said. That was my new word that year.

"My hip," said Grandpa.

"I'm sorry!"

"Get off me."

"I'm sorry I'm sorry I'm sorry . . ." I said, meaning it more than I had ever meant anything. I crawled off Grandpa's poor broken body. He screamed again. I put my hands over my ears and shut my eyes. I felt the Scarum licking at the back of my neck, his hot breath foul and damp.

"Billy," said Grandpa, "stay calm." His face was white and he breathed in high-pitched gasps. "You have to call somebody for help."

That, at least, was something I knew how to handle. I slithered my way over the slicked-up stairs into the kitchen, the Scarum panting hard at my heels. I knew that if I turned around at that moment I would see him. I chose not to look.

The phone was cold and black and very heavy. I held the receiver to my ear and listened. It was, of course, dead. So was every other phone in New York State. The ice storm had temporarily neutralized all the effects of modern civilization upon the world. It might have been 1877 instead of 1977. It might have been the dawn of time.

"Hello," I said calmly, hoping against reason that someone was listening anyway. I refused to let the desperation I was feeling drag me down into the abysmal blackness that was opening at my feet. "Hello!" I·shouted again. I was crying now, which made me angry; I hated crying. I slammed down the phone and ran to the door.

"It doesn't work!" I screamed. Later I would discover that the phone hadn't been working for three weeks, but since neither Grandpa nor I knew anyone to call and since there was nobody to call us, there was no reason to discover that fact until an emergency arose, by which time, of course, it would be too late.

"Oh, fuck a duck," said Grandpa, sounding more like his old self. That calmed me. "Okay, Billy," he said, "listen to me carefully. You'll have to take the Galaxie and get some help."

"The Galaxie!" I began to cry again. "No way! I don't know how!"

"Listen to me," said Grandpa. His face was growing whiter. "*Listen to me.* I can't move. It's very cold out here, and I'm going into shock. Do you know what shock is? It's when you're hurt very badly, and your body temperature drops. I could freeze to death, Billy," he said. "If I don't get some help soon, I could *die.*"

For some inexplicable and perhaps divine reason, as soon as Grandpa said that, my fear was gone completely. Even though I was only seven years old, I assumed the burden of Grandpa's life with the confidence of a man who'd lived my life span many times over.

From the diary:

> *Fear is a great obstacle to many things, but once it is removed, one can see clearly what needs to be done.*

I ran back into the house, found some blankets, and arranged them on top of Grandpa. Not even he had thought of that.

"Good boy," he said approvingly. He was in intense pain, breathing rapidly.

A sudden flash of inspiration hit me. It was almost palpable, as if it had been planted in my head by someone or something, some force that was watching out for me. "I'm taking the rider mower," I said. Even in agony, Grandpa was impressed.

"Beautiful," he whispered. "I've raised a genius."

The mower was kept in the carriage house. At some point in recent history the old solid oak door, which opened horizontally, had been replaced with a modern metal garage door, one that opened vertically; this, like everything else, had been iced over. Had it been fully shut, it would have been impossible for me to move. Mercifully, however, it had been left open enough for me to crawl under it. Once my eyes adjusted to the gloom, I located the mower and sat astride it. It was hard to see in there, but I had driven the mower so many times before,

I could have started it in total darkness. I pulled out the choke, retracted the blade—even though it was long gone—moved the throttle down to the picture of the turtle, which meant slow engine speed, and turned the key. The motor caught on the third try. I let it warm up for a few moments, gradually inching the throttle up to the picture of the rabbit, until it sounded ready. Then I stepped on the clutch and slowly shifted into first gear. The clutch slipped out from under my slick booted foot, and the mower and I hurtled forward into the mostly closed garage door, which was exactly what was needed to shatter the ice on it so that I could open it the rest of the way. I hadn't intended to do that, of course, but at age seven I was very superstitious, and this seemed to be a sign that things were eventually going to be okay, that someone really was watching out for me. I was reassured.

Cautiously I piloted the mower down the frozen driveway, still in first gear. I dared only one look over my shoulder at Grandpa. He was lying where I'd left him, his legs sticking stiffly out before him and his arms spread out to the side, looking oddly like a very large child in the act of making a snow angel. I wanted to wave, but I didn't dare take my hands off the steering wheel. I faced forward again and put the mower into second gear.

There was only one place I could go for help, and that was the Simpson house. In ordinary circumstances I would rather have cut off my arm than appear suddenly at their front door. For all I knew, Mr. Simpson would kill me on the spot and eat me for dinner. These, however, were not ordinary circumstances. Grandpa's phrase *I could die* rang in my ears with the urgency of an ambulance siren. It was dangerous to go above second gear, so I did my best to maintain a constant speed. When I got to the junction of our dirt road with the paved county road, I peered hopefully to the east and west, looking for a car, or a policeman, or an airplane, or anything. There was not a living creature in sight. The entire coast of Lake Erie had been immobilized. It seemed to me that the entire *planet* had been dunked in liquid mirrors, and only I, a seven-year-old boy, had survived the immersion to crawl about on its surface, a tiny and unnoticeable being living alone on a cosmic paperweight.

The mower skidded only slightly on the road. It was far lighter than a car, so even when I did skid there wasn't enough momentum to carry me into the ditch. The wheels spun maddeningly, however, and when I got to the base of the hill on top of which sat the Simpson house, they lost their grip entirely. The rider couldn't do it. I sat dejected, the motor humming incongruously under me in an otherwise silent world. It would take me forever to climb up the hill on foot. It was just too slippery. I could see the Simpson house far above me, glimmering and glinting in the sunlight like a tantalizing beacon of hope. I thought of Grandpa, slowly freezing to death in the yard. I almost began to cry again. I wouldn't let it out, however—I must be brave, like my father, I thought. My father never cried. Certainly not in situations like this anyway. He would have flexed his bronzed arms, grinned his bewitching grin, spit contemptuously on the ground, and gone straight to it. I would have liked to go straight to it too, but I had no idea what it was I needed to do.

And then I hit upon the solution that would later be reported in the Mannville *Megaphone* as the heroic feat of the century, a stunning example of youthful ingenuity under duress. I turned the rider around and went up the hill *backward*. I wish I could remember how I hit on that idea. It was a true flash of genius, for with the rider reversed, the greater part of the weight was forward; this, combined with the fact that reverse is usually the strongest gear of any machine, allowed me to arrive safely at the top of the hill, rear end first, having traveled exactly half a mile in about thirty minutes.

I maneuvered the rider through the maze of junked cars in the front yard and stopped before the sagging porch of the ramshackle house. There, standing in the doorway, was the girl I had seen playing in the yard several times before. She stared at me in astonishment, one finger in her mouth, her pigtails ratty and frizzed. I hopped off the mower and skated to the door in my boots.

"You better go get the man with the mustache," I said. "The mean one. My Grandpa fell down."

She kept staring at me.

"I know who you are," I said. "You're the only pretty one in the whole family."

I still had a lot to learn about how to speak to people I didn't know; one effect of my childhood solitude has been that I tend to get straight to the point, without observing social niceties, even now as an adult. Sometimes this is good and sometimes it's not, but in this case it was exactly the right thing to say. Annie told me much later, when we were teenagers, "I had no idea who in the world you were, but I fell in love with you on the spot."

"You're hurt," she said, pointing to my split lip. I'd forgotten about that.

"Annie!" came the voice—that deep, rumbling bass that always set the children crying and made me scurry off down the hill back to the farmhouse. "Who the hell is it?"

Annie didn't answer. Her eyes changed somehow—clouded over—and she stepped back from the door. In a moment I heard heavy footsteps and the man with the mustache and large belly appeared. He squinted at me through beady piglike eyes. He was much older than I'd previously thought. His hair was thinning and streaked with gray, and his face was like a streambed in summertime, with tiny cracks and wrinkles running all over it. He looked about as old as Grandpa.

"What the hell are you doing here on a day like this?" the man said. "Who are you?"

"I'm Billy Mann," I said. "My Grandpa had an accident." It was my fault, I did not add. I began to feel like crying again, but I wasn't going to do it in front of this man. Something told me I would get no comforting words or hugs from him. Suddenly I missed Grandpa very much. "He slipped on the ice and he says his hip is broken."

"Billy Mann," he repeated, his thin lips barely visible under his mustache. "Ooohhh. Eddie's bastard."

I wondered if he had read the note left by my mother. How else would he know my real name? He looked me up and down, appraising me like a piece of livestock, as if trying to determine how much of my father's legendary greatness had been diluted by the genes of my unknown mother. Then he opened the door.

"Come on in," he said gruffly.

I stepped inside. Every house has its own peculiar odor, but the smell here was almost overwhelming. It was composed of beer and stale cigarette smoke and old greasy cooking and just plain filth, and somewhere deep underneath it all was a layer of fear. I recognized this last smell immediately. It was the smell of the Scarum. I stayed by the door to catch the fresh cold breeze that wafted in.

"Close the damn door," said the man to Annie, and she did so immediately.

The man waddled into the living room and sat down on the couch. The inside of the house much resembled the outside, except for the ice. There were beer cans and paper plates and newspapers and car parts strewn about the floor, and the couch the man sat on was riddled with holes through which I could see springs lurking like long, ravenous worms. On a low coffee table sat a fascinating apparatus. It had knobs and dials and glass tubes in the back, and a microphone. Mr. Simpson lowered himself onto the couch with tremendous effort and flicked a switch. The tubes in the back of this thing began to glow orange. I wondered if this was the object that produced the flashing blue lights I was always seeing through the windows.

I remained in the doorway next to Annie. I could feel her looking at me but I hesitated to look back. I watched Mr. Simpson instead. When the tubes were a bright orange, he picked up the microphone and, to my astonishment, began speaking into it.

He used a strange language, one I'd never heard before. My heart chilled for a moment; the only other language I'd heard besides English was the one spoken by the foreign soldiers in my dream as they chased me through the forest. But I relaxed when I realized this one was different. The words were made up of recognizable parts: he said "niner" instead of *nine* and used numbers like "ten-four."

Annie took me by the hand suddenly. I jumped when she did it; her hand was like a live thing unto itself, soft and vibrant and pulsing. I didn't let go. Neither did she.

"C'mere," she whispered, bringing her lips close to my ear. "I want to show you something."

With another glance at Mr. Simpson, who ignored us as he chattered into the microphone, we crept down a hallway past a filthy kitchen to one of the back bedrooms. The door was open. A stronger smell seemed to issue from here. It was unfamiliar and very unpleasant; I could tell it was the source of much of the odor of the house.

"Look inside," said Annie.

I did. There on the bed was a man, or a half-man, under a sheet. He lay perfectly still, motionless because he had nothing to move. He had no arms or legs, at least none that I could see under the sheet, and his head was perfectly still. I couldn't tell if his eyes were open or shut. If they were open, he was simply looking up at the ceiling. The sheet he was covered with was dirty and gray and showed signs of having been repeatedly soiled without being washed in between. Tubes ran into his arms; they hung from clear plastic bags, several of them.

"What is he?" I whispered to Annie.

"He's my brother. Don't worry. He can't hear us. He can't hear anything."

"How do you know?"

"Because. He can't hear or see or talk or anything."

"What happened to him?"

"He was in a war and he got blown up," said Annie.

"What war?"

"Vietnam."

"Vietnam," I breathed, the familiar word oddly comforting in this sick and alien atmosphere. "I know all about Vietnam. My dad was in it."

"Come on," said Annie, taking me by the hand again. "He's almost done."

We went back out into the living room. The sight of the half-man unmoving in the bed had shaken me and I was breathing hard. I had a feeling I'd never known before, a different kind of dread than what the Scarum produced in me. How could there possibly be such a person as that man in the back room? I wondered. How could someone be so badly hurt and still live? When I thought of my father dying in his jet fighter I shuddered. If someone could have their arms and legs blown off and still survive, how badly was my dad hurt for him to die? The image was horrifying. I was fighting off the urge to cry again. Annie's hand in mine was soft and hot and I squeezed it hard.

"Ow," she said, but I could tell she wasn't mad. She squeezed back.

We were in the living room again. Mr. Simpson had finished speaking into the microphone.

"Idden 'at cute," he sneered when he saw us holding hands. "Annie got her a little boyfriend."

Annie said nothing. Neither did I—I was waiting to see what would happen next.

"Ambulance is comin'," said Mr. Simpson. "But if you think I'm gonna take you back down the fuckin' hill in my truck, you're outa yer fuckin' mind. Too much ice."

I looked away, embarrassed. I hadn't expected him to do anything of the sort. I felt a sort of gratitude to him for having called for help, but even at the age of seven I sensed that he'd done it because it was expected of him, not because he'd wanted to. My gaze fell on another device, a large box with a glass screen in it. My curiosity overcame my disgust and fear.

"What's that?" I asked, dropping Annie's hand to point.

Mr. Simpson snorted, superior and supercilious. "Ain't you never seen a TV before?"

"I've seen it plenty of times," I said defensively. I almost gave away the fact that I'd been spying on him and his family, but I remembered to keep quiet about that. A good spy, my father often told me during our games, never gives away his secrets. Grandpa told me that too—if the Munchkins captured me, I was never to talk, even if they tortured me.

"The damn women in this house have it on all day and all night," said Mr. Simpson. I wondered where these "damn women" were. As far as I could tell, the house was empty except for the three of us and the frightening creature in the back room. "These goddamn bitches," he went on. "They don't do nothin' but sit around and watch TV all day and all night. Annie too. She's gonna grow up just like her momma. Fat and useless and ugly."

I felt Annie flinch next to me.

"No she isn't," I said, before I knew the words were out of my mouth.

For a fat man, Mr. Simpson moved surprisingly fast. He was up off the couch and in front of me before I'd even noticed he'd moved, and one meaty hand was wrapped around my muffler, drawing it tight around my throat.

"You got a big mouth," he said. "Course, maybe you think 'cause you got all that money you can say whatever you want. Well, lemme tell you somethin', you little bastard. You Manns ain't shit. You ain't got any more money anyway. Ain't so great now that all those damn birds ran off on you, are you?"

I tried to swallow. My knees were trembling and I knew that in a moment the tears were going to come, no matter what I did to stop them.

"I know where you kids went," he went on, loosening his grip. "You went into the back to do bad things to each other. Grown-up things. Huh? Huh?" He had Annie by the arm now, and he was shaking her. "Did you touch each other back there? Did you? Did you touch her, you little bastard?"

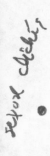

"No," I said miserably, but I was lying. I had held her hand. Was that bad? It must have been, to make him so mad. But she had grabbed my hand first. It wasn't my idea.

Mr. Simpson went into the kitchen suddenly. I heard the refrigerator door open and slam shut, and the shushing sound of a can of beer being opened. He came back out again, swilling from the can.

"You Manns think you're mighty fine," he said. "That old man down there always had his damn nose in the air. Too good to talk to us, too good to help us out. And his goddamn kid gets to be a pilot while mine has to join the regular infantry. Lemme tell you something, you little shit. I was in the goddamn infantry in the big one and there ain't nobody else there but niggers and spics and the white folks who ain't got the money to be pilots. And I didn't get no parade neither when I came home. I got off the train and there wasn't no crowd of people waitin' for me with signs and whatnot. I fought three years in France and I didn't get shit for it. I ain't ashamed to say it. My kid had to fight down on the ground with the niggers while his kid got to fly around in a nice cozy airplane. Huh. Well, if you were back there I guess you saw him. My boy ain't much now, but at least he came home. *His* didn't make it. And that's what he gets for havin' his damn nose in the air."

I couldn't even bring myself to say another word to Annie. I was out the door and back on the mower before I knew my feet were moving. It started with a roar. I headed back down the hill, weeping furiously, going far too fast. Before I was halfway down the hill I lost control of it and went sliding into the ditch. I was thrown up onto the far bank, smacking my lip for the second time on the ice. I tasted the familiar flavor of salt and copper that was my blood. I was crying even harder now because I knew I couldn't kill him until I was big, and that wouldn't happen for a long time yet.

I had no chance of righting the mower. I didn't even try. I left it roaring in the ditch, gasoline trickling from some smashed valve. I crawled back on the road and scooted down the rest of the hill on my bottom. If I hadn't been so furious I would have been delighted at the new game I'd discovered—sliding down the hill was even better than sliding across the yard. And if Annie's father hadn't been such a monster, maybe Annie and I could have played on the hill all day, sliding down and climbing up it, in another world where there were no people who spoke like that to children and who weren't filled with hate because of the things they didn't have. But these thoughts never entered my mind. There was nothing in me but blind rage, the impotent anger of a tiny male who would not be a man for a long time yet, and who had no choice but to submit to whatever happened to him, and for the first time that I can remember, I was angry enough to kill someone. It made me sick to my stomach, but at least I wasn't afraid any more. I didn't even give the Scarum a thought.

I skated on my boots once I reached the bottom of the hill, screaming and sobbing through the blood that trickled from my lip down my chin. The trip home was much faster than the trip up had been. Long before I arrived at the farmhouse I could see the flashing lights of the ambulance. When I arrived, I found the paramedics just loading Grandpa into the back of it on a stretcher. I forgot my sense of balance and tried to run, and I fell and hit my lip yet a third time, and that was how I got to ride in the back of the ambulance with Grandpa, because I needed to be stitched up.

I sat next to him and cried as he held my hand, too furious to explain any of it. It was all right, he said. He knew I was scared. He knew it was scary to be a kid when something bad went wrong. But it wasn't my fault. I mustn't worry and I mustn't cry. I didn't have to tell him I wasn't crying because of my split lip. He knew I didn't cry over little things like that. I was a daredevil, and the son and grandson and great-grandson of daredevils, and he was Grandpa. He knew everything about me, right down to the dreams I had at night, and he understood that I was crying because today I had caught a glimpse of how the world could be sometimes, and because that sight is horrifying to children.

* * *

I hadn't intended to tell Grandpa about what I saw at the Simpson house, but being young and excitable, the words were flying out of me before I could stop them. He lay wincing in pain as I rattled on—he'd been doped up already, so he was feeling much better, more like his usual self, but he was still conscious. The ambulance proceeded at about five miles per hour, and the siren, much to my delight, was blaring.

"They have a man in the back of their house with no arms or legs!" I told Grandpa. "He just lays there in bed and looks up at the ceiling, except I think his eyes are shut, and he was in Vietnam just like my father was!"

"There were lots of people in Vietnam," said Grandpa.

"Do you think they knew each other?"

"Do I think who knew each other?"

"My dad and that man in the back room."

"Just because they were in the same war doesn't mean they knew each other," said Grandpa. "It was a big war, though not so big as some."

"Yeah, but did they?" I sensed I was being put off about something Grandpa didn't wish to discuss, but I was tired of not being told things and I decided I wasn't going to let it go this time. "You never said if they did or didn't."

"Did or didn't what?"

"Know each other!"

"Billy, I'm tired," said Grandpa. We sat in silence for a while, the ambulance swaying gently as we got onto the county road and were able to pick up speed a little. A salt-and-sand spreader had been by recently and I could hear the tiny particles pinging against the bottom of the ambulance. The siren, to my disappointment, fell silent.

"Yes," he said finally. "Yes, they did know each other. But not in Vietnam. They were friends here in Mannville when they were little boys."

"How little?"

"Your age."

"They played together?"

"Yeah."

"What did they play?"

"I don't know. They ran around in the woods a lot. There were a hell of a lot more trees back then."

"Did you play Munchkins with them?"

A brief smile flickered across Grandpa's face. "Yes, I did," he said. "The three of us played Munchkins together."

"Just the same way? With dynamite and all that stuff?"

"Yeah. Just the same way."

"What's his name?"

Grandpa frowned. "Why do you want to know his name?"

"Because! You never tell me anything, that's why."

"Never tell you anything! Hah! Don't I tell you every story about this family I know?"

"I guess."

"You guess. You know more about your own family than most kids do, my boy, so no complaints. Knowing the kind of people you come from is just as important as knowing yourself. In fact, you can't know yourself if you don't know your people."

Grandpa may not have realized it, but at that moment he was para-phrasing something Willie Mann had written in his diary on precisely this subject, which I would read many years later:

> The Delphic Oracle urges one to "Know yourself," but how are Americans to know themselves? We have practically no history, and our future, although promising, is hazy. We have only our present, which we are continually creating and recreating. For one to know the self, one must examine the past, and inquire without hesitation into the nature of the people from whom he has sprung. This way, we can avoid making the same mistakes which were made by our ancestors.

I was confused. "How do you know yourself? You can't meet your-self and know yourself like how you meet someone else and get to be their friend."

"No, you're right," said Grandpa. "It's not like that at all."

"Well then, what is it like?"

"You'll understand later, when you're big."

"I'm pretty big now."

"You're seven years old. That's not very big."

"I'm going to be big enough someday to go back there and beat up that fat old man with the mustache!"

"What?" Grandpa was instantly alert. "Why would you want to do that? Did he do something to you?"

I was silent. I hadn't wanted to tell Grandpa about how mean Mr. Simpson was. That's how children are—when something bad happens to them, they tend to think it's their fault. This is true in a multitude of situations: divorce, abuse, molestation. On the other hand, children are also very bad at keeping secrets. I couldn't keep Mr. Simpson a secret from my Grandpa. I couldn't keep *anything* a secret from him.

"He yelled at me," I admitted, and my lower lip began to quiver.

Grandpa took my little hand in his big warm one. "Did he?" he said, his voice soft. "Did he yell at you?"

"Yeah." I was feeling miserable again, but I was glad to be telling him about it.

"Why?"

"He was mad I was talking to Annie."

"Who's Annie?"

"A little girl who lives there. She's my age. We're friends."

"So there's another one," Grandpa muttered.

"What?"

"Nothing. You say you're friends with this little girl?"

"Yeah."

"And he was mad about it?"

"Yeah. And he was mad about the man in the back of the house with no arms and legs."

"He was, huh?"

"Yeah. And he was mad about my dad."

Grandpa stiffened a moment and then relaxed, as much as one can relax with a broken hip. "What did he say about your dad?" he asked, letting go of my hand.

"That he was lucky because he got to fly and he didn't have to be in the intrafy—"

"Infantry," Grandpa corrected me.

"—and his nose was in the air and Mr. Simpson had to be down on the ground with the niggers in the war."

"Don't say that word."

"What word? War?"

"Niggers."

"What does it mean?"

"It means black people, but it's not a nice word. Only white trash use that word."

"What's white trash?"

"The Simpsons are white trash. Dirty and poor, but mostly dirty. There's plenty of poor people who aren't trashy at all because they know how to hold themselves upright like people, and they don't go around talking about other people who work harder than they do and calling them names. Mr. Simpson is angry for a lot of reasons, Billy, but mostly because he never worked hard at anything in his life. He always expected everything to be given to him. A Mann never expects anything to be given to him. That's the difference between us and the Simpsons. That's what makes them white trash. It has nothing to do with money."

"What are black people like?"

Grandpa smiled again. "What are they *like*?"

"Yeah. I don't know any. Do you?"

"I knew some in the Army," he said. "A few guys. They were very nice and they had a rough time because they were black. They didn't get any breaks. None. But they knew a lot of good stories and songs, and I used to talk with them a lot. I wasn't really supposed to, but I did anyway."

"You weren't *supposed* to?"

"No."

"Why not?"

"Because they were black and I was white."

"So?"

"That's exactly what I thought," said Grandpa. "I thought, *So?* An officer told me once I shouldn't hang around with them anymore because it was against policy. I thought, I don't give a shit about your policies, Mr. U.S. Army Guy. I didn't get shot down over the ocean and escape from sharks and live on an island with a Japanese pilot who saved me from starving just so I could come back and be told about Army policy against talking to black people by some little rodent from down South who happened to be an officer. God, those people were stupid. Back then they kept black people separate from whites. They had to ride in the back of the bus, use separate drinking fountains, separate bathrooms, separate schools, separate neighborhoods, separate everything. What a mess."

"Separate *drinking fountains?*"

"Yeah."

"Why?"

"Because white people were afraid they would get a disease if they drank from the same fountains as black people."

"Would they?"

"No, of course not."

"What was his name?" I changed the subject abruptly.

"Who? The black guys?"

"No, the man with no arms and legs. You never told me."

"Because I never tell you anything, right?"

"Just tell me!"

"His name was Frederic," said Grandpa. "*Is* Frederic, I mean. We called him Freddy."

"Did he like my dad?"

"Yes, he did," said Grandpa. "He liked him a lot."

"Did my dad like him?"

"Yes."

"Did *you* like him?"

"Yes," said Grandpa. "He was a very sweet-natured boy, and he didn't take after his father at all. He got into some trouble later, but when I knew him he was very polite. At least to me he was. Probably because I used to take them on little trips and play with them, which that fat old drunk never did. Excuse me, Billy, I shouldn't talk like that about Simpson in front of you. That's not good manners. Forget I said that."

"Okay. What kind of trouble did he get into?"

"He stole something."

"What did he steal?"

"A car."

"Who from?"

"From me," said Grandpa. His lips were tight.

"He stole your car? The Galaxie?"

"No. I had a different car then. A Chevy."

"Did you call the police?"

"Yes, but that was before I knew who took it. If I'd known it was him I wouldn't have called the police."

"Why not?"

"Because I knew that boy. I knew he was just acting crazy, that he wasn't really bad. And I knew when his father found out about it he would give him a hell of a beating."

"Did he?"

"Yes. The police found him and took him home and his father beat the daylights out of him. He had to go to the hospital afterward. The same hospital we're going to now. If we ever get there."

"Why did he beat him up?"

"Because he's mean, and don't ever forget it."

"He yelled at Annie."

"In front of you?"

"He yells at her all the time."

Grandpa eyed me suspiciously. "How do you know that?"

I said nothing, but I could feel my face getting red.

"Have you been going up there? Were you ever up there before today?"

"I don't know," I said.

"Yes or no. Don't tell me you don't know."

"Yes."

"Why?"

"I don't know," I said again. "I get bored. There's nothing to do!"

It was Grandpa's turn to be silent.

"Are you mad at me?" I asked him.

"No," he said. "I'm mad at myself. Connor was right. You need to meet other kids. You have to start going to school."

"*School?*"

"I was a fool to think otherwise," said Grandpa. "The county would probably get after me soon anyway. This isn't the old days anymore. You can't just do what you want. You have to go to school."

A sick feeling blossomed in the pit of my stomach. Before that day, I'd spent my entire life doing exactly what I pleased, whenever it

pleased me. Grandpa read to me and I read to him, and he taught me
what I needed to know whenever the opportunity presented itself. If
the Galaxie was in need of repair, we repaired it together, and I learned
in that way how to work on cars. If the roof needed shingling, I learned
how to shingle a roof. When Grandpa told me to bring half the books
that were in the second floor library to the basement and put the other
half on the shelves neatly, I learned to count and divide large numbers.
I thought I was learning plenty from Grandpa. I didn't see any reason
to go to school.

"I don't want to," I said.

"We'll talk about it more later," said Grandpa. "Don't worry about
it for now."

"Okay," I said. But I worried.

The ambulance pulled into the driveway of the Mannville General
Hospital. Mannville was really too small to warrant its own hospital,
but my great-great-grandfather had built one anyway, to cure the sick
and injured of the giant metropolis he was convinced Mannville would
someday become. It was an imposing four-story red brick structure
with three main wings to it, one of them especially for children. The
backdoor of the ambulance swung open and the attendants appeared.

"How you doing, Mr. Mann?" asked one of them. "Ride all right?"

The attendant was black. I stared at him unabashedly, wondering
if he'd ever had to drink out of a separate drinking fountain.

"I'm fine," said Grandpa. "Who's going to look after the boy?"

"Come on down, son," said the attendant. He took my hands and
helped me jump out of the ambulance. "Mind you don't slip on that
ice, now. Oooweee! Look at that lip! You busted it clear down to your
chin, looks like!"

"I fell down three times," I said.

"Three times! My, my. That's a mighty lot o' fallin' down!"

The attendants unloaded Grandpa's stretcher and wheeled it
through the swinging doors of the emergency room. I followed them.
They stopped beside a woman in a skirt suit. She had a pinched, dis-
tasteful expression, and she carried a briefcase.

"Get the boy stitched up. He's coming with me," she said to the
attendants.

"Yes, ma'am," they said together. The other attendant was white.

"Mr. Mann," she said to Grandpa, "I'm Elsa Wheeler, from the county children's services office. I understand you're the sole guardian of this boy?"

"Yeah," said Grandpa. "Why?"

"We're going to look after your grandson while you're recuperating."

Grandpa had done a lot of talking in the ambulance, induced by the painkillers the paramedics had given him, and now he was fading out. His eyes fluttered like the papery wings of an insect.

"Take care of my boy," he whispered.

Elsa Wheeler reached down and grabbed my hand. Her hand was thin and bony and cold. I struggled to pull free from her grasp but she only held on tighter.

"Hold still," she said sharply. "I don't have time to go chasing you all over the place."

"I don't want to go to school," I said, because I was sure that was where she was taking me.

"You're not going to school today," she said. "You're going to stay with one of our foster families until your grandfather is better. But you're going to school soon."

"The hell I am!"

Her hand flew loose from mine, swung around in a wide arc, and smacked me on the bottom. The sound of it caused the black ambulance attendant, who was by this time down the hall with my grandfather, to turn around and give Elsa Wheeler a long look. I was dumbfounded. In the course of my playing I'd been hurt far worse than her spanking, but it was the first time in my life I'd been struck by another human being.

"You just watch your little filthy mouth, mister," she hissed, "or you'll get another one of those, and you'll like it even less."

I knew I was going to cry now, and there was no helping it. My wails filled the emergency room lobby. I saw Grandpa lift his head up briefly from the bed and search for me before he collapsed weakly against the pillow again. The black attendant leaned down and said something to him. Grandpa shook his head.

Elsa Wheeler lost patience with me altogether. She dragged me by the arm into a large white room, where a doctor was waiting for me.

"Now, then," said the doctor. "You're Billy Mann, and I've heard all about you. You're a very brave little boy."

I stopped crying somewhat.

"Brave boys don't cry, do they?" said the doctor, and he stuck a needle in my lip and proceeded to sew it back together again. He didn't do a very neat job. That's why I grew a beard as soon as I was able, to hide the jagged white line that ran from my lower lip to my chin. It was always a physical reminder of the worst day of my life. I was eager to hide it from the sight of the world, so people would stop asking me where it came from and so I wouldn't have to remember the day I was taken, if only temporarily, from my grandfather.

4

My Seventh Year Continued; I go to the Shumachers'; I Encounter Trevor and Adam

I awoke early the next morning in a strange bed. The sun was not yet up and the room was predawn gray; I couldn't see where I was, only amorphous shapes of furniture that in the semidarkness seemed to levitate, as if they had wills of their own. Then I noticed what had awakened me. A large figure loomed over the bed, breathing in deep cavernous gulps. Petrified, I watched it move closer until it hovered directly over me. I caught a faint whiff of manure and milk, and also of tobacco; these, at least, were odors with which I was familiar. I clenched my eyes shut and pretended I was asleep, meanwhile leafing through my mental catalog of smells. Now who did I know who smelled like that? Someone, I knew. Oh yes. Now I remembered where I was. Relief flooded through me—I was at the Shumachers', and the Shumachers were nice.

The bed was damp. I remembered a dream, in which I'd been at home and had gotten up to pee in the bathroom. I wasn't at home, however. Apparently I hadn't made it to the bathroom after all. And it was only Mr. Shumacher standing over me.

Mr. Shumacher was a large, beefy man, and as he clicked on the lamp next to my bed I saw he was holding a newspaper inches from my nose. It was a copy of the Mannville *Megaphone*, the local paper from which I read to Grandpa every morning. My eyes focused first on the headline. It read BLOOD OF WAR HERO RUNS IN SON'S VEINS.

I looked next at the picture under it. It was a picture of me.

"Look! You famous boy!" said Mr. Shumacher. "Mutti!" he shouted over his shoulder. "We have a famous boy in our house!" He spoke with a heavy German accent. It sounded like he was saying, "Ve heff a famous poy!"

"Yah," said a woman from the doorway. "Famous Amos, we could call him."

"We could, if his name was Amos, like mine," said the man.

"I peed in the bed," I said. I got up. "Amos is my middle name," I added.

"Yah, time to get up," said Mrs. Shumacher, as if she hadn't heard me. She had an accent too, heavier than her husband's, and she wore an apron over her housedress. She disappeared from the doorway and I heard her clumping down the stairs.

"You go pee now too, yah? In the potty this time," said Mr. Shumacher kindly. He led me to the bathroom.

"I'm sorry," I said. I'd never wet my bed before and I was deeply ashamed.

"Shah, shah," said Mr. Shumacher. "Tomorrow night I'll wake you up so you can pee in the right place. We have a rubber sheet on that mattress anyway."

I peed again in the toilet. Mr. Shumacher filled the tub and Mrs. Shumacher reappeared to scrub me down thoroughly while I stood in it. I'd never taken a bath standing up before, nor had I ever been bathed by a woman. Her hands were swift and sure, the hands of a practiced mother, and I surrendered myself to her expertise. Mrs. Shumacher seemed to have bathed a thousand children, and she was much better at it than Grandpa. She gave me a professional scrubbing all over, even digging into my ears with the washcloth, until my skin glowed pink and raw and I begged her to stop.

"There," she said, with evident satisfaction. "Clean."

Then she dressed me in strange new clothes that didn't quite fit and I went downstairs with her to breakfast.

The Shumachers were a large and buoyant tribe of Pennsylvania Dutchmen, and they already had so many children one more could hardly be noticed. I learned later that they'd been taking in children for over two decades, most of them victims of some tragedy or other, like me. That was why they were hardly surprised when I wet the bed. Disturbed children often pee in their sleep. They knew that from experience, and were ready for it.

Besides the father and mother there were six Shumacher children, most of them teenagers, and one other child who was not theirs. The Shumachers were loud and Teutonic and vibrantly healthy, and they greeted me with happy shouts as they came in from their early morning work about the farm and sat down to an unbelievably large breakfast. There were platters of bacon, sausage, fried potatoes, pancakes, bowls full of scrambled eggs mixed with sweet peppers and onions, pitchers of ice-cold fresh milk and orange juice with beads of condensation standing out on them like sweat. Mr. Shumacher drank two cups of steaming black coffee without flinching before he even began to eat. I watched in amazement as his throat worked furiously. He set down his cup with a deeply satisfied "Ahhhh," and wiped his impressive mustache with a napkin; here was a man who appreciated small pleasures in a big way. When he saw me looking at him, he poured a small amount of coffee into a mug, filled the mug the rest of the way with milk, and sprinkled in some sugar. He set this in front of me.

"Drink that, boy," he said. "It makes you strong like me."

"It makes you fart like him too," said one of the Shumacher boys, and the table instantly erupted with laughter, Mr. Shumacher included. He picked up a sausage and pointed it like a gun at the boy. "I've had enough of you," he said, and this seemed to be the funniest thing the family had ever heard. They laughed until tears poured freely down their cheeks. Then Mrs. Shumacher clapped her hands once, and the joking was put aside. Only an occasional residual giggle now interfered with the serious business of consumption.

I, however, didn't laugh. Instead I sat in silence, overwhelmed by the attention and the sheer volume of food. Grandpa and I ate like birds compared to the Shumachers; also, there were only two of us, and the kitchen seemed empty even when we were both in it. I'd never been around this many people before. I couldn't bring myself to look up or to speak. Nor did I see what was so funny—in fact, I was beginning to feel lonely. The horror of the previous day was slowly revisiting me. I remembered Grandpa lying on the ground, old and soft and helpless on the hard ice that had nearly killed him. I remembered the half-man in the back of the Simpson house and the way Annie's eyes looked when her father yelled at her. The Scarum was reaching for me again, and I, still young and inexperienced in the ways of the world, had no idea how to escape his clutches.

Then the eldest of the children, also named Amos, who was in his early twenties and seemed to me very old, reached over and tickled me. I shrieked. More laughter. This time I joined in. Suddenly the Scarum was banished; I could almost hear his nails clicking on the linoleum floor as he dragged himself off to a corner, sulking. After that everything was fine, and I ripped into breakfast as though I'd never eaten before. I was, I discovered, very hungry.

That was how easygoing the Shumachers were. If they didn't know you, they tickled you, and then they knew you.

The other child who was not a Shumacher was named Trevor. He also wore ill-fitting clothes, the universal legacy of foster children. Amos tickled him too, but he didn't laugh. He ate little and stared down at his plate without taking part in the conversation, most of which was in German anyway. I didn't speak German, of course—I didn't even know enough to call it that—but it had a familiar, easy sound. I chattered along with them in English, laughing at jokes I didn't understand, which made them laugh at me, which made me laugh harder.

"You stay with us until your grandfatti gets better," said Mrs. Shumacher.

"Where is he?"

"In the hospital."

"When is he getting out?"

"Soon," said Mr. Shumacher. "Don't worry about him."

"How do you know?"

"We know your grandfatti," said Mrs. Shumacher. "He said you should stay with us while his hip gets better."

"He did?"

"Yah."

That was all I needed to be reassured.

After breakfast, Trevor and I were sent outside to play. Trevor spoke rarely, and when he did it was from the corner of his mouth, hardly seeming to move his lips at all. To me that was impressive. I decided to follow him around.

The world was still encased in ice. I tried to interest Trevor in my sliding game, but he didn't even bother to comment on it. I could tell he thought it was a child's game and that he was above such things. Instead we walked through the woods, breaking off frozen tree limbs and whacking them against the trunks until they shattered. We kept this up for a while. Then I trailed him to the back of the barn, where we sat on a pile of old lumber with our backs against the weathered wooden wall.

"How many homes you been in?" Trevor asked me.

I was confused. It was an odd question. "One, I guess."

"Liar. You wasn't born here, right?"

"No."

"So how many then?"

"Two."

"Huh. That's nothin'. I been in eight."

"*Eight?*"

"You deaf?"

"No."

"Parents dead?"

"My dad is. I don't know if my mom is or not."

"She must be, or you wouldn't be here."

"She might not be."

"She is," said Trevor decisively, and that settled that for him. He pulled a pack of cigarettes out of his jacket and lit one. I was shocked into silence. I'd never seen a kid smoke before. "What happened to your mouth? Cops do that to you?"

"I fell down three times," I said proudly. The doctor at Mannville General had given me seven stitches.

"Cops busted open my real dad's mouth one time."

"What'd he do?"

"Nuttin'."

"Did he go to jail?"

"Shut up," said Trevor.

"I was just asking!"

"None of your business. Got it?"

"Yeah."

"You ever smoked?"

"Uh-uh."

"Want to?"

"No," I said.

"Yes you do," said Trevor. "You got them cravin's all right." He took a cigarette out and handed it to me. "Put it in your mouth," he said. I lit it; it was the first time I had ever handled matches without Grandpa watching me, and I knew I could get in big trouble. I was thrilled. But the smoke burned my eyes, and drawing on the cigarette sent hot rivulets of pain down my stitched-together lip. I held it carefully away from me. It was the most miserable thing I'd ever tasted.

"Like it?"

"Yeah," I said.

"Smoking's good. Relaxes you."

"Uh-huh." I thought I was going to throw up.

"You just gonna hold it?"

"I don't want it."

"You have to have it now. I ain't wasting a whole cigarette on you."

"I can't."

"Jesus," Trevor said. "Gimme it back." I handed him the still-burning cigarette. "You got blood on it," he said disgustedly, and he threw it down in the snow. "That's one cigarette you owe me."

"All right," I said. I sat down. My stomach subsided somewhat.

"How long you gonna be here?"

"Just a few weeks."

"Huh. You're wrong if you think that. You're stuck here."

"No I'm not. I'm just staying here until my Grandpa gets out of the hospital."

"They pulled that one on me a few times too," said Trevor.

"What do you mean?"

"You'll see. They always come up with somethin' when there's somethin' happenin' they don't want to tell you about. I get moved around all the time. They always lie about it. That's how I know it's comin'."

"How come?"

"How come what?"

"How come you get moved around?"

"I break things," Trevor said.

"What things?"

"You name it. Glasses, dishes, windows, everything. Once I even wrecked a car."

"You *did*?"

"Yup. Guy I was staying with was passed out drunk and I took his keys. Drove it into a tree."

"How come?"

"I told you. So I get moved around."

"You *wanted* to get moved?"

"That time, yeah."

"Why?"

"That guy was a fag."

"A what?"

"A fag. A gay."

"What's that?"

Trevor eyed me suspiciously. "You kiddin'?"

I said nothing, hoping he would see I was not.

"A fag," said Trevor, "is a guy that likes to stick his dick in other guys' buttholes."

I absorbed this information in silence. I had no idea what a dick was, or why anyone would want to stick one in some other guy's butt-hole.

"Wow," I said.

"You ever done it?"

"What?"

"Stick your dick in another guy's butthole?"

Suddenly an image came to me. I thought I understood what a dick was then.

"No," I said. "You?"

Trevor shrugged and put out his cigarette. "There's other stuff you can do."

There's more? I thought. "Like what?"

"You put some guy's dick in your mouth and suck on it."

"Why do you do that?"

Trevor rolled his eyes. "You're an idiot," he said.

"No I'm not!"

"Yes you are. You go around to enough homes and some guy'll make you do it to him. Just you wait."

"I'm not going anywhere else. After this one I'm going back home. Mrs. Wheeler said."

"Wheeler don't know shit. You're staying here for the rest of your life."

"No I'm not!" A small sob escaped me.

"Look at you," said Trevor. "What a baby. You're gonna cry. That's how much of a baby you are."

"I am not!" But my lower lip was trembling, and my eyes filled with water.

"Jesus, what a baby. You're gonna be here forever, suckin' farmer dick. Your grandpa's dead and so's your mama. They just don't want to tell you 'cause they know you're gonna cry. See? There you go. You're cryin'."

"Shut up!" I screamed, and the next thing I knew I was sitting on top of him and beating the sides of his head with my mittened fists. I'd forgotten that he was older than me, that I'd wanted to be his friend. I wanted to kill him. Rage filled my tiny body until I felt it pulsing through me like a stream of Olympian lightning, and for the second time in two days I felt the ancient Celtic lust for war, or perhaps the utter disregard for death, that runs in the Mann blood.

Trevor scrambled out from under me and ran backward, crabwise, on his hands and feet. I chased him out from behind the barn and toward the house. He regained his balance, turned, and ran directly into Mrs. Shumacher, who had heard his screaming and my yelling and come running from the porch. Mrs. Shumacher had over twenty years' experience in breaking up fights between small boys and was utterly indifferent to their causes. She wasted no time interrogating us. She wrapped one meaty fist around Trevor's neck, grabbed me by the scruff with the other, and brought our foreheads together smartly. It was a precision blow, and if I close my eyes I can still feel it today. I'm sure

Trevor can too, wherever he is.

"No fighting," she said simply. She dragged us through the field of stars that had suddenly swum into my vision and into the bathroom, where she pressed cool washcloths to the lumps already forming on our foreheads. We were stunned into silence. My head hurt too much even to cry. "No fighting," she said again.

It was nearly time for lunch then, so dizzily, and under Mrs. Shumacher's direction, we washed our hands and went into the kitchen. The rest of the family reappeared soon after—Marky, a fleshy, apple-cheeked boy of twelve, easily twice my weight; Jan and Hans, eighteen-year-old twins who laughed nostalgically when they saw our knotted foreheads; two daughters, Elsa and Hildy, whose bosoms were enormous like their mother's, and who were always laughing about something secret; and then Mr. Shumacher himself, the biggest of all the Shumachers, his magnificent mustache a twin tapestry, his chest as thick as a horse's, and a broad, weathered face permanently reddened by cold and heat and always creased in a jolly smile. Amos, the eldest child, was the last to arrive. He looked exactly like his father except that he was slightly smaller and had no mustache.

The family sat at the long kitchen table, with Mr. Shumacher at one end and Mrs. Shumacher at the other, the eight of us arranged in between according to age. Mrs. Shumacher had begun cooking lunch almost immediately after cleaning up the breakfast dishes; she ran the kitchen with startling efficiency, and it never seemed to be dirty even when production was in full swing. The amount of food she created for each meal would have kept Grandpa and me in leftovers for a month; lunch made breakfast look like a kindergarten snack. There were platters upon platters of food, as if they hadn't eaten the hugest breakfast I'd ever seen five hours earlier: fritters, scrapple, spicy sausage that Mr. Shumacher made in his barn, ham sandwiches of homemade bread and slabs of ham as thick as my palm, homemade butter on those sandwiches, pitchers of milk, water, and apple juice, a large bowl in which I could comfortably have seated myself, filled to overflowing with potato chips. Mr. Shumacher brewed beer in the basement, and he and Amos Junior each helped themselves to a large stein of it, thick and dark with a soft brown foam. But first we prayed.

I learned by watching that praying consisted of ducking your head and acting embarrassed while Mrs. Shumacher intoned something out loud in German to someone who wasn't in the room. Later I was told it was God she was addressing—or "Gott," as she called him—and that sometimes he answered her, but that nobody else could hear him when he did. Whenever she had a problem on her mind, she would ask Gott, in front of the entire family, what to do about it. Today she said, "Dear Gott! Today two boys have been fighting. They also yelled and cursed. They are visitors here and won't be here long. What should I do?"

She was silent now, listening carefully to Gott's instructions and nodding her head from time to time. "Uh-huh," she said. "Yah. Okay."

The rest of the family dared not breathe. It was not often that Mrs. Shumacher decided to interrupt her regular prayer with a personal request, and to interfere with these conversations was considered a sin worse than murder.

"Okay," she said finally. "That's what I'll do then." And she lifted her head and said, "Amen."

"Amen," said everyone else.

I was horrified. So was Trevor. We looked at each other with wide eyes, wondering what would happen to us. Gott, it seemed, had seen everything, and hadn't liked it one bit. There was no doubt in my mind he knew we'd been smoking, too. I resigned myself to fate. Jail, I knew, was probably too good for the likes of me. Maybe Trevor was right— I wouldn't be allowed to go home after all. But Mr. Shumacher winked at me when nobody else was looking. With that simple dip of his eyelid, he communicated to me a thousand pardons, and the fear of Gott left my body and was replaced by hunger.

Then we ate. I watched in awe as these huge bellowing, snorting giants consumed food as if they'd never been fed before. The Shumacher body, I was learning, was a mighty machine in need of constant refueling. When I first saw on television those military jet planes that are able to refuel in midair, I thought immediately of the Shumachers. They would have benefited enormously from this method of eating while they worked except that it would have deprived them of the opportunity to talk to each other, which they did unceasingly as they ate. Mealtimes were the high points of their day. They shouted, laughed, cried, belched, clacked, slurped, smacked, and snorted. Most of the time I was too busy listening and watching to eat. I'd never imagined there could be such a thing as a Shumacher.

Days on the farm were extremely predictable. Even though Trevor and I were not expected to work—I because I was too young, Trevor because he was too bad—we were awakened at the same time as the rest of the family, long before sunrise.

The Mr. and Mrs. called each other Fatti and Mutti—German for "Dad" and "Mom"—and insisted that Trevor and I do the same; Trevor irreverently translated these names into Fatty and Muddy. Each morning, Mutti came into the room I shared with Trevor and the twins, clapping her hands and shouting, "Yah! This is a good time to get up!" So we got up. We formed a line outside the bathroom, the door of which remained open while we urinated in turn so that other members of the family could come in and out as needed. Life as a Shumacher included dealing on a regular basis with the facts of animal reproduction, and this translated into their daily affairs as a complete lack of modesty; the girls tittered at our morning erections as they came in and brushed their teeth, and it was at the Shumacher farm that I first saw a woman's breasts. They were Mutti's, stupendously large, and they swayed and jiggled violently like two live things as she brushed her teeth. I was embarrassed, thinking that I'd intruded upon some secret ritual, but she only laughed at me and gently closed the bathroom door.

Then we went downstairs in our long underwear to dress in front of the wood stove—the only source of heat in the large old house. Fatti generally appeared around this time, emerging from the subarctic wasteland that is New York in winter like a floundering polar bear, his eyes lighting up at seeing us out of bed. "Yah!" he shouted. "This is a good time to get up!" That, it seemed, was the basic Shumacher philosophy concerning mornings.

The first thing that needed to be done each morning was the milking of the cows. The cows were milked twice a day, regardless of mood, weather, or illness. Fatti had invested in an electric milking system of which he was fiercely proud. After the cows had been herded into their stalls, he and I and the other boys—except for Trevor, who wasn't interested in anything—stood around and watched as the milker sucked away in mechanical gasps and spurts at the swollen udders. The cows themselves swayed gently back and forth as they chewed their cud. The milker had only been there six months and it was still referred to as new. "You see that?" Fatti said, every morning. "That's progress. That sucks 'em dry in ten, maybe fifteen minutes." Everyone else already knew that, but they never tired of hearing it again, and it had to be said for my benefit. My visit to the milking barn put Fatti into seventh heaven. He had an excuse to launch into an endless lecture on the workings of the electric milker, which he did by showing me every tube and orifice of it, some of them twice. He substituted German terms when English did not suffice. That didn't matter, since I understood none of what he was saying, but I was happy because he was happy. I listened to him rambling, nodded at the appropriate times while he rested his hand on my shoulder, and a warm glow crept over me and settled at the base of my spine like a cat curling up to take a nap.

I avoided Trevor after that first morning. He was what Grandpa would have called white trash; not because he was poor, but because he was ignorant and mean, like Mr. Simpson. The Shumachers weren't poor, but they weren't rich either. I knew they weren't trashy at all. Grandpa would have called them "solid folks" or "salt of the earth" because they worked hard and expected nothing for free. I saw the difference clearly, but I don't think Trevor did. He seemed to hate the Shumachers. He didn't respond when spoken to, he sat sullenly and kicked at the table leg during mealtimes, and he merely snorted in derision when one of them tried to involve him in conversation.

I was afraid of Trevor. His stories of strange men making him do awful things had the opposite effect on me from what he intended. Far from being impressed, I was appalled, and because of that, and also because of our fight, I wanted nothing more to do with him. I rambled through the woods alone, as I was used to doing. The Shumachers lived in Eden Township, next to Mannville, and the woods were familiar; same clear cold smell of trees, denuded and dormant, and the Lake still there, not visible but breathing its wet breath gently upon everything. The ice was starting to thaw. The sun shone again and warmed the mirrors that covered the world, and they dripped slowly away into the earth, as in a Dali painting, and were gone. I played my old imaginary games with my father and looked halfheartedly for Munchkins, but it wasn't any fun without Grandpa's imagination to help me along.

Instead I climbed about in the hayloft and made a fort of the massive bales stacked there. Sometimes I spied on Trevor.

Trevor mostly sat behind the barn, staring out at nothing, smoking an occasional cigarette. Being beaten by a younger boy was a humiliation he felt keenly. He had withdrawn completely and spoke to no one. Mutti was worried about him. Hildy, the eldest girl, tried to tickle him once at dinner and he kicked her viciously on the shin, raising a large knot. The next day Mrs. Wheeler came in her long red car and sat in the kitchen talking with Mutti and Fatti. She smoked thin brown cigarettes as they talked, surrounded by a cloud of harsh perfumed smoke, and when she left, Trevor was with her, carrying his small cardboard suitcase. I watched from the hayloft of the barn. He didn't look back as he got into the car. His face was turned to the window, and though he couldn't see me, I imagined his set expression was being displayed for me to look at. It wasn't sad; it was triumphant, as if to say, I *told* you I'd be moving on soon.

At night, the nightmares came back to me. I was the girl again, whoever she was, fleeing desperately through the woods in my soft bare feet. The soldiers snarled at me in words that now sounded vaguely familiar. I screamed for Mutti and Fatti in my high girl's voice and hoped they would appear from behind the trees to save me, but they never did, and the dream always ended in the same way: me lying on my back, one heavy booted foot planted on my chest as the sword came flashing down and all went dark. I awoke every night with my head in Mutti's lap, her thick hands caressing my head. "Shah, shah," she whispered over and over, until my cries diminished and I grew sleepy again. I was aware of Fatti standing nearby, in the doorway perhaps, watching in confusion, trying to fathom what ancient demons could haunt a boy so young. If I'd had the words, I would have explained to him that they weren't just my demons; it was an old dream, and all of us Manns had it—Grandpa had told me so. But it wouldn't have made any sense, because I didn't understand it myself, and it would be many years yet before I discovered the diary of Willie Mann and the whole matter was explained to me in a way that would peel back the layers of dream-consciousness to reveal the truth that lay underneath.

The next day a new boy arrived. He was only five years old, and he was afraid of everything. His name was Adam. Something horrible had happened to him, but that we knew only from Mrs. Wheeler, because the boy himself couldn't speak. His vocal cords had been damaged, and when he tried to talk there was only a hoarse squeaking. Fatti told me it was because his stepfather had grabbed him by the throat. Adam was small even for five, and he had a shock of white-blond hair that looked as if it had been cut with the aid of a soup bowl. He was afraid of Fatti, Amos, Marky, Jan and Hans, Mutti, and Elsa. He was also afraid of bowls, knives, bathtubs, dogs, large pieces of wood, and the tractor. But of Hildy and me he was not afraid at all. There seemed to be no logic to his phobias. He held my hand tightly as we walked around the farm together, I showing him all the things I'd become familiar with in the last several days. We looked at the cows as they stood meditatively in their stalls. He wasn't afraid of them either, although they could have crushed the life out of his tiny body with one careless flick of their hips, and he squeaked excitedly when they looked at him with their large, limpid eyes. I showed him my secret fort in the hayloft, and we played a new game I'd invented, called simply "Vietnam." This game was played by launching myself from the top of a high stack of hay bales onto a soft landing platform of loose hay. That was me flying my jet fighter, and on my way down I made airplane noises and shot at enemy aircraft. Adam wouldn't jump, but he watched enthusiastically, squeaking as I flew. He became my shadow. When someone besides Hildy wanted to tell Adam something, they had to do it through me. He sat next to me at the table and ate whatever I ate. If I went to the bathroom, he sat outside the door and waited until I came out again; his eyes, blue and large and panicked, would resolve themselves into puddles of relief when I reappeared. At night he crawled into bed with me and snuggled up under my arm, where he stayed until Fatti came in to take me to the bathroom, and gently hoisted him out of my bed and into his own.

One night I awoke from the nightmare to find Fatti standing over me, watching silently. When he was perturbed about something, he twirled his pendulous mustache with his fingers. He did this now. When he saw that I was awake he kneeled next to the bed.

"What were you dreaming?"

"Soldiers," I said. "Chasing me."

"What soldiers?"

"I don't know."

"What do they do?"

"Kill me."

"Why?"

"I don't know," I said again. "I did something wrong."

"Nah," said Fatti. "You're a good boy."

"They think I'm bad."

"Why do you speak German when you're sleeping?"

"What?"

"German," said Fatti. "You speak German almost every night. But when you're awake you don't know German."

"*You* speak German," I said.

"Yah. But not you."

"The soldiers speak German."

"They from the war?"

"I don't know. What war?"

"The world war."

I knew a little about the Second World War from Grandpa's stories. I shook my head. "Different," I said. "They chase me and I trip over my dress and they cut off my head."

"You trip over your what?"

"Dress," I said. "I dream I'm a girl and they're chasing me."

Fatti pondered this in silence. I could see his massive bulk outlined against the moonlight, which glinted off the snow.

"A *girl*?" he said finally. "What kind of uniform do they wear?"

"Green," I said. "With big pointy hats."

"What do they tell you?"

"To stop. To *halte*."

"What's your name in this dream? You know?"

I thought for a moment. I didn't know for sure, so I said the first girl's name that popped into my head. "Mary."

Fatti nodded. That seemed to settle something for him. I got out of bed, and he took me to the bathroom so I wouldn't pee in the bed again, which I hadn't done since that first night anyway—it was just a precautionary measure. Then he tucked me back in and planted a loud wet kiss on my forehead. From his bed across the room, Adam gave a tiny whimper, engrossed in some nightmare of his own. Jan rolled over in the bed he shared with Hans and smacked him on the forehead with his arm. "Strudelkopf," said Hans in his sleep.

"Guten nacht, boy," said Fatti.

"Guten nacht, Fatti," I said, and I fell asleep again, this time free of nightmares.

The next day was Sunday. Working on Sundays was absolutely forbidden, not by Fatti and Mutti but by the mysterious and all-powerful Gott; so after the milking, which Gott didn't seem to mind, the entire family dressed in their best clothes and went to church. Ordinarily the Shumachers conveyed themselves to the Lutheran chapel in a convoy consisting of two pickup trucks and a sedan, but today was different. During breakfast, Fatti verbally commandeered one of the pickups. He and I, he announced mysteriously, were not going to church, but somewhere else, somewhere secret; it was personal business, and nobody was to ask me about it afterward. Adam, who after only a few days on the farm already couldn't bear to be separated from me, would come also.

Mutti looked worried. A day of worship missed was an open invitation to the devil, she said; though she didn't continue this thought out loud, I could tell she feared that Fatti was putting my mortal soul in danger for some fool reason that had popped into his head out of nowhere. Gott would not like it one bit if I wasn't in church that morning. I didn't volunteer that I'd never been to church in my life. This information would have shocked Mutti beyond speech. There was no telling what strenuous exorcism would have to be performed over me to set me right again, but whatever it would be, I knew it would be awful, and I wanted to avoid it.

This was the closest they ever came to having an argument in my presence. Mutti shot Fatti a look over the table that was loaded with unspoken admonitions, speeches, and protests; Fatti, normally not at all despotic in his nominal role as head of the family, nearly wilted under her steady gaze, and appeared to be caving in. I was intensely excited, but I said nothing that might jeopardize his position. I had no idea where he intended to take me, but I wanted to go very much.

The battle between them raged all through breakfast without another word being spoken. The Shumacher children watched this with great interest; this was how major issues in the family were decided, not with arguments but through some kind of marital telepathy between their parents. First Mutti folded her hands and rested her chin on them, staring at Fatti without blinking. Fatti busied himself with tucking his napkin into his shirt, taking an extraordinarily long time to do it. He smoothed out any possible wrinkles and made sure it was symmetrically aligned over his buttons. Then he picked up his fork and looked at Mutti with his eyebrows raised, the picture of husbandly innocence. Mutti rolled her eyes and began eating. But after one bite she put her fork down and looked at him again, this time with her arms folded. Fatti raised his hands in a hopeless gesture, as if to say he was obeying some higher law that could not be ignored; though he wouldn't say it, or perhaps even dare think it, the implication was that this law superseded even Mutti's authority, and therefore must be very great indeed. In fact, it could come only from Gott himself. There was even a hint that Gott had perhaps bypassed Mutti on this issue and gone straight to Fatti. It was not unheard of. It had happened before. But if Mutti was going to put her stamp on it, some hard evidence would have to be presented that this was the case.

Fatti put a forkful of pancake in his mouth and, chewing it mightily, put his elbows on the table and looked at her, secure suddenly in his decision. Mutti's shoulders slumped and her head went to one side. She wouldn't look at him for several moments. Then she sighed heavily, picked up her fork again, and began eating. The argument was over; Fatti had won, although it was clear he would pay a heavy price later. All the children, who had been watching with baited breath, breathed out the tension that had been mounting inside them and began to eat.

"You're not taking him to the circus, are you?" said Marky miserably, and the entire table exploded into mad laughter. Marky winced. It was explained to me later that when a county fair had been held in Eden a year ago, Marky had had a broken leg and couldn't go, and for a Shumacher child to miss a yearly fair—which they called "the circus"—was only slightly less heartbreaking than the death of a loved one.

* * *

Fatti steered the pickup into the driveway of a tiny house and turned off the engine. He didn't immediately move to get out; instead he appeared to be thinking hard about how best to proceed. His giant knuckles rapped out a tattoo on the steering wheel as he watched the house carefully.

"Yah," he said suddenly. "Okay. She has seen us."

"Who?" I said, alarmed.

"Frau Weiler," he said, "who is the lady we're visiting now. Okay. Listen. Whatever she does, don't be scared. She's a nice lady and she won't hurt you. Don't say anything unless she talks to you first. Okay?"

"Okay," I said, not at all sure what it meant, and we got out of the truck and walked toward the house.

The front door opened before we could knock. There before us stood a wizened old woman, only slightly taller than I was, stooped with age and heavily wrinkled. She wore a long black dress with a black shawl over her shoulders, and on her head was a white lace bonnet tied under her chin. Adam got behind me and wrapped himself around my leg. I nearly did the same to Fatti, but he had removed his hat and was speaking to the woman in low, respectful tones, not in English but in German, and I didn't dare move. The old lady nodded as he spoke, and when he finished speaking she opened the door and stepped aside to let us in.

The interior of the house was lit with two kerosene lamps, which did little to penetrate the darkness. I could see dimly that it was only a two- or three-room house, sparsely furnished. It smelled of some strange smoke that I didn't recognize. There were no photographs on the wall and no mirrors; nor, it appeared, was there any sort of electrical appliance. The old woman pointed to a long bench against one wall. The three of us sat down on it. Fatti got up again to drag a straight-backed wooden chair over. Frau Weiler sat in it, facing us, and fixed me with her eyes.

I was transfixed. Frau Weiler's eyes, unlike the rest of her, burned with fierce youth. They were a clear gray, her pupils twinkling like sunlight on the Lake in summertime; and though the rest of her was grim and fearsome, and her close-set lips did not alter in the slightest, her eyes were laughing, not at me but at something much bigger than I, than she, than all of us combined. It was not a mocking laugh. It was a laugh of joy, of recognition. I looked into these eyes and began to feel as though the old lady was communicating something to me. Then she looked at Adam, who was still clinging to me, and her eyes changed, softened somewhat. She looked as if she might shed a tear or two. Tiny Adam looked back at her, unafraid; slowly his grip on my coat loosened, and he leaned back against the bench, put his head on my shoulder, and, incredibly, began snoring.

The old woman spoke to Fatti now—her voice, though scratched like an overplayed record, was strong like her eyes—and he got up again and retrieved a small high table, which he set next to her. The table had a single drawer in it, and from this Frau Weiler produced a candle, some matches, and a small tin, which had once held throat lozenges. This she opened with reverence and set upon the table. From it she produced a sort of green stick that looked vaguely plant-like. She lit the candle with the matches and held the green stick to the flame. It began to smolder and give off a pungent odor. She held it under her nose, wafting it back and forth for several minutes, breathing in the smoke. Gradually the cloud grew and encompassed me, and I couldn't help but inhale it; it was nothing like cigarette smoke, but infinitely more pleasant, almost flavorful. I began to relax a bit more. I'd never smelled this kind of smoke before, but many years later, when I smelled it again, I would flash back instantly to that Sunday morning in the old Mennonite witch's house. It was the smell of marijuana.

The old lady fixed me with her eyes again, and this time I looked into her eyes and saw many things there, things that seemed familiar, but that I hadn't known I knew. I don't know what they were now; they weren't objects, or images, but more amorphous kinds of things: feelings, perhaps, or moods, or ideas. Everything made perfect sense at that moment; I've never felt the need to sort it all out in a logical way. We continued to look at each other for some time.

"Tell me your first name," she commanded me suddenly, in unaccented American English. "Nothing else. Just your name."

I told her.

Instantly she began speaking in German again, addressing herself to Fatti but still looking at me. Her voice was low now, singsong, and sent me into a kind of trance. The pitch and volume of her voice remained constant and she went on for a long time, just talking, and instead of growing uncomfortable or bored, I listened and let her words come into me. I was aware of everything, but my attention seemed to focus of its own accord on some little pinpoint of consciousness somewhere indefinable. I watched this little pinpoint as it grew into a larger thing, slowly taking me over. I surrendered to it, and it was warm and good.

The next thing I was aware of was that we were back in the pickup truck. I came back to myself in gradual stages. Adam was still sleeping against me, as if we hadn't moved or been moved but had suddenly materialized in the pickup from the bench in the little house. Fatti was relaxed, driving carefully on the still-slippery roads, occasionally laughing a little at some private joke. Nothing more was said about Frau Weiler for the rest of the day, and in accordance with Fatti's instructions, no one asked me where we had been or what had taken place. I spent the rest of the day in dreamtime, watching the family go through their Sunday routine. Occasionally the memory of Frau Weiler's eyes came back to me.

That night as I lay in bed, Fatti came into the room again to take me to the bathroom. I hadn't yet gone to sleep; I wasn't restless, just quietly looking up into the blackness beyond the thick rafters of the ceiling. The Shumacher house was even older than the farmhouse I shared with Grandpa, and in the ancient timbers one could still see the adze marks of the men who had hewn the beams out of living trees. It was the same in the barn, where I played among the hay bales. There were old messages carved into some of the beams, graffiti so old that they were no longer considered vandalism but history: WILHELM SHUMACHER SLEPT HERE, 1898. ELLA LOVES GERHARDT. EDEN ÜBER ALLES.

"That old lady told me something about you," said Fatti.

I'd been waiting all day for him to interpret what had happened.

"She says that dream is old. You too are old. Other things happened to you, in other times. Another body too. That girl you dream of—she was you. Or you were her."

I said nothing, digesting this. Fatti was staring out the window at the moonlit pastureland. It was a clear night and there were no streetlights to interfere with the stars. The Big Dipper hung low over the horizon, its handle pointing the way north, to the lake and to whatever lay beyond it.

"I go to see her sometimes," said Fatti. "Not too much. Every few years. When I have a question. When I was a young man, I went to her to ask her what should I do. I wanted to go to sea, you know. Be a sailor, like my Great-Uncle Wilhelm. But I also loved Mutti, before she was Mutti. I wanted to marry her, but I knew I couldn't do both things. If I went away to sea she would marry some other guy. So I went to Frau Weiler. She said, 'Amos, you do what your heart says.' She looked at me like she looked at you—strong, with those eyes. Even then she was old. That was almost thirty years ago. She don't give answers, that old lady. She just tells you the question another way, so you understand it. But she knows everything. All she needs is your name, and she knows you."

"What did she tell you?"

"That you are old, much older than seven. And you have been here before, like the rest of us. And that you are here again to find something."

"What do you mean, I've been here before?"

"We always come back," he said. "We come in groups."

"Who?"

"Souls."

Fatti turned away from the window and looked at me carefully. "Does your grandfather tell you stories?"

"All the time."

"Which ones?"

I shrugged. "About the war, when he was on an island. And about my dad. And about his dad. And Willie Mann."

"What about Willie Mann?"

"Just stories. He was in the Civil War."

"Yah. I know. Everyone knows about Willie Mann," said Fatti.

"They do?"

"Yah. It's a popular story."

"Which one?"

"How he found the money," said Fatti.

"Found the money?" I'd never heard this story before. "You mean how he got rich?"

"Yah. You don't know that story?"

"No. Tell it."

in me. I wanted to ask him about how Willie Mann found the money, but whenever I talked to him I cried and forgot to ask. But I knew I'd be seeing him again soon because he was almost better; and we would live together in the old farmhouse like we always had, and he would continue to tell me stories. And after Christmas I was to go to school.

I was still opposed to the idea of schooling, but I had held several lengthy conversations on the subject with Marky, who told me that school was not at all bad if you kept your mouth shut and were polite to everyone, most of all to the teacher. He dwelt particularly on the charms of a certain girl who sat in front of him. I lost interest after she came up in the conversation—I even walked away in the middle of it, and I believe Marky kept on talking about her to himself for several minutes anyway—but I was somewhat reassured about the whole business.

I was engaged in teaching Adam how to talk again. His vocal cords were returning to normal, and he was able to say a few words before he had to stop. I hadn't told him I was leaving. I knew he would want to come with me, but I'd overheard Fatti and Mutti talking one day and I knew they were going to try to adopt him. After that, they would stop taking in other children. Trevor had soured them somewhat. The twenty-year-long parade of strange children marching through their home was coming to an end. Adam was too fragile to withstand a child like Trevor, should another one happen along. They'd decided to adopt him because Adam's real father had shown up a week earlier.

He was white trash all over, a real Simpsonesque kind of guy; I could tell that from the moment he got out of his car, a brown Trans Am with an orange ball on the antenna. He was drunk and smelled like sour beer. I was playing out in the yard. Adam, for once, was not stuck to my side. He was in the house with the girls. It was a lucky thing, too, or things might have gone much worse than they did.

"Hey, you kid," said the man, "where's Adam?"

"I don't know," I said. He was a small man, but he looked danger-ous. Behind me I heard the front door slam. I didn't turn around. I was afraid to take my eyes off him. He was that sneaky-looking.

"You're lying," said the man. "You lie like a rug." He advanced toward me. I stepped backward and fell down.

"Aw," he said, "kiddo fall down and go boom?"

Fatti shook his head. "Not right," he said sadly. "I wish I could, but I can't."

"How come?"

"Frau Weiler said not to," he said simply. "Your grandfather knows it. He didn't tell you yet?"

"No."

"Then there must be a reason for that," Fatti said firmly. "I am not your blood, and it's not right for me to interfere with his wishes. He'll tell you when he is ready to tell you."

"Is it a secret?"

"No. It's not a secret. Everyone knows it. So I don't know why you don't know it. But there must be a reason, or he would have told you. It has something to do with this dream you are having every night."

"Does Mutti know it?"

"Yah."

"Does Amos Junior know it?"

"Yah."

"Do Elsa and Hildy know it?"

"Stop it, boy. Don't ask any of them. Ask your grandfather. He'll tell you."

"Okay," I said, resigned.

"You want to pee now?"

"Yah," I said. I was beginning to talk like a Shumacher. I got up and peed and then went back to sleep, and when I dreamed again that night I was free of the nightmare. I dreamed instead of Adam. In my dream, he could talk, and he wasn't afraid of anything. We played in the woods together, and there were no soldiers in green uniforms and pointed hats to chase us; and I wasn't a girl who had lived here long ago and whose soul had come back to find something, but myself, Billy Mann, son of fighter pilot Eddie, grandson of Grandpa, great-great-grandson of Willie Mann, the most famous man in Erie County.

Three more weeks passed and Christmas drew near. I'd spoken several times with Grandpa on the telephone. His voice was strong and healthy now, and when I talked to him a great homesickness welled up

"Shut up, you fag," I said, using the word I'd learned from Trevor. I got up again.

"*What* did you say?" He came toward me faster.

"Fatti!" I screamed. "Amos Junior!"

The man hesitated. "Aw, don't do that," he said. "I just want to get my kid."

The front door opened again and I heard the welcome sound of heavy male footsteps on the porch. It was not Fatti, but Amos Junior. Even though he was smaller than his father, he was easily half again as large as this smelly little man.

"Hello," said Amos Junior politely. "You have to leave. Now. No discussion." This was somewhat of a routine for the Shumacher family. From time to time the unruly parent or parents of one of their temporary children would appear and demand them back. The Shumachers had established a drill they followed: either Amos Junior or Fatti was around the house at all times, just in case someone showed up, and they politely but firmly escorted the parent from the property while one of the women called the police.

"I got rights to my kid," said the man. He had a nose like a rat, and his voice was whiny now that he was dealing with someone larger than himself.

"Actually, you don't," said Amos Junior. He was still trying to be polite, but it was becoming an effort. He'd grown very fond of Adam himself, even though the boy was still afraid of him. "You lost your rights to him when you grabbed him by the neck and pinned him to the wall. Don't you think so? Am I right?"

"That wasn't my fault!" shouted the man. "It was an accident!"

"It was not an accident. You were drunk out of your mind, just like you are now," said Amos Junior. His voice was shaking. "Get out of here. The cops are already on their way."

"Bullshit!"

"I called them the minute I saw your car. Brown Trans Am, license plate New York State 290JEY. Sound familiar? I've been waiting for you to show up, you dirtbag. You make me sick. You want to beat on someone, beat on someone who stands a chance against you. Now get out of here."

"Make me!"

"I will," said Amos Junior. "Believe me I will. I would love it, so just give me a fucking reason." Boy, I thought, he must really be mad. Swearing was forbidden in the Shumacher home.

"Here's your reason, you goddamn redneck," said the man, and he launched himself toward Amos Junior in a hopeless flying tackle.

Amos didn't even bother getting out of his way. He threw a slow, lazy uppercut, the trajectory of which was timed perfectly to coincide with the flight path of Adam's father. It caught him hard on the chin and flipped him over on his back. He lay on the ground moaning, blood pouring from his mouth. Then he sat up and tried to say something, but there was something wrong with his mouth; the sounds came out wet and garbled.

"Oh no," said Amos Junior. He was a very gentle boy and it was the first time I'd ever seen him hurt anything. He was polite to everyone, even the cows.

Adam's father spit something out on the ground. He looked at it for a moment in disbelief and began to scream. It was the front two inches of his tongue. He'd bitten it off when Amos punched him.

"Oh no," said Amos Junior again.

"Hah!" screamed the man. He got to his feet unsteadily. "Hah! Heeh! Hunh!" he said. Blood was pouring freely from his mouth. Already the front of his thin winter jacket was covered with it.

"Jesus, mister, why did you make me do it?" said Amos Junior miserably. He made a snowball and gave it to the man. "Put this in your mouth," he said. To me he said, "Billy! Go tell Mutti to call an ambulance!"

I ran inside the house. Mutti, the girls, and Adam were sitting at the kitchen table. Adam was crying; his voice was like a puppy's, soft and whining and inconsolable.

"Amos Junior punched him and he's bleeding, and call an ambulance," I said.

"Mein Gott," said Mutti. She went to the phone.

"Don't cry, Adam," I said. "Amos beat him up with one punch. He bit his own tongue off," I added, "so now he can't talk either. Okay, Adam? You're even with him now." I could hear the man's inarticulate wails from the front yard as Amos tried to calm him down. The sound just seemed to frighten Adam further. He crawled under the table and wrapped his head in Hildy's skirt. I went back outside and stood on the porch. The man was kneeling in the snow, sobbing in a high woman- ish voice. Amos Junior was making another snowball; he'd picked up the man's severed tongue and was packing it in snow, in case they could sew it back on.

I heard a siren approaching. The sheriff pulled in a moment later, a short, balding man with a large belly. He joined Amos Junior and Adam's father. In another minute the ambulance had arrived and the attendants were hurriedly loading the little man in. With a thrill, I rec- ognized the black man who had driven Grandpa and me to the hospi- tal after he'd broken his hip.

"Hey!" I shouted to him, waving. "Hi!" The man flashed me a peace sign, grinning hugely.

"Hey, little brother," he said. "How's that lip?"

He got back in the ambulance and they pulled out with a roar and a spray of snow and mud and were gone. The sheriff came toward me.

"You see what happened?" he asked.

"That guy tried to hurt Amos Junior," I said.

"Hurt him how?"

"Tried to tackle him."

"Amos Junior hit him?"

"Yah."

The sheriff looked at me more closely. "What'd you say your name was?"

"Billy Mann."

"Oh," said the sheriff. "That's right. Where's Mr. Shumacher?"

"Here I am," said Fatti, appearing from behind the porch. He was red-faced and blowing hard from his run—he'd been in the fields, fix- ing fences. He and the sheriff stepped out of my hearing and conversed secretively for a few moments. Then the sheriff went back to Amos Junior, who was standing there holding the snowball that contained the man's tongue. He'd forgotten to give it to the ambulance atten- dants. I crept up behind them to listen.

"You mind coming down with me, Amos?" said the sheriff. "Just to take a statement."

"Yah," said Amos. He looked as if he was going to cry. "I didn't want to hurt him that bad," he said. "God, I'm sorry."

"You're not in trouble, Amos," said the sheriff. "He had a restraining order on him. Wasn't supposed to be within a mile of this place, and he knew it. Far as I'm concerned, you could have shot him. I know that guy. Done business with him on several occasions. Repeat customer. Used to beat his wife up, before she got wise and hit the road. Too bad she left the boy behind. He's scum, Amos. Don't lose a minute of sleep over him."

"Okay," said Amos. He tossed the bloody snowball away and got in the backseat of the police car.

"Don't sit back there," said the sheriff. "Want everyone to think I arrested you?"

Amos grinned sheepishly and got in the front seat. They pulled out of the driveway and headed down the road. Fatti, beside me, sighed.

"You see some crazy people in this world," he said philosophically. "It's sad."

"Why sad? That guy was a jerk."

"Yes," Fatti said, "but he was a poor jerk, and now on top of everything else he has no tongue."

"He hurt Adam's throat," I reminded Fatti.

Fatti looked at me. "You love Adam," he said. "And he loves you. That's good."

"Are you going to keep Adam?"

"Yah," said Fatti. "I hope so."

"Me too," I said. "Can I come visit you after I go back with Grandpa?"

"Yah," said Fatti. He hoisted me up on his shoulders and we crunched through the snow toward the house. "We love you, boy." He said it simply, thickly—it sounded like "Ve laff you, poy." And we went into the house, where Adam had emerged from under the table, and Fatti made jokes and Mutti made hot chocolate until everyone felt better again, and with the amnesia that blessedly comes to children, I forgot about the visit from Adam's father.

I went home on December twenty-second. Mrs. Wheeler came again in her long red car to get me, and she sat smoking her thin brown cigarettes at the kitchen table. She smelled strongly of perfume and lotion; her foreign, citified odor had the effect of stupefying Fatti, and of sending Mutti into a territorial cleaning frenzy at the kitchen sink.

Mrs. Wheeler sipped thick black Shumacher coffee. Her lips left livid smears of paint on the rim of her mug.

"Are you packed?" she said to me.

"Yah, he's packed," said Mutti, sniffling.

"Best to get it over with right away then," said Mrs. Wheeler. "They get attached quickly at this age."

"Yah," said Fatti.

"Okay, then," said Mrs. Wheeler. "Did you thank the Shumachers for taking such good care of you?"

"He doesn't have to thank us," said Mutti.

"Thank you," I said shyly.

"See what a good boy he is?" said Fatti proudly. "He thanked us anyway."

Fatti carried my suitcase out to the long red car and put it in the backseat. Mutti stayed in the house. Fatti put his hands in his pockets and then stuck one out to me. I took it and we shook. Suddenly he picked me up by my armpits and crushed me against him.

"Remember everything Frau Weiler said," he told me. "Remember everything you have seen here. Yah?"

"Yah," I said.

"You come back soon."

"Yah."

"Auf weidersehen."

"Auf weidersehen, Fatti."

Fatti clamped me against his massive chest for a moment longer. I could hear his heart thudding in him like a bass drum. Then he put me down and stepped backward a few paces from the car. The other Shumachers came out in the driveway; the boys shook my hand stiffly, unaccustomed to such formality; Elsa and Hildy kneeled down and drew me to them, crushing me against their pillowlike chests without mercy.

"Let's go," said Mrs. Wheeler gruffly.

I got in the car. "Wait," I said, before the door was shut. "Where's Adam?"

"He's playing," said Fatti vaguely. "We'll tell him you said good-bye." So I knew Adam had been decoyed, and that he didn't know I was leaving yet, nor would he until I was gone.

Fatti shut the door and Mrs. Wheeler started the car. We pulled out of the slush-filled driveway and made our way slowly down the dirt road. Mrs. Wheeler turned on the radio and lit another cigarette. The radio gave off a harsh, tinny sound. On the way back to the old Mann farmhouse, we passed an Amish buggy, drawn by a single horse. It occupied the middle of the road. The driver hadn't heard us come up behind him, and Mrs. Wheeler leaned on the horn hard. As the car roared past it the horse reared in its traces. I turned to watch as the man driving the buggy stood up on the footboard to get control of the frightened animal. He wore heavy overclothes, his long beard protruding from under his muffler. There was a woman next to him, also heavily wrapped, her bonnet with its long brim shielding her face. "They never look at you eye to eye," I remembered Grandpa saying. "They don't want to know we're here."

"Buncha weirdos," said Mrs. Wheeler, of the Amish couple.

I turned to look at her. I was suddenly angry.

"You're the weirdo," I said.

Instead of spanking me again, she gave me a surprised look, and we drove on in silence.

Twenty minutes later we pulled into the driveway of my ancestral home. Grandpa was standing out in front of the house, wearing only a thin sweater against the cold. He had lost a great deal of weight, which he hadn't been able to afford; his neck was thin and scrawny, and he looked much older. I got out of the car and walked slowly toward him. He smiled shyly.

"Almost don't recognize me, do ya," he said, and in truth I didn't, but his voice was still the same, and it all came over me in a surge of emotion. I ran and wrapped my arms around his waist.

"Oof," he said. "Careful. I'm still a little sore."

"Sorry," I said.

He put his hands on my head and looked at me for a long time.

"You've grown three feet, I think," he said. "Go get your suitcase."

I ran back to the car and got my suitcase from the backseat. Then Grandpa and I went into the house together. I heard Mrs. Wheeler's car crunch out of the driveway. I hadn't said good-bye to her. Neither had Grandpa. She didn't exist anymore. I was home again, amid the same familiar smells of living and the sounds the old house made when you walked through it. I sat down at the kitchen table.

"Hungry?" Grandpa asked me.

"Yah."

"Yah?"

"Yeah, I mean."

"Whillikers," said Grandpa, as he stooped stiffly to retrieve the frying pan from a low cupboard. "You been hanging around with a bunch of Krauts, sounds like. Fried baloney all right?"

"Yeah," I said. Fried baloney would always be all right, as long as Grandpa was the one who made it. We sat together at the kitchen table and Grandpa watched me eat, and he asked me what I had been up to, and I began to tell him the whole story. I picked up speed and chattered away until the whole thing was told: the Shumachers, how much they ate, how big and loud they were, Trevor, Adam, Adam's father, the cows, the visit to the Mennonite lady. I went on and on until my tale was spun, even telling him how Mrs. Wheeler had honked her horn at the Amish buggy and nearly caused their horse to bolt. Then I arrived in the present, and the whole thing was history. It was just me and Grandpa again, sitting in the kitchen, and he ruffled my hair and made me another sandwich.

5

My Thirteenth Year; More of Annie; The Steamroller

I returned from my sojourn with the Shumachers a changed boy. I'd ventured into the outside world and come back in one piece, proving to myself and to Grandpa that such a thing could be done successfully and with no lasting harm; also, I'd met other people, and now considered myself worldly enough that the idea of school no longer held much terror. I was learning, in my own seven-year-old way, that there were at least two kinds of people in the world: the Trevor types and the Shumacher types, the bad and the good, the scary and the safe. And I learned also that even though the former could ruin things for you pretty quickly, they were made up for by the latter, by the secure, kind, warm Shumachers. Perhaps I would like school after all—if Marky Shumacher liked it, then it couldn't be so bad. So I acquiesced to Grandpa's will and allowed myself to be enrolled in the second grade. Grandpa himself would have preferred to continue teaching me at home, in his informal but effective way, but he in turn was acquiescing to the state, as personified by Mrs. Wheeler.

My earliest school memories are of being examined by a battery of specialists, all of whom were intent on discovering just how much I knew. They tested my reading, writing, and numbers, Mannvillian standards of education not having progressed much beyond the three R's in those days; in retrospect, I can see now that they were also testing Grandpa, to see whether he'd really taught me all he claimed. They seemed dubious at first, but they were forced to conclude that Grandpa had told them the truth: I was, in fact, educated, at least to a point. Though I was only seven, I could read and write as well as any ten-year-old, and my mathematical abilities were decent. As a result I was allowed to skip kindergarten, first grade, and the first half of what would have been my second-grade year, and was put into Mrs. Schmeider's second-grade class at Mannville Elementary, right where I would have been if I'd been in school all along.

I was late for my first day of school because the Galaxie wouldn't start. When I walked into the classroom, I was clutching a brown paper bag with a fried baloney sandwich and an apple in it, and wearing a brand-new pair of Zips sneakers of which I was immensely proud. Grandpa, recognizing the import the moment held for me, had purchased them for just this occasion. I hung up my jacket in my cubby and joined the class on the floor, trying to ignore the sea of curious faces staring at me. For a moment the old fear of strangers surged up in me; but that fear had been planted by Grandpa's paranoid warnings, and it was soon overcome by my natural interest in my new surroundings—I had never been inside a classroom before. Also, Mrs. Schmeider was reading us a story. Although Grandpa read to me often, it was never children's material—usually it was from a newspaper or a magazine. I was spellbound by the bright pictures on the shining pages of the book the teacher held. And then I felt a cold little hand work its way into mine and squeeze it in welcome. I looked at the hand, and then at the arm attached to it, and then at the owner of the arm. To my astonishment, it was her—the little girl from up the hill with the long braids. It was Annie. She leaned over and whispered, "Did your cut get better?"

I nodded, too surprised to speak.

"That's good," she said.

To say that I was overjoyed to have found Annie again would be a gross understatement. I had to take two time-outs in the corner that day because she and I wouldn't stop talking. That was all right, though. For the first time in my life I had a friend. After that first day I bounced out of bed bright and early every morning, urging Grandpa to hurry up and make my lunch, and asking was he sure the car was running today because I didn't want to be late to school again. If I was late, Annie might think I wasn't coming, and I couldn't let her down.

"Of course it's running," he barked one morning when he couldn't take any more. "It just didn't run that one day because I was in the hospital for so long. A car needs constant attention, boy. Just like some people around here I could name."

Meaning me, I suppose.

Second grade passed for Annie and me in this manner, and so did third, and then fourth, and the years rocked along like the cars of a speeding train. None of my classmates seemed to mind that I was a Mann; the Fiasco of the Ostriches, it appeared, had been forgotten by everyone except Grandpa, and nobody made fun of me for it. And Annie's hand stayed in mine right up to the year we turned thirteen, or so it felt, which was when things of note began once more to happen. Perhaps the holding-hands part is merely my imagination, because thirteen was when I began to feel shy around her. But shyness notwithstanding, we were together, and before I knew it we were in eighth grade, which was the year of The Steamroller.

Early each morning of that year, just as she had every morning for the last several years, Annie walked down the hill from her house and met me at the corner of Mann Road and the County Road. The County Road never had a name except for just that: the County Road. It was like everything else in town: The Square, The Oak, The School, The Steamroller. In a town the size of Mannville, where there is generally only one of everything, there's not much point in giving things a proper name; everyone knows what you're talking about.

Annie's father didn't know she and I were walking to school together. If he had, he would have found some way to stop us, maybe even by forbidding her to come to school altogether. He hadn't spoken to me since the day Grandpa slipped on the ice, six years ago now. That was because I'd done my best to avoid his presence, never going into the house or any nearer to it than I needed to let Annie know I was waiting. He sat in front of the television all day, leaving the house only to buy beer, which he drank on the couch until he passed out. I knew this only from Annie, of course. I hadn't dared to set foot inside the Simpson house again. His belly, according to her, was growing ever larger, his skin turning the sallow shade of death, his eyes smaller and beadier and more and more like the devil's. She shuddered when she spoke of him. I learned not to bring him up.

On the way to school Annie and I compared lunches, and if she didn't have enough I would give her some of mine. She packed her own lunch every morning, but often there was little to put in it: a hard-boiled egg or two, or a peanut butter sandwich. Doritos were her favorite. Mine too. They were the only thing I was jealous of giving her. Anything else I had was hers unconditionally, even my fried baloney sandwiches.

She asked me once if I didn't ever get tired of eating fried baloney sandwiches.

"No," I said, truthfully, although today, as a grown man, just the thought of eating one will make me nauseous. I calculated once that I had probably eaten around four thousand fried baloney sandwiches by the time I was thirteen.

"You do your homework?" I asked her.

"Yes!" Primly said, always, as though she was shocked I would have thought otherwise. Annie *always* did her homework. She did it in the trees behind her house when the weather was fine, or in the public library when it wasn't, or sometimes at my house. She couldn't do it at home because she had no desk and she shared a room with three sisters. Besides, he wouldn't have let her alone long enough. "Did you?"

"I did some of the math. I already read this damn novel a couple of years ago, though." I'd had to read *Lord of the Flies* for English class. I thought it was one of the scariest books I'd ever read because it was so true. Even if it hadn't actually happened, it seemed like the type of thing that was not only possible, but probable. A gang of boys marooned on a desert island, the way Grandpa had been, hunting down another boy because he was fat and slow and different and because they had reverted back to their animal instincts: it happened every day, in small ways, really.

"Don't swear."

"Why not?"

"It's mentally unhealthy," she said. "And someone with your vocabulary ought to be able to think of other ways to express himself."

"Mentally unhealthy?"

"You need a sound mind in a sound body," she said. "So you can be strong enough to rescue me."

I smiled at that. We were just barely teenagers now, but she still remembered the great plan I had contrived to rescue her when I was small. Many years later, she would tell me that not only hadn't she forgotten it, but she thought about it every night as she went to sleep. Sometimes, she said, even though it was only the fantasy of a little boy, it was the only thing that kept her going: the idea that someone, someday, would come barging in and change everything for her.

We were forced to meet in secret at the base of the hill, as we'd been doing almost every day since we were seven. The need for secrecy was something we never mentioned. We skirted around it. Whenever we said, "Meet you later," it meant "See you at the bottom of the hill, safe from his eyes and close to the woods, so he can't get you and so we can hide if we need to." "So you can rescue me" was only half a joke. Annie was seriously in need of a four-alarm rescue mission, complete with commandos in camouflage and face paint. The problem was, I was the only one who knew it, and I didn't know how to do it myself.

It was a three-mile walk to school. Grandpa offered repeatedly to take us in the Galaxie, but I shunned the idea. Mornings with Annie were a rosy, luxurious time, and I lengthened our walks as much as possible. I know now I was already completely in love with her. We'd stopped holding hands and we never kissed, but I thought someday we might, and the anticipation hung over me as thickly as if I'd been spread with jam. We brushed arms sometimes as we walked. Her skin was soft, her arms covered with a fine golden fuzz, barely visible unless the light struck them just right. They were lovely, perfect arms, although she often had to wear long-sleeved shirts to hide the bruises from where her father had grabbed her. Touching her sent a thrill through me so powerful I could scarcely breathe; it was a rapid surge of energy, beginning in my groin and shooting simultaneously out the top of my head and through the bottoms of my feet. Any boy who has ever been in love knows this feeling. It consumes you, controls you—

you have the feeling it has grabbed you by the nose and is just pulling you along, leading you closer to your final goal. I myself had no idea what that final goal was. I knew it was there because I could feel it. I thought it probably was "making out."

Making out was something I'd heard of at school. Some people did it and some didn't. It was common knowledge into which category each person at Mannville Junior-Senior High School fit—whether you had or hadn't made out with someone—and I had been in the latter category for too long. Soon it would be time to make the move. There were some minor obstacles to overcome first. First, Annie was four inches taller than I was, and I wasn't sure how I was going to circumvent that. Standing on a chair to kiss her was out; it was too undignified. I felt I ought to be able to sweep her into my arms and pull her to me so that her petite shoes were dangling just off the ground. First, however, I needed a magical growth spurt to bring me to the level of her lips.

Also, I hadn't the slightest notion of how to begin kissing someone. Grandpa and I still didn't have a television, or I might have had some idea of how these things worked. It was my understanding that people kissed on the television all the time. I'd watched a few shows at other people's houses, and I was shocked at how openly this kissing took place, as well as at other things I couldn't quite believe I was seeing. It was from television that everyone else my age learned their way around the adult world, and as a result I was at a serious social disadvantage.

I was also having another problem. It was The Steamroller.

The Steamroller was not a piece of construction equipment. It was a person, specifically David Weismueller, who had sacked more quarterbacks than any other linebacker in Mannville history and who occupied my father's old place as football hero of the town. He was famous; he had his picture in the *Megaphone* almost every weekend, just like my dad. It was ironic, that, because my father had been a quarterback himself and would have gone face-to-face and toe-to-toe with David Weismueller had they known each other on the scrimmage field, and would have put him in his place. Not only would my father have eluded Weismueller, he would have beaten the living daylights out of him. That was what I imagined, anyway, because David "The Steamroller" Weismueller wanted to beat the living daylights out of me, to steamroll me mercilessly until I was flat, and there was nothing I could do about it.

David Weismueller was handsome; I was ordinary. He was muscular; I was puny. He shaved every morning; I dreamed of it, and conducted weekly inspections of my chin in the mirror, all of them so far futile. He drove a red Corvette, which his father had bought him; I walked everywhere I went, or I rode in the back of Grandpa's Galaxie like a little kid. He'd been going steady with a cheerleader named Sherry Anderson for two years, and everyone knew they did it—*it*, the big It, the only *it* that really matters to high-school boys—on the weekends; sex was so far removed from my world that I couldn't even begin to fathom the road The Steamroller must have taken to get there. David Weismueller was what Jane Goodall would have called an "alpha male." If we had been gorillas, she would have taken copious notes on him, and ignored me altogether.

The Steamroller had taken it upon himself to shove me around whenever he saw me, which was why I had to keep my fists at the ready at all times. I was hoping for the chance to nail him in the balls one day. I hadn't had the chance to do it yet, but things were coming to a head, and my genetic warlike instincts were becoming aroused for the first time since my battle with Trevor six years ago. I was small, but I knew I could hurt him at least a little. I didn't know why he'd chosen me to pick on. I suppose he had to have somebody. Life, I was beginning to realize, was *Lord of the Flies* all over, every day. The real reason I hadn't wanted to read the book again was that it was too much like my own pathetic existence.

"I don't see it," said Annie. She was referring to his Corvette.

"He'll be around," I said grimly.

"I don't see why you don't tell someone."

"It's not so bad as that."

"Yes it is."

"No it isn't."

"There's no reason for you to put up with it."

"There's no reason for you to put up with it either," I said, and we both knew that I was talking not about David Weismueller but about her father, which was not something I was supposed to bring up. I had just violated an unspoken rule.

"I'll see you later," Annie said, her mood unreadable, and she left me to head toward the eighth-grade classrooms. We were both still in junior high, but next year I would skip ahead to the tenth grade, which meant I would be in the senior high building while Annie was still in the junior high. I wasn't looking forward to that. If anything, it was she who should have been ahead of me. Annie was a genius. She was teaching herself to speak French from a series of language tapes she'd bought with money she saved from doing odd jobs for neighbors, or pilfered from her father. She was, she said, going to become fluent in French and move to Montreal after high school; and I had no doubt that if that was what she wanted to do, then she was going to do it.

Just as Annie walked away, I saw him. The Corvette was cruising like a hungry shark down Frederic Avenue, which ran in front of the main doors of the senior high building. I neither slowed nor hurried my pace, but my heart began to thump rapidly and I felt hot blood pulsing through every inch of me. It was definitely David Weismueller. I knew that car well. Dreams of him in his Corvette were beginning to supplant the dreams of soldiers chasing me through the woods.

A moment later he saw me, stepped on the gas, and roared up to where I stood. Then he unfolded himself from the driver's seat and stood before me, a splendid example of *Homo erectus* more than *Homo sapiens*, but bent over considerably so that he could push his face threateningly into mine.

"What did you say?" he said.

This was his most common opening, to pretend I'd just said something to him that no man of honor could ignore. It was useless to protest, although I usually did anyway. But this morning I was feeling different. My eyes swept him from toe to head, taking in his sneakers, his jeans, his letterman's jacket, and finally his eyes, which were as vacant and glaring as two laminated meatballs.

"I said your mother sucks large dicks," I replied. "She sucks for bucks. Ten dollars a pop. I think you're the only guy on the football team who doesn't know."

David Weismueller's neatly shaved jaw dropped about three inches. I knew it would be wise to shut up, but it was already too late. I threw caution to the wind.

"Or maybe you do know," I said. "Maybe she practices on you.

Maybe she taught you how to suck 'em too."

"You're gonna die," he said.

"We're all going to die someday."

"You're gonna die today," he said, and at that moment I believed him. I dropped my backpack on the ground and stepped back two paces. Then I raised my fists and squared off.

"Bring it on," I said.

But he was too smart for that. There was already a small crowd around us, and from the corner of my eye I could see the parking lot monitor running toward us. If he'd hit me then he would have been in big trouble.

"Watch your back, shithead," he said. He was shaking with rage. "Don't go to sleep. Ever. I'm goin' faggot-hunting, and you're the faggot."

"All right, you guys," said the monitor, a teacher's aide named Drew. "You want to get written up, Weismueller? Or you, Mann?"

"I really don't care," I heard myself saying. I was seeing red.

"What was that, Mann?" said the monitor.

I said nothing more. I picked up my backpack and headed off toward the junior high building, feeling the disbelieving stare of David Weismueller burning twin holes in the back of my head. He was right; I was doomed.

A feeling of calm resolution settled over me for the rest of the day. It was almost a relief, actually. Now that the inevitable was imminent, the fear was gone, and I was clearheaded and ready. I went through the motions of going to classes like a condemned man who eats his last meal. I never paid much attention in class anyway because I knew most of the time what the teacher was going to say before he said it. The only time I allowed myself to get involved in anything that day was during a discussion in English class on *Lord of the Flies*.

"What happened with these boys while they were on that island?" my English teacher, a tall, gangling man named Mr. Doddy, had asked. "Why did they behave like animals?"

"Human beings *are* animals," I heard myself saying.

"And what exactly do you mean, Mr. Mann?" Mr. Doddy was thrilled—it was rare for a student to actually participate in one of his discussions, especially me.

"They were far from society," I explained. "They had to make their own laws. Also, they had to survive, which meant they had to kill. Like how they killed the wild pig."

Mr. Doddy had his hands folded in front of him and was staring at the ceiling in a kind of professorial rapture. "Please continue, Mr. Mann," he said. "This is most fascinating."

I grew red in the face, self-conscious, but I continued. "Their killer instincts were awakened. When we live in society, we put those away because we have to get along. But they were on a desert island, and they didn't have anyone to make laws for them, so they had to make their own. But they weren't like the laws we have. They were the old laws, the ones we had to obey when we were living in tribes."

"Yes, indeed, Mr. Mann," said Mr. Doddy. "What you are suggesting, then, is a kind of *reversion* to a way of life that no longer exists today, but that was most common when we had to fight a daily fight just to survive. Correct?"

"I think those laws pretty much still exist," I said. There were a few snickers from those who had witnessed my confrontation with The Steamroller that morning. I ignored them. "We're still bloodthirsty. Like animals."

Many years later, I would read what my ancestor Willie Mann had to say on the subject of human nature with respect to our animal instincts:

> *In most of us, the ancient urge to kill the weak has been sub-orned by the need to co-exist with other humans in society, accord-ing to modern laws. But we are fooling ourselves if we think we no longer carry these animal desires within us, just because we are "civilized." They lurk just beneath the surface, ready to reappear at a moment's notice, and they are as well oiled and smooth in their functioning as if they had never been dormant. Let none of my descendants forget that we are, at best, fancified apes who have shaved our fur and put on airs; and indeed, we have been putting them on for so long now we think they are our nature. They are not. Put the question to any veteran of any war, and he will tell you of the blood lust that erupts in mortal combat in all of us men, from private soldier to the highest general in the land,*

as naturally as though we had descended from the trees only last week.

But neither myself nor Mr. Doddy had ever heard of Willie Mann's diary, or perhaps we would have referred to it in our classroom conversations. I like to think it would have replaced all other classroom texts in use in the world then, simply because it contained all the ideas ever heard of in Willie Mann's diary. But it hadn't been returned to me yet, and the world was proceeding on its tottering circular path, unilluminated and ignorant of the genius of my great-grandfather.

I managed to send a note to Annie during lunch. It said:

The shit is hitting the fan today after school. You'd better walk home by yourself. I'm in for it.

She wrote back:

I wish you'd tell someone. But if you won't, I hope you kill him.

I grimaced at that. I felt exactly the same about her; and her situation, to my way of thinking, was far more desperate than mine. I didn't live with David Weismueller, after all. At least I was safe when I went home.

Our usual route home was to walk down Frederic Avenue to Third Street, down Third Street to the County Road, and then to our separate houses, mine at least warm and welcoming, if haunted, hers a cold and terrifying place. That day, however, instead of following this route after school, I crept behind the school buildings and ran crouching through a number of backyards. A few people were out weeding or mowing their lawns, and they stared at me curiously as I sneaked along across their property. I merely waved and grinned at them. "Playing Capture the Flag," I said. "Seen a bunch of guys come through here?" And they would shake their heads and smile, thinking, no doubt, "Boys will be boys," or something like that. If only they had known. Only my pride prevented me from throwing myself on my knees in front of them and begging safe haven, or perhaps a ride home to the farmhouse, with me in the backseat under a blanket hidden safely from The Steamroller.

I made it to the County Road without incident. Once there, I ducked immediately into the trees and followed the road for several yards. I'm going to make it, I thought, at least today.

And then I stopped.

Why, I wondered, should I allow this Neanderthal to ruin my peace of mind? If he doesn't get me today, he will tomorrow, and if not tomorrow, then next week. It's not fair. It's not fucking fair. I'm sick of it. I'm going to fight him. Maybe he'll kill me and maybe he won't. But I'm done hiding from him. I'm just as good as he is. What's more, I'm a Mann. And an accomplished stunt artist. And a Celt, goddamn him. I'm a crazy Celtic warrior with blue paint on my face and the skins of three foxes wrapped around my waist. Send him to me, God. Bring him on to me right now.

I could practically hear the bagpipes wailing and screeching away, from somewhere deep in my mind.

As Willie Mann wrote in one of his less esoteric but just as philosophical moods:

> *Be careful what you request of Our Maker. He grants all heartfelt prayers; but he doesn't give us what we want, only what we need.*

And just as this final prayer to the Almighty left my lips and floated upward, I saw David Weismueller's Corvette cruise by in second gear. Even the car seemed out to get me. The sight of it went straight to my gut in a cold lance of anticipation. This is it, I thought. Today is a good day to die.

I jumped out from behind the trees. He must have seen me immediately, for the Corvette ground to a halt in the dusty road. I announced myself anyway.

"*Weismueller!*"

There was the sound of a clanking transmission as the Corvette went into reverse.

"Come out and play!" I screamed. I was feeling crazy. It was delicious.

Weismueller stepped on the gas and the Corvette zoomed backward. I stepped into the ditch again; I felt a slight breeze as the car passed, barely missing me. He was not playing, I realized. He'd gone insane. He really wanted to kill me.

I jumped back into the road again and faced the car. Weismueller was not alone; there were two other football players in the car with him, and they were all staring at me with the same kind of mad-dog look in their eyes.

I stood in front of the car. Weismueller inched it forward until the front bumper was touching my knees. I held my ground, hardly daring to breathe. I wasn't going to move first. He had the power in his sneak-ered right foot to kill me then and there if he so chose, simply by step-ping on the gas. We stayed like that for a long time, although exactly how long I never knew. It seemed, of course, like an eternity. More likely it was three or four seconds.

Instead of stepping on the gas, he got out of the Corvette. I breathed again; at least it wouldn't be death by car. The other two also got out. They were also linebackers, large and powerful boys who were publicly lauded every Friday night for their ability to disable and even maim rival football players. They were the modern warrior-heroes of Mannville, and for the moment they had decided their brutal energy would be focused on me. It was highly ironic, I thought. I posed no threat to them. I didn't want to score goals on them. I just wanted to get on with my life.

"This is between me and Weismueller," I said to the two lineback-ers. "You guys stay out of it."

Grinning madly, the two looked at their leader. He ignored them, choosing instead to lock eyes with me. I stared back at him. My knees filled with water.

"C'mere, you little faggot," said Weismueller. Instead I stepped back two paces, which seemed to infuriate him. "What's the matter? You afraid?" he roared.

"Think about it, you moron," I said calmly. "There's three of you, and you're all bigger than me. Of course I'm afraid."

They said nothing. One of them snorted. I could see that my logic hadn't registered.

"I didn't start this," I went on. "You decided to pick on me for no reason. That's the kind of guy you are. You like hurting guys smaller than you? Fine. You're the coward. Not me."

"Shut up," said one of the two linebackers. I think his name was Pfeiffer. The other was named Olmacher. In eight years Olmacher was going to die in the Gulf War, his transport destroyed accidentally by an American missile. But at that moment he was very much alive and towering over me, blissfully unaware of his fate.

"No, I won't," I said to him. To Weismueller, I said, "I don't know why you want to beat on me, but if you're going to do it, then let's get it on."

"He's darin' ya, Dave," said Pfeiffer.

"I know it," said Weismueller.

"I'll fight you," I said. "I don't know what you think you're proving, but I'll fight you if you force me to, and I'm going to hurt you as much as I possibly can before I go down."

"You'll go down," he promised.

"Sure I will," I said. Then I executed the move I'd been rehearsing in my mind for the last several weeks. I stepped forward, dropped to one knee, and sent my fist crashing into where I surmised Weismueller's testicles were lurking, nestled like two soft and unshelled eggs in the recesses of his jeans. I hit him as hard as I possibly could. I was small, but not weak, and Weismueller was completely unprepared. He hit the ground as if he'd been shot, in too much pain even to cry out. Then I was on him. I'd forgotten completely about Pfeiffer and Olmacher. Later, in thinking it over, I realized they had intended to let it be a fair fight, as much as was possible considering the difference in size between Weismueller and myself. They let us go, standing over us, shouting encouragement to their warlord.

I used both my fists on Weismueller's face. For as long as I had him down I was going to make the best use of my time. I was once again the mad Celtic warrior. My blows were surgical and precise, not wild but well aimed. The first one flattened his nose, and blood leaked from him suddenly in thick rivulets. I hit him several more times before one of the other two—I never knew which—pulled me off, stood me up with one hand, and backhanded me with the other. It was only one hit, but that was all it took. I lay on my back and looked up at the sky. Something had cracked deep in my head. I didn't feel like moving.

"That was dirty, Mann!" shouted Olmacher, or perhaps Pfeiffer. "You hit him in the nuts!"

I had no choice, I thought to myself. Someone was kicking me in the ribs, but it might as well have been someone else they were kicking. I had left my body completely. Then I heard the car start. I wondered idly if they were going to run me over. They came close; the tires passed inches from me. Then I closed my eyes.

I must have been unconscious for a while because the next thing I was aware of was Annie standing over me, calling my name frantically. I opened my eyes but had to close them immediately. The sun was like tiny daggers at the back of my head. I tried to sit up.

"Don't," said Annie. "I already called the doctor."

"What doctor?"

"Connor," she said, concerned. I knew full well that there was only one doctor who would make a house call, or in this case a side-of-the-road call. She was worried, she told me later, that I would be simple-minded for the rest of my life. They had hit me that hard.

"How long have I been out?"

"A few minutes," she said. "I saw the whole thing. Don't get up! Don't."

"I have to."

"You can't."

I tried to get up anyway and collapsed immediately into a sitting position. "All right," I said.

"You probably have a concussion."

"I don't think so," I said.

"Yes you do. I saw him hit you. He hit you hard."

"I hit him hard too."

"You certainly did. You hurt him a lot worse than you got hurt."

"Really?"

"Think about it," Annie said. I thought about it.

"You're right," I said happily, as the warm glow of victory began to settle over me. "I bet I hurt him pretty bad."

"Which is exactly what he deserved," said Annie. She was looking at me differently now. It was a curious look, as though I'd just done something totally unexpected and wonderful and her opinion of me had changed because of it. Perhaps she thought me capable now of rescuing her from her father once and for all. Perhaps she knew now that I wasn't kidding about it.

Doctor Connor's car pulled up next to us and he got out with his black leather bag. I hadn't seen him in several years, not since his argument with Grandpa; he looked no different than I remembered him, tall and lanky, with the same pair of glasses forever sliding off the end of his nose. He had aged, with the peculiar grace of old country doctors, hardly at all.

"Hello, young William," he said sternly. "I haven't seen you in quite some time. Been fighting?"

"Yeah."

"Win? No, don't answer. Nobody ever wins a fight. Foolishness, all of it. Hold still." He felt the back of my head gingerly. I winced. He clucked over me for several minutes, asking me if I could move this, wiggle that, while Annie told him what had happened. One or two cars came by and slowed as the drivers looked at us curiously. I knew the story would be all over town by evening.

"You probably have a concussion," he told me.

"See?" said Annie. "I told you."

"I don't," I said again. I'd heard enough about concussions to know that I didn't want to have one, regardless of whether I actually did or not.

"I'll take you home," said Connor. "Your grandfather can take you to the hospital. Where, I might add, I insist you go. Today. Tonight, at the latest."

"Grandpa's missed having you around," I said. I don't know why I said that; I didn't even know that it was true, but it flashed into my head. "He's sorry about everything."

Doctor Connor said nothing to that, but in the softening of his eyes I could see he had heard me. He and Annie helped me stand, waves of nausea washing over me, and put me in the backseat of the car. Annie sat with me and I laid my head in her lap as we drove the short distance to the old farmhouse. Grandpa was standing out in the yard as we pulled in. The sudden appearance of Connor in our driveway seemed to stun him momentarily. Then he came toward us as Annie and Connor got out and helped me from the backseat.

"Connor," said Grandpa shortly.

"Tom."

"What happened?"

"Fighting," said Connor.

"Right. Thanks for bringing him home."

"Why don't you guys just shake hands," I remember mumbling. "Shake hands and get it over with."

But I don't remember if they did or not.

They took me into the house. Doctor Connor hovered somewhere in the background as I was put to bed. Annie stayed with me as he and Grandpa conversed in the hall outside my room, their tones low. I was reminded pleasantly of Connor's frequent visits to our house when I was younger, and how the rumble of their deep old-man's voices had soothed me as I drifted off to sleep at night. I was once again the subject of their conversation, except this time Grandpa merely listened and agreed instead of arguing, as Connor lectured him on what needed to be done with me; and this time I wasn't falling into the magical sleep of a young child, but lurking on the far side of wakefulness as my body set about repairing itself. Annie stroked my forehead as the two of them talked in the hall. Then I heard Connor's departing footsteps and Grandpa came back into the room.

"Fighting," he said simply. For a moment I was reminded of Mrs. Shumacher when she grabbed Trevor and me by the scruffs of our necks like two half-grown puppies and smacked our foreheads together. "No fighting," she'd said, which in her lexicon meant not only that fighting was wrong then, but that I was never, ever to participate in it again in my life. I had disobeyed her, but not without reason.

Grandpa sighed. "You gotta do what you gotta do, sometimes," he said, thinking perhaps of his journey to the South Pacific to kill the Japanese. "Who started it?"

"I did."

"No he didn't," said Annie. "Mr. Mann, there's this guy at school named David—"

"*I started it*," I said. I didn't want Grandpa to know. I still don't know why I lied to him that day. All I knew was that I would rather have him thinking I picked a fight with David Weismueller for no reason than that he'd been picking on me all this time. Scenes from *Lord of the Flies* played through my mind repeatedly. I didn't want Grandpa to think of me as some pathetic little weakling being chased around an island. I was, I think now, delirious with concussion, and also with the onset of a fever that I could feel already sneaking into my bones.

I spent the rest of the evening drifting in and out of strange dreams. In some of them I was on the island with Grandpa and Enzo Fujimora, and they were chasing me around with a wooden spear, chanting, "*Kill! Kill!*" In others, the three of us roamed around together, each of us armed with a spear, but there was nobody to chase; desolate, we searched every rocky crag and tiny jungle glen for a victim, but we couldn't find any, and finally we gave up. I dreamed too of Annie, and these dreams led me into the mysterious region where only grown men could go, the region I could only hint at to myself when I was awake. It seemed she was already there, waiting for me, and all I had to do was find the path. But you had to be a man to do that, and I was still only a boy.

"I'm a man," I must have muttered in my sleep, for I woke to hear Grandpa say, "Yes, you are a Mann, and you're the best damn one of them so far."

Annie had told him the real story while I was asleep. That was the thing about Annie. She absolutely could not tolerate another person's lie.

I didn't go to school the next day. I went to the hospital instead, where they x-rayed my throbbing head and told me I did indeed have a concussion. Grandpa had wanted to take me in right away, but I begged him to wait—my head hurt too much to move. I spent the rest of that day in bed, and I knew I was truly sick because I didn't grow restless. Instead I welcomed the chance to rest. I dreamed throughout the day and slept all night without waking once.

The next morning I awoke with the sun and went downstairs. Grandpa was already awake, as always; he still arose before dawn each morning, to water livestock that no longer existed and to ride along fences that had long since been jumped by ostriches and then bulldozed. He'd ransacked his ancient store of preserved herbs and was brewing up a concoction for bruised heads, which he made me drink without argument. I obeyed. It tasted awful, but I knew from experience that Grandpa could cure anything with herbs. We sat together at the kitchen table, he sipping a small glass of whiskey and I drinking his potion.

"Who started it?" he asked me, of the fight.

"He did."

"Why?"

"I don't know. He just started picking on me."

"When?"

"A few months ago."

"He ever hit you before?"

"No."

"Really?"

"Yes."

"And how did you feel when you were pounding him?"

"What do you mean?"

"You know what I mean," he said. "Annie told me how you settled his hash for him. Good. I'm glad. What I want to know is, how did it feel when you were beating his face into mush?"

I was silent. It was a disturbing question because I didn't like the answer. What was worse, I knew Grandpa already knew what I would say. He just wanted to hear me say it.

"Good," I admitted.

"Huh."

"I mean . . . I'd rather it never happened, but still . . . while it was happening, it felt . . . just good."

"You're your father's son, all right."

"What does that mean?"

"He used to say the same thing," said Grandpa. "Kids used to pick on him a lot. And he had to fight them. I never punished him for it because they left him no choice. Eddie wasn't a mean kid. He didn't like fighting."

"Neither do I."

"But when he got going on a kid, it wasn't pretty. He got mean. He got crazy. A couple of times I had to talk to the police about it."

"The *police*?" I was shocked. My father, a delinquent?

"Yeah. Nobody ever pressed charges, because there was never any doubt Eddie was defending himself. But he went beyond defending himself. He went berserk."

"How?"

Grandpa kneaded his knuckles uncomfortably. "I don't like telling you this, but you're getting older and you need to know. Can you handle this?"

"Yes."

"Okay." Grandpa sighed heavily. "Once he bit a kid's ear off."

"You've gotta be kidding me," I said, nauseated.

"No. I couldn't believe it myself. He didn't even remember doing it. At least that's what he said, and I believed him. He felt horrible about it later, too. He said he tried everything he could think of to get out of fighting the kid, but when he saw he had no way out, he made up his mind and the world changed color. Does that sound familiar?"

I thought back to the fight. The world had changed color for me too. It seemed red, as though my eyes were coated with a thin film of blood. And the power that surged in my arms was intoxicating, all the more so because it was power I didn't ordinarily possess. For a few brief moments, I realized, I had been entirely capable of killing David Weismueller.

"Yes, it does," I admitted.

"Be careful of it."

"Why?"

"It's not easy to explain. There's a lot more to it. Violence is usually a bad idea, just put it that way. Only use it as a last resort."

"It was a last resort!"

"I know. You were justified. That's not what I'm saying."

"Then what are you talking about?"

"Some families," said Grandpa, "have bad tempers. Really, when people say they have a bad temper, they're just making excuses for themselves. Everyone has a bad temper. It's just that some people are better at controlling it than others. Now we Manns," he continued, "are actually quite good at controlling ourselves. We're not mean. We don't pick on people because they're smaller than us."

"How could we? Everyone's bigger than us!"

"You know what I mean. A Mann is the nicest fellow you'd ever want to meet, until something or someone he cares about is in danger."

"Or himself."

"Or himself," said Grandpa. "But we don't worry about ourselves as much as we worry about other people."

"We don't?"

"Think about it. Think about Annie. You worry about her all the time."

"Yeah," I said.

"What I'm trying to tell you is you need to be careful of your temper. It's a genetic thing. We have a history of . . . of going above and beyond what's required, if you know what I mean. In certain situations. Once we decide to blow our cool, that's it. Bad things happen."

"What do you mean? What kinds of things? Like biting people's ears off?"

"Yes. Like that."

"Or worse?"

Grandpa shuddered. He had the faraway look in his eyes again, and I could tell he was remembering something he didn't want to remember. "Just remember what I'm telling you. And don't ever get started on this stuff," he said, pointing to his glass. "Pure poison. It'll kill ya. You ever been drunk?"

"Don't change the subject!"

"I'm changing the subject because I'm an adult and I want to change the damn subject, Okay? Answer the question."

"No. I have never been drunk."

"Good."

"I'd like to try it once, though."

"What? Drinking?"

"Just getting drunk."

"Why?"

I shrugged. "Seems like the kind of thing everyone oughta do once."

"It's ruined me, that's for sure."

I said nothing. I didn't think he was ruined. I thought he was disappointed. No farm left, all the money gone, and not an ostrich to show for it. And me the only living descendant of the once-great Mann clan—besides him, that is.

"Did you talk with Doctor Connor much when he was here?" I asked this to change the subject of my own thoughts.

"A little," he said.

"Are you guys gonna be friends again?"

"I don't know."

"How come you guys fought that one time?"

"How often do you see that Simpson girl?" This was to tell me it was none of my business. I took his cue this time and we changed tack in unison.

"What do you mean?"

"Just what I said. How often do you see her?"

"Every day, I guess."

"You ever kiss her?"

I blushed. "Shut up," I said.

"Did you or didn't you?"

"No! Okay? No!"

"All right," said Grandpa. He appeared relieved. "That's all I wanted to know."

"Why?"

"Never mind why. You'd just be better off not getting mixed up with those Simpsons."

"There's nothing wrong with Annie," I said.

"I'm not saying there's anything wrong with her. I'm just saying it would be better if you didn't get involved with her."

"She's not like the rest of them."

"No, you're right. She's beautiful. Smart, too. Nobody would ever know she's even halfway related to that fat bastard up the hill. Oops. Forget I said that."

"Why?"

"Oughtn't to speak ill of folks," he said, reciting for the thousandth time some trite piece of country wisdom he'd learned in his childhood.

"Everyone speaks ill of everyone, seems like."

"Not everyone. White trash. White trash sit around saying things about people. Quality folks don't do that. Gentlemen. Ladies. Decent folk. Simpsons do."

"Annie's a Simpson."

"No she isn't," said Grandpa. "Being a Simpson is a state of mind."

"Something has to happen to him."

"I know it."

"I've seen bruises all over her."

Grandpa raised an eyebrow, not joking. "All over?"

I blushed again. "I mean on her arms and stuff."

"Does he just hit her?"

"What do you mean? Of course he hits her."

"But I mean is that all he does?"

"I . . . I don't know for sure."

"She doesn't say?"

I shook my head.

"But you think he does more than that?"

I nodded.

"You should tell someone."

"She told me not to."

"Now why did she say that?"

"She said in a few years she'll be old enough to move out. Then she won't ever see him again. She's saving money and she's teaching herself how to speak French. She wants to move to Montreal."

"Huh," said Grandpa thoughtfully.

"She already knows a bunch of it." I was, I realized, proud of her.

"My mother wanted me to learn to speak French," said Grandpa. His head was suddenly forty-two years in the past again. "She wanted me to go to Europe instead of the Pacific. So I could get some culture."

"I know. You told me."

He shook himself slightly, as though he had been immersed in a shocking but somehow pleasant liquid. "Sure I did. I tell you everything."

"Not everything, actually."

"What now?"

"How is it you never told me how Willie Mann found the money?"

Grandpa turned pale. "*What?*"

I was suddenly not so sure of myself. But I pressed on.

"You remember when you broke your hip?"

"Yeah."

"And I went to stay with that German family?"

"Yeah."

"And I was already having the nightmares?"

"Yeah."

"Mr. Shumacher took me to an old lady who told me what they were about."

"He *did?*"

"Yeah."

"What kind of lady?"

"A witch."

"A *what?*"

"Some kind of fortune-teller. A real old lady. A Mennonite."

"Well, for Chrissakes," said Grandpa. "I guess I do remember you saying something about that, now that you mention it."

"He says everyone except me knows the story of Willie."

"Probably so," said Grandpa.

"So how come you never told me about it?"

"I was waiting."

"For what?"

"For you to get older."

"Well, I'm older now."

"It's a bloody story."

"I've seen blood before," I said.

"I'm not sure I remember all of it. Most of it's written down in the diary. I'm afraid I'd get it wrong."

He was stalling, I knew, but I let him. "What if he doesn't bring the diary back from Japan? That fighter pilot?"

"Fujimora?" Grandpa took a deep breath. "Then there will be a lot of stories that you'll never hear."

"That's not fair."

"I'm sorry. You'll know everything you really need by the time I go. Don't worry, kid. One of the reasons I was so glad you came along was so I would have someone to tell my stories to."

I was looking out the kitchen window as we spoke. As I watched, something appeared around the bend that caused me to forget the conversation we were having. My jaw went slack with astonishment.

"Amish buggy coming," I said.

Grandpa didn't look.

"I knew it," he sighed. "I knew it when I was dipping into my herbs last night."

"It's coming *here*," I said, as the buggy wheeled into our driveway.

"Of course it is," said Grandpa. "Things are starting all over. They always do."

This was exactly the sort of cryptic comment about which I would have loved to press him further, but I was too distracted.

"There's an old man with a beard driving it."

"Gray?"

"Sorta."

"Short guy?"

"Why don't you turn around and look for yourself?"

"Because I already know who it is," said Grandpa. "Go out and talk to him. He won't come in. I have to get some things out of the basement."

I went out on the porch. The buggy was a two-seater, pitch black, drawn by a single chestnut mare. The man sat alone on the bench-board in the buggy with a pipe held loosely in one hand. Smoke drifted lazily from the bowl as he puffed on it, creating tiny cumuli around his head.

"Good morning," I said.

The man turned and regarded me curiously. His gaze was frank and appraising, and all the more discomforting because I was still in my pajamas.

"Hello, English boy," he said.

To the Amish, it didn't matter where your family had originated. If you weren't Amish, you were English. It was how they thought of everyone else. But I only knew this from Grandpa's stories; this was the first time I'd ever spoken with an Amishman. A strange feeling wove its way through me, a snake of unreality and disbelief. Perhaps hundreds of buggies had driven up to our door since the house was built, but this was the first one I had witnessed. An odd sense of history was taking over the morning.

"You can come in if you want," I said, but he dismissed that with a wave.

"Where's your grandfather?"

"In the basement," I said. To my surprise, he spoke with an American accent, just like the old Mennonite witch who had told me the source of my nightmares.

"Did he know I was coming?"

"Yeah."

The Amishman chuckled. "I thought so," he said. He sat smoking,

his hat shading his eyes, his beard falling down his chest in a magnificent wave. He said nothing more. The horse sidled over to the grass
that grew next to the driveway and began chomping at it. Unable to
think of anything to say, I went back into the house. Grandpa was in
the hallway putting on his shoes. There was a black bag next to him
much like Doctor Connor's.

"He's *smoking*," I said.

"So?"

"I thought they weren't allowed to do stuff like that!"

"Their rules are complicated. Not all of them are as strict as everybody thinks."

I absorbed this. For some reason, the sight of a smoking
Amishman struck me as blasphemous. The Amish were a common
sight around Mannville. Sometimes they came into town to do some
shopping, and I would watch them in Gruber's to see what they were
buying, but to my disappointment I found they bought the same things
as everybody else—a pocketknife, a ball of twine, clothespins, overalls.
If you got too close to them in the aisle, they either quit talking to each
other until you moved away or sidled away from you. But they had
never, as far as I knew, bought tobacco.

"I'm going with him," Grandpa told me.

"Where are you going?"

"To his farm, no doubt."

"Why?"

"His wife is having a baby."

"How do you know?"

Grandpa sighed yet again, but it was a patient sigh. "Because I
know. Same as you would know, if you bothered to slow down and pay
attention."

"Pay attention to what?"

"To things," he replied vaguely. "To all the things around you."

I wanted to argue with him and tell him that I did already pay
attention to everything, but time was suddenly short, and I wanted to
go with him.

"Can I come?"

"You have a concussion."

"Not really. It's mostly better."

Grandpa paused. He knew my concussion couldn't possibly be better, but the best thing about Grandpa was that he sometimes chose to ignore the obvious in favor of what he would rather believe was true, even when it patently wasn't. "I would really like you to see this," he said. "You might never get the chance again in your life." And I knew I was going.

"I'll get dressed," I said. I had to walk slowly up the stairs, hanging onto the banister, because my head was still spinning. But I felt much better than I had two days earlier. I changed and went back down to the porch. Grandpa was waiting for me in the buggy next to the Amishman. He indicated the back of the buggy, where there was luggage space, or something like it; I couldn't imagine that the Amish had luggage, or if they did, what they would need it for.

"Hop on up there," he said. The Amishman himself said nothing.

"Eddie's boy," said Grandpa.

The Amishman nodded.

That was the last word spoken by either of them for an hour. Silence, I have since learned, was a quality once valued among men because it was necessary for survival; and in men older than myself, such as Grandpa, or in men from different worlds, such as the Amishman, I have often witnessed this taciturnity and marveled at it. I've never been able to keep my mouth shut for very long. But then I've never spent entire days hunting in the forest, as Grandpa had in his youth. Nor have I labored day in and day out at bringing in the hay or sowing corn, as the Amishman did. These are not times for idle chatter. These are times to be quiet, to focus on the job at hand; and I think those two old men were remembering that as they sat side by side, occasionally jostling each other's shoulders as the buggy swayed with the dips and bumps in the road. There was work ahead. This was no time for talk.

We pulled off Mann Road and swung onto the county road, heading away from Mannville. I sat with my legs hanging over the end of the buggy. An old Chevy sedan passed us, the teenagers in it staring at me uncertainly. I smiled. One of them waved. Then a familiar pair of legs appeared in the corner of my vision, headed the opposite way. Same old swinging arms, same lovely head held high. It was Annie, on her way to school alone.

"Hey!" I shouted.

My grandfather said nothing, but I felt him turn around and stare at me. I had broken the silence. I was instantly ashamed. Annie stopped and turned. When she saw me sitting in the back of the buggy, it was several moments before she could think of anything to say.

"What are you *doing*?" I heard faintly, over the clopping of the horse's hooves. But I could only smile and shrug my shoulders as we slowly drew away from her. We watched each other disappear, and I caught some of her final words, drowned out by distance and the clopping of the horse's hooves: ". . . supposed to have a *concussion*, I thought . . ."

We drove on and on. It was late September, the mornings still warm, and over the creaking of the wheels and the ring of the horse's iron-shod hooves on the dirt and stones I could hear cicadas already chirruping. I lay down in the back of the buggy, my still aching head cushioned on my arms. Through cracks in the floorboards I could see the road passing beneath us, moving at the speed of a lazy earthen river.

I must have dozed because the next thing I knew, Grandpa was shaking my shoulder. I sat up and looked around me. The buggy had stopped and we had left the present altogether, or what I thought of as the present. This was another present, and now that I was in it I couldn't imagine a different one. Time travel, I thought, is possible. You just have to hop in an Amish buggy and fall asleep.

On a distant hilltop I saw a lone farmhouse. Spreading away from it and toward me were fields and pastureland, broken by an occasional line of trees. The road was of dirt, and it wound over the hill back the way we had come, smudged in green and brown and black pastel colors like a chalk drawing. I got out of the buggy. We'd stopped before another house, a two-story home that reminded me of the Shumachers'. There were no telephone poles, no tractors, no cars, no antennas on the houses; the road was unpaved and rutted; across it was a barn, and against the barn leaned one or two farming tools that haven't been used by most farmers in America for at least a century and possibly more: a scythe, an adze, and a giant two-man hand drill. Scarcely a sound penetrated the morning, except for the whickering of a horse somewhere. There were no airplanes in the sky, not even a far-off jet. The air smelled of manure and grass, and was tinted with the smoke of burning leaves.

The Amishman was walking into his house. Grandpa followed him, carrying his black bag. I stayed close behind him. As I looked up at the house I saw a curtain swish violently shut. It was in the window of one of the second-floor rooms. There was someone watching us up there, someone curious.

The house smelled of kerosene and sweat, but clean sweat. The builders of the house hadn't bothered with an entrance hall. We passed through the front door and were in a large dining room, the floor of which was polished wood, like ours at home. The walls and ceiling were whitewashed and completely unadorned except for a row of hooks. These, Grandpa explained to me in a whisper, were where they hung the chairs when they needed the space; there were sixteen of them. A long table stretched from one end of the room to the other, and around it were the sixteen chairs. The mother of this family had given birth to fourteen children, and was trying at this moment to deliver the fifteenth.

"She's in here," said the Amishman. He opened a door and disappeared behind it.

Grandpa turned to me. He had a look of fierce concentration in his eyes.

"Don't try and talk to me," he said. "Don't interrupt me at all. Don't talk to anyone. If I tell you to do something, just do it. If you can't figure out what I mean, do it anyway. This woman is very sick. She's been in labor for almost two days."

"I'm coming in?"

"Yes, you're coming in. Remember what I said."

Without another word he opened the door to the room, shoved me in ahead of him, and closed the door behind us.

"My apprentice," he said to the room in general.

Introductions in this place hardly seemed necessary, or even appropriate. The air was close and fetid and reeked of woman's sweat and blood and other things I couldn't identify except for their distinctly human smell. The walls of the room were lined with standing women, how many I didn't know, and they were all dressed alike: white bonnets, floor-length black dresses, and white aprons. When I ventured to look up at them I saw they were all looking at the floor, away from me and Grandpa, and yet I knew they were keenly aware of our presence. In the center of the room, on a large, bloodstained bed, was a middle-aged woman, naked, her belly red and grotesquely distended. Her hands were held on either side by a pair of the black-clad women. She breathed in high-pitched wheezes. Suddenly she gave a scream, but it was not a scream like that of any animal or person I'd ever heard, not a scream of pain but from the realm beyond pain. It was low, hoarse, drawn out at the end, without a hint of hope to it. The woman was dying. Even I could see that.

"Open the bag," Grandpa said to me.

He'd set his bag on the floor at the foot of the bed. I knelt. When I opened it I was confronted with a jumble of bottles, tubes, and shining steel instruments. I looked up at him expectantly.

"Hensbane," he said.

I searched through the bottles until I found the right one. I handed it to him.

"Open it, damn it," he snapped. I did.

"Hand me the hose."

I gave him the rubber tube.

"Petroleum jelly."

There was a large tub of it in the bag. Grandpa slathered it on his hands and began to rub the inside of the woman's vagina with it. I ventured a look. Her genitals were swollen and bleeding, and a stream of yellow and black liquid oozed slowly from deep inside her onto the sheets. The smell was overpowering. I looked away quickly.

I heard the bottle being uncorked and the glug of liquid being displaced by air.

Grandpa sighed.

"Now we wait a moment," he said.

Instantly there began a low hum from the women. They were speaking to each other in Low German, and though I knew none of their words, I could tell they did not approve. One of them stepped forward from her position by the wall.

"She has waited too long," she said to Grandpa, and she stepped immediately back to the wall again, her face red.

"What I gave her will cause contractions," explained Grandpa.

Nobody said a word in response.

"Otherwise I will have to cut her!"

"Then cut her," said the man who had brought us. He was standing behind us, leaning against the door. The expression on his face was a turgid mixture of emotions. He was struggling hard to control himself. He clenched his unlit pipe in his teeth.

"All right," said Grandpa. He looked down at me. "Scalpel," he said. The urgency had gone out of his voice suddenly, and I knew by that he did not expect things to go well. "It's the knife thing in there."

I handed it to him carefully. He swabbed it with alcohol. Then he bent down over the woman's spread legs so that I couldn't see what he was doing. I heard the sound of flesh being suddenly rent. One of the younger women against the wall fell without a sound toward the floor. Two others caught her and carried her out.

"It's coming," said Grandpa.

"Heilige Gott," said the Amishman.

The women crowded around the bed. I was surrounded suddenly by a wall of black skirts. I backed out of it against the door and found myself standing next to the Amishman. He reached down and put one hand on my shoulder, squeezing me hard. I put my hand on top of his. He relaxed his grip.

There was a gasp, a spank, and the sudden shriek of a new voice. The baby was born.

Grandpa emerged much later from the knot of women. We hadn't been in the room an hour, but he looked exhausted. He came slowly to the Amishman. His hands were covered with blood.

"Levi," he said, "your wife will not live."

The Amishman took the pipe from his mouth and put it in the pocket of his black jacket. He brought one hand to his brow and held it there, covering his eyes. Grandpa clutched him firmly by both of his shoulders. They stayed like that, poised in an awkward moment of male grief. I watched them and listened to the soft sound made by the women as they wrapped the baby.

"Go outside, Billy," said Grandpa. He maneuvered Levi away from the door in a weird slow dance, and I opened it and darted out of the room. It closed behind me. I fled through the dining room, ignoring the throbbing in my head. I went out the front door, past the buggy, which still stood waiting in front of the house, and continued across the road and over the adjoining field. I couldn't be sick and I couldn't blame anyone, not Grandpa or Levi or the woman, but for the moment all I knew was that I never wanted to see anyone again for the rest of my life. Most of all, if this was what being human meant, I didn't want any part of it. Nor did I want anyone else to have to go through that either. It was too horrible. Somewhere underneath all of it was the suggestion that life was like this sometimes, but this was not life I had seen. It was death. Its presence was as oppressive as the odor of the Amishwoman's insides, as stifling as a blanket thrown over my head and held there by massive and inescapable arms.

I kept running across the field. It rose up gently to a small ridge. When I got to the top of it I stopped running and stood still, and I stayed like that until my breathing returned to normal. My head hurt terribly. It was dark, and I was waiting for it to get light again, thinking that perhaps something had shut off my sight inside my head because I had seen what I had seen. But after a time I realized I had my eyes squinted shut. That's good, I thought. I'll keep them that way.

I stood there trembling and blind, feeling a gentle breeze move across my face. There was a taste of cold in it. When I smelled it I knew Indian summer was over and fall had arrived in New York.

6

My Fourteenth Year; I Become a Man; How Willie Found the Money; the Rory Curse; I Become a Writer

Fall arrived with the death of the Amishwoman and the birth of her baby, and then faded without further event into winter. I thought of Levi Miller's wife often as the leaves fell and then were followed in their earthward path by snow. I was haunted for months by her tortured face, her lips twisted in pain as she tried to create a new life even as hers was leaving her. I'd seen cows give birth before, and once a horse, and not found it particularly disturbing. But watching Mrs. Miller *had* disturbed me—not because it was different from horses and cows, but because it was precisely the same. Nature, I discovered, ruled the world under her own terms; and those terms were harsh, bloody, and nonnegotiable.

There were two women in my life, Annie and my mother, and Annie was only my age and my mother was gone altogether. Thus I knew little about females, nothing of motherhood. I was familiar with the mechanics of sex and birthing, but women themselves were to me largely mysterious. Part of it was that I simply wasn't used to being around women. They seemed strange and fascinating creatures, foreign to my world and slightly unnerving in their ways. Even Annie, who was my best friend and counterpart, was often these days showing signs of inscrutability. She had sudden mood swings, and sometimes wouldn't speak to me for days, for reasons that were obvious only to her.

But part of it also was because of this strange property women had of being able to produce human beings from somewhere inside their bodies. To me this ability suggested power; but when I saw the poor Amishwoman splayed out on the bed, stripped of her clothes and covered in her own blood, she didn't look powerful at all. She looked helpless and pathetic. I felt sorry for her, and wondered what it would be like to be a woman, living, as the Amish did, buried under the weight of a hundred years.

Levi Miller's wife was also the first naked woman I'd ever seen. The sight of her, the whole experience of watching her in labor, seemed to be the catalyst for deep changes in myself. My body began to grow taller and stronger; I grew hair in strange places; my voice changed, became deeper. The whole process seemed oddly familiar; I felt as though I had been reminded of something I'd been forgetting, something I hadn't known how to remember. It was as if my body had been waiting for some clue to its biological purpose before puberty could begin. By Christmas of that year it was in full swing.

So it was with Annie too. In fact, she'd gotten a head start on me, as girls do. Being with her now was an entirely new experience, electrifying, tantalizing, even physically painful sometimes. To my deep shame, I suffered in her presence from constant erections. They happened not only around Annie, but all females in general, even older married ones, and sometimes even when there wasn't a female within sight. Anything could inspire an erection. They arose unpredictably and lasted for hours. They were there when I awoke and kept me awake long after I was to have been asleep. I no longer answered questions in class for fear I would be called to the blackboard; the entire world would have seen the madness pulsing in my pants, and the embarrassment would have been unbearable. I took to wearing long shirts and leaving them untucked, or carrying my books in front of my crotch. And I despaired at the arrival of summer. Shorts, in my condition, were dangerously revealing. It was almost safer to stay at home.

My hormones demanded things of me that no sane person would have attempted. They surged in me like a tidal wave. One Saturday, I'm certain, I broke all previous world records by masturbating six times. I was so sore I could barely walk, but the satiation was temporary; by Monday I was healed and ready to try again. Sometimes desire—for anything, for anyone—would wash over me so strongly I would feel I either had to copulate or die. Yet my shyness and my youth conspired against me. No woman, I knew, would want to have sex with a fourteen-year-old boy, even if he was going on fifteen. And it was definitely a woman I wanted. Not a girl, not someone my age. I wanted a grown, fully developed woman, one who would teach me everything she knew before graduating me into the world. She would train me in the arts of love until I was a skilled master, instead of a masturbator. And I knew I had to find one soon, or I could not be responsible for the consequences.

I remember these times as having a sort of glow about them, although whence that glow emanated I'm now not sure—from youth, I guess, and nothing more. Annie and I danced around each other in that painfully shy adolescent way. I concealed my lust from the world as best as I could. Grandpa drank his way through his days. Time passed in Mannville.

During Christmas break of my fourteenth year I worked for Mr. and Mrs. Gruber, stocking shelves in their store and occasionally delivering groceries, and after vacation was over they invited me to stay on as a regular employee. I showed up after school and worked for about four hours each evening. Mr. Gruber was generous; he insisted I take weekends off, even though I offered to work them. It was almost as if he foresaw certain things that lay in my future. When I told him I wanted to work full time, he said, "You're going to need your weekends."

"Why?" I asked. "There's nothing to do around here."

"How old are you?"

"Fifteen," I said, though of course Mr. Gruber knew very well I wasn't. I knew he remembered that day in 1970 when Grandpa had come in, flustered and in a hurry after he'd discovered me on the doorstep, and he was not so old that the date had become fogged in his mind. He didn't mind my being under the legal working age as long as

I never reminded him of it. The fact was that he and Emily were too old to deliver groceries anymore, and they knew I was one of the few dependable boys around. I was a Mann, after all, and the Grubers had never lost faith in us, even after the Ostriches.

"Fifteen?" he echoed.

"Yessir."

"Well now," he said, "how time does fly."

"Yuh," I said, "it sure does."

"Boy gets around your age, you'd be amazed how many things there are to do all of a sudden," he said.

"Yessir."

"Especially on the weekends."

"Yessir."

"You better keep your weekends free."

"All right, then. Weekends free."

"I know what I'm talkin' about."

"Yessir."

"I once upon a time was young myself, though you wouldn't know it to look at me now. Which reminds me of a story. There was this one time—"

"Harold, bejesus, shut up, would you," said Emily, who was Irish by birth, German only by marriage, and had heard her husband's stories ten thousand times too many.

I began to meet people now. I carried armloads of food to homes all over town, and by the time the old year had rolled over and died and the new one was begun I knew upwards of fifty adults by name. Most of them were elderly and had trouble getting out in the snow, which was deep again that year, but they were all the more interesting to me because they *were* old, and it was exciting to talk to them. All of them had known my father, and they never failed to comment on how much I looked like him, acted like him, talked like him, and walked like him. Sometimes I got a delivery order for families with small children and busy schedules who couldn't make it to the store. Of those families, two were single women with children; and of those two women, one was to me the most tantalizing symbol of femininity I'd ever seen.

Her name was Elsie Orfenbacher. Elsie was divorced, or maybe never married in the first place, and had a small boy about three years old; nobody seemed to know who the father was. I wonder now if even Elsie knew. She was notorious for having a steady stream of casual male visitors, occasionally married ones. This practice drew down the wrath of the more virtuous women of Mannville, and so Elsie suffered from a curious sort of social pariah-hood—other women wouldn't acknowledge her in public, but she was wildly popular with the men.

Elsie was plump, short, energetic, large-breasted, and radiated a kind of sexuality that seemed to affect everyone in one way or another. At least I knew it affected me. After my first delivery to her house I was captivated by her smell. I imagined it was everywhere, hanging over the town like an invisible veil, and all I had to do was crane my neck upward no matter where I was to sense it. She smelled of fresh warm bread and perfume, with a bit of hair spray mixed in. She ordered canned fruit, peanut butter, grape jelly, soap, orange juice, and a package of pork chops, and when I dropped them on her kitchen table she gave me seventy-five cents' tip and said, point-blank, "Who the hell are you, anyway? I don't know you from anywhere."

"Billy Mann, ma'am," I said, blushing. I was grateful for my long winter coat, which covered the part of my body that was in constant danger of exploding.

"How come I ain't seen you before?" She cocked her head to one side and winked at me, smiling.

I shrugged. "I dunno."

"You're Eddie Mann's boy."

"Yuh."

"I remember Eddie. He was a cute one. So are you, kiddo."

I grew very hot. Suddenly her little house seemed stifling. Her son was sitting on the floor between us, playing with a red fire truck.

"You knew my dad?"

"Every girl in town knew your dad," said Elsie, smiling again, and her body seemed to be vibrating with some kind of energy, part sex and part joie-de-vivre, although at the time it seemed all sex to me. It was too much for me to handle. I began to want to escape. I looked around wildly in terror, my eyes resting for no reason on the sink; it was scrubbed clean, not a fork or a cup in evidence. She was a neat house-keeper.

"I gotta go," I said. "Thanks for the tip."

There came a knock at the backdoor and George Lemmon walked in. George owned an auto shop near the high school. He was about forty and had a large beer belly. Most men in Mannville had one. Looking at him was a powerful argument against drinking beer.

"'Lo, Else," he said. "Hi, kid. Hi, Billy." He looked embarrassed.

"Hi, Mr. Lemmon," I said.

"Workin' for the Grubers now?"

"Yuh."

"Good job?"

"Yuh."

"That's good."

"Well, I gotta go," I said again.

"You come about my car, George?" said Elsie as I left, and her tone was such that I knew she knew George had not come about her car. As I walked past the front of the house I sneaked a peek in the front window. She and George were sitting in the living room, he in a chair, she on the sofa. He had a beer in his hand. I walked faster.

The next day, as Annie and I were walking home after school, I said, "Let's go on a date."

She stopped in her tracks. "Beg pardon?" she said.

"A date," I said. "Not like anything serious. A movie or something." I was listening to myself in astonishment. Some new part of me was speaking, a Smooth Operator version of my old personality. What had Elsie awakened? I hadn't encountered this part of myself before. I stepped back and watched to see what it would do.

"You're a maniac," she said. She began walking again.

"Just for fun," I said, or the Smooth Operator said. "What the hell else is there to do around here?"

She smiled, but said nothing.

"Life is short," the Smooth Operator philosophized grandly. "We might as well make the most of it. Besides, I've only been to one movie in my life." It was true. Going to a movie theater was something Grandpa simply never thought of. I had money of my own now, and the Smooth Operator wanted to spend it lavishly. *Return of the Jedi* was playing at the Bijou. I'd been dying to see it for weeks. "Besides, you're the only girl in my life. You're the one for me, baby." The Smooth Operator was speaking in a fake French accent now, deliberately bad.

Annie shrieked with laughter and blushed. "You are the one who makes the sun go up and down. You make the moon go round and round. You make the leaves grow and the white white snow."

Annie looked at me out of the corners of her eyes. "Are you making that up?" she asked.

"We shall watch Luke Skywalker, the great Jedi warrior, as he conquers the evil forces of the galaxy, and we shall rejoice together in his victory. And we shall eat popcorn."

"Have we *met*?" Annie said.

"'Ow do you do," I said. "I am Jacques le Snock."

"You're crazy."

"Not crazy. I am *French*, baby."

"Oh my God."

"Come on, Annie," I said in my normal voice. "It's no big deal. It's just a movie. Just come with me."

She was looking at me now with round eyes, her face betraying some emotion I'd never seen in her before. "You had me with the white white snow," she said, and I knew by the sound of her voice that something had changed with us, and that I had caused it, and that it was good.

I walked whistling up Mann Road to the farmhouse. I could hear Grandpa murmuring to himself as I came in the kitchen door. He was sitting in the living room with a glass of whiskey. He had gotten his banjo out, but it lay ignored and unplayed on the floor.

Occasionally, when I was younger, Grandpa used to play old folk songs on the banjo for me—"Oh, Susannah," "Cripple Creek," "Soldier's Joy." We sang the words together while he played and I banged out the rhythm with a pair of spoons. But it had been years since we'd done that together. Lately he'd taken to getting out the banjo and then just sitting and staring at it, as though he'd forgotten what it was for. I wasn't sure what this meant. Grandpa seemed like an old man to me all the time he was alive, but I know now he wasn't old at all; it was only the perspective of my youth that made him seem so. Yet his actions, his appearance, his habits were all those of a man much older than himself. Even his hands were growing crabbed and useless, as though he were eighty-nine instead of only sixty. Maybe it was that arthritis made it too difficult for him to play anymore—arthritis can hit you at any age, and in the Mann family it runs pretty strong. But Grandpa never complained about arthritis to me. He just sat and stared at the banjo, occasionally strumming it with one bare toe as it lay in its case.

In fact, Grandpa wasn't saying much of anything these days. It seemed as if the whiskey was making him drunker and drunker, as if his drunkenness had reached the point where it never left him, and every sip of whiskey only made it worse. Somewhere along the line he'd surrendered to it. I wasn't sure when this had happened. It was a gradual process, I guess. It happened a little bit more every day. You never see these things when you're right on top of them. But when I compared the Grandpa I'd known as a little boy to the Grandpa of my early teenage years, I could see the difference right away. The old Grandpa sang, talked, laughed, bellowed challenges to the Munchkins. This Grandpa was a specter. I found myself wishing he would just die and get it over with. Then I hated myself for thinking that.

And so it went.

Anyway, Grandpa spoke often enough, to be fair, but rarely to me. He talked to himself instead, or to someone I couldn't see.

"I have a date," I said. I liked to keep up the pretense that he and I were a normal family, to pretend that we had conversations about things that mattered.

He looked at me with vacant eyes. Slowly they focused on me.

"Swell," he said, with an effort.

"Yuh. Movie. With Annie."

He began to murmur again, gently. He was telling himself stories.

"Quit it," I said. "Wait until I get my notebook."

He fell silent.

"You hungry, Grandpa?"

I'd become the cook for both of us. I also cleaned the house, did the laundry and the dishes, shoveled the snow from the driveway, and did the million and one other things that must be done to prevent a house from reverting back to a state of chaos. Grandpa never asked me to do these things, but I knew that if I didn't the whole place would fall apart in a matter of days. I don't think he ever noticed this either. Perhaps he thought the servants of his childhood had moved back in. More likely, though, he just didn't care.

"You hungry, Grandpa?" I repeated.

But he never answered.

I threw my books on my bed, went into the kitchen, and made two peanut butter sandwiches and two cups of hot chocolate. Then I went upstairs again and got my notebook. I set one sandwich and one steaming mug of chocolate next to Grandpa—though I knew he would never touch them—opened my notebook to a fresh page, and waited. He was talking to himself again now, oblivious to my presence. When he muttered loud enough for me to hear, I wrote down what he said. In this way I was learning the story of how Willie Mann found the money. I'd gotten several pages of snippets in this manner—because sometimes, if your history has been stolen from you, you have to steal it back. They were something like this:

"*. . . the iron triangle . . .* "

"*. . . was the field Pop told you you could have once you got married . . .* "

"*. . . made in England . . .* "

"*. . . a big old letter R on it . . .* "

"*. . . cut off their heads . . . put' em in a barrel . . .* "

"*. . . Daddo had to set on the other side of the kitchen . . .* "

Grandpa was speaking not about someone, but to someone; and that someone, I had determined, was the ghost of Willie Mann. He'd been with us for some time now. I remembered when the strange things stopped happening, and things got calmer. Keys no longer disappeared, I no longer heard footsteps upstairs when both Grandpa and I were sitting downstairs. The end of those events had marked not the removal of ghosts from our house, but simply a change in the kind of ghost. The old poltergeists had been replaced by a serious ghost, one that seemed to have a purpose and did not have time to play around. It all had something to do with me, I imagined, but as of yet I didn't know what that was. I wasn't even sure what I was waiting for, but I knew something was coming, and that it would happen soon.

About once a week I gathered everything I had recorded from Grandpa and added things in the middle to make them fit. I was in the process of turning it into a story. When it was finished I was going to send it off to a magazine and publish it. I wanted to be a writer when I grew up. I *had* made up those things I'd said to Annie about the moon and the white white snow, although I was too shy to tell her so. Words came to me all the time. I saw them typed out in my head as they were spoken by other people. I wrote poems in the privacy of my bedroom, and some of them were not too bad. This exercise with Grandpa was my first attempt at a short story. It seemed to be taking forever, and it was a strange way to go about it, but I didn't know that then. And in my own way, I was enjoying it.

The week passed on without anything earth-shattering happening: my painfully throbbing symbol of adolescence remained my own secret, although I still lived in constant fear of someone noticing it. Had I known that every other boy my age in Mannville and, in fact, on the entire planet was suffering from the same malady, I would have relaxed somewhat. But my lack of social contacts was still affecting me, and I had nobody to compare notes with.

It wasn't that I hadn't had the chance to make friends; I simply hadn't wanted to. Other guys my age bored me. I used bigger words than they used, thought about different things than they thought about, and felt that most of what they did was ridiculous and boring. They rode around on their ATVs, chewed tobacco, and worked on cars. Sometimes they got in fights, but it never seemed to be over a matter of principle, which to me was the only reason for fighting. They seemed to fight for sheer enjoyment. This struck me as almost animalistic, just another lingering relic of our days as tree dwellers. They were fighting to establish social hierarchy, and I knew that in fifty years this hierarchy would still exist among them because none of them were ever leaving Mannville. What was worse, none of them wanted to.

Saturday arrived. The movie began at seven-fifteen. Around three o'clock I was too excited to wait any more, so I began to get ready. First I took a shower, during which I carefully scrubbed every square inch of my body with a washcloth. Then I brushed each tooth, back and front, and rinsed with mouthwash for a full minute. I cleaned out my ears, my eyes, and my nose. I meticulously trimmed finger- and toe-nails. I shaved, even though it was completely unnecessary, and then cauterized my raw face with aftershave, which brought tears to my eyes. Then, thoroughly sterilized and reeking of bay rum, I spent a further half-hour getting dressed, putting on each item of clothing very slowly and exactly and making sure it fit just so. When I was com-

pletely ready it was five o'clock. I still had two hours before I was supposed to meet Annie at the hill.

Writes Willie Mann:

> *There is nothing like the ritual of courtship to bring out what
> is simultaneously the bravest, the most ridiculous, and the most
> vulnerable in men. Our vanity overtakes us, and we preen our-
> selves like birds. This seems all the more ridiculous when one con-
> siders that the end result of all this is to gain the privilege of
> removing all our finery, and in fact all of our clothing, in the pres-
> ence of the one for whom we don it in the first place.*

I looked at myself in the mirror. I'd finally started to grow.
Although I would probably never reach the six feet I so earnestly
desired, at least I wouldn't spend the rest of my life looking up at other
people. Annie was only an inch taller than I was now, and that distance
was shrinking rapidly.

At six-forty-five an idea occurred to me. I sneaked the keys to
Grandpa's Galaxie from the hook on the kitchen wall, started it up, and
drove slowly to the base of the hill. Grandpa himself had been passed
out all afternoon in the living room, and I knew he wouldn't notice
that the car was gone even if he woke up. I giggled to myself as I guided the clattering Galaxie down Mann Road. Driving was a brilliant
idea; now I would have a car in which I could make out with Annie,
should the opportunity arise.

She was waiting for me at the foot of a giant oak. The headlights
of the Galaxie caught her like a rabbit, and for a moment she froze,
confused. She'd been expecting me on foot. I turned out the headlights
and opened the door.

"Come on," I called.

"Oh my God," she said. I opened the passenger door for her and
she slid in next to me. "Billy, this is *dangerous*."

"Don't worry about it."

"Do you know how to drive?"

"Of course I do!"

"I mean *really* drive!"

"I've been driving since I was five," I reminded her.

"Lawnmowers don't count, Billy! You have to be sixteen to drive a car! What if Madison sees you?"

Madison was Mannville's police officer. He usually spent his Saturday nights parked in the square, which was where the movie theater was. Annie was right; I'd forgotten about him. But there was an easy way around that one.

"We'll park behind the bank," I said. "Then we can just walk across the Square to the theater. He'll never see us."

Annie said nothing. I was crushed. Here I was, being gallant and manly and daring, and she thought I was just being stupid.

"Are you mad?" I asked her.

"It's not that," she said. The tone of her voice had changed suddenly. It was flat and dead, as though another person was speaking. I knew instantly what that meant. Her father had been after her again. I stopped the car and turned on the interior light. Then I took her chin in my hand and gently examined her face.

"No bruises," I said. I brightened my voice to hide the sudden twist of apprehension in my bowels. "You look all right."

"Yeah," she said. "I *look* fine."

"You still wanna go?"

"Yeah."

"You okay?"

She began to shake, just barely noticeably. I was still holding her chin. I thought now might be a good time to kiss her, but something told me not to; instead I put my arms around her shoulders and drew her to me tightly. Her arms remained down at her sides.

"Hug me back," I whispered in her ear.

"I don't know how," she said.

"It's easy," I said. "You just pick up your—"

"Billy," she said.

"What."

"I know how you feel," she said.

"What?"

"I know how you feel about me," she said.

I pushed back from her quickly, horrified. Had she brushed against my crotch by accident? Did she know what a pervert I'd become? "What do you mean?" I asked, trying to appear casual.

She smiled weakly, but there was no mirth in her eyes. "You're going to hate this," she said. A sick feeling shot through me. My secret is out, I thought. She knows what I really am. I'm a three-legged monster. I'm a demon of lust, a sex-wanting maniac. I'm damned.

"You're the sweetest guy in the world, Billy," she said. "I think you're wonderful, and I want to feel the same way about you. I really do. But I can't feel that way. In fact, I can't feel anything at all."

"What are you talking about?" I said.

"Nice boy meets nice girl and they fall in love," she said. "That's how it happens, right?"

"I guess," I said guardedly. She was suddenly sounding much older than herself. And I was still waiting for the accusation.

"Well," she said, "I want you to know something."

"All right." *Here it comes.*

She sighed. "No. Wait. First let me tell you something else."

"What?"

"I was really happy that you wanted to go on a date with me."

"You were?"

"Yes, I was. You were perfect. The way you asked me. All silly and sweet. Just the way a nice boy should ask a girl on a date. Just like I always imagined it would be, if anyone ever asked me out."

"Well, good," I said, thoroughly confused.

"But now I have to tell you the other thing."

"I'm listening," I said.

"I'm not . . . I'm not a nice girl."

"Well now, there you have something," I said. "You're not *always* nice. To me, I mean. Sometimes you get kind of bossy."

"I'm not joking around. Please."

"Oh. Sorry."

"I mean I'm not a nice girl like you meet at school. Or innocent."

"You're not?"

"No."

"I kind of thought you were." I was still trying to tease her, but it was failing miserably. It was too late to make this into something light-hearted. It was not me she was accusing; it was herself, and I hadn't the slightest clue what she was talking about.

"Well, you were wrong," she said. "I'm not innocent."

"What do you mean?"

"I mean," she said carefully, "that I'm not a virgin."

I stared at her. This was worse than if she'd accused me of something. This was not what I'd expected at all. The Galaxie was parked on the side of Mann Road, the engine running. The heater was finally starting to work.

"Well, I . . . um . . . "

Annie almost laughed.

"Don't you know what I mean?" she said.

There was a long silence.

I'd always known what she was about to tell me, or at least I'd known it for long enough that it felt like always. But I didn't want to hear her say it. Not now. Not tonight. I'd been gibbering with excitement all week about our big date, and this is how it was: scary. That was it. I was scared. Of her, a little bit. Of how she sounded so much older. And of the fact that what we'd tacitly agreed never to mention was about to be said out loud.

"You don't have to say anything," I said.

"I have to," she said. "Please let me say it."

I looked at her.

"If you really love me, Billy, and I know you do, you'll let me say it. I have to tell someone. And you can't tell anybody."

"Okay," I said.

"Do you promise?"

"Do I promise?" I echoed.

That night brought about a number of changes between Annie and myself. The first was that she told me the truth for the first time, there in Grandpa's old Galaxie. The second was that I flat out and deliberately lied to her. I lied through my teeth, and I looked her in the eye while doing it. And this was my great lie: "I promise," I said, "that I will never tell anybody."

She turned her gaze to the windshield, looking out at the whiteness.

"The reason I'm not a virgin," Annie said, choosing her words carefully, "is because of my dad. And that's why I'm not nice and innocent like the other girls are at school. And you deserve someone like them. You're a sweet guy, Billy, and you're the best friend I have. But

I'm not what you need. I'm a load of problems and I'm going to be crazy when I get older. In fact, I'm probably crazy right now."

I couldn't speak.

She said, "You could at least not stare at me."

"You're not crazy," I said. It was all I could think of to say.

She looked at me again.

"My dad is fucking me," she said.

I must have flinched, looked away. My ears didn't quite believe the word she'd just used. She never swore like that. Ever.

"Did you hear me?"

"Yes."

"Did you hear me say what I just said?" Her voice was growing higher and her shaking was visible now.

"Yes," I said.

"You don't like to hear it, do you?"

I didn't answer.

"Well," she said, "then just imagine how it must feel to have it actually *happen*."

"I can't," I said. I was shaking now myself.

"No. You couldn't. Nobody can."

Annie looked out through the windshield at the quiet, frozen night. Grandpa was right; there was nothing Simpsonlike about her, not a trace of the sloping brow or jutting jaw. Her nose was long and thin, her lips beginning to fill out with the first flush and fullness of womanhood. She'd cut her hair perhaps only three times since I'd known her, and tonight it fell down her back in a long single braid, soft and clean and reddish-brown. She was beautiful. Not in the same way I thought Elsie Orfenbacher was beautiful; more so, somehow, not in a womanly sort of way, or yes, like a woman, but like something else too, maybe like . . . I didn't know. She was just beautiful.

I cleared my throat.

"You've always known, too," she said.

"Yeah. Or I kind of knew." *What the hell am I supposed to do now?* I asked myself.

"I want to know what you think of me," she said.

"What I think of you?"

"Yes, Billy. What you think of me."

"I . . . still think the same," I said.

"Would you still ask me on a date now, if I'd already said it? If I'd already told you?"

"Of course!"

She examined me closely.

"You're lying," she said. "You're lying about something."

"Stop it," I said. "It's not a fair question. I always knew. You just told me that yourself. And you were right."

"You didn't know. You *guessed*. That's not the same thing."

"No. I always knew. I used to spy on you when I was a little kid," I said suddenly. "Did I ever tell you that?"

"You *what*?"

"I used to sneak up the hill and hide in the trees."

"What on earth for?"

"Because I was in love with you," I said. "I've always been in love with you. You used to sing to yourself all the time. And you had imaginary friends."

"Oh my God," she said.

"Do you remember them?"

"Yes, you *creep*," she said. "You *spied* on me?"

"I was watching out for you. I used to hear him yelling. That was when I decided I was coming after you. I've always loved you, Annie," I said again. "I always will, too. No matter what happens."

"Where on earth were you watching from? I mean exactly?"

"None of your business," I said. "I have to keep some secrets, you know."

"But *why*?"

I shrugged. "At first it was just because I was bored. There was nothing to do, so I started wandering around. I could see your place from my place and—" I almost said, *and Grandpa warned me never, ever to go up there, so of course I had to*, but instead I said, "—and I was always curious about who lived there. And then I saw you. So I came back, time after time."

"To watch me."

"Yeah. To watch you."

"And you heard things."

"Yes."

"What kind of things?"

"Shouting," I said. I was shaking harder now, and I was afraid to look at her. "Crying," I said. The word came out of me hoarsely, like I was coughing up a burr.

"Oh my," said Annie. "Oh my, Billy."

She reached over and took my hand. I was ready to shriek, to start punching the roof. I began to choke on tears. I went on: "I don't think you're crazy. Not in the slightest. You can get over this. I know you can. You're the only person in this town our age with any brains."

"I will be crazy," she said. She sat up demurely, looking suddenly like a very little girl again, the way she had when I first met her. She'd been running around the yard by herself then, wrapped up in her fantasies, singing to the chickens. Had he been doing it to her even then? It was a chilling thought. How could something like this be allowed to continue? Why didn't someone kill him? Why didn't I?

"I will be crazy because I can't stand my life. As if this wasn't enough, I have to be a Simpson too? The lowest family in town? The poorest, dirtiest, stupidest family, the one that everyone makes fun of? And look at me with you! Who do I think I am? You're a Mann, for crying out loud. You're not even humans. You're like superpeople. Rich, smart, talented, popular, good-looking . . . "

"That's not me," I said. "Come on. That's not us anymore. We don't have any money at all left. You know that. And none of those other things are really true either. That was just my dad. He was the superhero, not me. Besides, Annie, look at yourself. You know you're the smartest kid in town."

"Yeah? Then why did *you* get to skip a grade?" She screamed this. The sudden volume was startling in the confines of the car. I jumped, startled, and she saw it, and there was something in her glance at that moment that said, *You see? See how crazy I am? You're scared of me!*

She was crying now too, and not just little tears either. They were tears for a life that had so far been disregarded, not by herself but by others—it was the worst possible crime against her. Annie's life had been stolen, and she wanted it back. Her face was contorted in agony and her chest heaved for breath as she sobbed. "Why is everything so easy for *you*? You never do any homework! You never do anything, and you still get all the grades!"

"I do too do homework," I said, but it was a lame defense. She was right. Things came easier to me, not because I was smarter than she was, but because I was a Mann and she was a Simpson. Teachers expected me to do well, even if the Fiasco of the Ostriches had ruined us and made our brilliance suspect. She, on the other hand, was doomed. No Simpson had ever made it through high school without getting arrested at least once, and none of them ever went to college. Plus, she was a girl. That worked against her in the classroom. None of the other girls raised their hands nearly as much as she did, and even though teachers knew she was smart, they still acted surprised when she said something right. Some of the other girls hated her for her brains. Nobody knew what to do with a girl who refused to act the way a girl was supposed to act.

I couldn't think of anything else to say, so we sat there in the car with the engine running. I held her hand and stroked it lightly. Gradually her sobs quieted, and I put one arm around her shoulder and leaned over and rested my head against hers for a moment. Then I sat up again.

"I don't care if you're crazy or not," I said. "I love you. I mean it. I do. Do you still want to go to the movie?" What she had told me was almost too big to conceive. The implications were huge. I could only think in little steps. Suddenly the next thing we did seemed very important, no matter what it was; and all I could think of to tell her was that I loved her.

She smiled, sniffling. "I'm sorry," she said. "We've probably missed the beginning."

"That's all right," I said. "I can catch the beginning some other time."

We parked behind the bank and walked across the Square. Madison was exactly where Annie had said he would be; he waved and greeted us by name, and we did likewise. Then we went into the theater and watched the horrible truth of Luke Skywalker's parentage unfold. I'd known it was coming, but I still couldn't quite bring myself to believe that Darth Vader was Luke Skywalker's father. It seemed too incredible, and yet somehow it made sense. In the end, I reflected, everything comes together, the good with the bad. When the movie ended we walked slowly out with the crowd, and I took her hand in mine, and she let me. I'd been thinking about her as we watched the destruction of the Empire on the screen. I didn't care if she wasn't innocent and pure—those words meant nothing to me anyway. She was just Annie. I wanted people to see us together. I was proud of her.

We drove out of town the back way to avoid Madison and went back to the base of the hill. I could tell she was already thinking about what she would have to say when she went back in the house. Her mind had already pushed the entire evening into the background.

"Good night," she said. "Thanks for the movie." She got out. I watched her climb the hill, her long braid swinging like a pendulum in the headlights.

Then I went home. That was it. My first date was over.

Grandpa was still sitting where I had left him, lolling in his recliner, unconscious. I took the glass of whiskey from his side and dumped it in the sink. Annie had missed her childhood. How much of mine had I missed? I had no father, no mother, and my grandfather, though kind, was largely absent. He was too drunk most of the time to take care of me.

I sighed. I could have had it a lot worse, I thought. He didn't have to take care of me, after all. I wasn't really his problem. He didn't make me. He could have taken me to an orphanage when I was a baby. He could have just left me with the Shumachers. There was no point in complaining, or in feeling sorry for myself. Yet I had the same feeling that Annie had. There was something irrevocably different about my life, about who I was and how I came to be, that made me nothing like other kids my age; and what was more, it was too late to do anything about it. It always had been, in a sense. I was doomed to be a freak.

I scrubbed out the whiskey glass and went upstairs to my bedroom. There I took out my notebook and opened it to the last page of writing. Having no idea how the story ended, I couldn't tell how close I was to the finish, but I had a sense that things were drawing to a close. Grandpa's mutterings were beginning to add up. I was learning to decode him.

I scribbled away until midnight, adding things here, taking them away there, trying to make sense of a story that was being given to me in tiny bits and pieces. I could not afford to let my mind register fully the events that had unfolded with Annie in the car. But one little corner of my brain began to focus on the sound of Grandpa's footsteps coming up the stairs. He was walking more slowly and heavily than usual and it sounded like he was dragging one leg. I heard him come up the hall and stand outside my bedroom door, where he paused to look in at me, breathing heavily.

"I had a good time," I said. I hoped he hadn't figured out I'd taken the Galaxie. Not that he'd have minded—we Manns made our own rules, he often said, and they didn't always coincide with what the laws were. But he said nothing.

"Want to know what I'm doing?" I said.

"*Writing,*" he said, except the voice was not his. It was deeper and older, a strange voice, yet familiar. A horrible chill shot through me. I whipped around to look at him.

There was nobody in the doorway.

"Jesus Christ," I whispered. The air in the room had suddenly grown very cold. The hair on the back of my neck stood up.

"Willie," I said.

There was no sound except for my own rapid, panicked breathing.

"I'm trying to get it right," I said. "How am I doing?"

Again, I heard nothing. But he was there. Or had been there. I was sure of it.

Gradually the temperature of the air returned to normal. My raised hackles subsided and I calmed down.

"You have to help me," I said sleepily. "I can't do it by myself."

This was the last thought that came to me that night. I woke up in the morning, tucked snugly into my bed, though I didn't remember getting into it.

Doctor Connor and his wife lived on the second and third floors of his house. It was a large Victorian mansion, built around the same time as our farmhouse. There was a well-kept lawn in front and back and a row of tall hedges lining the sidewalk. Pasted to the front door was a small hand-lettered card that read PLEASE DO NOT RING DOORBELL. This meant you were just supposed to walk in. Underneath that, it said in smaller, less optimistic lettering, PAYMENT IS EXPECTED AT TIME OF

SERVICE. That, as everyone knew, was just a formality. Doctor Connor's patients were mostly those who didn't have insurance and couldn't use the doctors at the hospital; as a result, payments were not only often not made at time of service, but sometimes never made at all. That didn't bother Doctor Connor. He was not in medicine for the money, he once told Grandpa. Any doctor who was could have done better becoming a stockbroker.

A bell tinkled behind me as I closed the door. There was a small waiting room, which in previous times had been the front parlor of the house. It boasted a coffee table smothered in magazines and a couple of easy chairs that reclined only so far before they bumped into the wall. Doctor Connor himself was sitting in one of these chairs reading a fishing magazine. A large gape-mouthed bass glared at me from the cover. Doctor Connor peered at me over his glasses as I came in.

"Well, hello there, young William," he said. "Nice to see you. Come for a checkup?"

"Sorta."

"Um-hmm," he said. He led me down a narrow hallway to his examination room, where he pointed to the paper-covered table. "Have a seat," he said.

"There's nothing really wrong with me," I said.

"I know," he said. "I can tell just by looking at you. You Manns are as healthy as rocks. But it never hurts to check, as long as I've got you here." *Healthy as rocks* was one of Doctor Connor's favorite phrases; I was never sure how to take it, but since I was never sick, I assumed it was good.

Connor felt my throat and looked into my ears, eyes, and nose with his light scope. He tapped my knee with his rubber hammer; obediently my leg swung out and back again. "Head bother you since your little run-in with that football player?"

"No."

"Heart still beating?"

"Yuh."

"Brain functions normal?"

"Huh?"

"Joke. Sexually active?"

"I—" My face burned suddenly, a deep and humiliating red. "I'm not here for a checkup!" I said again, beginning to wish I hadn't come.

"Relax," he said. "I'm a doctor. I'm supposed to ask you these things. You don't have to answer."

"No," I said. "Not yet."

"Good. Bit young yet. How old are you now?"

"Fourteen."

"Yes," said Connor. "I knew that."

He sat down in a chair in the corner and indicated the other one. "Hop down from there," he said. "Examination over. What is it you really wanted to talk to me about?" Because, being a healer like my grandfather, he had developed a sort of X-ray vision. He could tell things about people just by looking at them. That was why I had decided to pay him a visit in the first place.

I looked around, not knowing how to begin. In fact, I'd forgotten exactly what it was I was going to say. In desperation I folded my hands in front of me and stared at them, hoping the answer would come if I looked at them hard enough.

"Something wrong?" His voice was kind, warm.

"Did you know my dad?"

It was not what I had intended to say, but there it was. I'd meant to ask him about Annie. Doctor Connor took off his glasses and put them in the pocket of his white lab jacket, which he wore everywhere, including to Gruber's Grocery to do his shopping.

"Yes," he said. "I knew him quite well."

"What was he like?"

"Doesn't your grandfather ever tell you about him?"

"Not much," I said. "It makes him too sad."

"That's understandable. He was a lot like you."

"He was?"

"Yes he was. About your height. No, shorter. Same eyes. Same personality, even—intelligent, friendly. Good-looking."

"Am I good-looking?"

Doctor Connor laughed.

"You really wouldn't know, would you?" he asked, and laughed again, but his laughter was mixed with some sadness. "You teenagers are all alike. So shy, so uncertain! I was the same, of course. Everyone was."

"Was my dad shy?"

"Was he?" He cocked one eyebrow and appeared to look into space for a moment. "Well, you know . . . your dad was different from the rest of us, Billy. He had a kind of glow about him. He was always confident. But never overbearing."

"What do you mean?"

"He was never stuck-up. Didn't have a cocky attitude. He easily could have, you know. He was perhaps the most popular person in town. Everyone knew him, and he knew everyone, and what was more, he liked everyone. Genuinely liked them. He was always going out of his way to do things for people. Opening doors for them. Helping little old ladies across the street. That sort of thing. Anyway, I never answered your question, which is the burning question for all of us when we are young. Yes, Billy, you are good-looking, and you will be a handsome man, barring any unforeseen mutilation, of course. So be sure and always wear a seatbelt."

"What?"

"When you're *driving*," he said sternly. He gave me a look then that told me that somehow he knew I'd driven Annie to the movie in the Galaxie. Had he seen us? Spooky, I thought. But I chose to pretend I didn't know what he was talking about.

"There's . . . "

"Hmmm?"

"I, uh—you know, I was . . ." I was stuttering badly.

"When someone as bright as you hesitates, it's probably because he wants to ask me a question about sex," said Doctor Connor, who was a genius at reading the minds of teenage boys. I was amazed.

"How did you know?"

"It's not hard to figure out what someone's thinking about when he only thinks about one thing," said he, winking, and I blushed again. "Hormones," he said. "Testosterone. That is the force that rules your body, and that in fact rules the world."

"It *does*?"

"It makes things happen," he said. "I shouldn't say *rules*—that implies superiority, and men are not in all things superior. But it is what makes us want to do things."

"What things?"

"Stupid things, often," said Doctor Connor. "Sometimes good

things. It makes men act brave, or foolhardy, or careless, or sometimes downright cruel. It was testosterone that made Columbus sail across the ocean and murder the Indians."

"It *was*?"

"Well, perhaps that's a little oversimplified," he admitted, "but it's basically true. Men have a tendency to want to go out and *do* things, to *cause* them. Sometimes it's not for the best of reasons. We want to take things that belong to someone else, or hurt someone, or kill them. Most of history was written by men because it was men who caused it, but that doesn't make us necessarily noble, or better than women. Some idiot gets an idea in his head that he ought to go murder the tribe that lives next door and take their land and their wives and daughters. So he does it, because his testosterone is making him crazy. It fills him with blood lust. And that's how Rome was born, and why it lasted a thousand years."

I was silent. This was news to me.

"It makes us do good things too," he went on. "We have families because of it. Athletes thrive on it, male and female. Did you know most women athletes don't menstruate?"

"No."

"Nor do they grow breasts, often," he continued. "Or maybe just small ones. It seems odd, but it's completely explainable by science. It's because their bodies are producing too much testosterone. And scientists, too, are driven to achieve partly because of their testosterone, although they might deny it, and women scientists can also do just as much as male scientists without testosterone—and I know for a fact that women scientists both menstruate *and* grow breasts. But men discovered things. We built bridges, skyscrapers. It was testosterone that sent us to the moon. The rocket ship was merely the vehicle. Is that good or bad? Who knows? Nothing is absolute. But this is really not of any concern to you, is it? You want to know why you're growing pubic hair, why you have constant erections, why all you think about is sex. Is that right?"

I said nothing. My face was aflame and I couldn't bring myself to look at him. Nevertheless, a stifled laugh escaped me.

"Silence is consent," he said, smiling. "There is absolutely nothing to be ashamed of. You are a healthy, normal boy, soon to be a man.

Your testosterone is simply raging through you right now like Niagara Falls being forced through the eye of a needle. That's how it's supposed to be. Eventually it will calm down."

"When?"

"When you're about thirty-five, maybe, if you're lucky." He laughed.

"But—"

"Look," said Doctor Connor. "It's like anything else. You can use it as you wish. You have this energy in you that is telling you to do things. Therefore it means you have power. It's up to you how you're going to use it, or whether you will let it use *you*. But you have a responsibility to the people in your life to use it wisely. To be a *good* man. Especially to the women in your life."

"There aren't any women in my life."

"There's the Simpson girl, isn't there?"

"She's not my girlfriend, though."

"It doesn't matter. You know each other, you interact with each other. And there will be more. Women aren't like men, and there are too many of us on both sides who don't understand that, or respect it. Take them for what they are. They may drive you crazy sometimes, but that's all right. We drive them crazy too. It would be a lousy world without them. And listen," he went on, "if you ever feel like hitting a woman—which you probably will, someday—don't. Get away from her instead until you calm down. We have the advantage over them in strength. But it's not fair of us to use it."

It occurred to me then that Doctor Connor was perhaps the most unusual person I'd spoken to in quite a long time, and maybe even a bit insane, but even so he was making a lot of sense.

"Do you know who my mother is?" I asked him abruptly.

Doctor Connor was silent.

"Because if you do," I said, "I have to know. I can't stand not knowing. Grandpa won't tell me. He won't even hint if he knows or not. I don't know anything about myself. I didn't know my dad, and I never will, but my mom is out there somewhere. She might even be here in Mannville. I have to find her."

"Why?"

"*Why?* Why do you think? She's my mother!"

"But what will you ask her, when you see her?"

"I don't know!" I was exasperated. "I just want to see her!"

"Are you certain of your motives, young William?"

"What do you mean?"

"I mean, have you ever considered how seeing you might affect *her*?"

"Do you know or not?" My voice was suddenly rising in pitch and volume. I could feel trails of wetness working their way down my cheeks. "Tell me! Do you know?"

"No, Billy, I don't know who your mother is," he said. "If I did, I would tell you."

"Swear?"

"Yes. I swear it. I would tell you if I knew."

"If you're lying—" I said, but I didn't finish that sentence. That was the boldest statement I had ever spoken to an adult in my life, and I was suddenly afraid he was going to be angry. But Doctor Connor was not like most adults. He could see through me, right to who I was, and I knew he wouldn't be angry at me no matter what I said.

"Son," he said. "Everything will resolve itself in the end. You have burning questions. You need to know things. That is what will give you purpose. Follow your nose. Someday you'll find out. Don't get disappointed when things aren't immediately available."

We sat in silence while I wiped my nose and eyes.

"What are you going to do when you grow up?" he asked me. Coming from him, it didn't sound like the same mindless question adults always ask of children. He was actually curious.

"I'm going to be a writer," I said.

"Ahhh," he said. "A writer."

"Of short stories," I went on. "And maybe novels. I'm writing a short story now." Not even Grandpa knew that about me; not even Annie knew.

There came a small tinkle from the bell on the front door. Someone was waiting in the parlor.

"I would like to see it, when you finish it," said Doctor Connor. "If you wouldn't mind, that is. Not to criticize it. What I know about literature wouldn't fill a thimble. Just to read it."

"Just to read it," I repeated.

"Think about it," he said, getting up. "I know how hard it is to show these things to others. But I will always be interested."

"There's one more thing," I said.

"What is it?"

I took a deep breath. I wanted so much to tell him about Annie, to tell him everything she'd told me. But there in the office the events in the Galaxie that night seemed unreal. That, I remembered now, had been my original reason for coming to see him—not to talk about myself, or my father, or my mother, but Annie. But I found myself unable to say it, or else I didn't know how. I was beginning to wonder if she'd really said the things she'd said, if it was all true. I wonder now if things would be any different if I'd told him then. Somehow I don't think so. I think things would have turned out exactly the same anyway. And I had promised her that I wouldn't tell, after all. I still meant to. I was going to tell someone. I was going to do something. But for some reason, I didn't do it that day.

"Nothing," I said. "Never mind. Just—thank you for talking to me. You're the only one I can say these things to. I appreciate it."

Connor smiled, his wrinkled, kindly face creasing with pleasure.

"I've always felt like you were sort of a son to me, Billy," he said. "And I will talk with you about anything you want. Any time at all."

If I'd been younger, I would have hugged him. Instead I shook his hand. He patted me on the shoulder and gripped my hand warmly, strongly, in his large hairy fist. Then without warning he drew me to him and clasped me against his chest, just for a brief moment. His arms were around my shoulders in a fatherly sort of way, and I smelled him, his odor of pipe tobacco and cologne and disinfectant soap. Then he released me and I went out of the examination room and down the hall and out the front door, avoiding the eyes of whoever it was sitting in the parlor.

Mr. Gruber put down the phone and handed me a slip of paper with an order on it. Mechanically, without reading the address, I grabbed a brown paper bag and began filling it with items from the slip. Pork chops, soap, tampons, canned fruit, bananas, beer, a pack of cigarettes.

Then I checked the address, to see whether or not I would have to take the bicycle.

I hoped not. I always felt like an idiot riding around on the Gruber Grocery bike; it had a basket on the front and a big red flag on the back, which Mrs. Gruber had insisted on installing to protect me from maniacal drivers, and—what was probably the most humiliating touch of all—a bell on the handlebars for me to ring in times of distress. Some guys from school had seen me riding this bike once, and the ribbing that followed was, though not mean-spirited, definitely unacceptable. Once was all it took; I had vowed never to ride the bicycle again.

The address was 1213 Evergreen. It was Elsie Orfenbacher.

"It's getting to be closing time," said Harold jocularly. "Might as well just go home after you finish that one." He was, I noticed, not looking at me.

"Pay the lad," said Emily, because it was Friday.

"Yah." Harold went to the register and hit the NO SALE button. He counted out my week's wages in bills and change and handed it to me. I put it in my pocket without counting it. It would, I knew, total fifty-seven dollars and forty-three cents. That was how much I made every week, not including tips, which generally added another fifteen or twenty dollars. I'd been working for the Grubers now for over six months. In my very own bank account there resided nine hundred of my own dollars, which was enough to buy almost anything I could think of. I was practically a millionaire. It was late August of 1984; I was still riding high on the feeling of turning fourteen; life was good, and soon I was thinking of buying a car, just to have around. Something to work on in my spare time.

"I think I'll just walk, long as I'm going home," I said, with a casualness that belied the tremendous hurry in which I suddenly found myself.

"Yah, that sounds fine," said Harold, who seemed to understand without being told.

"Take the bike home for the weekend, why don't you?" said Emily, who either knew nothing or was pretending to know nothing.

"No thank you," I said.

"Might as well—save you the walking."

"Emily," said Harold, "he hates the bike."

"Why does he hate the bike? It's a perfectly good—"

"Well, see ya," I said. I grabbed the groceries and slipped out the door before I could get swept up in another of their interminable arguments.

It was a ten-minute walk to Evergreen Street. I let myself in the backdoor as I had been instructed to do. I put the groceries away in the kitchen and then went down the hall to the back of the house, where the bedroom was. There I knocked.

"Come in," she said.

Elsie was sitting up in bed, smoking and reading a magazine. She wore a large T-shirt, and the covers of the bed came up to her waist. I knew that under the blankets she was naked.

"Hi," she said.

"Hi," I answered. I was getting used to this. I wasn't nearly as frightened as I'd been the first few times, when I had been practically incoherent. But I was still eighteen years younger than she was; she was, in all things, the boss.

"Come give me a hug," she smiled, putting down her magazine. I obeyed, kneeling awkwardly next to her on the bed. I was, she had told me, allowed to touch her anywhere I wanted, anytime, as long as we were alone and nobody could see us. It was part of my education. I lifted up her T-shirt and slipped one hand under there, feeling for her breast. They were my first breasts and I couldn't get enough of them. Their softness was inconceivable.

"Still like 'em?"

"Yeah," I grinned.

"My own little Mann," she said. She ran one hand through my hair. "Who ever would have thought it?"

"You forgot to pay me for the groceries last time," I said. "I had to pay for them myself."

"Oops. How much?"

"About twenty-seven bucks."

"Jeez. Sorry."

"It's okay."

"That really that much money to you? I thought you were millionaires!"

"No," I said patiently. I had explained this to her before, but I thought it was charming how she persisted in her notion that we were still rich. "We don't really have any more money. We're broke. But we still have the house."

"You must have *some* left," she insisted. "All that money doesn't just disappear overnight."

"Grandpa has a few investments. They're old, left over from a long time ago. That's what we live on. They're just enough to make it." This, I didn't add, I knew from bitter experience, for in the last year it had fallen to me to add up the bills every month and pay them with money from the dwindling dividend checks. Funds were running appallingly low. But I didn't want to think about that right now. "Lift up your arms," I said.

She lifted up her arms and I took off her shirt.

"I still can't believe this," I told her.

"I could go to jail," she said, in a perfectly willing and agreeable tone. "But I won't, because you need me here, don't you?"

"Yes," I agreed, as I removed my clothes. Because Elsie had volunteered to provide me with exactly what I had been looking for—a teacher, a tutor, a private instructor in the ways of the sexual world.

It had begun on my second visit to her home. I'd dropped her groceries on the table as usual, but this time, to my astonishment, she was wearing only a short bathrobe, and as I stood waiting for her to tip me or tell me to get lost or whatever she was going to say, she had opened it with a deliberate calm and shown me her body.

"See this?" she'd said.

The room reeled around me. I thought perhaps I was going to faint. She had just taken a shower and her body was glistening wet.

"You need a woman," she'd said. "I can tell."

"You can?"

"Everyone can."

"*What?*"

"Don't worry about it." There was something in her manner oddly similar to Doctor Connor's when she said that; it was reassuring somehow. "It's perfectly natural. It's all part of the dance. Come here."

I stepped closer. She unbuckled my belt and loosed my pants so that they dropped down around my bottom. Then she reached into my underwear, freed my cock, which strained upward in its eagerness like a thing possessed, and began to stroke it. I came almost immediately.

"Jesus," she'd said, laughing. "You are a horny little guy, aren't you?"

"Sorry," I murmured. My knees were buckling. I could barely stand.

"If you ever tell anyone about this," she said, "I'll tell them you're making it up. And that will be the last time you ever see me."

"Don't worry," I said.

"Now go home," she said. "I'll see you in a few days."

That was the first time. I went home and lay in my bed, staring in disbelief and wonder at the ceiling. I moved through the rest of the week with a renewed sense of vigor. Every time the phone rang at the grocery I forced myself to remain calm. She would call again, she'd said; I was not to call her, or to come over unannounced. Also, I was expressly forbidden to fall in love with her; she was not going to have some lovesick kid following her around with puppydog eyes, writing her sappy poetry. Those were the rules. I was terribly afraid that she wouldn't call again.

But she did, once a week, which was neither more nor less frequently than she had ever called Gruber's before, and in this way we kept things a secret.

I got in bed next to Elsie now and she stretched herself out along the length of me. She reached her hand under the covers and grabbed my penis. She manipulated me under the covers until she had me dangerously close to the edge again.

"Wait," I said. I got on top of her. She was not yet ready, and I entered her after much fumbling, nearly giving it up once as hopeless. She put up with this with a sort of bemused smile, wincing now and again.

"Slow down," she said, gently.

I slowed down.

We moved together as she had taught me, and soon she began to make her noises again, which made me go faster, and she told me to slow down again but this time I couldn't and things were over soon after. But I was getting better, she said. I told her if she didn't make so much noise I wouldn't be done so soon, but the way she did it made me crazy. It sent shivers through me. We laughed and she gave me a cigarette, another new thing she was teaching me.

"Do you think I'm a slut?" she asked.

"What? No!"

"No," she sighed, blowing smoke upward, "you're too sweet for that, aren't you?"

"I guess."

"You're not like most guys," she said. "Even though you're so young."

I said nothing. I had already known that.

"Most guys think they can just come over and do whatever they want with me and then take off," she said. "They even want me to be grateful. Jesus."

"They do?"

"Oh, come on. You must have heard stories about me."

"No," I lied.

"Whatever. I like sex, that's all. What's wrong with that?"

"Nothing!" I said, with conviction.

"Have you told anyone?"

"No. I promised, didn't I?"

"My, my, a man who keeps his promises. How wonderful!" But it was not because I was wonderful that I hadn't told anybody about her. It was because there was nobody I could tell.

"Come back next week," she said as I got dressed. "I'll call in another order."

"You still owe me twenty-three for this one," I reminded her. "Plus last week's."

"Cover me, can't you, lover? Things are pretty rough for me right now. I'll pay you back next check I get."

"Sure," I said. "I guess." There was something romantic about taking care of a single woman and her child. It made me feel all the more manly. But it suddenly occurred to me that she didn't really believe we were poor, and perhaps that had something to do with why she had decided to take me under her wing.

But none of that mattered right now. I was getting laid, and life was good. I walked whistling down the street through the square, down Frederic Avenue and up Mann Road, the same walk I had taken every day of my life since I'd started school. It was about six o'clock. The air was soft with evening and smelled of honeysuckle and swimming pools. A small boy, one of the MacDonalds, rode by me on his bicycle, a beach towel safety-pinned around his neck like a cape. "I'm Superman!" he shouted at me.

"I know how you feel," I said. The boy stared at me and then darted off down the street.

I went home and got out my story. It was finished—all I needed to do was type it out. I'd found an old Royal typewriter in the attic and fixed it up. I opened a package of typing paper, set it next to me, opened my notebook to the beginning of my notes, and started typing. From time to time I lifted my fingers to my nose and smelled the aroma of her, which lingered over my entire body for hours.

7

In Which I Present My Very First Short Story, Entitled "Willie Mann and the Rory Fortune"

Willie Mann was digging up his garden. It was early spring, and the weather in western New York State—along the southern shore of Lake Erie—was still cold and wet. The sun refused to shine and storms still arose without warning. There was one brewing now, far off over the Lake. Willie could smell it.

The earth came up dark under his shovel, just barely thawed and smelling dank and wormy. Willie grimaced in pain each time he forced the shovel into the ground. There was a Confederate musket ball buried in his thigh, which the surgeons on the battlefield at Antietam had been unable to remove because it was too deep. But Willie didn't pay any attention to the pain. He knew he was lucky to have kept his leg at all. Many men hadn't been as fortunate as he. They had to ride home from the war in the backs of wagons, or limp along on crutches because they had only one leg left. It hurt Willie greatly to dig, but every time his right foot came down on the shovel and the pain shot up his leg, it was a reminder that he still had a leg to feel pain with, and so he never complained.

He was digging up a piece of land that his father had given him. It sat next to the family property, and it was his for when he got married. Willie was about to turn twenty-one years old, and although he had no immediate plans to find a wife, he knew it was wise to prepare in advance for the day when he would have one. There were many rocks in the soil, which would have to be removed before planting could begin.

Digging rocks was a process that could go on for months. The plot of land he was working was about an acre, and at one end of it there was a pile of rocks three feet high, which Willie had already unearthed. When he was done digging up the garden, and his corn and vegetables were planted, he would use the rocks to add onto the knee-high wall that already partially encircled the Mann fields.

It was nearing noon. In a few minutes his mother would ring the iron triangle for dinner. Willie stabbed his shovel into the earth again and struck another rock. It was a big one. Sighing, he dug around it and dropped painfully to his knees. Then he began to scoop the loose soil out with his hands. He hoped the rock wasn't so big that he would have to hitch up the horse and pull it out. That would add at least another hour to the work ahead of him, and he was hungry.

But as soon as he had finished scooping out the loose soil, Willie forgot all about dinner. He also forgot about hitching up the horse and about the pain in his leg. He focused his attention instead on the top of the iron-bound chest he had just uncovered, which lay just a bare six inches under the ground. He reached down and touched it—the rusted iron almost gone, the wood eaten away by damp and decay. The thing looked *old*.

Willie sat back on the ground and squinted up at the sky. He was not an excitable man. He needed to think for a moment. Far away, at the other end of the fields, his mother rang the dinner triangle. It was a shrill, nerve-jangling sound, one that usually never failed to send him limping eagerly off to the house. This time, however, Willie ignored it. He picked up his shovel again and dug around the sides of the chest carefully, so as not to rupture the fragile wood. He excavated the chest entirely, so that every inch of it lay exposed. It had large wrought-iron handles on either end. When he tugged on one of them it came off effortlessly in his hand.

"Well," he said to himself. He sat at the edge of the hole for a while, twirling the ancient handle on one finger, contemplating this new turn of events. The chest had a lock on it, also badly eaten by corrosion, but on it was still visible the letter *R*, molded long ago by an English craftsman, if the legend was correct. Willie recognized it immediately. It gave him such a shock that he was only able to sit and blink stupidly for several moments.

He thought about the history of the chest, and of how strange it was that he should be the one to find it; and he reflected also on the unusual feeling he had of having been suddenly plunged over a century into the past. Willie reached into his jacket and plucked one or two chest hairs. Yes, it stung. He was not asleep then. He felt like a character in one of his own dreams. Best not just go rushing off into the next thing just yet, he thought. Chances are a thousand to one nothing like this will ever happen to me again.

"Well, well, well," said Willie. Without a further thought about anything at all, he went to the pump and washed his hands and face in a bucket there. Then he went into the tiny house that he had shared all the years of his life, minus his four war years, with his mother, father, grandfather, and two brothers.

The rest of the Manns, except for Daddo, his grandfather, were already seated around the table in the middle of the tiny house. The house had only three rooms. There was the kitchen, which was the largest area and in which they also ate, sat, and read the Bible on Sundays. There was one bedroom for Willie's parents, and another that Willie shared with his brothers and his grandfather. Willie slept head to toe with his brothers in one bed, while Daddo had his own cot. Daddo was not at the table. He ate in the bedroom, by order of Willie's father, because he had no teeth and made too much noise when he ate.

The family was in the middle of praying over the food. Willie removed his hat and bowed his head until they were finished. Then he hung up his jacket and sat down in his chair. Nobody spoke. Willie's mother got up again and began serving dinner. First she served Willie's father, then Willie, then Andy, then Poky Boy. She put some mashed peas and potatoes on a plate and took it into Daddo, roaring at him what it was because he was mostly deaf and half-blind. Finally she served herself, sat down, and the family began eating.

"Finish that field, did ye?" said Father.

"No," said Willie. "Won't for ages."

"Rocky, is it?"

"Aye. Same as the rest of this place."

"Right, so."

"Ham," said Poky Boy. Mother got up and served him another ham steak.

"You're not hungry, then?" said Andy to Willie. "Mind if I eat your steak?"

"Work away," said Willie.

"And why are ye not hungry?" said his mother, alarmed. "Be ye sick?"

"Naw."

"Ye must be, workin' all mornin' and not hungry!"

"Woman," said Father sternly, "if he says he's not sick, then he's not sick."

Mother fell silent and picked at her food.

"Excuse me," said Willie. He got up and limped into the back room where Daddo ate. He could feel four pairs of eyes burning at the back of his head. Something was going on, they knew, but they also knew better than to ask him what it was. Willie had been very quiet since his return from the fighting. He'd been gone four years, and when he returned he barely spoke at all, not even to tell them the story of how he was wounded. War did that to a man, counseled Father. Best let him work it out on his own, and he'll tell it when he's ready. The Manns had been waiting for nearly a year now for Willie to start talking. So far, he showed no signs of it.

Willie sat down heavily on the floor at Daddo's feet and tapped him on the knee so the old man would know he was there.

"Eh?" said the old man. "Who would that be?"

"Me, Willie!" shouted Willie.

"Willie!"

"Aye."

"What is it, then?"

Willie paused, unsure of how to begin. Daddo was very old, old beyond counting, and Willie didn't want to excite him. Daddo himself had no idea when he'd been born, but he had fought the English in the

War of 1812, and had already been past his youth then. Daddo had come from Ireland. So had most of the other residents of Clare, which was the town just a few miles down the road. He still spoke with a thick Irish accent. His son, Willie's father, also spoke with an accent, but not as thickly. Willie's accent, like those of his brothers, was mostly American, with a touch of a drawn-out *a* or a rolled *r* here and there, even though they still spoke in the same lyrical Irish rhythm.

"You remember that story of the Rory treasure?" Willie said.

"Aye," said Daddo. "Why d'ye ask?"

"Tell it," said Willie.

"What! Now?"

"Aye."

"Bejesus," mumbled the old man. In the eating room, all sound had stopped. The family was straining to hear.

Daddo, like many old folks, was a wealth of stories. He had a reputation for being great entertainment at gatherings, and he was always invited to weddings and funerals and barnraisings, where he was given an honored place by the fire and someone was always sure to keep his glass full. He knew ancient stories from the old country, stories of the New World, stories of battles, ghosts, heinous crimes, horrible betrayals, of love affairs doomed from the start. His memory began centuries before his own birth, for the stories he told had been told to him as a little boy by his father, who'd learned them from his father, and so on; by the time Daddo heard them, they were already ancient legends.

But the story of the Rory treasure was a relatively new one. It had happened around the time of the War of Independence; had happened, in fact, probably close to the time Daddo himself was born in County Clare, across the sea. Everyone in Clare Town and other towns for miles around knew the tale well. They had been brought up with it, and all of them hoped that someday they would be the one to find the Rory treasure, because it was rumored to be a great one.

But few people Willie's age believed in the Rory treasure. This was why he wanted to hear the story again. He had to make sure of every detail of it, had to make sure he remembered it exactly as it was supposed to be told, because he knew this story was about to become very important to him. When he repeated it later in his life, he wanted to be sure he got it right, because up to this moment, Willie had never believed in the Rory treasure either.

"'Tis a strange time to be askin' for stories," said Daddo, "with the whole day ahead of ye and work to be done."

"I have my reasons," said Willie. He put his hand on Daddo's knee again, this time warmly. "Tell it, please."

Daddo put down his plate. When he recited, he drew himself up to his full height, but remained seated, as befitted his age and dignity. At gatherings, his clouded and useless eyes stared mistily over the heads of his listeners, except when he came to a frightening part, when he made a point of staring directly at the youngest children in the room, who would scream in terror. Daddo had a grand flair for the dramatic. He pulled out his pipe and filled it. Willie lit it for him with a match.

Daddo paused for a moment to collect his thoughts. When he told stories, it was as if he was reading from a script in his head. He never told a story the same way twice, but somehow it always came out with the same ending.

"There was once a Scottish clan by the name of Rory," he began, his *r*'s and his vowels rolling roundly from his mouth. "They were among the first to settle in the Colonies, brought here, like the others, by the scent of money, which drifted across the Atlantic and tickled their freckled and greedy noses. They had a land grant from the governor of New Amsterdam, and half of their time and money went into farming there, with the benefit of free labor from Indian slaves. The other half of their money was invested in a different kind of slave. The Rorys owned a dozen or so ships, which loaded their hulls with stolen human beings, two-legged cargo taken from their homes deep in Africa and sold in African ports with names like Mozambique or the Ivory Coast. They shipped these slaves across the ocean and unloaded them in the Colonies.

"This brought them huge profits until the Colonies went to war against England. Then the English tried to press the Rory ships into naval service against the rebellion. The Rorys themselves cared nothing for the rebels, but being Scots, their hatred of the English overcame even their love of easy profits. They scuttled all their ships—one of them was still loaded with unsold slaves when they burned and sank it—so that the English couldn't get their filthy hands on them. The English king was so furious he sent a detachment of specially trained mercenaries—Hessians, the bloodiest and most murderous bastards in all of Europe—to kill every Rory man, woman, and child, seize all their goods, and turn them over to the Crown.

"The story has it the Hessians began their work in Scotland, where many poorer relations of the New World Rorys still abided. They cut off the heads of seventeen Rory men, women, and children, put them in a barrel, and shipped it off to England. Within two weeks, every sailor on board that ship was struck blind. That was the beginning of the Rory curse. The tale spread across the world, via the shipping lanes. It was a proven fact that anyone who harmed a Rory would lose his sight. Of course, what none of the blind sailors would mention was that they'd secretly been sipping away at the alcohol that preserved the heads in the barrel, not knowing themselves what else was in it. It was pickling alcohol, not spirits, which makes you blind. To the sailors it made no difference, y'see. They only knew it was alcohol. And when the alcohol was gone, the heads began to rot, and a dreadful stench came over the ship. Then the captain got wind of what had been happening. But that's another story."

Daddo paused to puff at his pipe, chuckling at the joke. One of his eyes was better than the other, and he squinted through it now at Willie, who sat patiently on the floor like a small boy, his wounded leg stretched out before him. The rest of the family was still sitting quietly at the table, listening and waiting. Daddo shook his head for a moment before continuing.

"Among the Rorys that had come to the New World," he said, "there were two brothers. One of them was very handsome and charming, named Malcolm. The other was as ugly as it is possible to be, and he was James. Though opposites in appearance, they were the same in temperament, both being cruel and evil men. They each had their own favorite method of indulging their vices. James, the ugly one, had a taste for young slave girls. He bought them strictly for the purpose of dressing them up in fine clothing, giving them perhaps the best meal they had ever tasted in their lives, and then beating them to death. He also did other things to them, which I won't mention, because of your mother in the next room. He sometimes kept several of them for just this purpose, young African or Indian girls, who never knew why they were being treated so decently until it was too late.

"Malcolm, the handsome one, was far more brutish than his brother. He tended toward more simple violence. He loved to get drunk and then feign insult from one fellow or another in the taverns. He would confront an ordinary man, demanding that he repeat something all knew he had not said, which Malcolm pretended he had heard as he passed by. Malcolm was widely known, of course, and nobody would dare to speak up in defense of the unoffending man. The Rorys were feared that greatly. Malcolm would work himself into a rage, all for the pleasure of being angry, and demand satisfaction from the man. Whoever the victim happened to be, he had no choice. He had to step outside the pub, unaccompanied by his friends, who were very few by this time, no matter how well liked the man had been earlier in the evening. Despite his delicate features, Malcolm had great strength. He had once killed a calf with a single blow to the head. So these fights were usually of short duration, taking only as much time as required for Malcolm to pound the man's skull into jelly against the pavement, after which he could always claim he was only defending his honor.

"As might be expected of a devilish breed like that, the brothers Rory hated each other deeply. James hated Malcolm for his beauty and brutish ways, and Malcolm hated James for his affected manners and his ugliness. However, in the days before the war, they had no choice but to remain business partners, although they plotted against each other constantly.

"When word came that a squad of Hessians were after their heads, the brothers knew they had to be united against them. But neither of them cared for the safety of the other. They only cared for keeping the family fortune safe from the English. They took all their holdings to bankers to be turned into gold, and when this was done they had seven large iron-bound chests filled with gold pieces minted in France, Spain, Russia, and Holland. The brothers then set about the nasty business of hiding the chests.

"They did none of the actual digging, of course, since they considered themselves too gentle for that. They had slaves do it for them, and when the hole was dug and the chest placed into it, they murdered the slaves and put their bodies on top of the chest, so that they could never tell where the gold was hidden.

"Six of the chests were hidden in this fashion. Finally there remained only one. Of course, anyone could see what would happen next. Since the two brothers were the only ones who knew where the other six chests were buried, each hoped to murder the other and return after the war to dig them up.

"They put the seventh chest in a wagon and rode far, far to the west, farther than they had ever been before, until they were well out of the territory of New Amsterdam and into what was then Penn's Woods. They wanted the last chest to be so well hidden that nobody would ever think where to look for it.

"What they hadn't counted on was their sister, Mary. Mary was a Rory, but for all that she had a good heart. She was half-witted, or at least everyone treated her as such, and she had never begged the difference. Mary was never told that the true source of the Rory fortune was slavery. She always believed, or pretended to believe, that it was tea. The brothers took her along with the seventh chest for safekeeping, since each knew he was safe from the other for as long as Mary was with them. They also took her for her own safety, since the Hessians were believed to be close by, and the story of the seventeen heads made everyone's blood run cold, even the blood of two heartless murderers such as James and Malcolm.

"James and Mary rode in the wagon, while Malcolm followed behind on horseback. They went on in this manner for several weeks, the brothers very much on their guard against robbers and each other. They hardly dared to sleep at night out of fear for their own necks. Mary, of course, knew nothing, or pretended to know nothing. During the day she behaved as if she was on some lovely little outing, and at night she slept the sleep of the innocent, wrapped up warmly in the wagon between her brothers.

"Finally it was agreed they had ridden far enough. This time, since there were no slaves with them, they had to dig the hole by themselves. With Mary still asleep early in the morning, they dug deeper and deeper, until the moment came at last.

"While Malcolm's back was turned, James took a shovel and struck his brother with the blade of it in the back of the neck. Malcolm never had a chance. His handsome head rolled cleanly off his shoulders and into the hole. Mary, awaking suddenly, began to scream, but James ignored her. He threw his brother's corpse in after the head, dropped

the chest of gold on top of it, and filled in the hole. When he had finished, he turned to Mary, and was amazed to see her pointing a large
pistol directly at him.

"'This is what you were to me, brother,' she said, and she fired.

"To understand the bravery of such an act, you must remember
that in those days pistols were not of the sort they are today. They were
matchlocks, big, slow, and unreliable. They failed more often than
they fired, and when they did work they often missed their mark. And
if you shot at a man and missed, you'd better be fleet of foot—there
was no time to reload. But Mary had nerves of steel. The pistol fired,
and her aim was true. The ball passed through her brother's heart and
he fell dead.

"Mary had known all along what the brothers were plotting, y'see.
She also knew the bloody ways in which her brothers amused themselves, and she was never really as ignorant of the true source of her
family's money as they thought she was. Nor was she half-witted; it was
only to her advantage to pretend that she was so. Her plan was to
avenge the innocents whose lives had ended at the hands of her brothers, and also to return someday for the gold. But she never returned.
Soon after that, near the spot where her brothers fell, the Hessians
found her. They chased her through the woods and cut her head off,
and it was shipped back to England for the King to gloat over. And that
was the end of Mary Rory, and in fact of the whole Rory clan, as well
as their fortune. The English found the first six chests of gold, but they
never found the seventh, and from that day to this, men have sought
for it in vain."

Daddo finished his story with a self-satisfied expression, puffing
away on his pipe.

"Now that half the afternoon is wasted, ye may as well bring me a
dram," he said.

Willie reached into his shirt and pulled out the old rusty lock from
the chest. He hefted it for a moment, enjoying the weight of it in his
hands. It must have weighed three pounds. It was so rusty it had come
off with only a few blows of the shovel.

"Feel o' that," he said, handing it to his grandfather. The old man
squinted at it. He held it in his hands, turning it over and over. Then
he traced the letter *R*, which was worked into the face of the lock.

"Jaysus," whispered the old man.

"Would you say that lock is about a hundred years old?" asked Willie. "And would you say it came off the Rory treasure, Daddo?"

The old man could not speak.

"You'll have as many drams as ye like, from now until the end of your days," said Willie, struggling to his feet. "Come on. I've somethin' to show everyone."

That night, while the festivities were still raging, Willie dragged himself off to bed. His entire family, even his mother, was drunk on whiskey, and the neighbors had begun to stream in from as far off as Clare Town to see for themselves whether the story was true.

Willie'd had to tell over and over again the story of how he'd found the money, until he was sick to death of it. And there were, remarkably, some folks who had never heard the story of the Rory fortune itself. It was decided that the whole tale should be told over by Daddo, this time with the open chest of gold as a backdrop, as well as the fragments of bone that had lain under it, and his audience now numbered nearly a hundred people instead of just Willie.

Those bones troubled Willie greatly. There were just enough of them remaining to identify: a rounded sort of half-dome, obviously a piece of a skull, and a couple of ribs. The rest of James Rory had disintegrated into the earth from which it had come. The bones were a grisly reminder that this gold was blood money, earned not through honest labor but by murder and treachery and slavery, and that more blood—*family* blood—had been shed in the defense of it, which showed to what lengths some people would go to stay wealthy.

Willie had always thought of the Rorys as a band of horned, fire-eating devils, born evil because they were damned. But when they pulled up the chest and saw the bones of James Rory underneath, Willie suddenly understood that the Rorys were probably once a family just like the Manns, simple and poor and honest, and that somehow money had turned them against themselves and each other. Furthermore, he realized, no person was completely immune from that kind of transformation, not even his family, not even himself.

And that night, as he slept, he had a disturbing dream.

He was running through a deep dark forest. The trees reached up to blot out the sky, and scarcely a single shaft of sunlight penetrated the dense canopy of leaves. He ran in a panic. And while he knew he was still himself, still Willie Mann, he also knew that he was not. He looked down at his feet. They were bare, small, delicate, not his own feet at all. And he was holding a skirt up around his legs so that he wouldn't trip on it.

Behind him he heard shouts in a strange, guttural language. He heard the clanking of equipment and the pounding of large booted feet on the ground. Willie dared one look back over his shoulder. There were several men chasing him, dressed in green uniforms with white crossbelts and carrying muskets. One of them was holding a sword. And Willie knew that they were Hessian soldiers, and they meant to kill him.

Suddenly his foot caught in a root and he went headlong to the ground. He tried to get up, but he tripped on his skirt and fell again, and by then it was too late. They were upon him.

One of them kicked him over on his back. Another, the one holding the sword, planted one massive boot on his chest. Willie heard himself screaming, felt himself struggling to get away. A rifle butt came smashing down into his face and he felt his jaw shatter. Then the soldier with the sword held it high above his head, looked briefly down at Willie to gauge his aim, and brought it down swiftly to his neck.

All went black.

Willie awoke to hear the sounds of the party still in full swing. He was alone in the room. The night was chilly, but he was soaked through with sweat.

"Mary Rory," he said aloud into the black room. "It was Mary Rory."

The door burst open and Poky Boy came staggering in.

"Come on, Willie!" he shouted. "'Tis no time to be sleepin'! Ye've made us rich, brother! We want to drink your health!"

"Go away, Poky," said Willie softly.

"Eh? Are ye mad? It's the greatest day of our lives!"

"Go away, I tell ye!"

More revelers came stumbling in the door. Soon the room was full of them. Several grabbed Willie by his limbs, paying no attention to his wounded leg, and pulled him out into the main room of the house. A cheer erupted from all when they saw him. A glass of whiskey was put into his hand.

Willie looked again at the open chest sitting on the dining room table. Andy and Father were guarding it fiercely, allowing no one too close. They were both drunk, and Willie saw his brother snarl at a man who reached out to feel a piece of the money. The expression on his face was savage; not quite murderous, but close.

"I just want to touch it," said the man, who was also drunk.

Andy grudgingly relented. The man reached out one tentative hand and picked up a piece of gold. Still holding it, he turned to speak to someone behind him. Andy followed his gaze, relaxing his watch on the piece the man held. This was precisely what the man had planned. Casually, he slipped the doubloon into his pocket and began to walk away.

Hardly had Willie seen this when Andy realized what had happened. He dropped one powerful hand on the man's shoulder and spun him around. With the other he made a fist and sent it crashing into the man's soft mouth. The man flew backward, striking heavily against the wall, and slid to the floor. Andy advanced on him. The man attempted to rise and Andy hit him again, on the top of his head this time. The man went limp. Andy went through his pockets and retrieved the gold piece. He put it reverently back on the pile of gold in the chest. Then, after a brief conference with Willie's father, they closed the lid and locked it tight.

The party was going full steam ahead, and hardly anyone seemed to have noticed what had just taken place.

Willie put the glass of whiskey down on the table. He had already been forgotten by everyone. Nobody saw him limp out of the house and out across the field, still in his nightshirt. He went to the hole he had dug earlier that day. There he lay down on his back, staring up at the clouded night sky, the dew soaking through his nightshirt. He closed his eyes, found himself seeing into the future, and he wished, quite simply, that someone else had found the money. Nothing was going to be the same for the Manns from now on.

The End.

8

My Fifteenth Year; I Kill Mr. Simpson

"Willie Mann and the Rory Fortune" was my first short story—the first thing I'd ever made from beginning to end, the first thing I'd accomplished entirely on my own. Maybe that was why it was so hard—because it was also, up to that point, the *hardest* thing I'd ever done in my life. There was nobody to help me with it, nobody to talk to about it when I got stuck. In my more reflective moods, I realized that I didn't even know why I was doing it.

I began work on that first short story of mine the summer I turned fifteen, and I didn't finish it until just a few months shy of my sixteenth birthday—just over nine months in the making. An adult woman can produce an entire human being in that time. I, a juvenile male, was happy with fifteen solid pages of prose. When I began the story, my face was smooth, my skin still clean and soft with childhood. By the time it was done, I had, to my immense delight, ten or fifteen whiskers on my chin. Less thrilling was the appearance of that dreaded stigma of adolescence—zits. My body was evolving even as I sat hunched over my clattery old Royal.

It seems to me entirely characteristic of myself in those days that while other boys were looking forward to their driver's licenses, their first cars, their first dates, I was sitting up in my bedroom endlessly rewriting the same story and teaching myself how to type at the same time. I used the hunt-and-peck-with-the-index-fingers method at first, a poky and frustrating business. Soon I developed a more efficient three-finger method, then a promising four-finger style. Four-fingered, I could type faster than I could write with a pen. Then I hit the point that I have since heard other writers describe as the moment when they knew for sure they were meant to be writers—I could type at the speed of my thoughts. The words seemed to flow out of me like a river, limited only by the need to stretch my aching lower back, or to race frantically into town on foot to buy a new ribbon—or to race even more frantically to the always enthusiastic Elsie Orfenbacher, to relieve the frequent and lightning-fast urges I felt for her warmth and softness. By the time the story was finished, I had learned two things: I could type like a professional, and I was utterly ignorant of what to do next. A novel? Another short story? Was I done? Was I any good?

It was a lonely business, teaching myself to write.

That fall had passed by with barely a glance from me, and then the winter, and then the spring, the succession of seasons the only thing that reminded me there were other things going on in the world. Annie and I still walked to school every day, but we saw less of each other than we used to. I knew without asking that it was because of what had passed between us in the car that night.

"You already know me," she said. "There's nothing left to say."

"Oh, bullshit," I said.

"No, really," she said, but she didn't look me in the eye anymore, and she was quiet much of the time as we walked. Sometimes she didn't say anything at all. I decided she was embarrassed she'd told me. I had to admit I was sort of embarrassed too.

"Have you told anyone?" she asked me once.

"No," I said—because I hadn't, even though I was going to. Any day now. In fact, I didn't know why I hadn't yet. "Of course not."

"Good," she whispered. Head down, feet shuffling through the dirt. She never used to walk like that. She was being beaten down. I was losing her. The time was coming for me to do something. But I still didn't know for sure if telling was the right thing. Maybe I had to do something myself. But what? It was a big job. I had to have a plan, and none seemed to be forthcoming.

And to tell the truth, though I'm ashamed to admit it even now, I had other things besides Annie's plight on my mind.

To my surprise, I found myself dreading our morning walks to school. Also, school itself had begun to seem so irrelevant that one day I decided simply to stop going. It was that simple. I made it in once or twice a week for roll call, and then I just went home. Amazingly, nobody seemed to mind. Certainly we never got any phone calls from the school about it, although that may have just been another period when I forgot to pay the phone bill. And Grandpa never noticed I was playing hooky, or else he pretended not to notice; actually, I doubt he even knew I was home. He spent a good deal of his time passed out in the rocking chair, or else sleeping off his latest drunk in bed. On the few occasions when he asked me what I was doing at home, I told him school had been canceled for the day. He always accepted that without further questioning—if he even heard me, which I doubted.

Grandpa drank more now than I'd ever seen him drink before. I bought his whiskey for him at Gruber's, so I had a clear handle on how much he was drinking and when—a bottle and a half a day, no more and no less. Mr. Gruber sold me the whiskey at a discount, a case at a time, with a wink and a friendly nod. It was against the law, but he knew it wasn't for me.

"How's the old man these days?" he'd ask every once in a while— or maybe he was asking, "How's the old Mann?" But that was mostly just for form's sake. He knew how it was with Grandpa and me.

"Same as always," I would say.

That's a small town for you. We ignore the most obvious things— Jack Simpson up the hill molests his daughter, Elsie Orfenbacher is banging a fifteen-year-old boy, old Thomas Mann is an alcoholic and his grandson has to buy his booze for him because he can't even make it out of the house anymore.

I guess if I'd known how alcohol, like a cat, will torture its victims mercilessly before dispatching them, I would have been alarmed at how much Grandpa was drinking. But I was a teenager, and teenagers rarely bother to look beyond the ends of their own noses—at least I know I didn't. Too, it must be remembered that I grew up with Grandpa drinking. No, not just drinking—drunk. Constantly. I thought it was normal, so I didn't worry about it much. I thought instead about becoming a writer, and sometimes about Annie, and sometimes about Elsie. That was about it.

Of course, as I was writing the story, I thought about the Rory fortune and how it had changed us. That was when I really began to understand what had happened to the Mann family in the last one hundred and twenty years.

It was hard for me *not* to think about the story of Willie Mann's money, because everything around me had been created by it, or at least affected by it in one way or another. The old farmhouse Grandpa and I lived in had been built by that money. The original Mann home, the tiny three-room shack in which Willie once lived with his family, had stood on the same spot where the farmhouse stood now. I'd heard about it in little snatches here and there from Grandpa. Destroying the shack and erecting the farmhouse in its place was just one of the many improvements Willie would make with the blood money of the Rorys. He was able finally to give the Manns what they desired most: not just plush living quarters, but privacy. Privacy had been hitherto unknown to the Manns. It was the greatest luxury he could imagine. He wrote:

> To be able to sit at my little desk and write at whatever hour of the day or night I please, without being disturbed by any person, is to me a source of deep joy.

But Willie, like me, was also tortured by an ancient guilt:

> I must never allow myself to forget that I live like a king because thousands of others lived like animals. To enslave a person is to rob them of their dignity, their rights, their past and future. I am tormented by nightmares, and by one nightmare in particular. Even though it was not I who traded decency for gold, I still reap the benefits of that transaction.

Willie also made sure the house contained a special room for Daddo, one not isolated from the others. It was placed in the geometric center of the house, so that Daddo was sure to see everyone as they passed back and forth on their daily business. It was a small room, a point that Daddo had insisted on, and plainly furnished, according to his taste, but it had doors in each of its four walls, which were left open so he could watch his family in the course of their comings and goings. It was the nexus of the farmhouse. Grandpa and I still referred to it as "Daddo's room." Willie had sensed the pain the old man's enforced solitude had caused him, and felt it almost as keenly as the old man himself.

"No one should have to be alone when they are old," he instructs us.

But perhaps the greatest reminder to me that this story needed to be written was the nightmare. During the time I was writing my story, the nightmare, which had been absent for a couple of years at least, came back in full force. I had it every night. It abated somewhat as the story came, but if I happened to stop work, it returned like a raging disease whose treatment has been discontinued too early. I had no choice but to finish the story, for I knew that as soon as I did, the nightmare would leave me for good. I knew it the same way I knew that the ghost of Willie was watching me, not always but from time to time. And I was right. I haven't had the nightmare since. And I also knew that if for some reason I were not to finish the story, Mary Rory would never leave me, and eventually would drive me mad. A person can only have his head cut off so many times, after all, before he starts believing it is gone.

Soon after I finished my story I took it to Doctor Connor. I needed the opinion of an adult; I wasn't sure if it was any good. Mannville was pretty short on writers, and Connor was the only person I knew who'd been to college, so he was the logical choice. He read it in his consulting room while I toyed with the paper on his examination table. His eyes, when he finished, were glowing with excitement and elation.

"Where did you learn to write like this?" he demanded.

"I didn't learn anywhere," I replied. "I taught myself."

"My God!"

"Do you like it?"

"*Like* it? I love it! It's fantastic!"

I blushed. A warm feeling of success swelled up in my chest.

"It's not like I made it up," I said modestly, because the events of the story were all true, and I had gotten them piecemeal from Grandpa. History had invented this story, not I.

"That doesn't matter," he said. "There are a million different ways to tell a story. You chose one that works. You have a vivid imagination."

"But I didn't imagine any of it!"

"That doesn't matter," he repeated. "You had to figure out how to tell it, didn't you? That takes imagination. What are you going to do with it?"

"Publish it, I guess."

"Do you know how?"

"I'll just send it away to someone. A magazine or something." It had never once occurred to me that I wouldn't become a real writer, a published writer, even though it seemed like awfully hard work, and to turn out only fifteen pages in nine or ten months was not exactly the mark of greatness.

But Doctor Connor dismissed these concerns with a wave of his large hairy hand. It wasn't how much I wrote that mattered, he said, but how good it was. He promised to take me to the library and show me where to look up the addresses of publishers. It wasn't as simple as I made it sound, he said. He himself had tried to publish one or two articles on medicine, and even though it wasn't fictional writing and there was a very specific kind of publication that would accept his work, it was still confusing and difficult, and he usually met with failure.

"You're coming along splendidly, my boy," he said. "Just splendidly."

I looked at him with gratitude, and I realized at that moment that I trusted Connor completely. It was then I knew I had to tell him about Annie.

"Doc," I said, "I have something to tell you."

And I told.

It was several days later when Annie appeared at the front door. I was in the kitchen when her shadow fell across the porch, and I caught it only out of the corner of my eye. She didn't knock or ring the bell. I went down the long hallway to the door. She stood turned to the side, so that I could see only her profile; that was how I knew she had something to hide again.

"Where have you been?" she said, speaking away from me, out into the yard.

"Look at me," I said.

"No."

I stepped out onto the porch and gently turned her face toward me. Her left cheek was bruised black and green, swollen out of proportion to the rest of her face. Her eye was puffy and closed.

"You haven't been going to school," she said.

"What happened?"

"I didn't go to school today either," she said. "And I have you to thank for it."

"I'm taking you to the hospital. Right now."

"No. You're not taking me anywhere."

"Annie, please."

"You lied to me," she said. "You broke your promise. You told."

"Annie. *Please* understand. I had to."

"I trusted you," she said. She didn't say it vindictively. It was simply a statement of fact.

I felt my face begin to flush with rage—at her father, but also at her. She was letting this happen. *She* was allowing it. *She let him do this.*

"How can you let him?" I asked her. "How much longer are you going to let him keep this up?"

"It's nobody's business," said Annie. "Okay? It's not yours or Connor's or the county's. It's mine."

"It's *not* just yours. It's mine. It's everybody's."

"I can't fight him, Billy," she said. "He's too strong. If I fight him he hits me. So I let him drug me. That's how it happens."

"What are you talking about?"

"When he does those things to my body," she said. She was staring far beyond me. It was as if neither she nor I were there, as if she were talking about someone else. "I know he's going to do it to me. There's nothing I can do about it. So I let him drug me, and at least then I don't feel it. And if I don't feel it, then everything's all right. It never happened—that's how it feels. But after those people came, this is what he did to me. And he didn't drug me first, and I felt every bit of it."

"I'm going to fucking kill him," I said.

"No you're not."

"Oh, yes I am."

"Nobody is going to do anything."

"If that's what you think, then you really must be nuts," I said. I was in the grip of full-fledged anger now. "I'm going to murder him. I'll kill him!" It wasn't me speaking, suddenly. It was the Celtic warrior again, the same one who had pounded David Weismueller's testicles into jelly, the same one who'd beaten Trevor's head into the snow all those years ago. *Well, hello there*, I said to the Celtic warrior, who gave me a cold, bloody smile. *Haven't seen you in some time. Got some work to do.*

"I trusted you," she said again. "And you told. And I'm never telling you anything again."

"Oh, goddamn this," I said. The Celtic warrior was waiting, a barely contained tsunami of fury. He sat down impatiently and began to sharpen his ax.

"Do you have any idea how it made me feel to have those people come to my house? To ask me questions that are *none of their business?* To snoop around, poke into things, interrogate me, interrogate *him* even, like we're some kind of criminals? Bank robbers or something?"

I knew then that Connor must have called the county, and the county had sent its people over. That must have been the only way Connor knew to go about it, and in most situations it would have been the right way. But not this one. I knew it couldn't happen for Annie the way it was supposed to happen. I'd always known I would have to take care of it myself. And I decided right then and there, although I didn't say anything to Annie about it, that I *would* take care of it myself, the way my father would have done it if it was him instead of me. The way a real man would do it. This was a job for a superhero, a daredevil. This was a job for Billy Mann.

Abruptly she stepped off the porch and headed back down the driveway.

"Annie," I called.

She turned.

"Yes?" Her voice was vacant, void.

"I told because I love you," I said. "That's why."

"That's nice," she said. She turned again and headed up the road. I felt, as she left, that Annie had not been there at all.

The Celtic warrior inside me went to the river and gathered clay. He mixed it with water and painted his naked body blue. My father, shirtless, grinning, smiled and slapped his hands together. He spit contemptuously on the ground and flexed his muscles.

Let's get to it, I said to him. *We have a job to do.*

Says Willie Mann, my long-dead but always relevant ancestor:

> *Have no fear of anger, for then anger has no power over you. Anger is a tool. Wield it, but use it wisely, never rashly. That is the way to turn it to one's advantage; that is the way to keep it from taking over Life.*

I—by which I really mean myself, the Celtic warrior, and my father—was going on another mission to the Simpson home. If Annie wasn't going to save herself from her father, then I was.

It had been years since I'd practiced the gentle art of spying. Of *espionage*. That was a beautiful, smooth-sounding word, an exotic word, hinting of foreign cities and meetings with shadowy characters in dark alleys. But this mission would not be to Casablanca or Algiers or Berlin. It would be to the top of a hill just half a mile away, to a filthy white house where great crimes were being committed on a regular basis.

I dug through closet after closet until I came up with what I was looking for: a box camera with the word BROWNIE on it, circa 1936. It was the sort of camera you had to hold at waist level and look down into. It had once belonged to Grandpa's mother, Lily. I'd used it once before, years earlier, when Grandpa had caught a large walleye out of the Lake and wanted a memento of it. The picture had come out blurry. In the lower left-hand corner, Grandpa's head was barely visible, and the fish not at all. I shook the camera and was rewarded with a papery rattle. There was still film inside. Probably expired, I thought, but it would have to do. I would have to take the chance.

I spent two days in preparation for my mission. During this time I stayed away from school and Annie stayed away from me, but I sent her telepathic messages: *I'm coming,* I would think, standing on my porch and staring up at her house. *Don't give up.* I drew maps in my head—a good spy never commits anything to paper—rehearsing exactly how I would go about the whole thing. There was a large tree just outside the Simpson house, which would afford me some cover, and if I climbed it I would be able to see into both the first and second floors of their house. I had no idea which room was my target; that was something I'd have to figure out when I got there.

I chose my clothing carefully: dark pants, black sweater, and, for the final touch, a ski mask I'd purchased at Gruber's Grocery with my employee discount, ignoring Mrs. Gruber's arched eyebrows as I did so.

I was ready on a Tuesday. I stood on the porch again, clenching and unclenching my fists, staring up at her old hilltop house.

I'm coming, I told her again with my mind. *I'm ready. But when?*

And perhaps it was purely my imagination, but this time I heard her voice come back to me, faint but distinct, clear. It was just one word: *morning.*

What? I thought. *What do you mean, morning? Which morning?*

But there was no further answer.

I went back inside and thought about it some more. Mornings seemed the likeliest time to make my run—early mornings. It had to be. The more I thought about it, the more it made sense. As much as it disgusted me to admit it, Mr. Simpson and I probably had at least one thing in common with all the other males of the world: we woke up with hard-ons. Annie would still be sleeping, or perhaps just waking up, when he came to her. She'd be powerless and groggy, and he would be strengthened by his testosterone, perhaps emboldened by his lingering drunkenness. It horrified me to think that Mr. Simpson might feel the same urges toward his daughter that I felt, that we had anything in common at all. But the fact was that male lust ruled both of us. I could take comfort in the fact that at least I knew what was taboo and what was not; just the fact that I felt lust didn't make me a criminal. But it was difficult not to feel some degree of self-loathing, simply on the grounds of commonality.

If I didn't catch him on the first run, I would simply come back again and again until I got it right. But something told me my hunch was accurate. As I thought about it, I remembered that Annie was often most subdued in the mornings, sometimes downright silent. My conviction grew inside me. And since I was ready, there was nothing holding me back. Before the sun rose again, I vowed, I would have done my best to accomplish my mission. One way or another, things would be different for Annie from now on.

I was certain that even though she'd told me she didn't want any help, there was a part of her that was begging for it. That part of her, the hidden, nearly absent part that had been pushed down so far it was in danger of disappearing forever, was the real Annie. That was the part of her that had answered me. That was the part of her I was saving.

I went to bed early that night, my gear laid out on a chair next to my bed: dark clothing, camera, ski mask, sneakers, small flashlight. My alarm went off at four A.M. I awoke instantly, sprang out of bed, and dressed. I was moving up the road within fifteen minutes, the dust of sleep blown rapidly from my mind as I walked and inhaled the fresh breeze. When I hit the base of the hill I entered the trees; this was why I'd brought the flashlight, to navigate among the large trunks and fallen branches. I didn't bother with stealthiness yet, being still a quarter-mile from my target, but even though there was nobody to hear me, I was sure my crunchings and crashings echoed all over town. I hadn't brought a watch—I didn't even own one—but calculated the time to be around four forty-five. When I had finally cleared the trees and climbed the hill, it must have been nearly five o'clock. The sky to the east was slowly graying as false dawn approached. I was at the outer boundary of the Simpson yard . . .

. . . where I stopped and hit the ground like a man under machine-gun fire. I had caught a glimpse of orange on the porch. It was the glowing end of a cigarette butt, brightening and then fading as someone drew on it. Annie didn't smoke, and her older sisters had all left home by this time; it was just him and her now. Therefore it had to be Simpson himself, the great criminal. I hardly dared breathe. I lay on my belly next to a large birch, hoping fervently that I wouldn't stand out against its white bark, certain he'd heard me. How could he not have? I was blown, I thought. Mission aborted. Time to evacuate the area.

But nothing happened. There was no shout, no approaching footsteps. I could barely make out the figure on the porch now as the eastern sky began to brighten. It was him, all right.

It was then that everything for which I had *not* planned began to occur to me. I cursed myself for being an idiot. It would be too dark for photography, and of course the ancient camera I carried had no flash. *Why am I always fifty years behind the times?* I wondered. I could never take a good picture in this light. I would have to make it a long exposure, meaning that the camera would have to be held perfectly still for perhaps as long as a minute, and the figures I would be photographing would certainly move during that time, meaning that their features would be blurred and unrecognizable. And how could I be sure that the deed would take place this morning, of all mornings? I'd no idea how often it happened, or even if my guesswork was correct. Perhaps it wasn't a morning event at all. Perhaps it happened in the afternoon. Perhaps it happened only once a month, or even once a year. After all, Annie had never said how often he did these things to her. *Once in a lifetime*, I thought grimly, *would certainly be enough.* Maybe he'd just gone crazy one day, taken it into his pickled brain to bang his daughter, and it had never happened again. Maybe it wouldn't happen this morning after all. Maybe I was completely fucked, lying there on my belly on the cold, dew-covered ground, clutching a hopelessly outdated camera and with a plan that even the worst spy in history would have scoffed at.

But something told me it wasn't just an isolated event. I could see that in Annie's eyes. It was a constantly recurring thing, one that was gradually battering her into submission, eating away at her soul like a cancer. And if it wasn't this morning, then it would be some other time. And I vowed then and there, my chin digging into the ground, the taste of grass and dead leaves in my mouth, that I would be there the next time it happened, even if I had to carry out a constant surveillance of the house and its miserable occupants for the rest of my life.

It was light enough to see now. I saw the orange cigarette butt arc toward me in a long, graceful line as the son of a bitch flicked it away from him. It skittered to a halt several feet from my nose. I heard him grunt with exertion as he stood on his spindly legs and went into the house, the screen door on the porch squeaking quietly behind him.

This was the first time I'd seen Simpson since the day Grandpa broke his hip on the ice. He'd grown fatter, waddled more. He was perhaps the most ridiculously proportioned person I'd ever seen. From his abdomen to his neck, his figure was almost a perfect sphere; but his legs were as thin as reeds, and the overall impression one got from looking at him was that of a ball of clay resting unsteadily on two toothpicks. The fact that he hadn't let the screen door slam gave me both fear and encouragement. Perhaps he was being sneaky, not wanting to wake his poor daughter up until it was too late for her to resist. My timing might possibly be dead on.

I crawled on my belly toward the house. When it became apparent that he wasn't coming back onto the porch, I rose and ran in a half-crouch until I gained the front door. My heart was throbbing in my chest. My ears were so alert I could hear only a high-pitched ringing, and the sound of my blood rushing through my veins at twice its normal rate.

I had abandoned the part of my plan that called for me to climb the tree. Instead I waited at the front door. I heard the thump of a glass being set down; he was close, but not too close, in the kitchen perhaps. I edged the screen door open, wishing I'd brought a can of machine oil for the hinges. But mercifully, they didn't squeak for me, though they had a moment earlier when he went inside. It took several seconds to open the door wide enough to slip in.

And I was back in the same living room where I had first met Annie, where she had held my hand for the first time. *Had it been happening even then?* I wondered. I didn't see how anyone, even the most dastardly of criminals, could be so morally bankrupt as to want to have sex with a seven-year-old girl. But it happened, I knew. You read about it in the papers sometimes. Maybe Simpson was that bad.

The house was filled with the same stench: shit, mostly, and stale beer, and urine, and greasy cooking. The living room was not quite as dirty as it had been seven years ago. Perhaps the people from the county had cleaned it up during their surprise investigation; more likely, though, was that Annie had done it herself, the sight of them pulling into the driveway sending her into a frenzy of tidying up, hiding the evidence of her wretched life. I moved quickly across the living room to the back hallway, listening with every part of my body for the sound of Simpson. I went to the back hallway first because there was a secondary motive to my mission. I wanted to see if the half-man was still there.

It seemed inconceivable that a human being could be kept in the same bed all this time, but I knew that in this house anything could happen, and that Simpson would if possible attempt to violate the one great rule of nature, which was that everything must change. He was like Grandpa in that respect, as much as I hated to admit it: he preferred to live in an earlier time, a time when things had been better, when his son had been whole and could walk and talk.

Moving through the living room was like having an old dream. I kept my hand over my nose as I approached the back room; the smell was nearly intolerable. The door was closed but not latched. I pushed it with one finger. It swung open, and there he lay, staring up at the ceiling, exactly the same as I remembered him, swaddled in the same filthy sheets.

I gagged as I stepped into the room. The odor of his unwashed body was overwhelming, almost animal. This was only a side trip, I promised myself. I had bigger and better things to be doing. But there was something about this man, this old friend of my father's, that drew me. I couldn't pass up the opportunity to look at him again, to see if I could draw from him any inkling of my mysterious past.

I stood at the side of the bed and looked down. He was unshaven, long-haired, a perfectly blank expression on his face, a man in his early forties who had checked out permanently when he was twenty or so. Where his arms and legs should have been were only four rounded stumps, cut and neatly trimmed by the U.S. Army. The same old tubes ran around him like so many plastic snakes, and the respirator clicked and hummed and hissed as it always had. This is what the Army does, I thought. It repackages you. And you always come home in worse shape than you were in when you left.

"What the hell happened to you, anyway?" I whispered. His eyes did not flicker in the slightest. He gave no indication that he knew I was there.

"Do you remember my dad?"

Nothing.

"My Grandpa told me about when you stole that car from him. He's sorry he called the police on you. He said he wouldn't have done it if he'd known it was you."

Nothing again.

"He knew you weren't a bad kid," I said. Then I realized that even if he could hear me, he would have no idea who I was.

"I'm Eddie Mann's son, Billy," I told him. "You were my dad's best friend."

Frederic—that was his name, I remembered—just breathed away. In thinking back on his condition now, I assume he must have had some sort of damage to the part of his brain that controlled his higher functions. He could blink and breathe, but that was about it. I never learned exactly what had happened to him to make him the way he was. It was possible that nobody knew. A direct hit by a mortar shell, perhaps, or maybe he had stepped on a mine in some rice paddy deep in the interior of Vietnam. It might have been that his mind worked perfectly and he was merely paralyzed, on top of being a quadruple amputee. I like to think that he heard every word I said, and understood me. On the other hand, I would prefer for his sake that he was not capable of thinking at all. For to be trapped in that filthy bed, in that house, completely aware of everything that was going on around you and unable to do anything about it, would be a fate worse than the worst kind of hell I can think of.

Time to get out of here. I stole along the hallway again, then through the living room to the stairs. I stopped there and listened again. There was an angry voice, muffled by walls. Then there was crying. My God, I thought, could I be right? Could it really be happening right now? I sneaked up the stairs. The sounds seemed to be coming from a bedroom to my right, just around the corner. The shouting was louder now. I had just identified which door it was coming from when it opened, and Mr. Simpson came out.

I drew back and froze. If he turned the corner to go down the stairs, he would see me. If he saw me, he would kill me. I didn't even have the strength to get down and hide. Terror shot through me like a flight of arrows. I felt my bowels clench and my stomach churn. But he didn't turn the corner; he went instead into the bathroom, next to the door from which he'd come. He closed the door and I heard him turn on the faucet.

I peeked cautiously around the corner. The bedroom door was open and the light was on. There was an item or two of clothing on the floor, and I could see the end of a bed. On it there was a naked foot. A small, slender foot. Annie's foot.

Without thinking, I crept down the hallway and into the room. I had lost all control of my plan now. Seeing Frederic had unnerved me, and I was thrumming with adrenaline. I was a spy wandering aimlessly, deep in enemy territory, and it was only through sheer dumb luck that I hadn't been caught yet. All instinct for caution had fled. I didn't even know what I was doing. I went quickly into the bedroom, my hand upraised to put over Annie's mouth if she should be startled.

She lay on the bed in much the same attitude as her brother downstairs, staring vacantly at the ceiling, unblinking. She wore a nightdress, which was lifted halfway up her thighs. Was I too late? I wondered. Had he already done it?

"Annie," I whispered. She didn't move.

"Annie!" Not a sound, not a glance. She stared upward, unmoving. I reached down and touched her shoulder. She didn't flinch, didn't shiver. I bent my ear over her mouth. Yes, she was breathing. There was a faint medicinal odor to her breath. He had drugged her. I was too late to stop that. But I wasn't too late to stop the rest of it.

Just then the sink stopped running and the bathroom door opened. I opened the closet door and slid inside, pulling it closed after me just enough so that I could see through a tiny crack. The heavy steps of Mr. Simpson came back down the hall into the bedroom. I looked through the crack in the door.

Simpson was taking off his shirt. I was horrified by the sight of his flabby alcoholic torso, his belly covered with stretch marks like a woman who has given birth not once but dozens of times. Not even Levi Miller's wife, with her fifteen children, had stretch marks like that. And I learned something I hadn't known about Mr. Simpson—he had a long scar on his chest, like a zipper, extending the length of his sternum. It was the mark of heart surgery. Somewhere, sometime, some misguided surgeon had decided he would try to extend this miserable life by ten or twenty years, as if it were worth saving. As if the world would benefit by the continued presence of a monster.

Simpson bent down and did something to Annie, moved her, or flipped her over; it was unclear what. But she didn't offer any resistance, or make a sound. She was out cold.

It occurred to me then that I was near the breaking point. I'd had no idea what I was getting myself into. Long ago, I had promised Annie I would rescue her from her father. But that was before I knew how evil he truly was. I'd always imagined myself kicking in the door, backed up by a detachment of Marines, perhaps, and spraying the house with machine-gun fire before throwing her over my shoulder and carrying her to safety. In my daydreams I was never scared or uncertain, and the outcome was never in doubt. But this was a different story. If Simpson caught me he would beat the living daylights out of me, and it would be worse than anything David Weismueller ever could have done.

I had to think.

There was no way I could take a picture of them. With a start, I realized I didn't even know where my camera was. I could have left it any number of places in the house. With my luck, Simpson would find it before I managed to escape. What was worse, the word MANN was written on the bottom of it in white indelible ink. If he saw that, he would know for certain I was there. My great-grandmother Lily had never imagined that she would be endangering my welfare by labeling her camera. It was, I thought furiously, another example of how history reaches out to fuck us over.

I heard the unzipping of pants and the clink as the belt buckle hit the floor. I was afraid I was going to be sick. It was now or never, I said to myself. I didn't know what to do, but there was no way I could stay there in the closet and listen to this man rape his daughter. I wished for a gun, or a knife, or anything to kill him with. Failing that, I wished for a modern camera. I wouldn't even be able to prove any of this had happened. Doctor Connor would believe me, but that was about all I could hope for. I was breaking as many laws as I was preserving. I myself could be arrested for what I was doing, sent to the boy's home in Gowanda, where I would probably be raped myself. I was almost crying. This was too much. It was more than any fourteen-year-old boy could be expected to handle.

But I was not, I remembered, just any fourteen-year-old boy. I was a daredevil, and the son of a daredevil. The blood of heroes coursed through my veins. And what was more, I was a Mann.

I pushed open the closet door.

"GET OFF HER!" I screamed at the top of my lungs.

The effect upon Mr. Simpson was immediate and dramatic, and better than anything I could have hoped for. He was just about to get on top of Annie, who had been rolled over onto her stomach, her nightdress lifted up now over her buttocks. He was naked, and completely unprepared for the sight of a black-clad, ski-masked stranger emerging from his daughter's closet. A lifetime of hard drinking, heavy smoking, and greasy food had already left its mark on his heart. He stood up rapidly, like a small boy caught in some misdemeanor, putting one hand on his chest. He spun around slowly to look at me.

"Ahhhh!" he said softly, his piglike eyes popping out of his head. "Ahhh! Ahhh!"

I stood and watched him, mesmerized.

"Waahhhh . . ." he said, in a deep, froglike voice, and slowly, almost gracefully, he toppled over like a short thick tree, hitting the floor with a house-shaking thud.

He seemed to take a long time to fall. The scene was replaying itself in my mind even before it was complete. For one revolting moment, our eyes locked. I couldn't look away. Down, down he went, sideways, and when he hit the floor the windows rattled, and I was sure the noise could be heard as far away as the center of town.

I stood there for several long moments. Simpson, lying on the other side of the bed, was invisible to me. I waited. After a time there came a hissing sound, like air being expelled through a tiny hole.

My God, I thought—*he's* deflating.

I waited another moment. His head did not reappear over the bed. He said nothing. Nobody moved. Annie was still unconscious on the bed. Delicately, I reached down and pulled her nightdress back over her bottom, not looking at her as I did so. So far, she didn't even know I'd been there, and it was beginning to look as if she never would. Phase Two of my plan was creating itself in my brain as the seconds ticked by, and it looked like a good one.

I stepped around the end of the bed and looked down.

A pool of urine was rapidly spreading around Simpson's body as his bladder relaxed. One eye was shut. The other was horribly half-open, the eyeball itself twisted around out of sight so that only the white part showed. His pudgy hand was still pressed to his chest, in a final, fruitless effort to encourage life to remain. I stood there for a long time, waiting, wanting to make sure but not able to bring myself to touch him. After five minutes or so of stillness, I was certain.

He was dead. And I'd killed him. I'd scared Mr. Simpson to death.

I had very little time to waste on reflection.

I ran down the hallway, back down the stairs, into the living room, and down the back hallway. There was my camera. It was sitting outside the door of Annie's brother's room—who, I hoped, would soon be going somewhere he would be taken care of. I ran out of the house and back down the hill, still avoiding the road. It was more important than ever now that I not be seen by anyone. It was also very important that I carry on with my normal life, that I not appear to deviate from my routine in the slightest. When Annie woke up, she would know what to do. Until then, I would have to wait. I couldn't just call her out of the blue and ask casually how things were going. I had never called her in my life; the constant malevolent presence of her father had forbidden that.

Annie would wake up from her drugged stupor, see her father on the floor, and call the police. There was absolutely no reason for anyone to suspect that I'd had anything to do with it. Nobody would question me, nobody would even think that I'd been there. I had carried out the perfect crime. It was all the more perfect because it had been spontaneous, not at all a part of my original plan. It wasn't really even a crime in the traditional sense. I hadn't intended to kill him. I had only wanted to prevent the awfulness from happening to Annie one more time. If killing him was what it took, then so be it. He didn't deserve to live anyway.

Willie writes of the gentle art of murder:

> *I am guilty of the murder of one of my fellow humans. I killed him during wartime, when murder is generally encouraged; yet his uniform was of the same color as mine, and therefore I was punished. Circumstances dictated that I should kill*

him, or else he would have gone on living, and that was not an
acceptable alternative. Yet my intention was not evil, and the act
itself was perpetrated without premeditation. My conscience has
troubled me greatly nonetheless. Persons in the future reading
this diary may wonder how it was that I came to kill only one
man in the course of my military career. Let them read on; all
shall be made clear.

It would be four more years before I read this entry. The relief it
gave me would be stupefying. I was not the only Mann to kill someone. Although my great-great-grandfather's crime didn't justify my
own, at least I could read of his guilt and somehow be strengthened
by it.

The sun had risen over the eastern corner of the Lake.

I hid my dark clothing in the back of my closet and ditched the old
Brownie camera in the attic. There was really no reason to hide anything. Nobody would be looking in my room for clues to Simpson's
death. They wouldn't even know it was a murder.

"I killed a Simpson," I whispered aloud, into the still, early morning.

It had not been the kind of killing that leaves one sick afterward
with the excess of rage. I had not bludgeoned, beaten, shot, drowned,
electrocuted, gassed, hung, or garroted him, nor had I used any of the
other methods humans have devised for killing each other. I simply
scared him to death, surprised him into heart failure. Perfect. It was
perfect.

It was now near six-thirty A.M. From the direction of town, I heard
the whine of Mannville's ambulance. I listened carefully. Gradually it
increased in pitch and volume as it drew nearer, and then abruptly
changed pitch as it sped past the foot of Mann Road on its way up the
hill. Don't bother hurrying, I thought. The doctors can't repair his
heart now.

This meant that poor Annie had woken up and found him. What
would she think? Would she wonder what had scared him? Would she
be scared herself, or would she fall on her knees, carefully avoiding the
puddle of piss that was her father's last gift to the world, and thank
God for delivering her? Would she ask herself whether he had forced

himself on her one last time before his sudden departure, or would she somehow know that he hadn't?

Not that it could possibly matter, I thought. There was no way for me to know how many times it had already happened; but once was enough. Annie would never quite be Annie again.

9

My Sixteenth Birthday; I Am Discovered, and Elsie Moves On; Mr. Simpson's Funeral; Grandpa Gets Better

It wasn't until late the next afternoon that I heard from Annie. Nobody had reported the death of Mr. Simpson to me yet, and I was still playing dumb, but my jaw ached from grinding my teeth all night, and there were bags under my eyes—the suspense was already beginning to tell on me. And I'd had a new nightmare the night before. It was a vague and dark one, full of shadowy, reproachful figures, and when I awoke I remembered nothing except the old feeling I'd had when I was young and the house was full of ghosts. It was the fear of death, and the despair that comes with it.

I went to work at Gruber's late in the morning. Mr. Gruber was oblivious to any changes in me, as he was oblivious to everything that didn't involve football or his grocery. The Buffalo Bills had been victorious the night before, and that was foremost in his mind; all he could talk about was Jim Kelly, the quarterback. Mrs. Gruber, however, darted sharp glances at me from half-lidded eyes as she totted up sums in her big black book. I knew I was behaving strangely, perhaps even guiltily. But there seemed to be nothing I could do about it. My actions felt beyond my control. Several cans of beans slipped out of my hands and dropped to the floor, and instead of picking them up I watched helplessly as they rolled under the counter, where they disappeared. Mrs. Gruber threw down the ledger in which she was writing and said sharply, "Come with me."

I followed her into the back of the store, my heart cold and shivering.

When we reached the rear exit, she said to me, "You're young."

"Ma'am?"

"*Too* young. For some things, anyway."

I said nothing. Too young to have killed someone? How did she know?

"From now on," she said, "you're not to deliver any more groceries to Miss Elsie Orfenbacher."

Jesus. So that was it. I'd forgotten all about Elsie. In fact, today was the day I was supposed to go to her place. For a "lesson," as we called it.

"You can't help the way you feel," she went on, her tone softening. "You're a young man, and soon you'll be old enough to do whatever you want. But when you're in this store, we're responsible for you. You're a minor, after all. And it's obvious you're upset about something. You're not yourself today, Billy. You haven't been for some time."

I still said nothing.

"It's *illegal*, Billy," she said. "She could be arrested for it. *We* could get in trouble for it too. You're too young even to be working here, really. Did you ever think of that?"

Numbly, too ashamed to look at her, yet relieved that our topic of conversation was merely sex instead of murder, I shook my head. The idea that I could get the Grubers in trouble with the law had never occurred to me.

"You don't have to worry about me telling anyone," said Mrs. Gruber. "And I've already called her and told her to buy her groceries somewhere else, so you don't have to worry about telling her either."

"You *did*?"

"Yes, I did." Her lips were set in a firm and self-righteous line, thin and dark like the rest of the lines in her face. The Grubers were getting old, I thought. In fact, they *were* old. "There are some things that are none of my business and some things that I can't keep my mouth shut about. This is one of the things I can't just sit back and watch happen. We're responsible for you while you're here. And that will be the end of that. Clear?"

"Yes, ma'am."

"You're not in love with her, I hope?"

I thought about that. I'd never given any consideration to whether or not I loved Elsie. Nor had it ever come up in our limited conversations, which usually consisted of her complaining about everything and everyone in the world, and me nodding my head.

"No, ma'am," I said. "I guess I'm not."

"Good," she breathed, relieved. "Then it shouldn't be any more difficult than it needs to be not to see her again. What you do after work is your own business, of course. You're almost sixteen. But while you're working for us, you stay away from her."

"Yes, ma'am."

She eyed me suspiciously.

"You seem to be taking this awful well," she said.

I shrugged. *I have other things on my mind,* I thought.

"I raised three boys of my own. Tomcats, all of them. I don't pretend not to know what's going on. I'm not a prude, like most people. I don't look down my nose at Elsie either, like most of the ladies do. A woman has to make her own way in the world, and sometimes it's not easy with men running the whole damn place. But I draw the line at stringing along a young kid like yourself. Kids need to run around. But they have to be careful. And they ought only to run around with other kids. Not with grown women who should know better."

"Yes, ma'am."

"What was she getting out of it, anyway?"

"What?"

"Why was she doing it? Don't tell me you just walked in there and seduced her. Not you. I don't believe it."

That hurt some, but I let it go.

"Free groceries," I said.

"*What?*"

"I paid for her groceries."

"With your own money."

"Yes, ma'am."

"Why?"

"She's always broke."

"Damn her," said Mrs. Gruber. "She's not too broke to go out to the bars every night, is she?"

"I don't know anything about that, Mrs. Gruber." In truth, I didn't. Elsie's other life, the ninety-nine percent of it that didn't involve me, was a total mystery. I'd never even thought about it. The news that she went anywhere at all came as a surprise. It occurred to me at that moment that I'd never seen her outside her house. Maybe she was nocturnal, like an owl, coming out to play long after I was in bed.

"You've been used," said Mrs. Gruber.

Well, I wanted to point out, so had *she*. It was more or less an even trade. We used each other for the things we needed, and as far as I was concerned I was getting the better end of the bargain. Mrs. Gruber may have had sons and a husband, but she would never know what it felt like to be a male, especially a teenage one. Sex was the greatest trophy there was, but it was more than a trophy—in fact, I had never bragged about my adventures with Elsie to anyone. Sex wasn't a conquest, not for me. It was a passport. It was a glimpse into the world of adults, the world I wanted to belong to so badly I would have paid any price to get in. I doubted there was a woman alive who really knew how boys my age felt. Not even Elsie knew, although she certainly sympathized. But I knew better than to say a word, except for the safest reply: "Yes, ma'am."

"She's little better than a prostitute, Billy."

"Now, just hold on there, Mrs. Gruber—"

"Don't you argue with me, young man. I won't have it. You go to Doctor Connor straight off and get yourself checked. You might have gotten something from her. She runs around with everyone. You knew that, didn't you?"

Vaguely, I had. It was something I preferred not to think about. I nodded.

"If you had parents, you would know all this. If you only had a mother." She sighed. "Or a father, at least."

"Grandpa does a good job," I said.

"I know he tries," she said. "But a child needs two parents. One can't cut it. There's just too much work."

Especially when that one is drunk all the time, I thought. But I could never bring myself to say that out loud. Not to anybody.

I headed home, despondent. I had no obligation to let Elsie go, of course. Mrs. Gruber had even said that what I did on my own time was my own business. But it had been going on for over a year now, and I'd spent nearly a thousand dollars on her groceries. I wanted that money back. I knew I wouldn't get it, but I wanted it back anyway. I'd worked for it. Mrs. Gruber had called her, she said, and no doubt she'd given her a piece of her mind. Mrs. Gruber was a short woman with a high-pitched voice, gentle enough with me, but I'd heard her rip into her husband once or twice and it hadn't been pretty. Mr. Gruber was stalwart, constantly smiling, and he seemed to believe it was his wife's duty to tear into him every six months or so. She didn't wait until they were alone, either. She was capable of saying things to her husband that made people's ears burn. I had learned much about the Grubers I would rather not have known in this manner; so had many Mannvillians who happened to be in the store at the wrong moment. So I could just imagine how her conversation, if you wanted to call it that, had gone with Elsie.

Abruptly my despondence disappeared. I changed course and headed for Elsie's place. I was young enough to be grateful that Mrs. Gruber had taken care of the hard part for me, but I was old enough to think that maybe I could put a different light on it for Elsie. Actually, it was embarrassing to have an elderly woman call and do your breaking up for you. If breaking up was the right word—Elsie had never claimed any romantic connection to me, nor I to her.

Parked in front of her house was a car I vaguely recognized. It was Wednesday, I thought—that's *my* day. Did she know? Did she already have someone new? I went around to the back of the house and opened the kitchen door. Elsie was sitting at the kitchen table, a mysterious shaven-headed stranger seated with her. Then I remembered where I'd seen the car before. It was David Weismueller's red Camaro, the Scarum of my early adolescence. And here was David Weismueller himself, minus his hair, three years out of high school and home on leave from the Army.

"H'lo, Weismueller," I said to him.

"Hey, Mann," he said.

Since our fight, my relationship with David Weismueller had changed dramatically. He no longer wanted to murder me; in fact, we seemed to have gained a respect for each other that only those who have fought nearly to the death can feel. This is a curious phenomenon among males—they might instinctively want to kill each other, and for reasons unknown perhaps even to themselves, but once they fight it out their tension is relieved and is replaced by a new sort of camaraderie. We'd gone so far as to have a conversation about football once. I even liked him, in a distant way.

"Hi, Else," I said.

"Hi, Billy. How's it goin'?"

"Pretty good."

"Yeah?"

"Yeah. Just stopped in to say hi."

"Well, I gotta get goin'," said Weismueller.

"Come back again," said Elsie, and Weismueller got up and went out the backdoor, our shoulders brushing casually as he passed me. I knew then that it was his first visit. Roles had switched suddenly: I was the seasoned hand and he was the new recruit, his training in the Orfenbacher method shortly to commence. Elsie wasted no time.

"Well," said Elsie, when he was gone.

"Mrs. Gruber told me she called you," I said, getting right to the point.

"Yeah."

"That go all right?"

"What do you mean?"

"Well . . . I mean, I didn't know she was gonna do that."

"I figured."

She lit a cigarette and looked at me with one eye through the smoke. She appeared different somehow. Mrs. Gruber's diatribe had had its effect on me. Elsie's lipstick looked too bright, her hair too blond. I abandoned my plan to ask her for my money back; suddenly I didn't want it anymore. Maybe Mrs. Gruber was right about her. I wouldn't ever think of Elsie as a prostitute, but my time with her was quickly taking on the air of a business transaction, the contract for which was about to expire.

"I guess it might be better if I didn't come over anymore," I said.

"All right," she said. She looked bored.

"Long as you understand."

"Understand what?"

"Just no hard feelings," I said.

Elsie expelled a burst of air in a short, sharp hiss. "No hard feel-ings," she said. "Yeah. Whatever."

"Thanks for everything."

She laughed. I'd never liked her laugh. It was loud, brassy, the wet guffaw of a smoker. It was naturally pitched to carry over the clink of glasses and the rumble of conversation in bars, so that everyone could hear it and know what a good time she was having.

"You're a sweet kid," she said, her manner softening. "You're not like most guys."

"Thanks," I said, though I had no idea what she meant.

"I thought you'd gone and told on us."

"Uh-uh. She figured it out."

"Well. I shoulda known."

"I'm not the kind of guy who goes around talking," I said. "I never told anyone about you."

"I appreciate it, kiddo," she said. "Not that it makes a difference."

"Why not?"

"You're probably the only one who doesn't talk," she said. "All the rest of 'em do. Why should I care? I have fun, don't I?"

"Sure," I said. I thought, *the rest of them?*

"Shit. I wish you were older. Or no—I wish I was younger. You're a catch. They don't make 'em like you too often."

"You neither," I said, though privately I believed exactly the oppo-site. But she beamed under the compliment like a bleached-blond lighthouse.

"You wanna go at it one last time for the road?" she said.

I looked at her hard: her makeup too heavy around the eyes, her hair frayed like used rope at the ends, the lines in her face that grew deeper and darker when she dragged on her cigarette.

"Can't," I said. "Gotta get home." I was trying to keep the new revulsion I felt for her out of my voice, but she squinted at me again, and there was a hurt look in her eyes. She'd detected it anyway.

"I guess you had enough of me," she said.

"It's not like that," I told her.

"Sure it is."

"Now knock it off. It is not."

"Whatever," she said. The bored expression was back. It was a wall, a defense; it was a trick to get me to try and break through again. But I wasn't interested anymore.

"You can just forget about those groceries," I said. "A present."

"Thanks," she said. I turned to go. "Hey."

I turned around.

"You really aren't millionaires anymore?"

"Jesus," I said. "I think you're the only person in town who thinks we still are."

"What happened to it all?"

"Why?"

"Curious."

"Ostriches took it," I said. "They grabbed it in their beaks and jumped over the fence."

"Ostriches," she said.

"You never heard the story?"

"No." Elsie wasn't from Mannville, I remembered. She was from Springville. I was relieved to find that our infamy hadn't spread that far.

"It's true," I said. "Ask anybody."

"I *see*."

"Yeah."

"Well."

"Bye, Elsie," I said. I'd closed the backdoor behind me before I could hear her reply.

Walking down Frederic Avenue I saw Madison, Mannville's lonely police officer. He was sitting in his squad car, staring blankly down the street. A chill shot through me. I had forgotten for the moment that I was a criminal, but the sight of him reminded me. I forced myself to wave at him.

"Hey, Billy."

"Hey, Officer Madison." He smiled at that; he was rarely called *Officer*.

"What's new?"

"Oh, *big* news."

"Yeah?"

"Jack Simpson's dead," he said darkly.

"No!" It was the first time I had repeated the script I'd so carefully prepared. I hoped desperately I wouldn't stumble over my lines.

"It's true."

"What happened?" Not too dramatic now, I cautioned myself.

"Well," said Madison, drawing out the word, "they *say* it was a heart attack."

"Wow," I said. "I can't believe it."

"You're a friend of Annie Simpson. Ain't you?"

"Yeah."

"You ain't heard?"

"Nope."

"Seen her lately?"

I thought hard and fast. Here was a question I wouldn't exactly have to lie to answer. I had seen her knocked out on her bed, of course, her nightdress pulled up to her waist. But we hadn't conversed, and she didn't know I'd been there. I hadn't seen her before that in several days.

"No," I said. "Not in a while."

"How long?"

"Eight or ten days."

"She didn't call you?"

"No, sir. We never call each other," I said. "He wouldn't allow it." Madison nodded at that. There was no reason to ask who *he* was; Mr. Simpson's temperament and habits were well known.

"She called it in herself," said Madison. "But when we got there she wasn't around."

"That's kinda weird," I said.

"And nobody's seen her."

"Huh."

"You *sure* you ain't seen her?"

"Yeah, I'm sure."

"Reason I ask is, the *circumstances* under which he was found were mighty *peculiar*," said Madison.

"What do you mean?"

"Well now, I can't reveal any details of the ongoing investigation," he said pompously. Madison had a special vocabulary that he reserved for discussions of criminal cases, the same kinds of words one heard on police shows. I suspected he'd gotten most of his law enforcement training from the television. "But lemme just ask you this. You see anyone wandering around in the woods back there around your place yesterday morning?"

"No," I said. I hoped I was able to keep the note of horror out of my voice. "What time?"

"Early," he said. "What time you get up yesterday?"

"Ten or so," I lied. "I think."

"Somebody reported seeing a suspicious individual. Dressed in black. Sneaking around the woods."

"Whoa."

"You didn't see nobody like that?"

"No, sir."

"Well, I guess it would have been too early for you," he said. "And it does look like a heart attack. No sign of foul play. But you know there's various *poisons* they got nowadays. Don't leave no sign. You shoot 'em with a blowgun and there's hardly a mark on 'em. Make it look just like a heart attack."

"Really?" I had read about these poisons, but I wasn't about to reveal that. In Madison's Barney Fife world, that would be tantamount to a confession.

"Government uses 'em all the time. Cover-up type stuff. For people who know too much."

"A blowgun?"

"Well now, this is just a little theory I have," said Madison. "No proof. Yet. Don't say nothing to nobody, okay, Billy? I don't want the perp to find out I know about it."

"The *perp*?"

"Perpetrator. It's a police word."

"I won't say anything."

"You know anybody with a blowgun?"

I was relaxing again. Madison was famous for his conspiracy theories, and the longer he entertained them in his bored and tiny mind, the bigger they became. With Madison investigating, I was in the clear.

"No, sir," I said. "I've never even seen a blowgun."

"Huh. And you don't know where the Simpson girl is?"

"No, sir."

"Well, when you see her, *if* you see her, tell her we need to talk to her."

I was genuinely worried about where Annie might be. "I will," I promised.

"You want a ride home?"

"Nah," I said. "I like walking. Exercise."

"Say hello to your grandad for me, then."

"Yessir."

I walked on, my mind slowly beginning to turn, my thoughts gathering momentum. I would have to start going to school again, so that nothing would seem out of the ordinary. Sooner or later someone was going to notice I'd been skipping classes, and suddenly I didn't want anyone to notice me at all.

Annie would have realized immediately upon waking what had been going on when her father keeled over. She would know that he'd been caught by his heart in the act of raping her yet again. She would have had to look at him naked, lying in his own piss on her bedroom floor. I wondered if she'd screamed. How long had it taken her to wake up from her drugged state? How long had he lain there before she'd come out of it? And where the hell was she?

"Annie," I muttered. "Come out."

We tried this sometimes, sending psychic messages to each other, beaming thoughts on mental airwaves because we couldn't use the telephone. It had worked once, although it might have been coincidence: I'd called her name in my head several times, and a moment later she'd come walking up the driveway, claiming to have heard me. "Annie Annie Annie. Where the hell are you?"

It worked again, though not in quite the same way. In our mailbox I found a handwritten note, containing only two words: MY HERO.

So she knew.

How much did she know?

I had no idea.

* * *

The entire town of Mannville searched for Annie for two weeks. Citizens formed rescue teams and combed through fields, woods, and meadows, looking for clues to anything at all. There was an unspoken commitment to finding her, which everyone seemed to share. Even though she was a Simpson, and the Simpsons were trash, she was one of our own. At least this is what people seemed to be saying to themselves. And we *knew*—that was the other thing they were saying, without saying it. We all knew what was going on up there. That was the part that would never be admitted, not by anyone. But there was an undercurrent of guilt running through our town, the feeling that all this could have been avoided if only someone had had the guts to speak up. But guilt can be covered up by busywork, so normal business stopped in Mannville for a time as everyone assuaged their conscience by forming lines and walking through the woods and fields, wearing yellow vests that said VOLUNTEER on them and calling Annie's name at the top of their lungs.

I participated in more of these searches than anybody else, but that was mostly for appearance's sake. I knew the whole business was useless, a farce. Annie, wherever she might be, wasn't going to be found. No evidence that she'd been kidnapped or murdered or that anything at all criminal had happened to her was discovered. In fact, there was nothing to suggest anything other than that she'd simply had enough of Mannville and the people in it, and the memories it would hold for her, and decided to seek her fortune elsewhere.

I was questioned once officially by Madison and perhaps two hundred times unofficially by everyone else. During these interviews I did my best to appear worried, perhaps even a bit remorseful, as if I was searching my conscience for anything I might have done to make her leave. But this was an act, and everyone else was acting the same way. I knew Annie was fine. I even thought I knew where she was, although I wasn't going to say anything to anyone. And I had no intention of showing the note she'd left me either. I ate it. Right there, standing next to the mailbox.

There was a funeral for Mr. Simpson, which was, to my surprise, very well attended. It seemed that everyone, not just Madison, found his death suspicious. Word had gotten out that he'd been found naked, and in his daughter's bedroom, no less. These circumstances, combined with Annie's disappearance, made for the biggest gossip mine in Mannville since the Fiasco of the Ostriches, and nobody wanted to miss out on the closing ceremonies of his scandalous life in case something dramatic would be revealed at the very last moment. Mannville was suddenly populated with amateur detectives. People shared theories, pieced together clues, and jumped to conclusions so far off base they were just distant spots on the horizon of credulity. One version had it that Mr. Simpson had surprised aliens in the act of abducting his daughter, and they had zapped him with their death-rays. The black-clad figure spotted in the woods—which was me, of course—was one of them. This theory was given credence by the report of a UFO sighting in Erie, an hour and a half to the west, the night before Simpson was found.

Grandpa and I went to the funeral in the old Galaxie. I'd roused him from his stupor enough to make him understand that Jack Simpson was dead; the news, amazingly, seemed to sober him up. He sat in the rocking chair, fully aware and awake, his chin in his hand and a thoughtful look on his face.

"How'd you say he died?" he asked me. He formed the words slowly, strenuously.

"Heart attack."

"Huh."

That was the longest conversation we'd had in years, or so it seemed.

Grandpa wore the same clothes to Jack Simpson's funeral that he'd worn to his mother's funeral when he was a young man, or so he claimed. Whiskey kept him thin, he said, by eating up his insides, which was why he was still able to fit into the old suit. But he drank no whiskey that morning as we were getting ready to go. The suit was patched and worn, over forty years old, and Grandpa, completely sober for the first time in years, stood stiffly at attention in the church-yard as if he were wearing a military uniform of embroidered gold, ignoring the stares we received.

And boy, did people stare. They stared because Grandpa and I were never seen together in public. They were used to seeing me alone, of course, carrying groceries around under my arm—or sometimes on the cursed Gruber Grocery bicycle. But Grandpa himself had hardly left the house in at least five or six years. There were some older folks looking at him out of the corner of their eyes, with expressions that said, "Oh, *yeah*," or "Jesus, he's still alive?" and I could tell they'd forgotten all about him.

"Why are you going?" I asked him, as we were getting ready. "I thought you hated him."

"I don't *hate* anybody," Grandpa explained. "I just . . . well, it's no good speaking ill of the dead. There's . . . there's an obligation."

His awareness of the world around him was beginning to return. I had no explanation for it, except maybe that the death of his enemy had reminded him that he was still alive, that he'd won some kind of contest. I was immensely relieved.

"What do you mean, an obligation?"

Instead of replying, Grandpa began muttering to himself. I knew better than to press him for details. I was just glad he was alive. I surprised him by throwing my arms around his brittle old frame and grabbing him tight. He stiffened, putting one hand on my shoulder instinctively as if to fend off an attack. But after a moment he appeared to remember that I was his grandson, and he put his arm around my neck and clenched me to him.

"Strong as an ox," he'd said. "Like your dad."

It seemed that everyone had forgotten about Frederic, too. He wasn't present at the funeral—not that I had expected him to be. But I wondered if anyone had noticed him lying there in the back room as they were hauling away the carcass of his father. I hoped he wasn't still there, gamely breathing away and waiting for someone to come back for him. There were, in fact, no Simpson family members at the funeral at all. Annie had disappeared, Frederic was simply Frederic, and Annie's mysterious sisters, whom I'd never even met, had stolen away over the years until it was just the three of them left: a ruined Annie, her demonic father, and her vegetative brother, a twisted and pathological trinity.

Grandpa and I stood together near the outer fringe of the gathering listening to the preacher intone his ritual speeches over the coffin that contained the last of Jack Simpson. Nothing exciting happened, as folks seemed to have hoped—no sudden appearance of Annie, no thunderbolts from the sky, no alien spacecraft. When it was over and he was buried, we got back in the Galaxie, and Grandpa said, as I was pulling out of the church parking lot, "Jack Simpson drank himself to death, didn't he?"

I shuddered as I remembered his zipperlike scar. "Yeah," I said. "More or less."

"I'm headed the same way."

I was startled to hear this. Grandpa rarely, if ever, indulged in reflections of this type. He knew he drank; I knew he drank; everyone knew it, and that was the way it was. The end result of a life of hard drinking was well known to everyone. You ended up like Jack Simpson, killed by your own abused heart. But this was the first time I'd ever heard him admit it.

"Yes you are, I guess," I said.

We drove in silence.

"How well did you know Jack Simpson?" I asked him after a while. "I mean, were you and he ever friends?"

Grandpa snorted. "No."

"Then what was all that stuff about an obligation?"

Grandpa thought. "We were never friends, but we knew each other," he said finally. "He was younger than me by some years, but not many. Below me in school. Our boys grew up together. Eddie and Frederic. I told you that."

"Yeah. I remember."

"Freddie used to stay over at our place all the time. When things got rough. Simpson used to beat on him and the girls when he got drunk. Up to the time he stole that car, he used to come over whenever he felt like it. Didn't even need to knock. He knew he was always welcome. He even had his own room, right next to Eddie's. But after he got in that trouble with the police, and his old man knocked him real good for that, he ran off. Joined the Army. Then he got hurt."

"Do you know what happened to him?"

"Land mine, they said."

"They said?"

"Or maybe a grenade. I don't remember which. Simpson was *always* mean," said Grandpa, returning to the subject of his nemesis. "He used to torture younger boys. I remember fighting him a few times myself. Never liked him. Got into a lot of trouble in high school. That family was trouble even then. Have been since forever. He took to drinking early too."

There was a pause.

"Like me," he added.

After another lengthy moment he said, "When you come right down to it, boy, there never has been a hell of a lot of difference between Jack Simpson and myself. I never knocked my kid around, but that's about it. We're both useless old drunks."

"Don't say that. There's nothing the same about you two."

"I know what I'm talking about. I've got hindsight, and you don't. You think it's too late for me to quit?"

"Do *I* think . . . ? No. Not yet."

"It might be."

"You could do it, if you wanted to." I looked at him out of the corner of my eye. He was staring out the window.

"All right, then. When we get home I want you to clean out the house."

"What?"

"Clean it. Top to bottom. Throw out every bottle you can find."

"Throw out the *bottles*?"

"I'm quitting," he said. "I'm going to check myself into the hospital for a while. When I come back I don't want to find any temptations lying around. Will you do it for me?"

"I . . . you're serious?"

"Yes, I'm serious." And to tell the truth, there was a determination in his voice that I'd never heard before.

"Yeah. Yes, I'll do it. Of course I will."

"Seeing Jack Simpson go to his reward without ever having made amends got me to thinking. I have some things to set right before I die. And I might not be living that much longer. I'm pickled," he said, "from the inside out. Drying out might kill me, but it would be better than living like I have been. And I owe you an apology."

I was speechless. My eyes were growing wet.

"I've hardly been any kind of father to you at all," said Grandpa, tears of regret welling up in his own eyes. "I've been drunk for forty years. I saw the way folks were looking at me back there."

"Who cares how they were looking at you? You always said that didn't matter."

"I care!" Grandpa put his fist to his lips. He was getting choked up. After a moment he regained control of himself. "It does matter. And I'm sick of it. I'm tired of living like a boogieman. Everyone thinks I'm a nut."

"No they don't," I said. "They just think you're eccentric."

Grandpa sighed.

"They're half-right," he said. "But listen. Something weird happened while we were in the churchyard."

"What was it?"

"Don't laugh."

"I won't."

"I left my body."

"*What?*"

"I just flew out of myself," he said. "I could see myself standing there, and you next to me—God, you're getting tall—and for the first time in I don't know how long, I could see myself as others see me. And it wasn't pretty," he finished lamely, his fist dropping back in his lap. "My nose is all red and my eyes are permanently swollen. I look like what I am. A drunk. And I could hear people's thoughts."

"Their *thoughts*?"

"About me. Not everything, just me. And they were thinking, 'That old drunk is still alive?'"

I didn't tell him I had read the same thoughts in their minds. I was getting spooked enough as it was.

"Well, yes I am!" he roared, smacking the dashboard. "I'm a long way from dead yet, goddamn it! And I've wasted enough years sitting around feeling sorry for myself. It's time for that to stop. So clean it out, boy. Clean out the damn house. That's a polite order. I'd do it myself, but I don't think I'm strong enough. If I picked up a bottle I wouldn't put it down."

"All right," I said, and with that simple acknowledgment, the redemption of Thomas Mann Junior had its beginning.

He sat in his rocking chair for the rest of the day. I called the hospital and told them we would be coming in tomorrow.

"They're getting a room ready for you," I said. "You want me to start cleaning out the bottles now?"

"Don't leave me alone in here," he said.

So I sat next to him on the couch and watched him reach for where his glass would be about thirty times. After an hour he held up his hand.

"Look at this," he said. It was shaking. "I'm as nervous as a long-tailed cat in a room full of rocking chairs. I better have a drink."

"No," I said.

"Just one, Billy. Just to keep me from shaking."

"It won't be just one," I said.

"A little one."

"No."

"All right, damn it," he sighed. "Will you make me something to eat?"

"Sure," I said. I went into the kitchen and got out all the makings of a fried baloney sandwich feast. When I stuck my head through the doorway to check on him, I saw him stowing a small bottle underneath the couch cushions and wiping his lips.

"Hey!" I said.

He started. I went to the couch and retrieved the bottle. It was a silver hip flask.

"What the hell is this?"

"Look," he said, holding up his hand again. It was perfectly still.

"I don't care," I said. "You have to get over these shakes the hard way."

"Don't throw it away," he said guiltily. "It's an heirloom."

I poured the whiskey down the sink and rinsed out the hip flask. After that I refused to leave him alone in the room. We ate with our plates balanced on our knees, with me staring at him and him looking at the floor. After we had eaten and some more time had passed, he began to shake again, but he didn't ask me for another drink.

We went to sleep early. I searched his bedroom before leaving him to sleep for the night. I found a bottle in the closet and another one under the bed. Before I went into my room, I made sure his bedroom door was open, as well as mine, so I could hear him. I lay with one ear cocked to listen for the sounds of rustling sheets or the unscrewing of a bottle cap. The house was still lousy with whiskey—I hadn't wanted to leave him alone long enough to start throwing away all the bottles he must have had stashed here and there. I looked up at the ceiling and thought disjointed thoughts.

I was awakened sometime after midnight by shouting. Alarmed, thinking maybe someone was breaking into the house, I raced to his bedroom and flicked on the light. I found him sitting in his underwear in the corner, rubbing frantically at his arms.

"Grandpa!" I said. "What are you doing?"

"Jesus!" he shouted. "Get 'em off me!"

I looked; there was nothing on him. But he continued to brush at himself in a panic.

"There's nothing there," I said.

"Snakes!" he shouted. "This fucking room is full of snakes!"

What the hell was this now? I wondered. "There's no snakes in here, Grandpa," I said. I checked under the bed, just to be sure. There was nothing there except a few dust bunnies. But Grandpa continued to scream. Large round tears, the tears of a small boy, began to roll down his face.

"Look," I said. I grabbed his hands. "Look at me. Look at my hands."

"Don't," he sobbed. "They're *biting* snakes."

"See my hands? There's no snakes on them, are there?"

"Yes there are, yes there *are*!"

"There's no snakes in here," I said. I was beginning to get scared. I sat down next to him and put one arm around his shoulders. I drew my feet up under me—just in case there were snakes after all. But of course there weren't. And my touch seemed to calm him; after a moment he relaxed, though he continued to sob in deep, hiccuping gasps.

"Oh, fucking snakes," he said. "Oh, I'm seeing snakes."

"They can come on me," I said. I pulled him tight. "I'm not afraid of snakes. Let them come on me. They won't bother you any more."

Grandpa began muttering to himself. He rocked back and forth, back and forth.

There was a phone in his room. I picked it up—mercifully, the phone bill had been paid. I heard a dial tone. I dialed Connor's number and listened to it ring. He picked it up after the third one.

"Hello, this is the doctor," he said. His voice was calm and perfectly alert, though I knew full well that five seconds earlier he'd been sound asleep.

"This is Billy Mann," I said. "Grandpa decided to go sober today and now he's seeing snakes. Can you come over?"

There was a moment of silence.

"Billy?"

"Yeah?"

"I'll be right there," he said, and he hung up.

I left Grandpa sitting against the wall and went downstairs to open the front door. Then I went back upstairs to Grandpa's room. He hadn't moved. Several minutes later I heard the whirring of Connor's Beetle pulling into the driveway. He came in the front door and headed directly up the stairs. He was still in his pajamas, and he was carrying his black leather bag.

"Howdy there, Tom," he said, setting his bag on the floor. "Hi, Billy."

"Snakes," said Grandpa.

"Haven't seen you in a while, Tom," said Connor, as calmly as if they'd bumped into each other at the grocery store.

"Yeah."

"Billy says you laid off the hooch."

"Oh, Lord," said Grandpa. He was rubbing his hands over his eyes, as if trying to wake up.

"Here's a little something to help you sleep," said Connor. He handed me a pill. I went into the bathroom and got a glass of water. When I came back into the room with it, Grandpa was in bed again, the covers pulled up to his chin.

"Here you go," I said. Grandpa swallowed the pill with a sip of water and laid his head back down on the pillow.

"You'll sleep now," said Connor.

"I'll sleep now," Grandpa echoed, his voice already fading.

"It's the hospital tomorrow for you," said Connor.

"We already called," I said.

"Good. I can check in on you there, if you want."

Grandpa nodded.

Connor motioned to me and we headed out of the room. We were nearly through the door when I heard Grandpa's voice.

"Connor," he said.

Connor turned.

"Yes, Tom?"

"That wasn't me that screamed at you that day," he said. I knew he was talking about the fight they'd had when I was still small, before I'd gone to school. His voice was barely a whisper. "It was the booze."

"I knew that all along, Tom," said Connor.

"You're my best friend, Connor. I'm sorry."

"I knew that too, you miserable old son of a bitch," Connor said.

"All right, then," said Grandpa. "Just so you know." He fell asleep.

Connor shook my hand at the backdoor and got into his Beetle. At another hour, perhaps, we would have talked, but it was so late, the events that had just taken place seemed already to be cast in a surreal, distant past. I listened to him drive down the road and then went back to bed.

I may have slept for an hour or two. I was awakened by the sound of a timid knock at my door. When I opened it, Grandpa was standing there in his funeral suit, a small suitcase on the floor next to him. He refused to look me in the eye.

"Will you take me to the hospital now?" he asked.

I wanted to ask him how he felt, but something told me I should never mention the events of the previous night to him. Instead, I dressed and drove him to Mannville General Hospital, where I waited while he checked himself in. It was the second time in my life I'd left him there. This time, though, there was no Elsa Wheeler from the county waiting to haul me off to the Shumachers. Grandpa and I shook hands formally at the admissions desk.

"I'll come see you tomorrow," I said.

"No visitors," said the nurse.

"Can he call me?" asked Grandpa. He was already looking jumpy; it was his second day without a drink, and he was nervously scanning the walls. *More snakes?* I wondered. I debated whether I should tell the nurse about last night.

"No phone calls tonight," said the nurse.

"This is my grandfather," I said. "I'm going to call him when I feel like it."

"Young man, we have rules here," said the nurse. "Particularly in *this* kind of situation." She nodded at Grandpa when she said that. "So if you can't abide by them, then you'll have to go somewhere else."

"Forget about it," said Grandpa. "Call me tomorrow."

"I will."

"You'll be alone on your birthday."

"That's all right," I said. I'd forgotten about that. I would be turning sixteen soon. And he would be turning sixty-four. "So will you."

"I'm too old to give a shit about birthdays anymore."

"We don't allow profanity in this hospital," said the nurse.

"I hope someday you can forgive me for all this," said Grandpa.

"Knock it off," I said.

"All right, then."

We hugged.

I turned and walked out of the lobby to the waiting Galaxie in the parking lot. Then I turned around and went back into the lobby. As I'd hoped, Grandpa was gone, and the nurse was sitting alone at the desk.

"Yes?" she said.

"I wanted to tell you about something."

She looked at me expectantly, her eyebrows arched, a pencil poised as if she was going to write down every word I said. I wanted to tell her about the snakes. I didn't know anything about delirium tremens yet, that seeing snakes or worms or spiders is common in those who quit drinking after years of heavy alcohol abuse. I was afraid it was one more manifestation of the Mann curse, like the nightmare of Mary Rory. But there was something in her manner, her supercilious attitude, that struck a chord of pride in me. Mann pride. I could not admit a weakness to this woman. I would not add to the gossip about our family. And I didn't like the way she'd spoken to Grandpa. So instead I said, "My great-great-grandfather built this hospital. We used to own this whole damn town and everything around it for a ten-mile radius. So I'll thank you to remember that when you're talking to my grandfather."

The nurse opened her mouth and then snapped it shut. I turned and walked out.

When I got home I made a thorough search of the house, from attic to basement, and collected nearly seventy whiskey bottles. Most of them were empty—Grandpa never threw anything away—but there were a few full ones. I took them in boxes out to the yard and threw them, one by one, into the old brick oven next to the carriage house. They each exploded with a satisfying pop, the full ones sending lovely arcs of amber poison through the air. When I was finished, I built a bonfire of paper and wood on top of the shattered glass, soaked it with gasoline, and set the whole mess on fire. It burned for the rest of the day, great black clouds of smoke roiling out into the Mannville sky. I sat in the yard in a lawn chair and contemplated the blaze, and the snakes, and the old farmhouse, and for the thousandth time in my life thought about what it was like to be part of the clan called Mann. There was this new thing with us now, these snakes, this disease. I wondered if heroes were supposed to get diseases. And I wondered what it would be like to live alone.

But I found, not entirely to my surprise, that I liked living alone. It was easier to write when I knew the house was empty. I settled down to some good serious work. My training in the Orfenbacher method was over, but the second round of my training, my training as a writer, had begun.

I'd learned, in the course of my reading, that all the great writers had routines. They woke up at certain times and wrote every day for a prescribed amount of hours. They either made sure they were drunk or that they'd had nothing to drink; that they'd eaten or had empty stomachs; that there was plenty of noise or that there wasn't a sound. The formula went on and on, diverging in endless confusing paths that seemed to lead nowhere. I'd been researching methods in the hope of finding one that would suit me. I quickly realized, however, that what worked for others wouldn't work for me, and that I would have to figure it out for myself.

So I awoke to my alarm clock at five each morning. I made a pot of coffee and opened a fresh pack of cigarettes, carried it all upstairs to my desk, and rolled a new sheet of paper into my typewriter. There I sat and stared out the window for several minutes, smoking and sipping coffee. When a word came to me I typed it out. The words came in no particular order and didn't seem to have anything to do with each other. The first one was the hardest. The second one was usually connected somehow to the first, but might belong before it instead of after, and the third would fit in somewhere. After I had twenty or so words like this, spaced out like distant cousins, I would set about figuring out how they were related. They were usually nouns. If I took each noun to symbolize a separate event in a story—a story that didn't exist yet—then I would have enough material to make something up. I moved the nouns around and joined them with text in between, sometimes several pages. It was a sloppy way of doing it, but it was all I could think of at first, and it's probably due to this half-assed noun formula that most of my early stories after "Willie Mann and the Rory Fortune" made absolutely no sense. But I didn't know that at the time. I was pleased that I was writing at all, even though it still hurt and I still hated it, in the way that athletes hate training—not a true hate, but a sort of grudging acceptance that it is necessary. Soon I was thinking of moving on to verbs.

In the weeks that Grandpa was drying out in the hospital, I wrote fifteen stories. My solitude, instead of stifling me as I had feared, seemed to enhance my creativity. And I was waiting for news about my first story, "Willie Mann and the Rory Fortune." I'd sent it to a magazine that Doctor Connor helped me pick out. He said that a fast response time was good, so when only a month passed and I found a letter from the magazine in the mailbox, my heart leaped with joy. Inside was a form letter. "Dear contributor," it said, "thank you for your interest in our magazine, but . . . "

A rejection letter. I took it upstairs and stuck it in one of my notebooks. It would not be my last, I knew.

Also, I bought a motorcycle. It was a 1977 Kawasaki KZ1000, an old cop bike I'd picked out of the newspaper one day. "Needs work," the ad had confided, but that was right up my alley—along with my father's tendency to throw himself off roofs and do stunts in midair, I'd inherited Grandpa's mechanical facility. I kept the bike in the garage. After I was done writing for the day—at least four hours every morning, I'd promised myself—I went out to the garage and worked on it. Grandpa assisted me over the phone in our nightly conversations. The snakes, he said, had stopped crawling on him, his hands no longer shook, and he'd actually made a friend there.

"I haven't had a friend in decades," he said. "Except for Connor."

I was happy for him, but I had other things on my mind. "Where do I get gaskets for these damn carburetors?" I asked. "The old ones are all cracked."

"Ask George. He'll have 'em. You know, we watch the news together every night."

"Who? You and George?"

"No, my friend."

"What's his name?"

"It's a she," he said. "Her name is Mildred."

"You have a *girlfriend?*"

"I'm too old for that nonsense," he scoffed. "Boy, she's a smart one, though. She's got something to say about everything. You'd like her."

"How old is she?"

"At my age, boy, you don't ask questions like that. You're just grateful for what you can get. What did you do on your birthday?"

"I forgot about it," I said. My sixteenth birthday had come and gone without so much as a nod of recognition from me. "I think I just worked on my bike."

"I'll bring you a present when I come home."

"I can't figure out how to straighten the handlebars," I complained.

"I'll show you when I get back."

"That can be my present, then. When are you coming home?"

"In ten days."

"I cleaned out the house."

"Good job. Thanks."

"Don't mention it."

What I meant, of course, was not "Don't mention it." What I meant was a million other things—such as *What took you so long to do this? What would our lives be like if you'd quit sooner? What would they be like if you'd never started?* But I didn't know how to say any of those things to him, and I was still too young to understand the implications of the spiritual rebirth of my grandfather. I focused on small things, took baby steps. I just wanted him home with me, so he could help straighten out the handlebars.

But I was able to straighten the handlebars by myself, and within a week the bike was running smoothly. My life was changed irrevocably and forever. I soared along the back roads of Erie County, breathlessly covering hundreds of miles, helmetless and limited only by how long I could stand to ride. Riding a bike is physically punishing; sometimes you have to hang on for dear life, clinging to the machine by your fingertips and toes. My chest stung with the impact of a thousand hapless insects, my eyes watered permanently from the wind, my hands became cramped in the shape of the handgrips. But I loved it. Little by little, I was making up for all the things I'd never seen and all the places I'd never been. I sped through tiny country towns so far off the main roads that Time seemed not to have bothered with them—little one-horse towns even smaller than Mannville, with maybe a gas station and a general store, and every third vehicle on the road an Amish buggy. It was nearing the end of summer, and evenings were the best time for cruising, with their soft warmth and gentle smells.

The odors of the country are myriad and unique: manure, fresh-cut hay, fields of burning cornstalks, the sweat of horses. I understood then why dogs like to ride in cars with their heads lolling out the window. Fully half the mysteries of the world are encoded in smells, smells that are hidden from those who ride, sheltered, in cars. I whirred along tiny country lanes, surprising men loading hay into giant wagons, zipping by the Amish buggies as though they were standing still. The taste for freedom began to expand in me like a slowly inflating balloon. I knew the time for leaving Mannville would be coming soon. It was as inevitable as the approaching winter.

Grandpa came home from the hospital in early September, nearly five weeks after he'd gone in. He'd put on weight, and his eyes were alert and clear. After cleansing the house of any traces of alcohol, I'd gone through it again with all the implements of purification: warm soapy water, bleach, oil soap, broom, mop, rags, lemon-scented furniture polish. It had taken me nearly two weeks to accomplish, but the house gleamed from the inside out. He stepped inside and inhaled.

"The old days are over," he said. I knew he was talking about his drinking days, the days when the house was falling into disrepair and decay, the days when he ignored me in favor of his bottle and his memories. He put his hand on my shoulder and squeezed it. Tears came to his eyes.

"I have so much to tell you," he said, in a broken voice, "that I don't know where to start."

"There's plenty of time," I said, embarrassed.

"Yeah," he agreed, wiping his eyes. "If drying out didn't kill me, nothing will."

Grandpa was not alone; he'd brought Mildred with him. She was a tiny, pretty woman with sharp gray eyes and a birdy way of talking that belied her tremendous energy. She nodded in approval as she stepped inside our farmhouse for the first time. "It's *clean*," she said, "and coming from me, that's a compliment."

"It's not always like this," I said.

Mildred smiled. "It will be from now on," she said, and that was how I knew she'd come to stay.

Mildred had raised seven children over the course of almost thirty years, Grandpa told me later, and her husband had beaten her regularly all the way through it. She'd stayed first for the kids, and later because she'd grown attached to drinking her way through her days, which was easier than leaving. I peered closely at her when I thought she wasn't looking. She didn't seem like the kind of woman who would drink at all, and I couldn't imagine anyone ever wanting to hit her— she was too little. But alcohol was insidious; it didn't choose its victims on the basis of appearance. I liked her immediately.

"Mildred's going to live with us," Grandpa said to me late that evening. "That is, if it's all right with you. It's as much your house as mine now. You're old enough to have a say in things now."

"Are you guys getting married?"

Grandpa snorted. "No," he said. "We know better than that."

"You mean you're going to *shack up*?" I was only teasing him, but his face grew red and he looked down at his hands.

"I didn't know you were so moral," he mumbled.

"I was only kidding," I said, remembering my adventures with Elsie Orfenbacher, and my so-called murder of Jack Simpson. I had no room to preach to anyone about morality. "I think it's great. Really. I like her."

"You do?"

"Yeah, I do."

"We're taking it slow," he said, and he was so relieved he wrapped his arms around me and squeezed.

I didn't understand what he meant by "taking it slow" until I helped Mildred move her few possessions into a bedroom separate from Grandpa's. It was on the second floor, and it had last been occupied around the turn of the century by one of Grandpa's ancient aunts. There would be no hanky-panky between Grandpa and Mildred, I gathered, at least not yet. Privately I wondered if they were too old for that sort of thing. They seemed to enjoy spending their evenings simply sitting together in the living room and reading aloud to each other, occasionally helping the other stifle the sudden urge for a drink. Grandpa had been in the hospital nearly three times as long as was normally necessary, partly because he had suffered serious liver damage. His body was accustoming itself to not drinking, but his mind was still restless. Sitting in the living room had always been one of his favorite pastimes, except he'd always had a glass of whiskey on his knee.

"Mildred helps me forget about all that," he said, "and I do the same for her. We keep each other's minds occupied."

Mildred herself told me she was grateful that I hadn't objected to her moving in with us. "Seven children I have," she said to me, "and not one of them has written or called in almost ten years. Not that I blame them, you understand. They hated their father, and I didn't lift a finger to change anything. I *couldn't*, you see. And my husband is dead now. So I would have been all alone, all alone in the world, if I hadn't met your grandad." Her explanation of her previous life went no further, but I thought I understood. I knew something about cruel fathers. I found myself tempted to tell her that I'd rid the world of another cruel father, one who used to live up the hill and who had done things even Mildred's husband would probably have found unspeakable. But I managed to hold my tongue, even though I think Mildred would have approved.

Mildred and Grandpa seemed to take to the sober life as though it had secretly been what they'd wanted all along. Mildred gravitated naturally to the kitchen, which soon became a bustling private enterprise that churned out cakes, cookies, roasts, and stews on a grand scale. She cooked enough food to supply a small restaurant. Grandpa and I both began to put on weight, and I gave silent thanks that I had eaten my last fried baloney sandwich. Grandpa began to take up his old hobby of tinkering with machines, and he spent most of his time in the garage, repairing everything he could get his hands on. Soon the house began to look as good on the outside as it did on the inside: shutters were painted, electrical fixtures were replaced, the yard was mowed. He pruned the trees and plowed up a garden.

"This is pretty damn near the spot where everything happened," he told me one day, pointing to his little spaded-up patch of earth.

"What do you mean?"

"The treasure," Grandpa said. "This is where Willie found it."

I stared at the spot, awestruck. Somehow the notion that the events of one hundred and twenty years ago had a physical location had never occurred to me. I was once again overwhelmed by the weight of our history. It thrilled through me like a bolt of lightning.

"We ought to put up a monument, or something," I said.

"No," said Grandpa, his voice dark and sad. "It wasn't all good."

"What do you mean?"

Grandpa had read my story, and found it amazingly accurate, considering how I had come by my information. "You hinted at it yourself in your story," he said now. "Don't you remember?"

"No," I said.

"Money is as much a curse as a blessing," Grandpa said. "Crazy things started to happen to the family after they became rich."

"What kind of things?"

"Greed," he said. "Greed moved in and decency moved out."

"What happened?"

Grandpa sighed. "I don't like to talk about it," he said. "Those things were still going on when I was little."

"You mean people were jealous of each other?"

"Something like that."

"Did they try to cheat each other?"

"Yes."

"How?"

"You remember Willie's brothers? Andy and Poky Boy?"

"Why did they call him Poky Boy?"

"Because he was so slow. Poky means slow."

"What about them?"

"Willie had told everyone in the family they were entitled to equal shares of the money, but only after he took his cut."

"So then *he* was the greedy one!"

"No. He didn't keep very much of it at all. He built the hospital, he built the farmhouse, he started up the farm. He didn't spend anything on himself. Everything he did was for the future. For *you*," he said, stabbing me in the chest with one finger, "except I fucked it up."

"You couldn't help it," I said loyally. In truth, since the money had never been mine, I didn't miss it.

"Well, God bless you for saying that, but you don't know what the hell you're talking about. Anyway. Willie's brothers didn't like what he was doing. They thought they should keep all the money among themselves. Divide it all up first, you see, and *then* spend it however they wanted to."

"I see," I said.

"That way, they would have more to blow on whatever they wanted. But Willie wouldn't let them, because it was his money. So there was fighting."

"Fistfighting?"

"Well, yes. Sometimes."

"You mean there was more than one fight?"

"Yes."

"What happened?"

"You ever read the Bible?"

"Little bits of it."

"Remember Cain and Abel?"

"Yeah."

"Brothers."

"Yeah." I was getting impatient.

But Grandpa was not to be hurried. He leaned on his shovel as he spoke, pushing his fedora back on his head.

"God punished Cain because he killed his own brother," he said. "And the reason he killed him was selfishness. Jealousy."

"And?"

"Well, Andy got drunk one night and started in on Willie. Pushing him around and such."

"Why?"

"Because he was mad at him for not giving them their share of the money right off. Willie wouldn't fight back. He couldn't anyway, because of his leg. And he always said he'd had enough of fighting to last him the rest of his life. So Andy just pushed him around, and Willie let him do it. He kept trying to leave, but Andy wouldn't let him. They were alone in the house. It was this house, in fact. In our very own kitchen."

"What happened?"

"Poky Boy came in in the middle of it. He asked what was going on. Willie wouldn't say anything. He just kept trying to walk out the door to get away from Andy, and Andy kept grabbing him and shoving him against the wall. And Poky Boy didn't like that. He was a softer, gentler kind of fellow, and even though he wanted the money too, he wouldn't have hurt Willie to get it. So he hauled off and hit Andy to keep him off Willie."

"He did?"

"Yes. And Andy beat the shit out of him," said Grandpa. "He beat him to death, right there in the kitchen."

"He *killed* him?"

"Right there where Mildred is doing her cooking. Knocked his head against the stove. Didn't kill him right away. He was laid up for three days in bed, unconscious, and they thought he might pull through, but he died one night. Wasn't nothing they could do to save him. Medicine in those days wasn't near what it is now."

"Oh my God," I said.

"Andy couldn't take it," Grandpa went on. "Nobody in the family would speak to him for the three days that his brother was laid up. Except Willie, of course, because Willie was that kind of guy. Andy begged Willie to forgive him, and Willie said he would. He sort of felt like it was all his own fault anyway, for finding the money in the first place. Then Andy told him that he couldn't stand to live anymore. Willie said he understood, but that he ought to make a go of it anyway. Andy said he would try, but he didn't mean it. And he hanged himself."

"Where?"

"Second-floor bedroom, last one on the left at the south end of the hall."

"Jesus." No wonder the house was full of ghosts, I thought.

"Then things went downhill," Grandpa went on. "Daddo died. Their mama died, mostly of a broken heart. Their father took to drinking hard, and it killed him off within a few years. That kind of thing is in the blood. Pretty soon Willie was the only one left in the house. He finally got married, just to keep himself from going crazy, and he had my father, and then my father died too young. Then I was born. Thank God," he went on, "Willie died before he could see how bad things finally got, after I came back from the war. Sometimes I think the dead are the lucky ones. Anyway. That's the story."

We stood in silence for several moments as I digested this new information and Grandpa reflected.

"You still have those nightmares?" he asked finally.

"No."

"That's good," he said, relieved. "Neither do I."

"Maybe it's over," I suggested.

"Well, I should hope so."

"Me too."

"I want to read the diary," I said.

Grandpa sighed. "Fujimora promised me he'd come back with it," he said. "He's not late yet, either. We swore to each other."

"How will you know when it's time to go there?"

"If he dies first," said Grandpa, "I'll just know. Same way I know everything else I know without being told. Just like you. Same way we all had the same dream. He and I are connected, and so are you. But I don't think I'll be going there. I think it'll be him who comes here."

"Not soon, I hope," I said, alarmed.

"No. Not soon."

Mildred came out on the back porch and rang the old iron dinner triangle. Grandpa and I started. We looked at each other and grinned.

"It's nice to have a woman around again," he said. "Isn't it?"

"I wouldn't know," I said. "I've never lived in the same house with one before."

"You'll like it," said Grandpa. "They make life worth living."

We went into the house together for lunch.

10

My Sixteenth Year Continued; Middlism; How I Decided to Conquer the World; I Have a New Dream

From the diary:

> Universal signs, those clues to our destinies, are everywhere. It is up to us whether or not we follow them—but they are there nonetheless.

And also:

> The extent of a man's greatness is determined by his ability to follow his proper direction. We create our own destinies, and yet we do not. We forge a new path as we proceed, and yet the path already exists beforehand, though it is not always well marked. This is the paradox of life; and a paradox is not a riddle to be solved, but a place to dwell in, if only for a brief time.

Early in the fall of my junior year, another strange wrinkle occurred in the fabric of my life. It announced itself as a letter in the mail. Insignificant details come back to me from that day: it was a Tuesday afternoon in mid-September, and the weather was clear and crisp. I was wearing jeans. None of this has anything to do with what happened later, of course, but the mind of a writer remembers best of all those things that seem to have nothing to do with anything, to have no connection to the general flow of events: a snatch of conversation, the luffing of a flag in the wind, the smell of someone baking cookies in a kitchen three blocks away. But writers understand, perhaps better than anyone—or maybe just *differently* than everyone else—that there's no such thing as an isolated incident, no such thing as an insignificant detail. Details are remembered precisely because they are important, because they can be pieced together later, added in tiny fragments one by one until they form a tapestry of considerable proportions. Life is composed of details as tiny as an unexpected letter in the mail on an autumn Tuesday. Such are the swatches from which my life is woven, the weather the warp, the letter the woof, that day the image that emerges.

Getting a letter in itself wasn't so unusual. I often received mail, mostly letters of regret from literary magazines. Every two or three weeks I gathered up my courage and my spare change, photocopied my short story about Willie on the rickety old Xerox machine at the Mannville Public Library, and mailed it off to various small presses around the country. Then I sat back and waited for the rejection letters to pour in. This process is known as *submitting*, which I've always believed is the perfect term for the whole business of trying to get published. I felt not that I was simply asking the editors of these magazines to look at my work, but that I was crawling before them in abject humiliation, my chest bared for the editorial knife, which they unfailingly plunged into my young and tender heart. "Dear Author," their rejections usually went, "we thank you for the opportunity to look at your work, but unfortunately at this time . . . "

Or something like that. The words varied slightly from letter to letter, but the overall message was "Not good enough."

The letters came trickling in one and two at a time throughout that fall. I was probably the only kid at Mannville High who raced home from school every day for news of whether or not he'd arrived in the literary world.

But this particular letter was unusual for two reasons: it bore no return address, and it had a Canadian postmark. I was nonplussed.

Although the Canadian border was barely an hour away by car, Canada seemed to me an utterly foreign land. I'd certainly never been there, and I hadn't submitted my story to any Canadian literary magazines. It had never occurred to me that Canada *had* literary magazines. There was an electric instant in which I realized what a fool I was: of *course* Canada had literary magazines! There was an entire nation directly to the north of me, not just a nation bounded by political borders, but a whole other literary universe to explore! So far, I reflected, I'd met with no success whatsoever in America. *But Canada!* I thought. *Maybe they want to publish me!*

But of course I hadn't yet submitted my story to any Canadian presses. Who, then, could be writing to me from Quebec?

Then I remembered: Annie.

I don't mean to imply that I suddenly remembered her. The fact was I hadn't forgotten her, not for an instant. How could I? Each morning I rode my motorcycle to school along the same route she and I had walked every weekday since we were small children, and I pretended she was with me, sitting behind me on the bike with her arms wrapped around my waist and laughing in my ear. And without her, I was completely alone. Since my battle with David Weismueller I had no enemies, and in fact—according to the peculiar laws of male social order, which I didn't yet completely understand—I'd earned a grudging respect from him and his athletic cohort. Nobody bothered me anymore. But I didn't have any friends, either. The boys of Mannville were generally suspicious of me, with my longish hair and my artistic pretensions, and the girls bored me with their endless nattering about who was going out with whom and who was getting married after high school. Annie'd been the only person of my age in Mannville who understood me. Things had come full circle. My world was once again reduced to the farmhouse, and to Grandpa. True, now there was Mildred, and also my bike, but life in general seemed hollow without someone to share it with. I would have liked it if Annie had been there each day to open the mailbox with me. The blows of rejection would have been easier to bear, I believed, with her matter-of-fact outlook on things: "Buck up, old bean," I could hear her say. "Those twerps wouldn't know a literary genius if one came up and spit in their eye."

Nearly three months had passed since the morning I murdered or did not murder Annie's father. Nobody, including me, had seen or heard from her in all that time. It was as if she'd simply vanished. I was even beginning to wonder if the wild tale of her abduction by aliens was possibly true. Madison had for a while kept a sort of unofficial watch on me, as the most likely candidate for her to contact if she was still alive. I knew very well that she *was* alive, but nobody else did, and though I felt vaguely guilty about leading everyone on, I knew it was better than telling them the truth. Nobody could know my suspicions about where Annie had gone. The success of her future sanity depended upon it.

All these thoughts flashed through my mind in less than a second as Grandpa handed this new letter to me. I checked his face quickly for signs of curiosity or intrigue, but if he'd guessed who the letter was from, he wasn't letting on.

"Mail for you," he said simply, and he went back out to the garage, where he was repairing a radio. He'd decided recently to branch out into electronics.

I pinched the envelope between my fingers. It was weighty and thick, a long letter. I took it up to my room and opened it. A light odor wafted out—not perfume; perfume was never Annie's style. It smelled foreign, somehow, like some kind of unusual cooking. Here and there the paper was translucent with grease stains. I began reading:

Dear Billy,

I presume you got my two-word note on that awful morning, that you knew it was from me, and that you understood it. That's one thing about you I've always been able to count on—you understand everything about me, usually without having to be told. I've never had a connection like that with anybody else, and I probably never will again, which is why it hurts me so much to tell you that I'm not sure I can ever see you again. And that too is something I hope you'll understand without me having to explain it, but I feel I owe you an explanation anyway.

I'm very confused right now. At the same time, however, I feel free. That's a first for me, and I want it to make you happy for my sake. I'm in Montreal. I told you once a long time ago that I dreamed of coming here, and I know you remember that. All those years of studying French on my own have paid off. I spoke like a typical American tourist when I first arrived here, but thanks to my hard work and a little luck, I'm picking up Quebecois pretty fast. Quebecois is a French dialect, and it's probably ruining my chances of ever speaking the French they speak in France, but that's all right. I like it here. I think I'm going to stay for a long, long time.

I have so much to tell you, and it all seems jumbled in my head. I'm not like you. Words don't come for me so easily. Thank God you already know so much about me, or this letter would be ten times harder to write. I guess there's no reason to start at the very beginning of everything, because that would just be repeating everything you already know. So I'll start where we left off, the last time we saw each other, or to be more exact, the last time you saw me.

I know you were in my house that morning. The drug my father used made me look unconscious, but I was still able to take in vague sensations, although—as I told you that horrible day, the last time we talked—I wouldn't remember anything very clearly afterward. I remember seeing you bend over me, looking at me to see whether or not I was dead. I could tell it was you even through the ski mask. And I knew you were hiding in the closet when he came back into the room, and I heard you jump out and scare him. I had been hoping you had a gun or something like that to kill him with. I didn't want you to get in trouble, or to have a murder on your conscience for the rest of your life, but all the same I hoped you would kill him, even though I'd told you I didn't, and you didn't disappoint me. Thank you, thank you, thank you. You really are my hero, Billy. You really did come to my rescue after all, just like you always said you would. And let your mind be at ease about the death of my father, because I know you, and I know you must feel guilty. It was really his heart that killed him, not you. It was only a matter of time before it went out on him. You were just trying to protect me.

I'm not sure I'll ever be able to forgive myself for allowing those things to happen to me. I hate it that I had to wait to be saved by

*someone else, but as long as that's the way it happened, I'm glad it was
you. I just didn't know what to do. There didn't seem to be anyone I
could tell besides you. I don't know if this makes any sense, but the
shame I felt over what my father was doing to me was huge. I was
afraid if I told someone, the whole thing would somehow backfire and
be made to look like my fault. It's irrational, I know. But I've been
doing some reading, and they say that kind of feeling is pretty common
among people like me.*

*"People like me." I hate it that I belong to a group of victims. I
hate whiners, hate helplessness. I despise weakness and I always have.*

*And despite the fact that you saved me from him, I'm not sure I
can ever forgive you for having sneaked into my house and seen me at
my most vulnerable. Does that make sense? I don't care, really, if it
does or not. I'm sorry if that sounds harsh, but that's the way it is. You
saw me with my nightdress pulled up. I don't care about that, that you
saw me naked. That's not what I mean. It's hard for me to explain.
You knew what was going on because I told you, and I even felt shame
over that.*

*There was a time when I thought you and I would grow up and
get married, or at least become lovers. But what I told you that night
in the car still goes. I don't think I can ever physically love a man,
ever. The very idea of it repulses me. That's partly what I'm trying to
tell you in this letter, to silence any doubts you might have about our
future and make sure everything is clear. I love you deeply, truly,
wonderfully, permanently, but we will never be lovers like you wanted
to be that night. It's not because of a lack of feeling for you. It's not
even that I don't find you desirable. Call it association. It's not you
that disgusts me—it's me, my own body. I don't want anyone to touch
it ever again. I hope you can understand that. You're a normal
healthy male but not so testosterone-ridden that you can't understand
what it feels like to be vulnerable, and not so egotistical that you think
you can talk me out of it. If you were to see me again—and that's a
big if—I want to make absolutely sure you understand this, so that
there's no mistake, no confusion, and no hurt feelings.*

I called the police only after I had managed to pack a bag and was sure I could get out of the house before they arrived. I would have just left him there to rot, but I had my brother Frederic downstairs to think of. It would have been weeks, perhaps months, before anyone would have found out that I was gone and he was dead, and Frederic would have starved to death before that. Poor Frederic; I've never known him. He was hurt before I was even born, and he's been like that now longer than he was healthy. Maybe I should have left him to die after all. He would have been better off. It's been twenty-five years since he's made a sound or moved, and it makes no sense to keep him alive, but my father would never hear of pulling the plug on him. I don't know why he insisted on keeping him alive in that kind of condition. It was pure torture. No, I do know why. It was because he was his only son, and I guess he didn't want to let go of that. My father believed girls were worthless. He must have told me a thousand times how disappointed he was when I was born. I hope wherever Frederic is now they're taking better care of him, and that they realize he's never going to get any better and they might as well end it for him. There's no point in keeping him in misery any longer. I am convinced he can hear and see and understand everything that happens around him but that he can't break out of himself. He must be insane by now. He must pray for death constantly. I hope it comes for him soon, and quickly. My father used to say he was the only one of us that was ever any good.

After I left the house, I disguised myself as best as I could and got on the main road. It was too risky for me to go into town and take a bus, so I hitchhiked, and I almost gave up the whole plan right there. It was a mistake. I was picked up by an older man who seemed very interested in taking me home with him, and it was only by begging and pleading that I got him to drop me off in Springville. I had to threaten to call the police, but I hoped like hell I wouldn't really have to because they would have hauled me back to Mannville. By then I was ready to kill every man I saw. I got a ticket to Montreal in the Springville bus station. While I was waiting in the depot, three men tried to hit on me, one after the other. By the time the last one came along I was screaming at the top of my lungs. People must have thought I was crazy, and I guess I was by that time. One of them tried to put his arm around me and I elbowed him in the stomach. The security guard looked up from his newspaper for perhaps a second, and then ignored me. It's a different world for women, Billy. Although I haven't had a day like that since then—I don't know what it was about that day, or the kind of energy I must have been sending out to attract those freaks—it could easily happen again, at any time, and I'm always on my guard.

So here I am in Montreal. I'm old enough to work, but barely, and for a while it didn't look like this was going to work out. I thought I would have to come back to Mannville. But I had managed to save up quite a bit of money. I've been saving for this move since I was little, you know. I knew the day would come and I dreamed of it every night as I stared out my bedroom window. I didn't think it would come quite so soon as this, though. I was still a little unprepared. But you saved me another two years of misery, Billy, and for that I will always be grateful. I couldn't bring myself to run away before he was dead. I don't know why. I was going to leave when I was eighteen. That way I knew there was no chance of me being brought back. If I had made it up here and he had found me and had me sent home, I would have killed myself. I know it. Sometimes I'm afraid I still might do it anyway. Sometimes I forget he's dead, and I imagine that he's out there looking for me. When I remember he's gone, that can be even worse—I'm afraid of his spirit more than I was of his body because it was his spirit that made him do those things to me. Now I worry he can see me all the time, that he stares at me in the shower and while I'm going to the bathroom. I worry that I'm losing my mind. But when I'm rational, I remember that hell is a place with no windows for him to see out of, and that perhaps I really am safe from him. Finally.

I have a job and a tiny apartment. I work in a Middle Eastern restaurant, cleaning toilets in the morning and serving food in the afternoon and evenings. I'm sure the owners know I'm here illegally and that I'm really too young to be working, but they don't seem too interested in who I am and that is a very valuable gift. Anonymity and secrecy are the things I value most right now. That's why I'm taking such a big risk writing to you. Please, please don't show this letter to anyone, and destroy it after you read it. I'm giving you my address, but please don't write it down anywhere. Memorize it. You can write me if you want. I might even like you to come see me. But be warned that I am not the same person you knew in Mannville. Already I have begun to change drastically, and I like it. I have no intention of being the person I once was ever again. I will always know you, always have you in my heart. But things will be very different with us from now on. And let me know first if you decide to come up. I will need to get a few things ready.

  I always tried to be normal. I always wished I was a normal girl from a normal family. I even had a picture of my father hanging on my bedroom wall. That was how bad I wanted to pretend everything was fine. But the time for pretending is over now, isn't it?

Love,

Annie

In October I said to Grandpa, "I think I'll take a trip up north."

He raised his eyebrows. "Really? And where did this idea come from?"

I shrugged, trying to conceal my unease. I didn't want Grandpa to know where I was going, or why, but I had to tell him something, and it was useless to lie. He could still read my thoughts, almost without effort.

"I have my reasons," I said.

"I'm sure you do," Grandpa replied. "But that's not what I asked you, is it?"

"No."

"What I'm asking you is what those reasons are."

"I know!"

We were silent for a moment.

"Are you going to tell me?" he asked finally.

"Do I have to?"

"Well," he said, "what kind of father figure would I be if I just let you go off without even asking where you were headed?"

"Not a very good one," I admitted.

He looked at me carefully.

"Is it about that Simpson girl?"

"Not 'that Simpson girl,'" I said hotly. "She has a name."

Grandpa smacked his knee. "Do you mean to say you've known where she's been all this time and you didn't bother to tell anyone?"

"I couldn't," I said. "I promised her."

"When? When did you promise her?"

Always, I thought. *I promised her always, from the time I first knew what was going on in that house.*

"Right before she left," I said. It wasn't exactly true, but it was true enough. Some promises didn't need to be said out loud.

"Well, I'll be goddamned," said Grandpa. "If that doesn't beat the hell out of everything I've ever heard. You knew. All this time you knew!" He took off his fedora and scratched his head. His right foot began tapping out a frustrated rhythm on the floor.

"Grandpa," I said. "Think about it for a minute. If you were me, would you have ratted on her? After everything that happened up there?"

"Up there," Grandpa knew, meant up in the big old white Simpson house on top of the hill.

"No," said Grandpa. "I wouldn't. But that's not the point."

"Then what is the point? Why are you so mad?"

"Because I thought she was gone for good," said Grandpa.

"Now wait a minute! That's not fair! Just because of her dad, you think she's a bad person! You told me yourself she wasn't like the rest of them! She's not! She's—"

"Just you calm down," said Grandpa. "I don't think she's a bad person."

"Well then, what is this all about? Why were you hoping she was gone for good?"

"I just don't want you to see her anymore," said Grandpa. "Ever."

"You can't do that," I said. My voice was low and shaking with rage. "You have no right to do that! And there's nothing you can do about it anyway! You can't stop me! Not without telling me why!"

"I can't tell you why," said Grandpa. "I can't. I just don't want you to go see her, wherever she is. It's not right for you to see her again. That's all. It's just not right."

I was shaking so violently now that my vision began to blur.

"Not good enough," I said. Then I turned and walked out of the house and out to the road.

Grandpa came to the door.

"Hey!" he shouted after me.

"Not good enough!" I screamed at him. "You can't keep things from me anymore! It's not fair! I have a right to know everything! I'm a Mann too!"

"You get your ass back here right now!"

"No!"

"Where are you going?"

Instead of answering, I shot him my middle finger.

"Goddamn it!" Grandpa roared. "You do as I tell you! Get back here!"

"You're not my father! I don't have to listen to you!"

"I raised you from a pup, boy! You mind me now!"

"You were *drunk*!" I shouted. "You were drunk the *whole time*! I raised myself, and you know it!"

There was a stunned moment during which Grandpa and I stared into each other's eyes across the driveway. I'd always sworn I would never say that out loud. There'd always been something in me that wouldn't allow me to blame Grandpa for who he was, for all his weaknesses. After all, he was my grandfather and my father and my mother all rolled into one, and when you came right down to it, he was all I had in the world. He was my entire family. But I said it then, even though I'd never wanted to, and it stopped him. I can still feel the twinge of pain I felt then as I saw Grandpa's shoulders sag and his eyes go hollow. He turned away from the door as if he'd been shot in the gut and went into the house.

There have been many nights since then when I wished I could go back and unsay that, long lonely nights when I couldn't get to sleep in those wee, dim, oddly reflective hours when we adults are haunted by the misdeeds we have done.

But there are other times when I think it had to be said. And you can't turn back the clock.

I turned my back on the farmhouse and began to jog. I ran down Mann Road and turned north onto the County Road, increasing my pace to a flat-out sprint. I wasn't headed anywhere in particular—I thought maybe I would go down to the Lake and throw rocks into the water for a while until I calmed down. The Lake was good for that. I could go swimming, maybe—I had no bathing suit with me, but there was a hidden stretch of beach where I could go skinny-dipping. Instead, however, I found myself turning up the long dirt drive that led up the hill to the Simpson house. I followed my feet, not really knowing what my intentions were. My rage abated as I drew nearer. I stopped at the foot of the hill and stared up at the house. Gradually I forgot about Grandpa, until there was only the house in front of me. It seemed to breathe chill waves of despair that washed down the hill and dwarfed me in their grandeur. I shivered.

Small-town people are funny. Morbid curiosity had flared in the wake of Simpson's death—it was the main topic of conversation in Mannville for months—and yet the causes of it, the story behind Jack Simpson and his fucked-up family and his gradually disappearing daughters, were themselves taboo. After all, if people had begun to raise those questions, the inevitable question, the most important one, would have to come up: *Why didn't we do something about it, before it was too late?*

We of small-town America still believe in placating ghosts, I guess. Or maybe it's just us Mannvillians.

In any case, the Simpson house had been left unmolested since the day Jack Simpson died. You'd think it would have become a popular make-out spot for teenagers, a place for kids to go make noise and break things. But I guess everyone had always known what was going on up there, and the wound was still fresh in people's minds. When folks did speak of the Simpson family, it was in whispers; not enough time had passed for the story to fade into legend, and people were afraid of conjuring up whatever evil spirits had driven the Simpsons to ruin. In any event, the house was left undisturbed, a monument to typical neighborly blindness.

But I've never considered myself a typical Mannvillian. And the criminal must always return to the scene of the crime.

A notice on the door informed me in large red letters that the property was condemned as unsafe. *Damned is more like it*, I thought. But nobody had taken the time to board up the windows or doors, and entering the house was as easy as walking in the front door, which was ajar.

"Hello!" I shouted.

Nothing, of course.

"Simpson, you fucker!" I screamed.

But there was no response. The house wasn't just empty—it was dead, as dead as Jack Simpson. The furniture—the same ravaged couch I'd seen the day I rescued Grandpa, the ancient and rickety kitchen chairs, the linoleum and the rugs worn almost into nothingness—all of these things had been left exactly as they were on the day Jack Simpson keeled over upstairs in his daughter's bedroom. The house was a monument to decrepitude. Even the same old television set was still there, the small gray screen set in the massive false-wood console staring back at me uncomprehendingly. I flicked the power switch—nothing. The juice had been cut off.

"I'll fix you," I said to the television. I went outside and hunted around in the yard until I found a rock the size of a softball. I heaved it through the television screen. It exploded with a satisfying crunch of bulbs and tubes and artificial wood.

That felt so good I went outside and gathered up a whole armful of rocks. Several windows had already been broken—some by the elements, some by Simpson himself probably, in one of his fits of drunken rage—but most were still intact. I set about remedying this situation. One by one, I wound up and pitched rocks through all the windows on the first floor. I was Sandy Koufax, I was Honus Wagner. There was nobody living close enough to hear the noise of breaking glass, but I wouldn't have cared if there had been. The house, I'd decided, had to go.

When I was finished with the first floor I got another armful of rocks and went upstairs. None of the windows there had been touched yet. I threw rocks through all of them except for those in Annie's room, feeling not anger but a cold and delicious satisfaction as each thin, clear, rigid membrane of windowpane popped under my barrage. There were mirrors, too, and these I flung against the walls with deliberate abandon—but still I avoided Annie's room. Soon the floors were crunchy with broken glass. *I could burn this place down*, I thought. I had a lighter in my pocket. I picked up a shred of newspaper from the floor and ignited it there in the upstairs hallway. It smoldered, flared up, and died. I let it flutter to the floor and stomped on it. Not here, I thought; her room. Let the fire come from Annie's room. Let it come and purify this house.

I went down the hall. The door to her bedroom was shut. I opened it slowly. The hinges grated as the door swung open. I stepped inside.

It was as though I'd entered another house, or another world altogether. Annie's bedroom, in defiance of the laws of nature, was still immaculately clean. Sunlight streamed cheerily through the windows, illuminating the made-up bed, the spotless floor, the pictures of unicorns and the photograph of her father hung neatly on the walls. It was ruffled and pink, a little girl's room, not the room of a teenager. The details of it had escaped me on my prior visit. Annie would have done all this herself, I thought. I could see her down at Jo-Ann's Fabrics, picking out exactly which frilly trappings would best portray the illusion of happy girlhood. "I'll take these, please," I could hear her say in her serious, studied way, pointing with a neatly manicured finger to the one sample among dozens that best promised to carry out the lie for her. She would not have looked up to meet the gaze of the saleswoman, because she wouldn't want her to see that it was all a lie. That it was part of the pretending.

Which was now over, if her letter was to be believed.

Here is the spot, I said to myself. This is the very piece of floor on which Jack Simpson breathed his last. And over here, ladies and gentlemen (for I was now conducting an imaginary tour group through the room), is the exact bed on which he often and gladly did things to his last remaining daughter which I won't go into here. The other daughters were all used up, you see. He drove them all crazy and then they skipped town, so she had to do. This is the scene of Mannville's greatest crime. No flash photography, please. And I myself am a criminal too—a murderer, yes, so take a good look if you've never seen one before. I'm the one who sent Simpson packing, and I've come back one last time to revel in my triumph over the forces of evil. No, no, don't applaud. It was just another one of my duties as the only son of Mannville's hero and ace fighter pilot, Lieutenant Eddie Mann, USAF (dec.), of whom you all no doubt have heard. I'm just keeping up the old traditions. I don't expect any thanks. And now, let's all proceed downstairs again and out of the house. In fact, you should all just go home, and don't come back. I have big plans for this room, and I don't want any of you to get hurt.

I had my lighter in my hand. My thumb rested on the wheel.

But instead I sat down on her bed. The covers had been neatly straightened and tucked in under her pillow. Even after three months, I marveled, there wasn't a wrinkle in them. That was Annie to the last. She would make her bed every morning even if the world was ending. I sat and listened for her, tried to smell her, waited for any sign that she was coming back. But I knew that was ridiculous. She never would come back, and I didn't want her to anyway, even though her absence felt to me like a bone that had been yanked from my body, as if our lives together were a tune so far only half played.

I sat in there for a long time, not thinking.

Suddenly I noticed the picture of Jack Simpson again: a black-and-white portrait, thirty years old perhaps. I took it off the wall without looking at it too closely. Then I went to the south window, opened it, and tossed the picture like a Frisbee into the yard. It sailed away gracefully into the trees. I listened for the sound of breaking glass, for the parting of branches before it, but I heard nothing. It was as if it had disappeared.

I leaned on the windowsill and stared out the window for a while. To my surprise, I could see the entire town from Annie's bedroom, the rooftops of the homes and businesses of Mannville poking peacefully above the trees. I could even see my house. I went to the north window. From there I could see across the Lake, which today glimmered turquoise and green. I hadn't realized Annie's perspective on things before, how much of our little world she was able to see. *Did she stand here at night and dream of a normal life, of escaping across the Lake to Canada?* I wondered. *Did she watch the rest of us going about our daily affairs, like Rapunzel in her tower, waiting to be rescued?*

No—not Annie. She'd rescued herself. I'd only helped her along a little. Life was not a fairy tale, and Annie wasn't a helpless princess. She was even braver and tougher than I was, and that was part of the reason I loved her.

Abruptly I put the lighter back in my pocket and went downstairs and out the front door.

I still don't know why I didn't burn the Simpson house down that day. I guess my anger was spent. I guess I figured enough violence had taken place there. It was time for quiet to seep in now. Eventually the house would decay into nothingness. Better to let it happen that way. Better to let nature take its course, as it was already doing.

I meandered back home. When I came into the living room, Grandpa and Mildred were sitting in their rocking chairs. Mildred got up upon seeing me and went into the kitchen.

"Grandpa," I said, getting right to the point. "I just have to go see her."

"I know," said Grandpa. He leaned back in his chair and looked up at the ceiling. "Hell, don't I know it? Haven't I spent most of my life sitting here with a broken heart? If there was anywhere I could have gone to make it whole again, believe me, I would have."

"If there's a reason you know of why I shouldn't go," I said, "I'd sure appreciate it if you'd tell me what it is."

"Someday you'll know," he said. "Until then, forget about it. Live your life the way you need to live it, boy. I can't stop you. I don't even want to stop you. You're a good boy. You'll be a better man than I ever was."

I could say nothing to that, but I knew he was right.

"I'm sorry I said what I said," I told him. "I shouldn't have said it."

"You had every right." He was looking at the floor. "I wasn't any kind of father to you. And now it's too late."

"You did a good job," I said. "I guess I'm gonna turn out all right."

Grandpa got up from his chair and put his bony arms around me. I had to stoop nowadays to hug him. I had risen to the height of five feet eleven and a half inches, and had every reason to believe I would attain my long-sought-after goal of six feet. I was, Grandpa said, the tallest Irishman he'd ever known, and certainly the tallest Mann in history.

That week I sent a letter to Annie, telling her I wanted to come see her and asking if it was still all right. I didn't tell her I'd gone into her old house, or that I'd flung the picture of her father out the window, that it had vanished into thin air, and I was afraid that was what would happen to my love for her if I didn't see her soon. I mentioned nothing about anything. She replied:

Yes. No. I don't know. You have my address. No promises. I have to warn you, I'm not the same person I was before. Come around Christmas if you want to. You might not want to.

Of course I want to, I thought. *How could I not?*

I bought a bus ticket to Montreal. I planned on going in mid-December, after school was out for the holidays.

About a week before I was to leave, I collected all the stories I'd written using the noun formula, put them in a box, and took them to Doctor Connor, whom I hadn't visited in a long while.

"Where have you been?" he asked me. Connor never shook my hand—instead he grabbed my head and looked into my nose. This, I'd come to believe, was how all doctors greeted people. He produced his little doctor flashlight and stuck it into my nostrils. "You've been smoking!" he said, disgusted.

"I've been *writing*," I said.

"Of course you have," he said. "Looks like you've been hard at it, too. Quite a lot of work here, isn't there?"

"I'm not sure if they're any good, though."

"Well, don't be too hard on yourself."

"Can you take a look at them?"

"I'd be glad to," he said. He picked a story out of the box and peered at the title. "'Mr. Woodcock and the Green Porpoise'? What the hell does that mean?"

"It's a new style," I said. "I invented it myself. It has to do with nouns."

"Nouns. I see," he said dubiously.

"I've been getting stuck a lot. After that first one they didn't seem to come so easy."

"And so you use nouns?"

"I write from the middle out," I said.

"Hmm. Interesting. A middlist, you are?"

"More or less. A middlist. Yeah." I had never thought of the word *middlist* before, but I liked the way it sounded: important and original.

"And so the school of Middlism is founded, right here in Mannville," mused Connor. He put one hand over his mouth for a moment and pretended to cough, but I could see he was hiding a smile. "Well, come back tomorrow morning. I should be able to look at a couple of them by then."

I came back the next morning, bright and early. Doctor Connor was just turning around the sign on his door from THE DOCTOR IS OUT to THE DOCTOR IS IN.

"Come in," he said. He didn't bother to look into my nose this time. I followed him into the examination room and sat on the table. Connor sat in his chair opposite me. He was holding "Mr. Woodcock and the Green Porpoise" but holding it daintily, by one corner, pinched between his thumb and forefinger as one might hold a dead rat. My heart, for so long flush with confidence in my literary future, was suddenly in free fall.

"You know I love you like my own grandson," he began.

"Oh no," I groaned, because with that kind of introduction, I knew that whatever was coming next was bad.

"And you know I would never say anything to hurt you," he went on, ignoring me. "Not unless I thought it would help you. You know that. Right?"

"Yes," I said. "I know that."

"Let me tell you a little story of my own, and I want you to listen carefully. Once I had to break a kid's arm," said Doctor Connor. "He'd already broken it once, and he didn't want to tell his mother, because he'd broken it roller-skating in the street and he wasn't supposed to be roller-skating. So he hid it from her—how, I have no idea—and it healed crookedly. You could see it right through the skin, where the two ends had come together all out of whack. This was in the old days, when I was still young. Just after the war. There was only one thing to do back then. Surgery was out of the question—people couldn't afford it then like they can today. So I grabbed his wrist with one hand and his elbow with the other and I snapped his arm in half on the edge of a table."

"Jesus!" I cried, involuntarily.

"It hurt him like hell, of course," said Connor. "He screamed and cried to beat the band. But that didn't bother me a bit because I knew

I would be able to reset his arm properly. Otherwise he would have gone through life with only one good arm. That was before anesthesia was used like it is now, too. If it had been a grown man I would have filled him up with whiskey first. But the poor kid had to have his arm broken stone cold sober."

He took a deep breath.

"This," he said, holding up the story, "is horrible. And telling you that is the hardest thing I've ever had to do."

I said nothing. I could feel my face growing hot with shame.

"It's like breaking that kid's arm," he said. "Except I have no guarantee you're going to get better, like he did. It's up to you. Bones heal themselves automatically, but people don't automatically hear criticism and become better writers."

I still couldn't speak.

"I've had to tell people their loved ones were dying of incurable diseases," he went on. "That was fun compared to this. I wouldn't be telling you this if I didn't think you were capable of doing better. You're very talented, Billy. But . . . well . . . "

He dropped the story back in the box. I knew without asking that he hadn't had the strength to read the others. The noun formula winked out of existence. Middlism was a failure. It died right there in the examining room of Doctor Connor's office.

"What are you *doing*?" he whispered, in the same tone one might use with a small boy who was eating wallpaper paste. "What happened? Your first story was so good!"

"I don't *know* what I'm doing," I said. "That's the problem. I don't know what to do." Secretly, in the deepest and most honest corners of my mind, I'd known the stories weren't any good. But I'd forced myself to write them anyway. I didn't know what else to do. "I was just trying whatever worked. I just don't know. I don't know how to do this."

"You're trying too hard," he said. "You're full of stories. All Manns are. And I know you. I knew you before you were even born, practically. You just have to let them flow out of you. Just say what happens, Billy. Forget this fancy formula stuff. Just tell the story."

"Okay," I said.

"But I'll tell you something good about your stories."

I brightened. "What?"

"You'll never make the same mistake twice," he said. My face fell again, but he ignored me. "You're too smart for that. Consider this all water under the bridge. It's practice. Like money in the bank. You've written this much, and now you have that much more experience. Make sense?"

"I think so."

"It will, if it doesn't yet. Go back to your original method, Billy. Write down the story of your family. There's plenty more besides the one about the treasure. When you run out of material, write down your own story. It will be good reading. Things will come to you if you just let them. And remember—just let it flow. Do you want these back?" He indicated the box of stories with his foot.

"I guess," I said.

"Don't be discouraged, boy," he said warmly. "You'll make it. I know you will."

"Thanks."

"You're welcome. Stop smoking."

"Yessir."

"I mean it."

"Yessir."

"See you later."

I took the box of stories home, dug a deep pit in the yard, and buried them. My face still burned as I shoveled dark and rocky Mannville dirt over my literary efforts, my life's work. What the hell had I been thinking? I would never be the kind of writer who could just make things up out of thin air. I was doomed to write about true events, maybe just adding a little twist here and there to make it more interesting. I was not a Hemingway, a Faulkner, a Dorothy Parker. I was a family historian, nothing more.

Maybe, I thought, I should be something else. Being a writer is just too damn hard.

Later that week, Grandpa and Mildred drove me to the bus station. I carried a basket full of Mildred's cooking, three packs of cigarettes, a blank notebook, and a copy of Jack Simpson's obituary.

"You know, I just realized something," said Grandpa. "That's the basket you were delivered in."

"What? Jesus!" I said. "I hope you at least washed it!"

"No, not *birthed*," he said. "Just dropped off in."

"It doesn't look very old," I said. "It looks brand new."

"You're right," said Grandpa. It was a curious property of things in our house: they gathered dust, but they never seemed to age. It was as if all Grandpa's efforts to stop time, to keep alive only those days when life was good for us Manns, had succeeded, but only as far as physical objects were concerned. To me he'd said once or twice that he thought it had something to do with all the whiskey he'd breathed into the air when he was still drinking. It had soaked into all the wood and clothing fibers and pickled them, he said. On the surface, it looked as if he was right. Furniture and clothing that should by all rights have fallen into disrepair decades earlier were still as good as new. But we both knew that explanation was ridiculous. It was instead some new, subtler kind of haunting, perpetuated by the ghosts who still couldn't bring themselves to leave us alone.

I shook hands with Grandpa—being older now, I had forbidden him to hug me in public—received a kiss on the cheek from Mildred, and I was off. Ten hours later the bus pulled into the Montreal bus station.

Annie met me at the terminal. I barely recognized her—she'd cut all her hair off. She hadn't just cut it—she'd *shaved* it. It had grown back some, but the sight of her skull under only a thin layer of hair was unnerving. I went to hug her, but she fended me off with one hand against my chest.

"First things first," she said. "Don't touch me."

I stopped, my arms outstretched gracelessly in midair.

"All right," I said. My arms fell to my sides.

"Second. I knew the whole time about that awful woman you were seeing."

"You *did*?"

"Yes. And may I say you suffer from a lack of taste?"

"Jealous?" I was trying to tease her, but it fell flat.

"Why on earth would I be *jealous*?" She stood with her arms crossed, a stony glint in her eye.

"Never mind," I said. I looked aimlessly around the bus station. For the first time, I was at a loss for words with Annie.

"Why in hell did you ever want to get mixed up with her?"

"It's hard to explain."

"I don't think it's really all that complicated," said Annie. "You have a penis, don't you?"

"Now wait a minute," I said. "That's not fair."

"Nothing," Annie sniffed, "is fair. That's what *I've* learned."

"I didn't do anything wrong."

"You were just *using* her for *sex*!"

"And what was she using me for?" I thought Annie ought to get together with Mrs. Gruber. Between the two of them they would sentence me to life in prison without parole. "You don't know the whole story, anyway."

"It's just a point I'm trying to make," she said angrily. "If I'd been fifteen years old going out with a man who was thirty-two, what would people have said about me?"

"Hi, Annie," I said. "Nice to see you too."

"You just don't get it," she said. "There's a big double standard out there. Girls have to be goody-goody, and boys get to do whatever they want."

"Maybe *you* just don't get it," I said. "Why are you angry at me?"

"I told you," she said. "I told you I wasn't the same as I was before."

You were very right, I thought.

I picked up my bag and followed her out of the bus station and down the street. We walked for perhaps half a mile, she in front, silent and walking fast, I struggling to keep up behind her. It was unspeakably cold. Mannville got cold, but it was never anything like this. This was the kind of cold that felt almost red-hot. I was wearing a light jacket and jeans, and within moments I began to wonder if my life wasn't in danger.

"This *hurts*," I said.

Annie said nothing.

"I'm not wearing the right clothes," I said.

Nothing.

"You could have told me how *cold* it was up here," I said.

She turned and looked at me. For a moment I thought her eyes softened, but then they glazed over again, and there was the same steel there.

"Deal with it," she said shortly.

We kept walking until we arrived at her place. I didn't say another word.

Annie lived in a second-floor apartment on Sherbrooke Street. Directly beneath her place was a Middle Eastern restaurant run by a couple of Palestinian women. Annie worked there twelve hours a day. The Palestinian women were short and stocky and hairy; one of them had a large black-tufted mole on her upper lip. When Annie introduced me to them they regarded me cautiously, as one might look at an emissary from an opposing army.

"Hello," I said. They stared at me, their eyes slitted and wary.

"Not hello," said Annie. "*Bonjour*. They don't speak English."

"Bon jer," I said. It was my first French word and I could tell by the smirks of the women that I was mispronouncing it.

"Bonjour," said one.

"Comment ça va," said the other.

Annie spoke to them in French. She was explaining something, speaking rapidly; her hands flew like birds, and occasionally she pointed at me. The women continued to stare at me, their expressions unchanging. I couldn't understand a word of what she was saying. I wondered if she was telling *them* about Elsie Orfenbacher too. Then she finished, turned, and said, "Come on." I followed her out of the kitchen.

"What did you say to them?"

"I was explaining who you were," she said.

"How did you learn to talk like that?"

"Practice," she said. "Necessity."

"You mean nobody around here speaks English?"

"Some do," she said.

"What's with those two? They didn't seem awfully glad to see me."

"They were raped by Israeli soldiers," Annie said, as we went upstairs. "That's what's with them, okay? Not just once. Dozens of times. So they don't really like men that much. I was explaining to them that you were all right. That you weren't going to hurt them."

"Holy cow," I said. "Why were they raped?"

"What do you mean, *why*?" asked Annie. "Is there ever a reason for that kind of thing?" She stopped on the stairs and faced me. Her lips were set in a tight line, small wrinkles of displeasure forming fissures around her mouth. For a moment she looked about forty years old.

"I guess not," I said. I almost said *Sorry*, but something in me wouldn't allow it. I didn't have anything to apologize for. I wasn't a rapist. I was only sixteen years old. But my belly quivered with nervousness, and suddenly I wished very much that I hadn't come.

Annie's apartment was a three-room affair, with a kitchen, bedroom, and small sitting area, and it was thoroughly permeated with an odor of grease and Middle Eastern spices that seemed to hover in a cloud over everything. It was the same smell that had clung to the letter she'd sent me.

I unpacked my picnic basket full of food. "Grandpa has a girlfriend now," I said. "She loves to cook."

"I see," Annie sniffed.

"Well, help yourself," I said.

"Does she love to cook, or is it that she's supposed to cook?"

"What?"

"You know. Keep 'em in the kitchen? Barefoot and pregnant?"

"All right. You know what?" I said. "This is fucking bullshit. You better get civil right now or I'm out of here. I don't know what the hell your problem is, but I don't deserve this."

"Look," Annie said. She ran a hand over her head. "I don't know what you expected in coming up here, but—"

"Annie," I said, thoroughly exasperated, "do not assume for one second that I want anything from you. I told you already. I miss you. I mean, I *missed* you. I wanted to see you, make sure you were all right, spend some time with you. Maybe I should go stay at a motel or something. Jesus. In fact, you know what? Fuck you. I'm leaving."

I picked up my bag and went toward the door.

"Wait," she said.

"No. *You* wait." I opened the door.

"Please, Billy," she said. "Just hang on. Just—"

I stopped.

She sat down and put her face in her hands. I sat next to her.

Automatically my arm went up around her shoulders. She started like a colt.

"Please don't do that," she said, but her voice was her old voice again—it was just a request, nothing more.

"I'm sorry. Habit."

"*I'm* sorry," she said.

"I'm on your side," I said. "I always have been."

"I know," she said. "It's just . . . "

"I know what it is," I said.

She was silent.

"Annie, you don't owe me anything, if that's what you're worried about," I said. "I didn't mean to come up here and make you remember a bunch of stuff you don't want to think about. I just wanted to make sure you were all right. I'm proud of you. I really am. Jealous. Do you know how much I'd love to have an apartment of my own?"

"You would?"

"Yes, I really would."

"It gets really cold here," she said. "I mean, even worse than this. It's not as great as it looks."

"Well, you know what I mean," I said.

"Billy," she said, "I'm glad to see you. I really am."

"Well, that's more like it," I said. "I'm glad to see you too." *Oh God*, I thought. *If only you knew.*

"Let's get out of here," she said. "I'll show you around. We can go get a beer."

"We can get beer?"

"You can drink younger here than you can at home," she said. "You only have to be eighteen."

"We're not eighteen, though."

"They never check," she said. "Just act natural, and they won't even bother you."

This struck me as a brilliant plan—a country in which teenagers could buy beer. America, which had already been faltering in my eyes as the country that would not publish me, slipped even lower on the scale in favor of Canada. We got dressed to go outside: long underwear, jeans, flannel shirt, sweater, winter jacket, scarf, hat, gloves, and two layers of socks under heavy boots. The sun was down, and when we emerged onto the street the cold hit me like a fist in the stomach. Annie was right. It had gotten even worse.

"Pull your scarf over your nose," Annie instructed me. "Breathe through it. Don't breathe straight air. You'll freeze your lungs."

I was nearly paralyzed. The temperature had plummeted a further twenty degrees or so in the short time since my arrival. I'd never imagined a cold like this was possible. It seeped through the cracks in my thermal armor and stung like hundreds of hornets. We walked rapidly to stay warm. Everyone else seemed to have the same idea. It was a Friday night, and the streets were filled with people, chattering in a melange of languages and striding briskly to and from bars, restaurants, clubs, and various darkened places that seemed to prefer discretion over advertising. I'd never heard French spoken before that day, but now it was everywhere. I thought it was a beautiful language, birdlike and airy even in this frigid weather—one expected the words to shatter in midair because of the cold. We passed two intoxicated men having an argument. They were bearded and large-bellied, the same sort of men one might see driving pickup trucks or tractors in Mannville, and it amused me greatly to hear them speaking this flowery tongue instead of western New York twang as they shouted, two potbellied and unshaven drunks insulting each other in the language of diplomats and kings.

We arrived at a small place with an unpronounceable name. Annie ordered a pitcher of beer. It was red and dark and glorious, and all the more delicious because it was my first beer in a bar. We sipped it slowly.

"Boreale Rousse," said Annie. It was the name of the beer. She made me say it over and over until I was close enough to pronouncing it correctly to satisfy her: Bo-ray-ahl Roos, except she was doing something funny with her *r*'s that escaped me completely, swallowing them while they were still only halfway out of her mouth. It was a great trick, and as I drank another beer it seemed to become even more remarkable.

"That's just amazing," I said. "Why does that make me so happy?"

"Be careful," she warned me. "This stuff is stronger than the beer at home."

"Let me ask you something else. Why did you cut off all your hair?"

She shrugged, taking a large sip of beer. "Men," she said simply. "There's something about baldness that kind of makes you invisible. They don't look at you, they don't hassle you. I did it because I wanted to be invisible."

"Did you really get hassled all that much?"

She looked at me in disgust, but it was no longer mixed with loathing; it was more pity for my ignorance, and the tiniest bit of amusement.

"You will never understand in a million years," she said.

"Understand what?"

"What it's like to be a woman."

"Well," I said, already a little drunk, "that's because I'm a man."

"I know you're a Mann."

"No, I mean a male."

"I was making a joke," she said.

I threw my head back and laughed uproariously.

"All right," she said, and now she was actually smiling. "I think we've had enough beer."

We went home, wrapped ourselves in blankets, and sat on the couch talking. There were perhaps ten thousand things I wanted to tell her, little details mostly. It was impossible to get them all out, and it was then I began to see that there was a segment of my life Annie had simply missed and would never understand, and that the same was true of me for her. But at least we were together again. We rubbed toes under the blanket. Words came more and more easily until we were talking freely and laughing; things began to seem more the way they had been and Annie began to seem more like Annie; and I realized I had passed a sort of test, although exactly when it had happened and of what it had consisted escaped me. We fell asleep with our legs entangled, sleeping like children, and late in the night she awoke and led me to her bed and snuggled in next to me.

Once, three-quarters asleep, I thought I felt a hand stroking my hair, and a voice whispering, "You're still my hero, Billy Mann."

But it was probably just a dream.

* * *

The days were not quite as cold as the nights, so while Annie labored in the kitchen of the Palestinians, I wandered around and explored Montreal. The sheer magnificence of the city plunged me into a state of culture shock. Even the mailboxes, which were tall and thin and red, seemed fascinating. My first morning there, munching cold falafel that Annie's Palestinians had given me, I headed down Sherbrooke to Mont Royal and listened to some hippies—at least I thought they were hippies, but I'd never seen hippies before and couldn't be sure—bang on their drums in the park. Then I turned around and headed downtown, pausing to explore the ruins of a burned-out cathedral. A flock of pigeons exploded from their hiding place among the exposed rafters and scattered skyward. I watched them go, noticing that the sky was a deep blue and the sun was warming the city. The influence of France seemed to be everywhere, in the architecture and the food and the language; I felt as though I'd gotten on the bus in Mannville and arrived some hours later in Europe.

It was an odd sensation, and I relished it thoroughly. I'd never been anywhere in my life. I realized with shame that I'd never even been to Buffalo, except to pass through it on the bus. I thought of my seventeen years of solitude and stagnation. No wonder I was such a lousy writer, I thought. I hadn't *done* anything yet. I needed to meet new people, eat strange food, learn foreign languages, worship bizarre gods, if only to see what it felt like to do these things. The hunger to see more of the world was blooming in me like a ravenous flower, demanding to be fed. Compared with Montreal, Mannville seemed like a depressing backwater, its inhabitants a bunch of ignorant hicks in baseball caps that said CAT on them, who chewed tobacco incessantly and said "ain't." No great writers would ever come out of Mannville. I didn't want to go home.

Around noon I stopped in a little bakery and bought some mineral water and a few pastries. There were several small tables with chairs on the sidewalk, but they were all occupied, so I sat on the curb to eat my lunch. I was nearly done eating when I heard a great commotion in the distance. I perked my head up and listened. Whatever it was, it was coming closer. It sounded like hundreds of voices singing in unison, accompanied by the tramping of many feet. I stood up and brushed my hands on my jeans, looking down the street in the direction of the noise. Others around me had heard it too; the sidewalk was crowded with pedestrians, all of whom suddenly fell silent and paused to listen.

Swinging into view around the corner I saw a line of men and women. They marched in unison, their arms swinging, bearing banners in French. I tried to pronounce the words on the banners to myself, but it was hopeless; they were protesting against something, or perhaps in favor of something, but I had no idea what it was. Another rank of people appeared behind the first one, bearing more French banners; they were followed by another rank, and another, and another, and soon the street was jammed with people marching and waving banners, passing only inches from me.

Among the many experiences I'd never had in Mannville, seeing a protest was chief among them. Protests were something I read about in the papers, involving total strangers upset about something that had nothing to do with me, or so I thought—unemployment, or nuclear disarmament, or logging. But these people were right in front of my nose, not on the front page of the *Megaphone*. It was possible, I thought, that I was witnessing an event of historical significance. I began to grow excited. This was great fun, whatever it was. This was the sort of stuff I needed to see if I was to become a writer. This was *real*.

There were hundreds of marchers, perhaps thousands, all singing the same song. The cement vibrated under the weight of their feet. All motor traffic had been forced from the street; I could have walked from sidewalk to sidewalk on the heads of the marchers, so dense were their numbers. The people sitting at the tables behind me stood up and began chattering to each other excitedly. One of them poked me in the ribs and said something in French.

"What?" I said. I had to shout to be heard above the roar of voices.

The man who'd poked me looked to be in his mid-forties. He had a thin, carefully curled mustache, and he wore a sort of beret tilted to one side. He was a very French-looking guy.

"You don't speak French!" he shouted.

"No!"

"Why you sing?"

"What?"

"Why you are singing?"

"I wasn't singing!" I said, but as soon as I said that, I realized I *had* been singing, in unison with the marchers. Their enthusiasm was infectious. I'd no idea what they were singing about, but whatever it was, I was highly in favor of it. It was the greatest cause in the world.

"What is this about?" I said to the man.

"Eh?"

"What are they protesting?"

"You don' know?"

"No! Tell me!"

A crafty look came over his face. "You are American?" he asked.

"Yes!"

"I do not like Americans," he said. "Not one bit do I like them."

"I'm sorry," I said.

"In fact, I *hate* Americans. You are all a bunch of drug-taking *pigs*."

"Well, hold on there," I said.

"But you I like," the man went on. "And for that, I will tell you what it is about. It is a march in favor of a free Quebec." The man had a strong French accent—he made his *t*'s into *z*'s, and he said "favair" instead of "favor."

"A free Quebec?"

"You like Quebec?"

"Oh yes! Very much!"

"Do you *love* Quebec?"

"I do!" I said. I was getting quite worked up; I could feel my heart pounding.

"You are American but you love Quebec!"

"I do love it!" I roared. "I love it more than anything!"

"Then you must *march*!" the man screamed. "You must tell the *world* 'ow much you are loving Quebec!"

"I will!" I shouted. "I'm gonna do it!"

"Go! Go! March your brains out!" the man howled.

I was nearly delirious with excitement. Without another word to the man, I threw myself out into the street and fell into step with the marchers. They opened their ranks briefly to admit me and then closed in again, and I found myself linked arm in arm with two burly men, each of whom were easily four inches taller than I was. They looked down at me briefly and gave me broad, toothy grins. I smiled back. I couldn't understand the words of the song, but I could carry a tune, and I imitated the lyrics as best I could. My heart pumped madly and adrenaline coursed through my veins with the heat of molten lead. *I'm protesting*, I thought happily. *I'm a demonstrator! If only Grandpa could see me now!*

We marched on for several blocks. I sang, I shouted, I took part. I knew nothing about the Canadian province of Quebec, but that didn't matter. Freedom was a great thing, and if I could march for it anywhere, I would. Freedom was the underlying principle of America. It was what we fought wars for, usually.

The streets were lined with people, but few of them were singing along; they seemed curious, but aloof, uninvolved.

This gave me pause. Although I'd only been in Quebec a day, I'd already heard much about how strongly the French-speaking Canadians felt about their independence from the rest of Canada. It was the sort of subject about which it was impossible for Canadians to be ambivalent. Yet few of the bystanders, most of whom I assumed to be natives, seemed moved by the marchers. In fact, one or two of them seemed to be jeering.

"Free Quebec!" I shouted.

"Fuck you, you faggot!" shouted a man from the sidewalk.

Faggot? I thought.

I looked around. Behind me, two women were carrying a banner. My French was atrocious, but I'd found that in the French language there were several words that matched the spelling of their English equivalents almost exactly, and in this way I was able to understand many of the signs I saw in shop windows. I'd been too excited to concentrate on reading the banners earlier, but it occurred to me now that perhaps this march was not, in fact, everything the very French-looking man had said it was.

I mouthed the words on the banner silently to myself. One or two of them stood out. VIVE LA DIFFÉRENCE, said one line. I'd read that somewhere before. It meant something like "Long live the difference," which in turn meant that different things were good, that one should encourage diversity. Well, that was nothing radical; I was in favor of that too. But it seemed a strange thing to protest about. I read on.

Suddenly my blood chilled. I'd recognized another word. It was
HOMOSEXUALITÉ.

I was not marching for a free Quebec. I was marching for gay
rights.

At the same moment, I realized that the gentlemen on my left and
right had relinquished their grips on my arms. One of them had casually sneaked his arm around my waist; the other was holding my hand.

I turned back to look at the crowd again. A leather-jacketed teen
on the sidewalk was attracting a good bit of attention to himself by
dancing around in a little circle with one limp wrist extended. Several
of his friends stood around him, laughing and pointing at the
marchers. At *us*. And near him, aimed directly at me at the moment I
happened to look, was a television crew complete with camera, wide-
angle lens pointing at myself and my two large companions. A heavily
made-up man stood in front of the camera with a microphone. He was
looking directly into my eyes.

"Excuse me, guys," I said to the men next to me, and I twisted out
of their grasp and jumped onto the sidewalk. I wanted to run, but I
tripped on someone's foot and sprawled onto the cement. A hand
grabbed me by the collar and hoisted me to my feet.

"Thanks," I said.

I was looking into the heavily made-up face of the television
reporter.

"Hi!" he said. "How long has it been since you came out of the
closet?"

"Excuse me," I said. "I was marching for a free Quebec."

I turned and headed back the way I had come, my face burning.

I had nothing against homosexuals; I believed they deserved all the
rights they could get, and now that I knew how it felt to be called a faggot by someone who really meant it, I had a new perspective on the
whole matter. It had hurt, and I wasn't even gay.

But I vowed that if I saw that French-looking guy again, I was
going to teach him a lesson in international relations.

I met Annie again at six that evening.

"What did you do today?" she asked.

"Oh, nothing," I said. "Walked around."

"I heard there was a big march today," she said. "Did you see it? We wanted to go, but we were too busy."

"You wanted to go?"

"Sure."

"Why?"

"Because we—well—do you know what it was about?"

"The march?"

"Yeah."

"No," I lied.

"Well, it doesn't matter," she said quickly.

I thought I understood then. The shaved head, the sexless appearance, her general anger at all things male and masculine. The Palestinian women.

Annie was becoming a lesbian.

"Look at this," I said, producing a magazine I'd bought at a bookstore. I had to change the subject because there was a sick feeling in my gut suddenly that I could not explain. *Oh, don't become a lesbian*, I pleaded with her silently. *How are we going to get married if you're a lesbian?* The magazine looked to be a literary journal, but I couldn't be sure because it was in French. *Lesbian! No!*

"*Le Journal des Lettres,*" she read out loud. "It's local. They publish short stories."

"What kind of short stories?" *Are you* already *a lesbian?*

Annie shrugged. "Any kind, I guess," she said, leafing through it. "Why?"

"How good are your translating abilities?" *You're not in love with those weirdo Palestinians, are you? Are they in love with you? Oh God.*

"You mean from English to French? Why?"

"Do you think you could translate my story about Willie into French?" *Don't, don't, don't*, I begged her in my mind. *We're not all like your father. I can be good to you.*

Annie pursed her lips. "Well, I suppose I could. I could do it literally. But I'm not sure it would still sound like a story. It wouldn't be as good as it is now."

"Maybe it would," I said. "Don't sell yourself short." *Shit. It's too late, isn't it? You've gone over.*

"I don't know. I'm not too good at idioms yet."

"What do idioms have to do with it?" I gave up my internal monologue. It probably was too late, I realized. Maybe this is how it really is supposed to be.

"You need them to tell a story," she said. "They're like sayings. Or just a general feel for the language, I guess. And to do that you have to really know it."

"Will you try it?"

"Are you thinking of sending it to these guys?" She tapped the magazine with a chapped and reddened finger. The Palestinians had Annie doing dishes constantly, and it was beginning to tell on her skin. Some women's libbers they are, I thought indignantly—taking advantage of her age, working her like a dog. And taking advantage also of the fact that she's here illegally. I wanted to say something about it, but I held my tongue. I didn't want to start tearing down what little progress she'd made in building a new life.

"Well, I'm not having any luck in America," I said.

"We don't say 'America' here," she giggled. "Say 'the States.' It's a little less dramatic."

"Whatever. Will you do it?"

"I'll try," she said. "But I can't promise you it'll be any good."

"Trying is good enough," I said. "I have faith in you."

She smiled at me shyly, her chin supported by one slender hand. I had a flash of how she was going to look when she was older. She'd be one of those women who attracts attention to herself without trying, just by existing, the kind of woman who radiates a certain calm purpose in everything she does, and she would be beautiful besides. And she would have children. I was certain of it.

"Nobody ever tells me that," she said. "That they have faith in me."

"You've been hanging around the wrong kind of people," I said.

"I was born to the wrong kind of people," she said, and her face darkened for a moment. I recognized a storm approaching. We'd agreed that we were never, ever going to discuss her father again. She'd decided she would reserve that for the therapist she knew she would need someday. When we were together, it was my job to help her forget about it.

"Drink your beer," I said. "I'm taking you to a movie. What do you want to see?"

She smiled.

"*Return of the Jedi* is playing," she said. "We can make the beginning this time. I hope you don't mind subtitles."

We spent the rest of that evening and the next several evenings in the same way: we walked, sometimes holding hands and sometimes not, and slowly I learned of all the little niches of Montreal that Annie had claimed as her own. They were frequented by others too, of course, but in my eyes the very fact that Annie was in a place made it hers and simply on loan to everyone else. She loved bookstores, cafés, parks, or just certain building facades, patches of sidewalk, concrete stoops that made her feel a certain way when she was near them, for no particular reason at all. She'd spent her first two weeks in Montreal just walking, she said. It hadn't been cold then, and she'd needed to know if she could be comfortable here.

"If you ever want to know a city, just walk around it for a while," she said. "Smell it. Listen to it. Every city has a mood of its own."

I thought this so lovely I wrote it down in my journal.

My last night we lay next to each other in bed, not speaking. In the last eleven days, I'd crammed more sights and sounds into my poor provincial brain than it had ever known before, and now that I was going home in the morning I felt a keen sense of loss. Life in Montreal was just too exciting. But gradually I began to fall asleep, and as I often do when drifting off, I had a waking dream.

I was standing in the cemetery of St. Jude's Church in Mannville, where Mr. Simpson had been buried and where five generations of Manns already lay. We'd accumulated an impressive amount of tombstones since our arrival in the New World, and I stood now in my dream looking at them, reading the inscriptions one by one as I'd done a hundred times before. This time, however, there was a new stone that I had never noticed. It was shuffled in with the rest of them, standing between Grandpa's, which he'd already placed years ago with the date of his death left blank, and my father's, which was not truly a tombstone because there was no body beneath it—it was only a memorial, his body never having been recovered. I peered closely at this new apparition, puzzled that I'd never noticed it. It was covered with a kind of writing I couldn't recognize.

"You'll be buried here someday," said a voice, "and so will I." I turned and saw not Grandpa, from whom I would have expected such a speech, but Doctor Connor. He was standing next to me in his white coat, his hands folded respectfully in front of his crotch, as though we were in the midst of some religious service. "I knew you before you were born," he added.

I turned and looked again at the new tombstone. The writing, I saw now, was Japanese. The characters blurred before my eyes, and then resolved themselves into English letters for a moment before they blurred once more and went back again. They read, "Enzo Fujimora is a very old man."

A shock of recognition went through me as I read the name. Enzo Fujimora was the fighter pilot who had Willie's diary.

"He's not dead yet!" I shouted happily to Doctor Connor. "Connor! He's still alive! He's still coming with the diary!"

But he was no longer standing next to me. In his place was Grandpa, and he said nothing but gave me a quiet, frightened smile.

"I don't understand," I said.

Then my eyes opened. Annie was shaking me gently, shushing me. "You're having a nightmare," she said. I struggled into a sitting position.

"Where are we?" I asked, confused.

"In my apartment," she said. "In Montreal. You were having the Rory nightmare again."

"No," I said. "This wasn't a nightmare."

"Well, you were shouting."

"What did I say?"

"They weren't words," she said. "Just shouts."

"I don't have the nightmare anymore," I told her. "Neither does Grandpa. It wasn't the nightmare."

"Well, that's nice," she said, but I imagined she was looking at me strangely.

"Don't look at me like that," I said.

"I wasn't looking at you like anything," she said, but whereas I had imagined it before, now she really was looking at me strangely. "Are you all right?"

"It was a different kind of dream," I said. "Something's happening."

"What?"

"I don't know," I said. "I have to go home."

"You're going home in the morning."

"I can't wait," I said. I got up and began throwing my belongings into my bag. "I have to go home right now."

"Billy, you're still asleep," said Annie. "Get back in bed."

"I'm not asleep!" I said.

"You're confused, then. You had a bad dream. Now get back in bed. It's freezing outside and we're not walking to the bus station in this weather."

But perhaps I really was asleep because, although I remember clearly the dream itself, my memory of this conversation is hazy, and I have no memory whatever of what happened next. Annie claimed, in a letter she wrote to me after my return to Mannville, that I said to her, "You used to be my mother, when we lived before, and that's the only reason I'm going to listen to you," and then I got back into bed and dropped instantly into unconsciousness. That had given her pause. Actually, she said, it did more: it spooked her so badly she was unable to get to sleep for several hours. My tone had been so intense, so convincing, that she felt the hairs on the back of her neck stand straight up, and she'd been chilled to the bone despite the layers of heavy blankets on her bed.

"Sometimes," she wrote in the same letter, "it's not easy being friends with a psychic."

Morning came and I awoke refreshed and rejuvenated. We breakfasted on hot coffee and cold falafel, courtesy of the Palestinians, who'd betrayed no emotion upon my arrival and who showed exactly the same stoicism now that I was leaving. I bid them each farewell in French, as politely as I knew how, and Annie and I walked together to the bus station. I wouldn't remember the dream until later. Just now I was dreading my return to Mannville and the boredom I was sure was in my future there.

"No sense in you waiting around with me," I said. "You ought to get back to work."

"Okay," she said.

"Are you ever coming home?"

"I am home," she said. Her eyes were suddenly wide and glistening. "I thought you understood that."

"Force of habit," I said, cursing myself for my careless words. "I meant coming back to Mannville."

"No. I'm not." She stood with her arms folded in front of her thin chest, looking up at me both in defiance and in expectation.

"I think this is great, what you're doing," I said because I sensed she was waiting for me to say something. Despite Annie's bravery and fortitude, her plan needed my pronouncement on it, either my blessing or my condemnation. But I would never condemn her for what she was doing, even if I thought the Palestinians were taking advantage of her. For her it was a question of survival, and I knew she would go on living alone in Montreal no matter what I said about it. And she would do it until she was done, and ready to go on to the next thing. "Really. I wish I was doing it too. I'm jealous."

"Consider my life for a moment, you dipshit," she said, smiling wanly. "How could anyone be jealous of me?" But her smile contained a hint of relief, and I was glad I'd said it.

"I guess I just wish I had more time with you," I said. I drew her to me and held her tightly for several moments.

She said into my ear, "Thanks for coming."

"It was my pleasure," I said, releasing her.

"It means something to me," she said.

"I know."

"I was really nervous about it. It was like . . . my past meets my future, you know? I was afraid there would be a collision or something. But there wasn't. It worked out just fine."

"I'm glad," I said.

"I wasn't sure it would."

"I could tell."

"Shit. I'm sorry I was such a bitch when you first got here."

"Forget about it," I said. "I understand. Don't forget to translate my story."

"I won't," she promised. "Tell your grandfather I said hi."

"Oh no!" I said. "I forgot the picnic basket!"

"It's still at my place," she said. It was too late to go back for it; my bus had just pulled up to the loading dock.

"Oh man," I moaned, "Grandpa's going to kill me."

"Over a picnic basket?"

"That's *my* picnic basket. The one I came in."

"You mean when you were a baby?"

"Yes."

"I always thought you were speaking figuratively when you told me you were delivered in a basket!" She was laughing.

"No, I wasn't," I said. I wasn't amused. "Listen. That basket is the only thing I have to remind me of my mother. It's the only thing I know for sure she touched. I have to have it back."

"I'll send it to you."

"No! It might get damaged in the mail. Or lost."

"I'll pack it up good," she said. "Don't worry."

"Please," I said. I was surprised at the sudden upwelling of panic I felt in my chest. "Please be careful with it."

"Jesus, I will," she said. "Don't you trust me?"

I was suddenly embarrassed. "I'm sorry," I mumbled. "I don't know what came over me."

"Don't worry," she said.

A garbled voice came on the loudspeaker and announced my bus. "Toronto-Buffalo-Erie-Pittsburgh and points south," it said.

"Sometimes we get hooked on things," said Annie.

"I'll write to you a lot," I said.

"I'll write back."

"I'll miss you."

"I'll miss *you*."

"Annie?"

"Yeah?"

Are you dyking out? Will you ever love me? Will you always hate men? Will we ever be together? Will you marry me? Isn't there something I can do to make things all right again?

"Bye," I said. I couldn't say those things to her—not now, not ever.

We embraced again and I got on the bus. I found an empty pair of seats and sat by the window. My panic over the picnic basket had subsided. I amused Annie, and distracted myself from my own despair, by putting my lips to the glass and puffing out my cheeks, until we pulled out and headed, as the announcer had said, for points south.

It wasn't until we were well under way that my dream of the previous night began to filter back to me in little bits and pieces. I wrote them down in my notebook until I was sure I had the whole thing recorded in the proper order. There was one line of Doctor Connor's that puzzled me greatly. He'd said it before in his office, too, while he was pleading with me, pained, to give up the noun formula of writing, but it had borne more significance in the dream than it had in real life. It was "I knew you even before you were born."

Connor believed seriously in reincarnation. He'd told me more than once of his belief that souls travel in flocks, like birds, following each other from life to life just as swallows go from tree to tree. Our roles may change, he said, but the souls stay the same; someone who was your brother in a past life may be your best friend in this one, or your sister now may have been your wife in ancient Rome. He pooh-poohed my objection that this would be incest. "What matters is that the souls are together," he said. "The bodies themselves are insignificant, and so is what you do with them." Any number of soul combinations were possible. He even believed people changed gender from life to life, as easily as people change clothes.

But I didn't believe in reincarnation. That is to say, I'd never paid any attention to him when he talked about it, and I never considered it when I thought of how I was connected to people, such as Annie or Grandpa or Connor himself. It would come as a great surprise when I received Annie's letter telling me what I had said my last night in her apartment, about her being my mother in a life before this one. Ordinarily I would have put it down to the fact that I was sleep-talking, or at least only semiconscious. But now I began to wonder what Doctor Connor knew, what he might have been hinting at. His knowledge had always seemed limitless to me; there was no subject upon which he couldn't discourse at length. He knew about medicine, cars, politics, economics, both world wars, all major religions, most of the great Western thinkers, and a few Eastern ones. I'd no trouble convincing myself that his learning had finally exceeded the bounds of the physical world and gone on to encompass the mysteries of the afterlife. I couldn't wait to talk to him. I would ask him point-blank what he meant by appearing in my dream, for I was talking myself into believing that even that power was in his repertoire.

Back in Mannville, I was met at the bus station by Grandpa and Mildred. Grandpa looked as if he had not slept in days.

"You leave for a while and the whole fucking world falls apart," he said, his voice cracked with fatigue. "I'm sorry to tell you this, Billy, but Connor's dead."

We stood in the churchyard, Grandpa and Mildred and I, having come straight there from the bus station. Before us was a freshly filled-in grave; the tombstone wouldn't be placed until the earth had settled. I'd missed the phone call informing Grandpa of Connor's death. I'd also missed the wake, the funeral, and the burial service; and now all these things were over and Connor was in the ground, and there was nothing I could do about it.

"I had no way to get in touch with you," Grandpa said apologetically. "And if I had I might have just let you alone till you got back anyway. I didn't want to ruin your first trip outside of Mannville for a funeral. And Connor wouldn't have wanted that either. Especially for his own funeral. Waste of time, he would have said. He would have preferred we just drop him in the Lake without any funeral at all, but you can't do that, of course. Against the law."

I was unable to speak.

"I hope you think I did the right thing," said Grandpa. "Not calling you, I mean."

"Annie doesn't have a phone anyway," I said. I was staring hard at the newly turned earth. "There was no way for you to find me."

"I know this is sudden for you, boy," said Grandpa. "It was for everyone. The whole thing."

Mildred, acutely aware, it seemed, of having recently walked in on a story that had already greatly unfolded, remained respectfully silent. One thin, birdlike hand reached out to take mine, and she squeezed it for a long moment before she let it drop again.

"He never knew what hit him," Grandpa went on. "The docs at the hospital said it was sudden, whatever it was. He'd left explicit instructions with them some time ago that he didn't want an autopsy. Said once he was gone it didn't make much difference how he went. But they think it was a massive stroke, a brain hemorrhage or something. His wife found him in his examination room. He was sitting at his desk, writing."

Writing. I squeezed my temples in my hands. The sun was nearly down, and the wind was cold and biting, though not nearly as cold as it had been in Montreal.

"How many people came to the funeral?" I asked.

"Whole damn town," Grandpa said proudly. "Even folks that owed him money." He straightened up and blew his nose. "I'm glad you visited him so much. I think he enjoyed talking to you."

"He was helping me," I said. "I don't see what he got out of it."

"You'll get it when you're old like us," said Mildred. "Nice to have young folks around."

"At least you made it up with him," I said to Grandpa.

The sun was completely down now, the sky overcast and seeming to loom just a few feet over our heads. I heard a clattering sound and realized it was Mildred's teeth knocking together. Then I heard another sound, a snuffling kind of sob, and I realized that Grandpa was, if only for a second, crying.

"Yeah. And now let's get home," said Grandpa. "This weather is just plain obnoxious."

Before we got back in the Galaxie I scooped a small handful of earth from the grave, tore a sheet from my notebook, and twisted it up with the dirt inside. I held the little package carefully on the slow ride home. It was exactly the sort of gesture Connor would have disdained making. "Ah, yes, *venerate* the sacred dirt," I could imagine him saying. "Never mind the fact that the rest of New York State is covered in billions of square feet of exactly the same stuff. Next thing you know they'll be erecting statues of me in the town square. Ridiculous. What good was I, anyway? I never even reproduced." But I needed it; I needed some kind of talisman. I'd missed the wake, missed the funeral, and most of all I'd never gotten the chance to ask him the questions I'd been formulating on the bus. I needed, at least, a small handful of the earth surrounding his body to remind me of him.

It was beginning to snow. Large soft flakes hit the windshield audible blows. In the morning Connor's grave would be covered with an inch or two of fine white frosting, and because it had no headstone, it would be invisible. Nobody would be able to find it until spring. It would be, to all appearances, as if he never was at all.

11

Doctor Connor's Letter, in Which Much Is Explained; I Visit Henry Hutchins

Dear Billy,

   By the time you read this letter, I will be dead. I don't know when that will be, of course, but it can't be too much longer now. I have seventy-two years under my belt, which is not so many by modern standards, but certainly more than enough by my own. I didn't think I would live even this long. Six months ago I suffered a mild stroke, which I told no one about because it didn't seem to harm me greatly; really, it was nothing more than a slight headache, but I recognized the signs. Last month I had another one. Then I knew it was only a matter of time. My father died in much the same way, having little strokes one after the other, until a big one sneaked up on him finally and carried him off. I know full well that I will go the same way, and that it will be happening shortly. I am resigned to it. Curious, even. I've always regarded death as a great adventure, and I must admit frankly, I've been excited about it for quite some time. I have both a clinical interest and a spiritual curiosity in what lies on the other side of this life. But I have some items of business to attend to before I go, and writing this letter to you is one of them, because there are some *things I need to tell you that may help you in your quest to become who you are.*

In late summer of 1970, very early in the morning, a pretty young woman whom I didn't recognize came to my office. I mention that I didn't recognize her because that was unusual—strangers almost never come through this town, as you well know. I've had the same patients for years, and there is hardly a person in Mannville I haven't seen naked. This young woman was a complete stranger, however, and what was more, she was in the final stages of pregnancy and had just begun having contractions. It was about five-thirty in the morning. She pounded on the door for me to let her in, and, when I did, told me that she was about to have a baby, and furthermore she intended to have it here, in my office. She'd been walking to the hospital, but realized she wasn't going to make it—the contractions were coming too strong and too close together—and as chance would have it, she happened to be right in front of my office when this fact became apparent. I offered to drive her to the hospital myself, but she was vehement in her refusal. Fate, she said, had decided when and where she was going to have the baby, and she believed in following the dictates of circumstance, not creating them. She was, in fact, what you call a "hippie," one of the few ever seen in Mannville. She wore a fringed leather jacket and had long brown hair, and she was quite lovely. She told me—and this is the only fact she willingly volunteered—that her name was Sky.

"Come now," I said. "Nobody names their child Sky. Surely you must have had another name at one point. What was it?"

So she told me her birth name—Eliza.

Eliza had another objection to going to the hospital, one she didn't tell me but that I deduced rather quickly. She knew that in the hospital, with all the forms one had to fill out, she had much less chance of keeping her identity a secret. This was of the utmost importance to her. Being an experienced doctor, it didn't take me long to figure out what the story was. She was unmarried, the father of her baby was obviously not present, and therefore she wanted her pregnancy to be kept a secret—probably from her family, who no doubt would disapprove of the whole business. It's an old story, one I've witnessed repeatedly in my career, with infinite variations on the same theme. I also knew without being told that her coming to my office was not as much of an accident as she wanted me to believe, for I had—and still have—a reputation as a doctor who will help young girls in trouble, and who will do it for free, if necessary. There is a subculture of the illegitimately pregnant. Word gets out, and when girls around here find themselves in trouble, eventually my name comes up. I do prenatal exams for free, and Eliza would not be the first woman to deliver a baby right here in my office. If a woman is having a baby, who am I to turn her away just because she hasn't any money? It would go against everything I believe in. It may surprise you also to know that I have performed numerous abortions in my day. My reasons for this should already be known to you—you know how I feel about overpopulation. I do feel a certain sadness during the procedure, of course, but that's just my own selfishness. I think my moral obligation extends further than the individual. I am more concerned with ensuring that a baby will have a happy life, with the chance for a happy future. There seems little point in introducing a new person to the world if nobody can help him get started in it. But my assistance to women is not limited to abortions, or to free obstetric services. There is, in fact, nothing I will not do to help a panicked young mother bring her child along. I didn't become a doctor for money. I did it for humanity's sake.

Eliza was too far along for an abortion, of course, and I was certain that if she'd wanted to have one she would have done so earlier. In the few minutes I'd known her, she had already struck me as very strong-willed and independent, entirely capable of making her own decisions and following through with them. This suggested to me that since she wanted the baby to come into the world, perhaps she had some means of assuring it would have a decent chance for success. But she also must have known I wouldn't ask any questions. That seemed very important to her. She wanted nobody to know her name. It was only with the greatest reluctance that she told me her real first name, and she begged me to keep it a secret. On the subject of her family name, she remained unmovable, and after one or two vain attempts to get her to divulge it, I let the matter rest.

I rang upstairs and told my wife I would be needing her assistance. She and I prepared the birthing room, made young Eliza comfortable, and settled down to the long business of waiting. Birthing is, for the most part, a waiting game. It can go on for hours. This is precisely what happened in Eliza's case. I changed the sign on my front door to read THE DOCTOR IS OUT, so nobody would wander in. My regular patients could go to the hospital if they were having an emergency. I timed Eliza's contractions with one hand on her belly and the other holding a stopwatch. While we were waiting, I asked her some questions on the pretext of needing a medical history. Thus I discovered that she was twenty-three, that this was her first pregnancy, and that she was not from New York State.

"And the father?" I asked. "What do you know about him?"

"He's dead," she told me, her eyes welling up with tears. "He died in Vietnam."

"I'm sorry," I said, and I meant it. I had strong objections to our involvement in the Vietnam conflict. There is nothing sadder to me than a young mother bringing her child into the world alone, and there were many children in America without fathers because of that stupid war. "Do you have friends to help you once the child is born? Or family?" I asked her.

She shook her head—unable to speak at the moment because a particularly strong contraction had just begun and she was trying not to cry out. She was brave and tough, and already I was developing a great respect for her. When the contraction was over, I asked her, "Were you very close with him?"

She laid her head back on the pillow. "He was beautiful," she sighed. I was silent. I hadn't asked her what he'd looked like; I sensed, however, that she wasn't referring to his appearance, but to some general quality he possessed. And I was right, for a moment later she went on, "He was totally right on. Totally clear. He just zoomed in on you in an instant. No head games, no power trips. His soul was clean. And old."

I translated this in my head. Her description, once I decoded it, sounded familiar. A few bells were starting to go off in my head.

"Was he from here?" I asked. "From Mannville?"

But she couldn't answer because another contraction was gripping her. I felt her cervix; it was fully dilated. She was ready to start pushing.

Mrs. Connor and I stayed with her all that day and into the evening. She dilated around noon, I remember. It was a long and difficult labor, and several times I wrestled with the question of whether I should have her transported to the hospital. But when I ventured to broach the subject to her again, she remained adamant in her refusal.

"This baby is going to need to be strong in his life," she said, her speech, under duress, becoming free of slang. "Better to find out now if he's got what it takes to make it."

That was the last time I asked.

She delivered the baby at around six o'clock that evening. It was a boy, nineteen inches, seven and a half pounds. The labor nearly killed her, and the baby too. Mrs. Connor cleaned him off and got him breathing while I stitched up young Eliza and got her cleaned up. I'd had to perform an episiotomy, which is normal during a woman's first delivery, and there was blood everywhere.

Eliza and her baby stayed for nearly six weeks—she confessed she had nowhere to go, and we were more than happy to let her stay with us. Despite her reticence, she was very likable. We gave her one of the guest rooms upstairs. Her recovery was rapid, and the baby, after the initial shock of his difficult arrival had worn off, showed every sign of a strong constitution.

Eliza begged us not to tell anyone of her existence. Seeing as how she was completely helpless, my wife and I respected her wishes, though of course we were curious. We were also perplexed by the fact that she hadn't given the baby a name. When we asked her about this, she said that it wasn't for her to decide what the baby would be called. She would leave it up to those who would know him better.

"I don't like this," said Mrs. Connor. "There's something strange going on."

"I know," I said. "But it's none of our business."

"I'm having a hard time remembering that," my wife replied. I thought I knew what she meant. She felt she was at least entitled to know what the real story was, after all we'd done for the young mother and her baby son.

"We promised we would never ask for payment of any kind from girls like her," I reminded her. "That includes information too. If she doesn't want to tell us, she doesn't have to."

"Well, I can still ask her," said Mrs. Connor.

It was then I did something I had never done to my wife before, and have never done since: I gave her an order.

"You are absolutely forbidden to ask her anything at all," I said. "If you can't do that, then you are to stay away from her."

Needless to say, my wife never quite forgave me for that. I wasn't just being difficult, however. I was reminding her of a promise we'd made. She seemed to want to forget about that promise, and of course I knew why—she was becoming attached to the baby, and didn't want him to go. Neither did I.

When Eliza was finally ready to leave, to my astonishment she produced a wallet full of cash.

"How much do I owe you?" she asked.

I did some calculating. At regular rates, including medical fees, groceries, and the price of a room, her bill would have come to something like three thousand dollars. I hadn't any intention of asking her for money, of course, but I did take the step of conferring with my wife, to get her opinion on the matter. She was in agreement with me—she usually was, which was why we married in the first place; we felt the same way on most subjects. But my wife wanted to take things one step further.

"Tell her we'll forget about money if she just tells us about herself," she said.

"That's blackmail!" I protested.

"It's not blackmail," retorted Mrs. Connor. "It's insurance. I have a feeling this information will come in handy someday."

"What are you talking about?" I asked her.

"It's just a feeling," she repeated. And I'm sorry to say that since my wife was able to give me no solid, rational reason for wanting to know more about Eliza, I contravened her will and told Eliza she didn't have to give us any money, nor did I ask her any more questions. This appeared to give her some relief. I had suspected it would. I knew she wouldn't stay around Mannville, and she would need the money to get wherever she was going. As I said before, I didn't become a doctor for money. And somehow I knew we wouldn't get any more information out of her. My wife never forgave me for this either, and as it turned out, she was right. This information would have come in handy later, simply for the sake of satisfying the natural human urge

to know something of one's origins.

The day Eliza left with her baby, Mrs. Connor sat in the kitchen and cried. This was unlike her, but I wasn't surprised. I was moved to tears myself. We had grown very attached to the young woman, despite her air of mystery, for it was obvious that she was well bred, and we admired her grace and strength. We'd also grown attached to the baby. Mrs. Connor and I had agreed even before we were married that children were not for us. She had her reasons, and I had mine, and though they were not the same reasons, our goals were identical, and things seemed to work out fine. But you can't watch a baby being born, and spend the next month and a half watching him grow, holding him and changing his diapers and cooing and clucking and doing all the things people do with babies, without feeling a strong bond. Eliza's departure was difficult for both of us.

Her last words to us were of thanks. "You've helped bring a little man into the world," she said. "A wonderful little man." And she was gone.

As things would turn out, however, we had misunderstood her. What she was saying was not "a wonderful little man" in the sense of a fine boy-child. She meant—and I'm sure you've deduced this by now, Billy—"a wonderful little Mann." For this baby was you, William Amos Mann IV, and Eliza was your mother.

The very next day, your grandfather came marching into my office with a baby in a picnic basket. I was hard-pressed to conceal my astonishment, my joy, my general excitement, for I recognized the baby immediately as Eliza's. A few questions sufficed to prove to me that your grandfather knew nothing of the mother. It was obvious to him, however, that the father had been Eddie, his own son. Once he pointed that out to me I could have kicked myself for not recognizing it sooner. And I knew you were Eliza's baby because of a birthmark on the back of your head. You probably don't know you have it. It's just above your hairline, between the two tendons at the back of your neck, and it's about the size of a quarter. If you were to cut off your hair, you would find it exactly where I'm describing it.

I said nothing to your grandfather about the fact that I already knew you intimately. But I can never describe the incredible joy that washed over me upon seeing you again, and knowing that you were, after all, going to be part of my life, part of Mannville. I felt as though you were my own flesh and blood. Your grandpa left you with me for a brief time to go buy some supplies, and as soon as he was gone I rang upstairs for my wife. She came down in a flash, and together we held you and cried tears of love and joy. We were barely able to contain ourselves. There was no sign of Eliza, so we knew that she'd abandoned you. It was—and I would not say this lightly—one of the defining moments of my life. My wife and I have always loved you beyond any reason, because we've felt that you are ours, and you'll never know how hard it's been not to show it more than we have. But we promised each other then and there that we would never tell your grandfather, or you, until you were old enough, the real story of your birth.

Now for the hard part. You may be angry with me just now for not telling you the whole story sooner. I beg you to remember that my wife and I are reasonable, intelligent people, and that we always have good reasons for the things we do. I'm not bragging—I'm explaining. There were several mitigating factors that caused us to make our decision. First of all, Eliza had wanted her identity to be kept secret, and for all the anger we felt toward her just then for abandoning you, we had to admit we didn't know the whole story. There may very well have been a good reason for you not to know more about her. Therefore, since we weren't capable of making an informed decision, we decided on secrecy. I still feel we made the right decision.

Secondly, we didn't want to interfere in any way with the bond forming between you and your grandfather, for the fact was, we knew you much better than he did at that time, and to behave otherwise would have created confusion. Later on, as you got older, things resolved themselves naturally, until it was simply too late to come out with the truth. We felt it was important for you to live your life with him and not be influenced by outside factors. Your grandfather was a very sad man, and to see him made happy again was deeply satisfying to both of us. He felt you were his, that God had brought you to him to save the Manns from disappearing altogether, and we didn't want to take away any of his joy by expressing our own.

Perhaps these reasons seem silly to you, but consider finally the fact that I am a doctor. My decision was made also for professional reasons, and ultimately I was bound by law not to reveal anything of Eliza's *identity. That was the deciding factor.*

But I'm dead now, to state the fact bluntly, and therefore no longer obligated to follow the laws dictated to me by the state. Where I am going, no lawyers are admitted, and I have no fear of prosecution.

You once asked me if I knew who your mother was. If you can recall the words of our conversation, you will remember that I neither admitted nor denied knowledge. I did say I didn't know her, and that was the truth; I knew almost nothing about her. But these are technicalities, and I admit I am splitting hairs to assuage my own conscience. I deliberately concealed from you the information I had concerning your mother, and that has, from time to time, caused me some guilt. But I ask you to trust that I had good reasons. What I told you that day was that you needed to concern yourself with what was now, and to focus on who you were. The truth, I knew, would come to you with time, and I wanted to wait until you were ready before I gave out all the facts. You're ready now. Very soon, I feel, you will be leaving Mannville and setting out on the sort of quest that most young people undertake at one time or another—to find out who you are, what sort of material you're made of. In your case, the question of who you are is a very literal one. To tell you earlier what I knew about your mother would have created endless problems of confusion and restlessness, and I didn't want to do that to you. You were always a happy child, despite the fact that you were raised in strange and unusual circumstances. I didn't want that happiness to disappear.

One of the few facts I was able to establish about your mother was that she was from the southwest. One could tell just by looking at her that she wasn't an easterner: her skin had a healthy tan glow to it, and her eyes—how do I say this?—were used to a bigger sky. She could see farther than most of us can. I have no idea what I mean by that, I'm sorry to say, but if you ever meet her, if she's still alive, you'll understand. She mentioned in passing certain places she had been through, some of which you'll recognize, perhaps: Santa Fe, Denver, Needles, Jackson Hole, Missoula. I looked these places up on a map; they are all out west. She was somewhat of a wanderer, I gathered, but there was nothing about her that suggested vagrancy. She was clean, free of disease, she had some money, she seemed mentally alert and stable and even happy, considering the circumstances. She was a captivating person, too, intelligent and quick-witted, and that made it all the more frustrating for my wife and myself, because she was the kind of person one would wish to know better no matter how well one knew her already.

I have no idea how she met your father. She would have been a year or two older than he, but there is nothing unusual in that. What struck me as really odd was the difference in their situations. Your father was the all-American type, clean-cut and dutiful and proud to serve his country unquestioningly. That sort of person generally didn't associate with hippies. You could say that they were from completely different camps, that they stood, at least on the surface, for completely different ideals. But it was easy to understand why any man would have been attracted to Eliza, and it isn't hard either to see how she would have been attracted to Eddie. Her description of him was perfect. It was almost as if he was simply an actor playing a part in life— one that he believed in, of course, but one that didn't limit him either. His role, his identity, was not all of who he was. He went much deeper than just being a football player, or a pilot. In speaking to him, I often had the feeling that I was really talking with someone who was much older than I, who understood much more than a small-town boy ought to. He was, in short, an oddity, an anomaly, and he knew it. Instead of becoming disenfranchised, however, he turned his situation around and used it as a way of elevating himself above the rest of us. Everything he did and said hinted at an awareness of something higher, of whatever it is that lay behind everything and gave it meaning. I have no doubt it was this quality in him Eliza was referring to when she said his soul was "old," for this is the sort of behavior you might expect from someone of great age and wisdom, not from a small-town football jock. They were a perfect match for each other, and I'm sorry it didn't work out for them to be together.

No doubt soon you will be ready to begin looking for her. I've told you as much as I can about how to find her. If I were you, I would look out west, perhaps in one of the places she mentioned having been through in the course of her journeys. Look for a tall woman, light brown hair, gray eyes, a Roman nose, a soft, husky voice. I'm sorry I can't tell you more.

And in closing I would like also to say that

The letter ended there.

Connor had been writing at his desk when the final stroke, the one for which he'd been looking over his shoulder the last six months, finally came for him, just as he'd predicted. It wouldn't have surprised me if Connor had known exactly when death was coming; it appeared, by the almost-finished state of the letter, that he had pretty nearly timed the end of his life to within a few minutes. Telling me about my mother was that last item of unfinished business he was referring to. He couldn't leave until this one final account had been closed.

I racked my brains trying to figure out what he might have been about to write in the last paragraph, but it was no good—you can't read the minds of the dead. I gave it up as fruitless. At least, I thought, he'd gotten the important parts down.

Mrs. Connor told me in a note that she took the letter from his cold hands, sealed it up, and had it delivered it to me the day after I returned from Montreal. I never got the chance to discuss the events of my birth with her. She was five years older than Doctor Connor— it appeared that he, like me, had a penchant for older women—and they'd been married for nearly fifty years, so it came as no surprise to anyone when she died peacefully in her sleep only a few days after Connor himself, in perfect health and with twenty years left in her, if she'd wanted to live them. Apparently, however, she hadn't. She'd chosen instead to rejoin her husband.

"Who could blame her, poor dear?" said Mildred. "Who would want to live alone after being happily married all that time?" And she put her birdy little hand on top of Grandpa's large hairy one, as they rocked side by side in their rocking chairs. Grandpa had made her a chair in his carriage-house workshop. An ornate carved eagle adorned the headrest. He'd turned the spindles himself on a lathe.

"Well, I missed this round," Grandpa said.

"What do you mean?" I asked.

"This round of three. Death always comes in threes. Simpson, Connor, his wife. It's a fact."

"That's ridiculous."

"Of course it's ridiculous," he said. "And it's infuriating. But it's the way it is. It always happens."

"I've never heard of that," I said.

"It's an old superstition, but it's true. And you're too young to have experienced much of it. Watch and see. The older you get, the more people you know start to kick off. And they go in threes. Anyway, what was in that letter?"

"News," I said. It was then that I realized Connor had never told Grandpa any of what I now knew. He had just as much a right to know as I did, so I let him read the letter. He read through it twice, right there in the living room. I expected perhaps that he would get angry, or emotional, or at least excited, but he only rubbed his forehead thoughtfully and said, "I want you to finish high school first."

"What do you mean?"

"Before you go traipsing off," he said. "You absolutely have to finish high school."

"What makes you think I'm going traipsing off?" I said, but before the words were out of my mouth I knew he was right. Once again, Grandpa had proved he knew me almost better than I knew myself. I hadn't had time to think it through yet, but once I had, there would be only one possible course of action. I would have to go west and find my mother, and I wanted to get started immediately.

"That'll take forever!" I protested.

"It will take exactly one and a half years," he corrected me calmly. "After that, you can do whatever you want. But if you leave now you'll be screwed. You can't do anything these days without a diploma from high school at least. And you ought to plan on college, too."

"College, shmollege," I said. "I'm going to be a writer."

"Writers go to college too," he told me. "They even have special writer's colleges."

"So what? That doesn't mean I have to go to one. It's experience that counts for writers anyway. Not some dumb piece of paper."

"You don't have to go right away," he said. "See a little of the world first."

"*You* never went to college," I pointed out.

"That," said Grandpa, "is precisely the reason you ought to go. There will never be any manuals written about how to live life according to the Thomas Mann school of thought. My mother wanted me to go to Harvard. I should have at least gone to the community college. Taken some courses in business or something." In previous times, he would have added, "so I would have known better than to buy those damn ostriches." But since he'd stopped drinking, he'd also stopped beating himself up over the Ostrich Fiasco.

"This Eliza person," I said. "Does she sound familiar? Ever see her?"

"No," said Grandpa. "I can't figure out where Eddie would have met someone like that. He didn't hang around with hippies."

"But he might have if he'd met one," I pointed out. "And obviously he did meet at least one. He wouldn't have been the type to look down his nose at people just because they had long hair. Would he?"

"No," Grandpa admitted. "No, he wouldn't. What Connor wrote was true. Everybody connected with Eddie, and not just on the surface. It was a deep thing. He had a way of looking right into people."

"Maybe she was the same way," I said.

"It sounds like she was," said Grandpa. And I could see he was thinking hard, trying to remember back to the days when Eddie was home last. "He would have to have met her while he was home on leave for the last time," he said. "Which was for a month, in November of sixty-nine."

"Did he stick around Mannville the whole time he was on leave?"

"No, he went to Buffalo twice," said Grandpa. "To visit friends. He had an Air Force buddy there who was on leave at the same time. Huh. I'll try and remember his name. Maybe he would have met your—this Eliza person." Neither of us could quite bring ourselves to refer to Eliza as my mother yet. After all these years of not knowing who she was, it seemed strange to have a name to put to her, and a physical description. The idea would take some getting used to.

"Yes," I said. "Try."

There was something else nagging at me, which I chose not to share with Grandpa. It was the note my mother had left on my basket. Why had she referred to me as a bastard? If she was so carefree and easygoing, why did she hate me? It seemed to me that if she was really a hippie—as far as I knew, hippies stood for peace and love and going with the flow of things—she would have kept me with her no matter what. But not only did she give me up; she called me names. It hurt me to think that if I sought her out she might still not want to see me, even after all this time. She might have another family, one with a husband and legitimate children who would despise me for being illegitimate. What if she was rich now? She'd think I was trying to get at her money. And if she was poor, maybe she'd think—as had Elsie Orfenbacher—that millions of dollars don't just disappear overnight, that there must be something left she could get her hands on. "It's me," I could hear myself saying, "Eddie's bastard—the one you didn't keep." And then—what? Tears of welcome? Shouts of accusation? Guilt? Happiness? Remorse?

"This is not so simple," I said. "There's a good chance she won't want to see me again, isn't there?" Maybe she was just trying to distance herself from me, I thought. Maybe she had to call me names so she wouldn't love me so much.

"Well, it's a big risk. You never know how these things are going to turn out."

"Do you think she thinks about me?"

"I'm sure of it," said Mildred. "Especially if you were her first baby."

"If she's still alive, that is," added Grandpa. "You have to consider every possibility."

"Your grandfather's right. She might have been sick, dying or something," said Mildred. "I can't imagine how she could keep a baby for six weeks and *then* give it up. Maybe she wanted to keep you but had a good reason why she couldn't."

"She could have been a criminal," I said.

"Now I really don't think so," said Grandpa.

"But there was that lady in the news who helped rob a bank almost twenty years ago—she was a hippie, wasn't she? She got married and had a family, and nobody suspected a thing. She had kids and everything. She was even on the PTA. Then the Feds came and busted her. Maybe my mother was on the lam."

"I don't think she was on the lam," said Mildred.

But regardless of whether she was on the lam or not, it was beginning to sink in that it was my mother we were talking about—my actual biological mother, about whom I'd never known enough even to speculate. Now she had a name, and a face, and I had several details I could put together. Over the next few weeks these details became bones, and I added flesh in little bits here and there until I had a real live mother in my head, one who walked and talked and was from a distant and mysterious place out west. I drew pictures of her based on Connor's description. Soon the walls of my room were papered with drawings of a young hippie woman with soft brown hair and a Roman nose. I discovered that I was a terrible artist, but it didn't matter. What did matter was that I finally had a clue about where to begin looking.

I alternated between soaring to new heights of elation and grumbling and grousing over my delay in leaving Mannville. I was ecstatic over Connor's revelation, furious at Grandpa. It was, in fact, the only time I could remember that Grandpa had ever expressly forbidden me to do anything. He'd never been much of a disciplinarian. I blamed that on his drinking. His recent sense that right and wrong must be enforced I blamed on his newfound sobriety. But when school began again in January I was resigned to it, and gradually I realized, to my immense annoyance, that Grandpa was once again right. I was at least comforted by the fact that my immediate future was laid out for me; even if I had no idea of where to begin looking for my mother, at least I had something to do when I graduated.

This seemed to put me in a class by myself among my friends at school. Nobody else my age seemed to have a clear idea of what they would take up when they graduated. Some of them wanted to go to college but didn't know what they would study. Others knew already that they wouldn't go to college but would go to work in garages or retail stores or the grain mill outside of town. Others didn't seem to care what happened to them; these were the ones who floated through life carelessly, getting what they could out of things without having to work too hard.

Privately, all three groups of people alternately amused and bored me. I didn't seem to belong to any of them. Neither had my father. And now that I knew something about her, I was sure my mother hadn't either. There always seemed to be another path than the most obvious one, and that was the one my people took. That was because we were Manns. Even my mother, although she must have had a different last name, was one of us in spirit. And we weren't normal people, for better or for worse. Normal things didn't happen to us.

Grandpa found a cigar box of full of letters in the attic. He'd stuck it up there among the rafters after the news came that my father was dead, in an uncharacteristic gesture of denial; it was more his style to keep relics of Eddie in plain view, such as the copy of *A Farewell to Arms*, which still sat on my father's desk and had not been moved since 1969.

Somehow in my wanderings, I had failed to discover the box of letters myself. My hopes surged when I saw it, but it contained only a few items of interest. There were three letters written on thin blue military stationery and a postcard from Thailand. There was also a funny-looking necklace, a choker with hundreds of tiny white beads. This I unclasped and refastened around my neck. It fit snugly, as though it had been made for me. Then I turned my attention to the postcard.

The front bore a picture of a man pulling a middle-aged couple in a rickshaw down a dirt road near what looked like a jungle. The man doing the pulling was small and brown and nearly naked, and the couple in the rickshaw were white and puffy-looking, like two fancy foreign pastries being delivered to a bakery. They wore excessive amounts of clothing and superior expressions on their faces. For some reason the picture revolted me. I turned it over and read:

> *Dear Pop—Am in Thailand. Rode in one of these things yesterday. Fun but I felt sorry for the guy pulling it. See you in November. Love Eddie.*

That was exactly how I would have expected my father to feel—relishing the feeling of riding in a rickshaw for the first time, but hating it that someone had to pull him. I imagined him hopping out and insisting that the bewildered coolie ride instead, then trotting around the jungle roads of Thailand in his blue Air Force uniform with the tired little man in tow.

The postcard was dated August 1969—it was likely that Eddie hadn't yet met my mother, or at least that she wasn't yet pregnant with me.

The letters were dated October 1969, January 1970, and May 1970. During the interval between the first two, Eddie had come home and created me. It was even possible that as he wrote the last letter, he knew I was coming.

I took the letters to my room and scanned through them. They were short, printed laboriously in cramped writing. The ink changed colors once or twice in each letter, suggesting that he wrote them in several sittings with different pens, and perhaps that it was difficult for him to put his thoughts on paper. I had every intention of reading them thoroughly, but I was too excited just then to do anything but scan them. First I wanted to find names. Any name at all would be a possible lead. I was looking first of all for the name Eliza, but it didn't appear. Neither did Sky. He mentioned his base commander, which gave me some hope, but in the next sentence I read that he had been killed in a Jeep collision, so I forgot about him. It wasn't until the end of the last letter that I saw another name, and my heart leaped up into my throat and pounded there insistently.

> *You remember that guy Henry Hutchins I went to visit in Buffalo when I was home? Well, he got lucky. He got a million-dollar wound right in the ass. A sniper snuck up close to the base and managed to nail three of our guys before we got him. Henry was the first one of them. I guess he had just bent over to tie his shoe when the gook pulled the trigger. Bingo—he gets to go home for good.*

A clue.
And Buffalo was only an hour or so away.

The Hutchins' home was one in a series of row houses in downtown Buffalo, all of them identical, separated from each other by only a few feet of dingy cement driveway. I grew claustrophobic just looking at them. Henry Hutchins himself explained to me that the entire neighborhood had been built by a tire factory for the purpose of housing its workers; it rented the homes to them at exorbitant rates, which they were just able to afford, thus ensuring that they would never be able to move somewhere else and work for another factory.

"It's an old system of exploitation," Henry told me. "It started with the first factories in England back in the seventeen hundreds, right at the beginning of the Industrial Revolution. That's when people first perfected the art of taking advantage of each other. Before then it was serfdom, feudalism, peasants working their fingers to the bone for the lord of the manor until they dropped dead. Like the southern plantations with their slaves. Factories are just another kind of plantation, really, except they pay a little better. My family worked for the tire factory for three generations. When I came home from the war I bought the house. God knows why. I always hated it. Come on in. You look just like your dad, you know. But I'm sure you hear that a lot."

Hutchins was a small, balding man who spoke quietly but forcefully. He wore thick glasses, the lenses of which made his eyes look the size of half-dollars. We entered the house and came into a darkened living room.

"This is my mother," he said, indicating a white blur in one corner. I looked more closely and saw a very old woman sitting in a recliner, staring at me vacantly.

"How do you do, ma'am," I said.

"She won't answer," Henry Hutchins said. "She has Alzheimer's." He confessed this in a whisper, as though afraid I would find it repulsive.

"Who is that, Jacob?" asked the old woman, in a high, trembling voice.

"I'm Henry," said Henry. "This is Eddie Mann's son, Billy, Mom. He came up from Mannville." To me he said, "Jacob was my brother."

"Poor Eddie," said the woman. "Is he here too?"

"No, Mom," said Henry. He indicated a couch to me and sat down opposite it. Then he stood up again. "I'm sorry. Manners. I don't get a lot of visitors. Would you like some tea or something?"

"Sure," I said. Henry went into the kitchen and ran water into a kettle. I looked again at the old lady.

"Who are you?" she asked. "Are you a friend of Henry's?"

"I'm Eddie Mann's son, Billy," I said.

"Poor Eddie," she said. "Is he here too?"

"No, Mom," said Henry from the kitchen.

"There's a man in here, Jacob," called his mother.

"Okay, Mom," said Henry. "Come on and take a nap."

"Am I tired?"

"Yes," said Henry. He led his mother from the chair into a bedroom at the rear of the house. I could hear him say, "Swallow it. Don't spit it out. Good girl . . . Want some more water?"

"No," she said. A door shut and Henry reappeared with a tea tray.

"Sorry about that," he said.

"Don't apologize."

"Company works her up. Everything confuses her now. Anyway."

"I hope this wasn't a bad time," I said.

Hutchins dismissed this concern with a wave of his hand. "I'm glad to have her here and not in some home," he said. "She doesn't have much longer left. It's pretty advanced."

He sat down and sipped his tea.

"I presume you're not just here to reminisce," he said, getting down to business. "I don't mean to sound rude, but this is the first I've ever heard of you. I was kind of skeptical when I got your phone call. I never knew Eddie had a son. But I'm sure you are who you say you are. Which means you must have been born after he was killed."

"That's right."

"Which also means you never knew your father, if you'll forgive me being so direct?"

"No."

"How sad," said Henry Hutchins. "I'm really sorry to hear that."

"It's okay," I said. "I mean, yeah, I guess I would have preferred to have him around. But I never knew him anyway. So it's not like I knew I was missing anything."

"You're a tough kid."

I smiled, but my smile was lost in the dimness of the house.

"Did Eddie get married?" Henry looked doubtful, pursing his lips. "No, he didn't," he answered himself. "He never had time. Which means," he said, a look of satisfied understanding coming over his mild features, "that you're here to ask me some questions. Am I right?"

"Yeah," I said. "You should have been a detective."

"That's what your father used to tell me," said Hutchins. For the first time he smiled. "Which proves you are who you say you are. Not that you'd have a reason to lie. If you don't mind my asking, who raised you?"

"My grandfather."

"Eddie's dad, you mean, or your mother's?"

"Eddie's."

"Ahh," said Hutchins. "I met your grandfather once. How is he?"

"Sober," I said.

Hutchins nodded. "Not an easy chore," he said. "I battled alcohol myself when I came home from the war. It nearly won. I'm glad to hear he stopped drinking."

"Yeah." I was surprised—Hutchins didn't look like my idea of an alcoholic. He was neat, composed, intelligent. For some ridiculous reason he struck me as too short to be a heavy drinker.

"So," he said. "What exactly would you like to know?"

"I'm trying to find my mother," I said. I'd intended to be a little less direct. There was something embarrassing about admitting to a stranger that my parentage was a mystery, but in the few minutes I'd known Hutchins, I'd come to trust him. It was easy to see how he and my father had become friends. And he himself had taken a risk in introducing his mother to me. We were baring our weaknesses to each other. I felt suddenly that I had a powerful ally in my quest.

Hutchins smiled again. "An ancient story," he said. "Young man in search of his origins. Yes. You want to find out who your mother was. Is she still alive? I mean, do you know that for sure?"

"I don't know anything," I admitted. "I know her name, and I know what she looked like. That's it."

"Tell me what it was."

"Eliza," I said. "Or maybe Sky."

Hutchins closed his eyes.

"Tall woman," he said.

"Yes!"

"Strikingly beautiful. Long brown hair. An earth child. A hippie, as they used to say."

"You've met her." A rush of elation surged through me. It was an effort to keep myself from flinging my teacup into the air and doing a little dance.

"Yes," said Hutchins. He opened his eyes and came back from whatever world he'd gone into. "I met her once."

"Only once?"

"Don't be disappointed," he said. "It was a significant meeting."

"When was it?"

"A party," he said. "When was that, now, let me think . . ."

"November of nineteen sixty-nine?" I suggested.

"You've been doing your homework," said Hutchins. "Yes, that's right. We were home on leave."

"And Eddie came up here to visit you."

"Yes."

"Where was the party?" I produced a small notebook and a pen and wrote down the word *party*. I looked up to see Hutchins trying to conceal his amusement. "Just so I don't forget," I said sheepishly.

"I'm not laughing at you," he assured me. "It's just that you're so serious."

"It's a big deal," I said.

"I understand. Do you know why?"

"Why what?"

"Why you want to find her?"

I was wordless. "I—well—why wouldn't I?"

"It doesn't matter," he said. "I'm not implying you shouldn't be looking. It's just that some people would be content never knowing. Most people, I guess. Most people are too lazy to look this far for answers. They'd give up. But you Manns are not like most people, are you?"

"No, we're not," I said, and I knew instinctively that I wouldn't have to explain myself any further, because I could tell by the way he moved and spoke and how he looked at me knowingly through his spectacles that Henry Hutchins wasn't like most people either.

"Anyway," he went on. "We were out on the town. It was a weekend, I remember, probably a Saturday. I was still drinking then, of course, and Eddie and I had a few slugs of booze under our belts. We were at a bar. Don't bother trying to find it—it's closed now. Fire. We were wearing our uniforms, which was unusual. We hated our uniforms."

"My father hated his uniform?"

"Well, not hated. He was proud to serve his country. So was I. But things in Vietnam had gone pretty sour. And neither of us really liked taking orders. I think we had the idea we were staging some kind of protest, going out and boozing it up so everyone would see us and think, *Look at those two clowns*. Not a protest against the war—a protest against the military. Our own personal protest, for our own private cause.

"A few people shouted insults at us on the street. They were hippies, I remember. I don't know if you know this, but there were serious doubts in America about why we were in Vietnam in the first place. A lot of people had the idea that we were over there just butchering people left and right. That we enjoyed it. Hippies in particular hated us, which"—he chuckled—"always struck me as ironic since they supposedly stood for peace and love. Anyway. We were walking down the sidewalk, kinda tipsy, and feeling too good to get into a fight. These hippies were shouting at us from the other side of the street. We went into the bar without paying any attention to them. No, wait—Eddie flashed them a peace sign. We had a good laugh over that. That made them even angrier, and they followed us in, I remember. There were three or four of them. Four. Three men and one woman."

"What happened?"

"They called us baby-killers," he said. "Boy, was that a mistake. It was a blue-collar type of bar, and a lot of the patrons were former servicemen themselves, veterans of Korea and the Second World War. Older men. They had a particular understanding of war that wasn't shared by these hippies. Most kids who had the leisure to grow their hair long and roam around the country came from families with lots of money, you know. They were able to afford college, and so they didn't get drafted. Which, as you might guess, caused a great deal of animosity among those who couldn't afford college. I couldn't afford it either, not before the war. I went on the GI Bill after I got back. But the war was never a moral issue for the working class, at least not until later, when it was over and they had time to think about it. Back then they didn't have a choice. You got called, you went. It's always been that way. It wasn't within their power to question the government. And if they had, they couldn't have done anything about it anyway. They just would have been causing trouble. Rocking the boat. You follow me?"

"I think so," I said.

"People still trusted the government back then," he said. "Although that was just starting to change. So we're in this bar full of beefy ex-Army and Marine and Navy guys, factory workers, and these hippies are hassling us and they follow us in, and suddenly they look around and think to themselves, *Oh shit, what have we walked into?*

Everyone in there had gotten quiet. And then there was this sudden explosion of people toward them."

"You mean they rushed them?"

"Yeah. They were about to get their asses kicked."

"Jeez."

"And I hate to confess I thought they deserved it," he said. "They had pushed me just a little too far. I kind of wanted to get in a few licks myself."

"You?"

"I know I don't look like the brawling type," he said. "But I was a different man when I was drinking. Anyway. I turned to Eddie and was about to say, 'Let's get in on this,' when I realized he wasn't there."

"He left?"

"No." Hutchins laughed. "Somehow he was suddenly in the middle of the whole thing. He was trying to protect them."

"Protect the *hippies*?"

"Exactly," said Hutchins. "He was standing between the hippies and the guys who wanted to get at them. Which caused some confusion on both sides, as you might imagine."

"What was he thinking?"

"He didn't want to see them get beat up," said Hutchins. "It was really as simple as that."

"Go on," I said.

"Well, what happened next was the kind of thing you might see in a movie. Eddie actually gave a speech. Everyone just sort of stopped what they were doing because he had taken them all by surprise. The hippies were surprised that he was protecting them, and the bar guys were surprised too. And Eddie just stood there in the middle of them. He wasn't as tall as you are, and I couldn't see his head through all the people. I could just see his hands, because he was waving his arms around while he was talking."

"What was he saying?"

"He was talking about peace," said Henry Hutchins softly. "He didn't want any more fighting. He hated fighting. Odd, really, considering how many people he probably killed as a pilot. But he told everyone that he and I were home on leave for only a little while longer, and he told them how good it was to be home again, because America was a peaceful place and to him it meant safety. He said that even though war was a horrible thing, and maybe the peaceniks had a point, just for that night he wanted everyone to forget about it and be friends. And he asked them to do that for our sake—mine and his. So that when we shipped back in-country we would have pleasant memories of home, and not of more fighting. I can't say it as well as he did. He was really eloquent, you know, when he got going. He couldn't write very well, but he could really sway people when he was in the mood."

"So what happened?"

"Exactly what he wanted. Which I knew would happen as soon as he started talking. Once Eddie decided he was going to convince you of something, he kept at you until you were convinced, and it didn't take him very long, either. What happened was he made them all shake hands."

"You're kidding."

"Hell no," said Henry Hutchins. "And then the hippies came in and sat at the bar. The whole place was still quiet. Eddie had taken control, you see, and everyone was waiting and watching him to see what to do next."

"What did he do?"

"All he did was sit down. I think they were expecting something a little more dramatic, but he disappointed them on that count. He brought the hippies over to the bar and ordered them a round of beers, and we all moved to a table and sat around it."

"And one of them was Eliza?"

"We didn't get to names right away," he said. "But there was only one woman with them. In fact, she was the only woman in the whole bar, but that didn't seem to bother her one bit. I don't think she was even aware of that. She was absolutely beautiful. I couldn't take my eyes off her. I never stood a chance with her, of course, not with Eddie in the same room. She was three or four inches taller than he was, but she was looking at him like he was a Greek god who'd just dropped by in his flaming chariot for a quick drink. And Eddie kept looking at her, too."

"He was putting the moves on her?"

"Don't get me wrong," said Henry. "Eddie was very aware of the

power he had over people, and he never abused it. He hated to dom-
inate a situation. Most of the time he just sat back and let things take
their course, except when he absolutely couldn't keep his mouth shut.
That was part of his power, even. That kind of sitting back. You were
aware of him even when he wasn't saying a word. But I think everyone knew right away there was something in the air between him and
Sky. Some kind of electricity, or chemistry, or whatever branch of science you wish to attribute it to. Curious, isn't it, that we speak of love
in such scientific terms? Anyway. No, Eddie wasn't the kind of guy to
put moves on women. Part of it was because he didn't have to—they
came to him instead. But part of it was that he thought there was
something indecent about it. He thought it cheapened women to get
hit on. Or maybe he thought it cheapened the men who were
making the advances. I don't know. He hated the whole business,
anyway."

"So how long did you hang out with them?"

"Well, we were in the bar for about an hour," said Henry. "And
then we went with them to some party somewhere. Needless to say, we
were the only guys at the party in uniform, and we got a lot of strange
looks. Most everyone there had hair down to their asses. They were
smoking a lot of grass and drinking wine, and sitting around playing all
these musical instruments, and some of them were tripping on acid, I
remember, because there was this one guy who came up to me and
stared at my medals for like ten minutes. When I finally asked him
what the hell he was doing, he said they were *singing* to him. It was
really wild."

"And Eliza came with you?"

"It was her party," he said. "It turned out it was her house. She did-
n't own it, but she lived there, with some other people. But she didn't
call herself Eliza. She was Sky. How did you find out her real name?"

I gave Henry a brief rundown of Doctor Connor's letter.

"She went to Mannville to have you?" he asked, surprised.

"I guess. That's where I was born."

"Why didn't she stay with your grandfather?"

"I don't know. She left me on the doorstep."

"On the *doorstep*?"

"With a note."

"Well," said Henry Hutchins. "That surprises me."

"Why?"

"Because she seemed like a very responsible person," he said.

"So you got to know her?"

"A bit," said Henry. "We actually ended up staying there all week-end. We were having too much fun to leave."

"And is that when I was conceived?"

"Well, it must have been," he admitted, "because they spent most of their time in bed." Henry Hutchins blushed slightly. So did I.

"They did?"

"They were inseparable," said Henry. "They didn't come out of her room. I was left to myself most of the time, but that was all right because there were people trooping in and out of the house constant-ly, and they were all very nice to me, even though I was in uniform. I was actually enjoying myself quite a bit. It was the strangest time I'd ever had. But that was what I liked about it. That weekend changed my life, actually."

"Why?"

"Well, between you and me, I took some acid."

"You did?"

"Don't take that the wrong way," said Henry Hutchins. "I don't recommend it to anyone. Especially young people. I'm not endorsing it. I took it on the spur of the moment. It lasted a long time, I remem-ber. It was really strong stuff. I've never taken it since."

"What happened?"

"Well, at first it was a lot of fun. I was laughing at everything, and everyone seemed wonderful, and life was suddenly revealed to be the big joke I'd always suspected it was. Aldous Huxley says it best—the doors of perception were opened for me. But about twelve hours into it I started having what they call a bad trip."

"What was that like?"

"Awful," he said. "Worse than war. Worse than the fear of death. It was just inescapable. I can't really describe it. It was just like this huge void had opened at my feet, and I couldn't look into it and I couldn't look away. That's when I really started to freak. I was think-ing about going back to Nam, and I just totally lost it. Eddie had to come out and talk me down."

"What did he do?"

"He just sat there with his arm around me. He must have stayed with me for something like six hours. He didn't say much, which was perfect. When he knew I was ready to do some listening he started talking me through it. It was like he was taking me on a guided tour of my soul. Somehow, he knew exactly how I felt."

"What did he say?"

Henry pursed his lips and looked thoughtfully at the ceiling. "Something about just letting it in. Not shutting anything out. Just letting it swallow me."

"Was he taking acid too?"

"No way," said Henry. "Not him."

"Then how did he know what to say?"

"That was Eddie," he said. "He knew how to do everything, even things he'd never done. Sometimes I got the feeling he'd lived before. I mean, supposedly everyone has lived before. At least that's what you believe if you're a Hindu or a Buddhist. But I sometimes wonder if Eddie didn't remember everything from his past lives."

For a moment I debated telling Henry Hutchins about my experience with the old Mennonite witch-lady when I was a little boy. But the evening was wearing on, and I still had the long drive back to Mannville to make that night.

"So what happened later? When you left, I mean. With Sky and my dad."

"Oh. Yeah. You know, I don't remember that part too clearly. I'm sure they exchanged addresses. They must have, for Sky to find out where your grandfather lived. Maybe they planned on getting together after the war. God, they would have been a beautiful couple."

"So Eddie had her address?"

"I would think so."

"What did they talk about while they were in that room together? Did he ever tell you?"

"No, and I didn't ask. But afterward he was sort of glowing, like he'd just had some sort of religious experience. That struck me as unusual. Women didn't usually affect him like that. He'd met so many of them, you see. I don't mean he was jaded. He just wasn't the type to go head over heels over a girl. That kind of behavior was sort of beneath him."

"But he did this time?"

"Well, he came the closest I had ever seen him come. He didn't talk much after we left. He just sat there and hummed to himself. I think he was very happy."

"What did you guys do after that?"

"We came back here, to this very house. And the next day Eddie went back to Mannville."

"And then you both shipped out again?"

"Three days later," Henry confirmed. "And it was the next February that he was shot down. I'm sorry. It must be hard for you to hear his death spoken of."

"I'm used to it," I said. "I never knew him."

"That's right. I forgot. What a shame that is. He would have loved you, kid."

"Anyway," I said, "you don't know where I might look for my mother?"

"I'm sorry, Billy," he said. "I never saw her again, and I don't think your dad did either. Maybe they wrote letters to each other. If they did, they should have been shipped home with his personal effects. Did your grandad get anything like that? A box of stuff from the Air Force?"

"I don't know," I said, feeling like an idiot. Why hadn't I thought to ask Grandpa that myself? *Because I'm an amateur,* I reminded myself. *I've never tried to track anyone down before.*

"Henry," said a high, shaking voice. "Who is that man?"

Henry and I turned to see his mother standing in the dining room, pointing a finger at me. She was completely naked.

"Jesus, Mom," said Henry. "I'm sorry, Billy." He got up from the couch with a blanket and went to cover her. I averted my eyes.

"Don't worry about it," I said.

"Let me know how things turn out," Henry called over his shoulder as he took his mother back to her bedroom. "I've enjoyed talking to you, kid. You're a chip off the old block."

I took that as my cue to leave.

"Thanks, Mr. Hutchins," I said. "I'll let you know what happens."

I let myself out into the narrow driveway and squeezed into the Galaxie, which Grandpa had loaned me for the trip. On the way home, I mentally searched the entire farmhouse in Mannville for something. Anything. I was missing a vital clue. I could feel its absence as though the gap itself was a palpable object, yet I didn't know what it was. But I was getting closer. I could feel that too.

My Eighteenth Year; the Next Round of Three; I Bury Frederic Simpson; Grandpa's Narration, and His Departure

From Willie Mann's diary:

We humans are a lot of monkeys running hither and thither, living in fancy cages of our own devising and slowly inventing the means to destroy ourselves. Before us also came a long line of monkeys, who through no grandiose intentions, but through the simple ability to procreate—or the inability not to—gave rise to us. For the most part they have been a depraved, murderous, hateful group, stealing land from other monkeys and wiping out other monkey tribes. Some of us modern monkeys seem to think much of our ancestors, and are proud to trace our monkeyhood back several generations, perhaps even as far as those original murdering monkeys, the Europeans. But I myself see little in our species' history of which to be proud. It is far too late to prevent our worst errors as humans. Even if they haven't been committed yet, the stage has already been set. My only concern now is for my family. I wish to keep this diary so that my descendants will know the mis-

takes we monkeys known as Mann have already made. Some mis-
takes are inevitable, but I do not wish the more serious ones among
them to be made again.

Willie Mann wrote those words as he neared the age of ninety. For
the last seventy-five years of his life, beginning when he was twenty-
one and just learning how to write, he made daily entries in his journal. He thought—he hoped—that by doing this he might have some
effect on the Manns who came after him. He didn't want fratricide, or
greed, to come tearing through his family ever again, even after he was
dead.

I hadn't yet read the entry above, of course. I hadn't even seen the
diary yet. It was still in Japan, and how much longer it would be there
I had no idea, but I hoped for its safe return because I knew its value
to me would be incalculable.

"I don't know how you could just give it away like that," I fumed
to Grandpa one day. "I mean, did you think nobody else was ever
going to be interested?"

"Think about it, kid," said Grandpa. "I was nineteen years old.
Your father wasn't even born yet. I was an only child. I didn't think I
was going to survive the war. You did things impulsively in those days
because the moment was the only time that was. Plus, I didn't like what
I read in it. I wanted to get rid of it."

Grandpa had hinted before that there was something revealed in
the diary that, at the time, he found too shameful to think about. He
still refused to talk about it, although whether his reticence was due to
pride or lack of memory I never discovered. Grandpa was adept at
feigning a tattered mind when it suited his purposes.

"You don't have an address for this Fujimora guy? Some way I
could write to him and make sure he's coming back?"

"He was from Nagasaki," said Grandpa. "Nagasaki was nuked.
Even if he'd given me an address, that house would just be a shadow
on the street now."

"How do you know he's still alive?"

"He's alive."

"But what if he doesn't show up at all?"

This was the big question, one that had been brewing in my mind for some time. This whole system they'd concocted of simply knowing when the other was going to die seemed far-fetched and unreliable. I would have preferred a slightly more certain method of notification, such as a phone call.

But Grandpa remained secure. "He's coming," he said. "I can feel it. And it won't be long now."

It wouldn't be long now because, according to Grandpa, the next round of three had begun with the death of Frederic Simpson, and he was convinced he would go in this round. His number was up, he said. He was about to hang up his hat, to check out, to buy the farm, to kick the bucket. He was so sure of himself that he asked for his grave to be dug now, while the earth was still thawing, so it could be drained periodically before he was put in it. He didn't mind the idea of being dead and cold, he said; but being dead, cold, and wet was intolerable. Ever since his involuntary dip in the South Pacific, Grandpa had hated water.

"Humor an old man," he said, and so I called the funeral director, and he called the cemetery, and the cemetery called their gravedigger, and the grave was dug.

I went out to see it without telling anyone. I had the crazy idea that I would get in the grave myself for a moment, just to see what it was like to be in there. I don't know why I wanted to do that, but I was eighteen years old, and I believe that explains a good deal of it. It was a poetic gesture of the sort only eighteen-year-olds are capable of conceiving. I did many things at eighteen that I've spent the rest of my life trying to understand. But when I arrived, the grave looked so unpleasant I changed my mind about getting in it. Grandpa was right. The earth was soggy and cold and dank, and I had the terrifying impression that if I poked my finger through the earthen walls I would touch one or another of the innumerable Mann coffins that populated this part of the cemetery so densely.

We would never have known of Frederic's death if it hadn't been for Mildred's morbid habit of reading the obituaries each morning. She read them first thing, even before the headlines, and when she found a name she knew, she read the whole notice out loud. It was a peculiar habit, one that unnerved me; but Grandpa said that when I reached old age I would do the same thing, simply because my deceased acquaintances would start to outnumber my living ones.

"You have to keep up with what's going on in the world," he said. "And when you're our age, what's going on is death, and lots of it."

Someone had written a brief notice for Frederic, describing his service in Vietnam and mentioning that he was "severely wounded," after which he was cared for by his "loving father, whom he survived." The notice made no mention of a sister named Annie. Most likely, I thought, it was written by one of the nurses at the VA hospital where Frederic had been moved. Only a complete stranger could have made the mistake of calling Mr. Simpson "loving."

I felt as if a huge burden had been lifted from my chest. I breathed more fully, more easily, knowing that poor Frederic was finally released from the prison of his body. It terrified me to think he might have had full use of his mental faculties all along. Even though that was unlikely, the mere possibility of it sometimes kept me awake at night, paralyzed with sympathy, pretending I couldn't move and never would again. After such a life as his, I often thought, the notion of hell would hold little discomfort. That morning I clipped the obituary out and mailed it to Annie in Montreal with something akin to joy; my relief, I was sure, would pale in comparison to hers.

Grandpa went matter-of-factly about the business of making preparations for his own death. He'd purchased an airtight, waterproof coffin, made out his will, and begun in advance the myriad tasks that a modern death enforces upon us. "Damn it," he sighed, on numerous occasions. "You can't just drop dead any more, can you?" When he heard about Frederic, he knew his time was not far off, and he decided formally to announce to me that he would be leaving soon. His liver had never recovered from the punishment he'd dealt it over four decades of hard drinking. It had been failing gradually for years, and according to the doctors at the hospital, it was about to go out on him completely.

"It could be another year yet," he told me, "so don't go around blubbering."

"All right," I said. I was trying to fight down the horrible feeling in my chest. It was the same feeling I'd had when Annie had disappeared, the same feeling I'd had as a boy when I thought about my lack of a father and mother. It was the feeling of being left behind, a deep, vague opening sensation, centered somewhere deep within me and radiating outward, like an explosion.

"I do not wish to be hooked up to any machines," said Grandpa. "I feel very strongly about that."

"Okay."

"There's just no reason for being hooked up to machines except pure selfishness. Old people have a duty to get out of the way. Think of poor Frederic Simpson. Think I want to end up like that? All tubed up? Fuck it! Better off dead!"

"Yessir." I was interested in changing the subject, but Grandpa went on.

"There's no reason for us to go on consuming valuable resources just because we're afraid of what comes next. Sometimes when I think of how long people are living these days it makes me sick. What's the point? They don't do a goddamn thing! They just lie there and complain. They're a burden."

"Could we stop talking about this now?"

"They say babies born in the year two thousand will have an average life span of one hundred years," he said contemptuously, ignoring me. "Ice Age man probably lived to be around thirty. We're not *supposed* to get older than that. We're supposed to die and turn into dirt. So flowers can grow in us, and all that shit. Jesus. People complain about pollution, but the real problem is people. We're cluttering up the earth."

I said nothing. It was strange to hear someone speak this way. Grandpa could, if he chose, prolong his life by many years, perhaps with a liver transplant. But the very idea made him snort in derision.

"Everybody ought to get one liver and that's it," he said. "Livers are like cars. If you can't take care of the first one, what the hell makes people think they deserve another?"

"I don't know," I said. "I guess I just figured people have an obligation to stick around as long as they can."

"Ridiculous. Nonsense. Why? What am I going to accomplish now? What good is an old man like me anyway?"

"You could tell me some more stories," I suggested. I was searching desperately in my mind for some argument to counteract his, but the horrible truth was I realized he was right. It was time for him to die. Nevertheless, every atom of my being sought for a way to rebel against the inevitable. I'd spent my entire childhood in the shadow of death. Everyone I was supposed to have known, everyone who could have given my life fullness and more meaning, was already gone. In fact, they'd left before I arrived, with barely a hint of who they'd been, and instead of meeting them I was left with the task of piecing together the clues of my identity with only Grandpa to help me. I'd paid my dues to death in full, I thought, and I didn't care to surrender any more of my people to the unknown, where I couldn't reach them. Perhaps this was why our house was full of ghosts when I was a child—my mournful ancestors felt guilty at leaving me behind, parentless, broke, and playing with imaginary friends.

But Grandpa said, "I've told you all the stories I know."

"All of them?"

"Literally all. You know everything I know. And they're all written down, right?"

For a moment I considered lying to him to get him to prolong his stay, but when Grandpa questioned me about anything it was nearly always a formality; he already knew the answer because he always knew what I was thinking. In the last three years, I had filled several notebooks with Grandpa's knowledge of family history as he repeated it to me. Recently I'd shown the whole collection to him, and even he was amazed at the scope and variety of the stories. "I can't believe my poor pickled head holds all that," he marveled, and then he began to laugh, wheezily, at some private joke.

"What's so funny?" I asked.

"It's just ironic," he gasped.

"What is?"

"My head being pickled. Just like all those poor Rory heads in the barrel."

It was then spring of 1988. I was going to be graduating soon. More than two years had gone by since I'd visited Henry Hutchins in Buffalo; during that time I'd occupied myself by searching the farmhouse for anything the Air Force might have sent home after my father's death, and for other clues—anything.

I also wrote long, rambling letters to Annie. They were enthusiastic, not really about anything. Infatuated with my own way of expressing myself, I made copies of them; in rereading them now, I see them for what they were: a desperate bid to get her to change her mind, to love me the way I loved her. She answered them at first, then she only answered every other one, then she wrote rarely. Time passed, as it always did. Then I heard nothing.

Forget about her, said an inner voice. It was a voice that had been speaking to me often lately, as I was getting older. *Just let her alone.*

As much as I hated to admit it, I knew the voice was right. I would never be able to forget about her, but maybe leaving her alone was the best thing. So I focused my energy anew on finding my mother.

But Grandpa had told me nothing had been delivered to him anyway, so there was no point in looking—there was nothing to be found. He hadn't thought anything of it at the time, and besides, he had a whole roomful of relics to keep him company and remind him of my father. But now that I brought it up, he too wondered what had happened to Eddie's personal effects.

I knew the Air Force must at least have had a record of what he'd left behind, even if it was nothing important: his toothbrush, perhaps, and other things like that. I spent several months making phone calls to various government departments before I was even able to determine which one would be able to tell me anything useful. Then I had to submit a request in writing, stating my reasons for wanting to know what Eddie's personal effects, if any, had been, and where they had been sent. It took them nearly three months to respond.

"It's a wonder we've ever won any wars at all, with this kind of military bureaucracy," I told Grandpa, who agreed; occasionally he still ranted at the clerical idiocy that had set him adrift in the South Pacific forty-seven years ago. But finally, that spring, there came a letter in the mail. It was a photocopied list, typed in 1969 by a Sergeant Jackson. Apparently it had been Sergeant Jackson's job to catalog the effects of dead men and mail them off to whatever address the deceased had put down for next of kin. The list contained mostly mundane items, as I'd suspected it would, but among them was the following entry:

Twenty-seven (27) letters, personal correspondence.

"Did you write Eddie twenty-seven letters?" I asked Grandpa.

He frowned. "Does the Air Force say I did?"

"No. They just say they found twenty-seven of them when he died."

"I wrote him one a month," said Grandpa. He closed his eyes and did some mental figuring. "He was gone for eighteen months before he was killed. So I wrote him eighteen letters. If that many."

"Who else would have written him letters?"

"Anybody with his address, of course," Grandpa said.

"But how many people had his address?"

"I don't know, boy. Probably half the girls in Mannville."

Of more concern than whom these letters were from, however, was where they'd been sent after Eddie's fighter jet disintegrated in a fiery cloud over the Indian Ocean. I was certain that was the next clue to the riddle of who my mother was. I imagined there must have been some kind of private agreement between Eddie and Eliza, some sort of arrangement about what would happen if Eddie was killed. I felt sure they weren't just randomly copulating. Henry Hutchins knew my father well, and if he thought they were in love, then they probably were. Perhaps they even suspected that Eliza was pregnant already, in which case she would want some memento of my father, some connection to ensure his return. Or perhaps Eddie, like Grandpa, knew in advance the day and manner of his death, and informed her of this as they lay together in bed in that party house in Buffalo, with poor Henry Hutchins tripping his head off in the next room, so that she could plan her life accordingly.

But the address to which the letters and other items had been sent was not included. I seemed to have run into a blank brick wall, built with infinite care by the Air Force. I fired off one last letter to the same department that had sent me the list of Eddie's personal effects, in the desperate hope that some blue-suited, soulless animatron would read it and take pity on me.

"I am attempting to find the answer to a question that has haunted me since my birth," I wrote. "You are the only ones who can help me. My father gave his life while in the service of the Air Force. I think the least you bastards could do in return is tell me where these letters were sent, and stop giving me the runaround."

"That's tellin' 'em," said Grandpa admiringly. Since his time with Enzo on their South Pacific island, he'd borne a strong distrust of the

Air Force, which during his war had been run by the Army. My father's death had only served to exacerbate his feelings.

"I don't think you should call them bastards," said Mildred. "You might get better results if you were nicer."

"It takes one to know one," I said, but I knew she was right, so I changed *bastards* to *gentlemen* and mailed off the letter.

I included a photocopy of the photocopied list that Sergeant Jackson had typed out eighteen years ago and mailed it back to the same department from which it had come. Perhaps it would be months before I heard a reply, I thought; perhaps it would be never. I marked the date on a calendar. It was then early Saturday morning, the fifteenth of March. With a start I remembered that today was the day of Frederic Simpson's funeral; he was going to be buried in the churchyard in two hours. I hadn't planned on going, but I knew suddenly that I had to be there.

I showered and put on my one good suit, which barely fit me any longer. It had belonged to Eddie, but I was taller than he by a good inch and a half, and my wrists and ankles were revealed by the retreating cuffs of the jacket and pants. In fact, according to Grandpa, I was the tallest Mann ever to exist, and the effect was that I could not continue for much longer the great Mann tradition of wearing antique hand-me-downs.

"We need to take that boy shopping," said Mildred, in disapproval.

Grandpa raised his eyebrows. He and I had never gone clothes shopping together in our lives. The very idea of it was simultaneously horrifying and intriguing. Somehow the notion had escaped me that one could simply buy clothes whenever they were needed. It seemed like a waste of money, when there were so many generations worth of perfectly good suits and hats and shirts lying around, packed in cedar chips and mothballs. So what if they were decades out of date? Clothes were clothes. Nothing in my wardrobe had been made after 1969. But Grandpa was not the same man he'd once been, and he found himself caught up in the idea of making sure I was well dressed.

"Mildred, you are correct, as usual," said Grandpa. "We'll get him suited up before he graduates."

"You're not coming to Frederic's funeral?" I asked.

"I don't feel well," Grandpa said. I said nothing to that; he didn't look well either, but I didn't want to mention it.

I parked my motorcycle in the gravel car lot of the church. There were only four or five other cars there, and I wondered for a moment if I had misread the date. But there was a small sign in front of the door, which read SIMPSON FUNERAL SERVICES, 11:00 A.M. I entered the church and sat in the back row of pews, letting my eyes adjust to the dimness of the church's interior.

"Come on up to the front, why don't you," said a disembodied voice. I squinted into the gloom. Standing up behind the altar was Father Kinney, the parish priest, and I could now make out the forms of several uniformed men sitting in the front row. They were soldiers. I tiptoed up and sat behind them. The soldiers sat stiffly at attention, ignoring me completely.

"I'm glad someone showed up," said Father Kinney. "Were you related to the deceased?"

"No," I said, and then as an afterthought I added, "I'm sorry."

"Oh, that's you, Billy," said Father Kinney. "I didn't recognize you. No need to apologize. Glad you could make it." He seemed more than glad. He seemed relieved that he wouldn't be performing the funeral ceremony to an empty house.

Frederic's coffin had already been placed at the front of the center aisle, draped with the American flag. Two more soldiers stood at the head of it, staring sternly at the rear of the church. Father Kinney said, "We might as well begin."

Besides the soldiers, I was the only member of the congregation. Although the Manns had always been Catholics, I'd never been baptized, and Frederic's funeral was the first Catholic service of any kind I had attended in my life. I was fascinated, as though I'd stumbled upon the rituals of some ancient and forgotten cult. I followed the lead of the soldiers, who knew when to kneel and when to stand, and who sang the hymns in loud, clear voices, completely bereft of tonality and rhythm but full of military enthusiasm.

Father Kinney said, "At this time, anyone who wishes to may say a few words and share their memories of Frederic."

There was dead silence. Father Kinney looked at me. I pretended not to notice.

"Billy? You're the only one here," he said.

I swallowed.

"Go ahead," urged Father Kinney. "Just a few words."

I stood up.

"Frederic Simpson was a good friend of my father," I said.

Father Kinney nodded from the pulpit. "I see," he said.

Encouraged by this, I went on, addressing myself partly to Father Kinney and partly to the soldiers, who continued to ignore me. "He served his country in Vietnam, and he was badly wounded. He's been in a coma or something ever since then. He doesn't have any family left, so I'm glad I could be here. He and my dad were pals. My father died in Vietnam."

I couldn't think of anything else to say, so I sat down, my face aflame.

"Thank you," said Father Kinney. "We will now proceed to the grave site."

In utter silence, the soldiers stood up and formed a line on either side of the coffin. With Father Kinney and an altar boy in front and myself behind, they walked slowly down the aisle, taking one short step at a time, the lead soldier counting a barely audible cadence. I watched their feet; they moved in perfect precision. With a shock of understanding, I realized that they hadn't known Frederic at all. This was merely their job. They were professional funeral soldiers. They probably never knew any of the dead they carried. They simply carried them, quietly and with great ceremony, to their graves.

We formed a small group around the open tomb. Father Kinney read another passage of the funeral service and the soldiers formed a single line. The soldier who had counted the cadence as they marched now produced rifles from somewhere, and each soldier received one. I stood with my hands folded in front of my crotch on the opposite side of the grave. At a quiet command, they raised their rifles and pointed them at the sky.

"Fire!" said the one who commanded them, and I jumped as their rifles cracked in unison. They did this twice more. Then the rifles were collected. They picked up the flag from the coffin, folded it with much ceremony into a thick triangle, and gave it to the commanding soldier, who turned with it and, after a moment of indecision, approached me.

"Sir, on behalf of the United States Army, you are presented with this American flag as a small token of appreciation and gratitude for the service rendered by"—here he paused, then remembered—"Frederic Simpson."

I couldn't quite believe he was offering the flag to me. I looked uncertainly at Father Kinney, but he was staring off into the distance at something that wasn't there. I cleared my throat.

"Thank you very much," I said, and I took it.

And the funeral was over. The soldiers marched carefully out of the graveyard, leaving me alone with Father Kinney.

"Saddest funeral I've ever performed," he said. "Smallest congregation, too. How exactly did you know him?"

"I knew his sister Annie," I said.

"Ah yes. The one who disappeared. Did they ever find her?"

"No."

"Well," Father Kinney sighed. "That's the end of the Simpsons, I guess. And here's the rest of them." With a sweep of his arm he indicated the surrounding tombstones.

My gaze followed the sweep of his arm. What I saw then took my breath away: dozens upon dozens of tombstones, perhaps one hundred of them, all bearing the name of Simpson. There were even more of them than there were Mann tombstones. I'd never explored this part of the burial ground, since my family occupied the opposite corner of the graveyard, and somehow it had never occurred to me that there might have been other Simpsons in other times.

"Jesus," I breathed, forgetting I was in the company of a priest. But Father Kinney appeared not to be offended. "There are so many of them!"

"Oh yes," said Father Kinney. "That's what makes this particular funeral so sad. Simpson was once the most common name in Mannville, before it was called Mannville, of course. In fact, we came darn close to being called Simpsonville. And now they're all gone, every last one of them."

I pondered the implications of this. Somewhere inside me, a small candle of understanding began to glimmer with a tiny spark.

"Do you mind if I look around here for a bit?" I asked. The spark of understanding burst suddenly into flame, tiny, but bright and strong. I had some exploring to do.

"Certainly not," replied the priest. "There've been Manns in this graveyard since this church was built. You have a right to." He picked his way neatly around the stones and made his way back into the church. "Thanks for coming, Billy," he called over his shoulder. "I'm sure it meant a lot to Frederic, if he's watching."

Then I was alone among the dead.

I read with interest the names on the Simpson stones. There were many with birth dates from the last part of the eighteenth century, as there were in the Mann section. They were carved out of the same white granite, probably once gleaming and bright but now dull and pitted with age and decay. Judging by the dates, there'd been many more Simpsons before the Civil War than after it. What had they been like? I wondered. Had they always been a bunch of fat drunks? Had they always lived in the big white house on top of the hill? And what had happened to them? What had caused them to die off?

Grandpa would know. I was sure of it. When I got home, Grandpa would have some questions to answer.

I turned to leave and was headed purposefully for my motorcycle when a familiar name caught my eye. Next to the rear fence I found the grave of Frederic Simpson, but not the same Frederic Simpson we'd just committed to the earth. This Frederic was born in 1848 and had died in 1864. The engraving on his stone depicted a pair of crossed rifles surrounded by a wreath, the sign of an infantryman. This Frederic had been a veteran of the Civil War, just like Willie Mann. He must have died in battle, or perhaps of fever, or infection, or any one of the endless afflictions that claimed the lives of soldiers in those dark days. He'd been only sixteen years old. I wondered if he'd known my great-great-grandfather.

I nestled Frederic's flag carefully under my leather jacket and rode home in a pensive mood. The Simpsons must have been guilty of great sins to have earned from fate the complete extermination of their line. Such a punishment, I'd learned in school, was usually reserved for the villains of ancient Greek mythology, those who committed patricide or fratricide or incest. But the gods of the ancient world were all asleep or dead, and had been for centuries; and even if they'd been alive, it seemed unlikely to me, a twentieth-century boy whizzing along on his motorcycle, that they would aim their vengeful thunderbolts in the direction of western New York State. Perhaps, I mused, the Simpsons hadn't done anything wrong at all, and it was only chance that they should have disappeared in this manner. Or perhaps the twisted soul of the Simpson whom I knew simply as Mister, father of Annie and the nastiest, most brutal human I'd ever encountered, was enough to cause their downfall. In that case, it was true, if outrageously unfair, that the sins of the fathers were visited upon the sons.

Which made me wonder, ever so briefly, if Eddie had really been some sort of secret criminal.

But I discarded that thought immediately without really admitting that I'd had it. I arrived home and stowed the flag in one of my dresser drawers. Then, on second thought, I took it out again, wrapped it in paper, and addressed it to Annie. I'd included no letter with the obituary I'd sent her, nor did I write one to accompany the flag. None was necessary. It was another eighteen-year-old poetic gesture, one that I hoped would be poignant enough on its own. Annie never required explanations of me. None were needed.

At the last moment, though, I didn't send it.

"Sure are a lot of Simpsons up in that graveyard," I said to Grandpa later that afternoon.

He and Mildred were sitting side by side in their rocking chairs, teetering gently back and forth in perfect unison. In the old days he'd have had a glass of whiskey in his hand. Now he sipped herbal tea.

"What? What do you mean?" he said.

"Well, I was looking around," I said, "and I guess I just never noticed how many Simpsons were buried up there."

"Yeah," said Grandpa. "Well, those are the good Simpsons."

"Why are they good?"

"Because!" He gave me an impish grin. "They're dead!"

Mildred whacked Grandpa on the knee. "Shame on you," she said.

"The only good Simpson is a dead Simpson!" Grandpa crowed. He laughed and sipped his tea.

"Hey," I said, "Annie's a Simpson."

The smile left Grandpa's face.

"Relax, boy," he said. "I forgot about her. I didn't mean her."

"Well, I certainly haven't forgotten about her!"

"Maybe you should," said Grandpa darkly. "No good can come of that."

"What do you mean?" I was growing irritated; it hurt me to hear Grandpa speak in this way of the girl I'd loved all my life.

"Never mind."

"What do you mean, never mind? I have a right to know everything!"

"Not everything, you don't."

"Damn it," I said in frustration. "There were more than a hundred Simpsons up there. They've been here longer than we have even. What happened to all of them?"

"Who cares?"

"I care. Have we been fighting with them all this time? Since the seventeen hundreds?"

"I don't want to talk about it," said Grandpa.

"Well, I do," I said.

"Well, so what?"

"What do you mean, so what? I have a right to know!" I was angry now. It was rare for Grandpa to pull rank on me, so to speak; he'd always treated me like an adult, or at least with respect for the fact that I had a mind of my own. But now he remained silent. He'd stopped rocking and I could see by the tightening of his lips that he was angry too.

"How long have the Simpsons and the Manns known each other?" I asked.

"Oh, I forget," he said coldly. "How's your bike running?"

"Nice try," I said. "Don't even think about it."

"About what? I was just asking—"

What happened next surprised even me. I picked up Grandpa's teacup and saucer and smashed them on the floor. They shattered into tiny shards. Then I leaned forward and rested my hands on the arms of his rocking chair.

"Don't you fucking lie to me," I said. "Don't you ever fucking lie to me again. I'm asking you some serious questions and you're going to tell me the answers. I've had it with you and your games. You think you're the only one who can take the truth? You tell me what happened. Now. Not later. Not sometime. Now. I have a right to know."

My voice was low and even. Grandpa leaned back in his chair and stared at me.

"Billy?" said Mildred.

I stood up.

"I'm sorry," I said.

"I'll get a broom," said Mildred.

"No, let me do it," I said. "I'll clean it up, Mildred."

"No, I want to do it," Mildred said. Her voice was shaking. I could see I had scared her. But Grandpa had not been fazed at all. I turned to him in embarrassment.

"I didn't mean to do that," I said. "I'm sorry."

Grandpa was staring out the window at the yard.

"I know you didn't," he said. "But you did it."

I said nothing.

"Let's you and me go out to the garage and have a little talk," he said.

"There was another Frederic," I said, once we were in the garage. "In the Civil War. He has a stone up in the cemetery."

"You were poking around up there, huh?"

"Well, yeah," I said. "Father Kinney said I could."

"Well, I kinda knew you had to find out sometime," he said.

"This other Frederic died in the Civil War?"

"Yes," he said.

"Did he and Willie know each other?"

Grandpa put a hand over his eyes.

"Grandpa? Did they?"

He took his hand away.

"Yes, they did," he said.

"How well? Were they friends?"

"No," he said. "I mean yes, they were friends, but they were more than that."

"What do you mean?"

"They were cousins," said Grandpa.

I sat in silence for perhaps a full minute, absorbing this. The connection this implied between Annie and myself was obvious, but my reeling mind chose not to look at it right away. I couldn't.

"Kid," Grandpa said, "there's a lot of things I haven't told you."

"How could you not tell me *that*? Of all the things you had to leave out, how could you not tell me that?"

"How could I?" Grandpa said. "How could I tell you the girl you were in love with was related to you by blood?"

He put his hand over his eyes again. He was leaning against his workbench, and he turned now and bent over it, resting on his elbows. Underneath his T-shirt I could see his thin shoulders begin to shake. *How could I ever have wanted to hurt him?* I thought. His old body was thin and frail and wasted. He'd never looked so small to me before. My grandfather is dying, I thought, and ten minutes ago I was shouting in his face. A wave of tenderness and regret washed over me with such enormity I had to sit down or I knew I would fall. The nearest object was the old riding lawnmower, the same one I'd ridden to Grandpa's rescue all those years ago. I slumped in the bucket seat and pulled my knees up to my chest. My eyes were hot and wet.

"Did Annie know?"

Grandpa pulled a handkerchief from his pocket and honked loudly into it.

"She might have," he said, "but I doubt it. He never told Frederic. His son, I mean. He was as ashamed of it as I was."

There was no need for him to say who *he* was. We both knew he meant Annie's father.

"That's why you didn't want me to go to Montreal to visit her," I said. "That's why you kept saying it wasn't right. Not because she's a Simpson. Because we're related."

Grandpa sighed.

"Yeah," he said.

"That's why you said you had an obligation to go to Mr. Simpson's funeral," I went on. "Because he was family."

Grandpa nodded dumbly.

"Jesus," I whispered. Simpson was family. *Family.* That meant *I* was related to Mr. Simpson too. Nausea welled up briefly inside me as

I remembered how Simpson had looked the morning he died, over-weight and naked, with his one open eye twisted back into its socket. *All along I thought we were alone in the world*, I said to myself, *and there I went and murdered my own flesh and blood.*

"Did my father know about this?"

Grandpa shook his head sadly. "I never got the chance to tell him," he said. "I was gonna, when he was older. But he didn't get older."

"So he and Frederic never knew they were related?"

"No."

"But you didn't mind that they played together when they were boys?"

"Hell no. In those days I thought there was a chance everything could be forgotten. I figured, why poison what the boys got going? Let them grow up with each other, and that way when they get to be men, once they found out the truth, they could just laugh it off. I never *liked* feeling bad toward Jack Simpson. I didn't see any reason to pass it on."

"So you kept it a secret from my father?"

"Every family has secrets, boy."

"But why keep it secret from *me*? Why? I'm the last Mann! I have to know everything! You told me that yourself!"

"I've never lied to you," said Grandpa. "But sometimes I leave things out. There's a reason for that. It's not because I thought you couldn't handle the truth. It's because there's some things that need to be pulled out of the world. If nobody knows something, then it isn't true any more. That's why there's things I haven't told you. To filter them out, like. To kind of clean things up. We're never going to get back to where we were if we stay stuck in the same old shit. The only way to purge badness is to kill it. Or to take it to the grave."

He sighed.

"But I never figured on Annie entering the picture," he said. "I felt God-awful bad for that girl, but I was relieved when she left town. I didn't know how much you cared about her. I should have seen it. I guess I just didn't want to. And now that you're asking, I can't lie to you," he said. "That was one thing I swore I'd never do. And I knew you'd find out someday, when the diary came back. But I figured by then I'd be dead and gone."

"All right," I said. "I understand."

"Did you and her . . ." He hesitated, blushing.

"What?"

"Did you and Annie ever . . . did you ever get together with her?"

"You mean did we ever . . . ?"

"Yeah."

"No," I said. "Never."

"Phew," he said. He seemed greatly relieved. "Okay. Sorry. I had to ask."

"So where did it all start?"

"You mean the feuding?"

"Yeah."

"It's a long story," he said.

"Well," I said, and then I paused. I wanted to pick my words carefully. My first instinct was to say, "No shit! Suppose you tell it anyway!" But I was disgusted with myself for smashing his teacup; in doing that, I'd hurt myself as much as I'd hurt him. I'd crossed some barrier in losing my temper, broken some silent taboo, one I'd never been aware of before but of whose violation I was now sharply aware. Thou shalt not throw one's grandfather's teacup to the floor. Thou shalt not threaten the elderly. Thou shalt not use the word *fuck* in front of Mildred. Inwardly I was wincing in shame.

"Grandpa," I said instead, "this is very, very important to me. Okay? I need to know it. And you know I need to know it." *And*, I did not add, *time is running out. You're dying. Tell me now, please. Please. You have a very limited supply of tomorrows left, and the next one might be your last.*

Because, to tell the truth, I'd never fully believed the diary was going to show up, and I was sure that if Grandpa didn't tell me himself, I would never know. And that was unthinkable.

But I didn't need to voice my most hideous thoughts. I looked at Grandpa as I thought them, and he looked at me, and he knew once again what I was thinking without my saying a word. A moment of understanding passed between us then. I sensed his body as though it was my own somehow, felt it growing frailer, felt his essence slipping slowly out of him. I had to grab with both hands onto the lawnmower; I felt, for a moment, that I was leaving my body. It was only a brief instant, but it was one of the more terrifying experiences of my life,

and I still believe to this day that for a fraction of a second I ceased to
be myself and became instead my dying grandfather, and moreover
that he'd somehow caused me to feel that way, on purpose. It was that
damned Mann telepathy again. Annie had complained once that it
wasn't easy being friends with a psychic, but that was nothing compared with how difficult it was to be one.

"All right, boy," he said. "You listen good. I'll tell you everything.
Okay?"

"Okay," I said.

Grandpa stepped up on a toolbox and boosted himself onto the
workbench. He looked absurdly like a small child sitting there with his
legs dangling off the edge. He stared for a moment at the wall behind
me. I knew he wasn't looking at anything in particular; he was, with his
considerable mental powers, pulling away the curtain that veiled the
past, to remind himself for a moment of what was there before he
started describing it. For most people, this is a difficult task, requiring
great energy and concentration. For Grandpa it had always been as
easy as pulling on his socks.

When he'd seen everything there was to see, and reminded himself of everything there was to be reminded of, he started talking.

"You know about as much about Willie as everyone else in this town
does," he said, "but you don't know as much about Willie as Willie
himself would have wanted you to know. He would have wanted you
to know the whole story, and if he were here, he would tell you himself. He felt shame, sure, but he got over it when he was an old man.
Willie understood how important it was to tell the truth. But he did-
n't go around town blabbing and confessing to everyone about what
he'd done during the war, not because he was ashamed of it, but
because he was a hero, and Mannville needed a hero bad. Every town
does. Look around you. We don't have much going for us. We have a
grain mill, we have a bunch of farms, a few stores downtown. A decent
beach. Your dad was the last real hero this town ever produced. Willie
built a hospital, a school, a library, all the stuff people needed to feel
like they were important. Like they were worth something. Like living

in Mannville wasn't a big waste of time. Willie wanted everyone to feel that way, and he knew that if people found out the truth about him, everyone would just want to curl up and die of embarrassment.

"But me—he wanted me to know the truth. He hadn't really been a war hero. That was just a story that got told around, kind of the same thing that happened to me when I came back from my war. People like to blow things out of proportion. Willie himself never made anything up. In fact, for years after he came home, he never said a word about the war to anyone. He clammed up tight, and that made everyone think he was just being modest. Next thing you know, he's a legend. Finding that money didn't help any, of course. Folks like to think there are a select few who are born to greatness. Willie was just that type, they thought. They figured if he was lucky enough to find the Rory treasure, then he was probably also a war hero, and the stories got bigger and bigger, and next thing you know they had him sitting next to Lincoln at the signing table at Appomatox, or giving advice to Grant on how to win battles.

"Anyway. None of that was the real Willie. The real Willie was a scrawny sixteen-year-old kid when he left home to join the Army, underfed, wearing raggedy clothes, barefoot. In those days the Manns were so poor they couldn't even afford shoes—in fact, one of the reasons he wanted to join up was so he could be sure of getting regular meals and having decent clothes. Willie was bright, too, and he was a hard worker, but like most smart kids he hated farm life with a passion. That's certainly understandable. I was none too fond of it myself. It's grinding, boring work, day after day the same thing, rain or shine, summer or winter, and there's always something broken that needs fixing, always some damn thing going on to get you out of bed or make you miss your dinner.

"So when a war comes along, farm boys are usually first in line to enlist. War is glory, they think. Lots of guys leave home for a few years and come back heroes; why couldn't it happen to them? They never stop to think that probably they're just going to get an arm or a leg blown off, or even get killed outright, or if they don't get hurt they'll be haunted for the rest of their lives by the things they did to other men just like themselves. Every veteran on earth has nightmares, I can guarantee you that. I have them still. Your father probably had them even before he came home. I'm damn glad we're not at war, boy, or you would most likely be in it yourself. You're just like I was at your age. Then you would know what I'm talking about, and I hope to God you never do find out what I'm talking about.

"So Willie hears about the war coming, and he gets all fired up. In those days there was just the tiny little shack here, three rooms, dirt floor, and there were—lemme see—six people living in it. Willie, his folks, his two brothers, and Daddo. So right there's another reason he jumped at the chance to fight. Better food, new clothes, don't have to live all cramped up in one little house any more. So Willie heads off down the road to Buffalo, which in those days was a good three-day walk along the Lake Road. He was barefoot, and he had an old gun Daddo gave him. It was a muzzle-loader. Willie said it was longer than he was and it weighed a ton. After one day of walking with that gun he almost gave up and came home again, it was that heavy. But he didn't. He stuck it out.

"On the way to Buffalo, Willie happened to meet up with his aunt and uncle, who were coming back from some trip or other. They used to go to revival meetings, which were big back in those days. If a famous preacher got within fifty miles, Willie's aunt was there to see him, and more often than not she dragged her husband and son along with her. Her name was Elspeth. She was, if I remember correctly, kind of the hysterical type. She liked to faint a lot. Not for real, but just to get attention. Fainting was very fashionable back then. All the fancy city ladies did it. They even had special fainting couches in their houses, and whenever something exciting or scary or just plain unpleasant happened, well, down they went. Willie's Aunt Elspbeth was just that kind of lady, although her fainting was kind of misplaced, seeing as how farm women didn't do that sort of thing, and Elspeth was, above all, a farm woman.

"So Willie stopped to talk with them. Young Frederic, their son, was with them. He was twelve that year. He and Willie were best friends, and they did everything together. It was no accident Willie had chosen to leave town while Frederic was away with his parents, because he knew he would have a hell of a time saying good-bye to them, and like as not Frederic would want to come along with him. As it turned out, that was exactly what Frederic tried to pull, too. He put up a hell of a fuss when he found out Willie was going somewhere without him. I imagine there must have been quite a scene there on the road, actually, what with Willie's auntie fainting all over the place and Frederic bawling like a calf. But it was out of the question for Frederic to go with him. That went without saying. He was too young. Willie himself was just barely old enough to heft that old gun, and he was already afraid the Army would turn him back once he got to Buffalo.

"So he kept on his way, and his aunt and uncle and Frederic kept on theirs, and Willie camped the first night in a stand of trees along the road. There was a lot more forest in those days, and you could camp wherever you wanted, pretty much. He was lying awake that night, already homesick as hell, feet sore, arms aching, hungry, tired, and starting to get scared, when all of a sudden he hears this noise coming from the road. It was a voice, calling something over and over. Willie had already worked himself up to such a frenzy about the Rebels that he figured they'd somehow got wind of his presence and sent a spy out to kill him, way up here in New York. He said later he just about wet his pants. He loaded up his gun, and he sat there in the leaves, listening to the voice and trying to see who it was, when suddenly he hears his name. He waits and listens again, and sure enough, it comes again. Whoever it is, he knows Willie. And then it comes to him—it's Frederic. The little rat had sneaked off from his parents and set out to find his cousin, and as chance would have it, he found him.

"Well, to hear Willie tell it, he didn't know whether to hug him or shoot him. He knew there was going to be a hell of a fuss when Frederic's parents found out he was gone, and an even bigger one when they realized where it was he'd gone off to. Willie tried to get him to turn around and go home, but of course Frederic wouldn't do it. He was bound and determined to become a soldier himself and head down South to 'whup Rebs.'

"Willie said later that what he should have done was just turn around the next morning and head back to town with Frederic in tow, tie the little bastard to a tree to keep him from following, and start his trip all over again. But for one reason or another he didn't do it. Later on he wished he had, of course, but by then it was too late. He was young, too young to think responsibly for the sake of others—he was just learning how to take care of himself. And he was glad of the company, because lying there all alone that first night he found out real quick he wasn't near as tough as he thought he was, and half of him was scared to death, and the other half was almost crazy with loneliness and homesickness.

"So to make a long story short, Willie and Frederic went to Buffalo and joined up. The Army didn't want to take Frederic, of course, but the boys lied and wheedled and whined, and finally they signed him on as a drummer boy. In those days nobody had any papers, and it was possible to lie about your age with no trouble at all. So they sign up, they get fancy new uniforms, they learn how to drill in formation, all the rest of it. They spent a month or so in camp and then they marched down South.

"Now on this march there was another soldier named Ferguson. A lot of the Irish liked to stick together, but Ferguson was a nasty son of a bitch, the kind of Irishman who made other Irishmen look bad, and the other soldiers didn't like him. He was drunk all the time, lazy, foul-smelling, and a bully. He was a big fellow, too, and he liked to push the smaller guys around. They had chores to do every night on the march when they made camp—one guy went for wood, another guy for water, so on and so on. You generally camped each night in groups of six or seven guys. Ferguson was in the same group as Willie and Frederic. He never wanted to go for wood when it was his turn, and if he was feeling particularly mean that day he would make some other poor slob do it for him. It happened to Willie a few times. Ferguson was too big for Willie to fight, and you didn't complain about things like that to your officers. So you either beat the hell out of the guy and settled it that way, or you put up with it. Willie chose to put up with it.

"That is, until one night when they were camped somewhere in southern Pennsylvania. It was Ferguson's turn to go for wood, and of course he didn't want to go, and he decided he was going to get some-one else to do it for him. Instead of Willie, though, this time he picked on Frederic. Willie was small, but Frederic was even smaller, being only twelve. And to top it all off, Ferguson started smacking the boy around. Well, that was all Willie could take. He lit into Ferguson like a bobcat, and next thing you know, Ferguson is dead, and Willie gets taken off to jail."

"*Dead?*" I interrupted.

"As a doornail," Grandpa said.

"Willie *killed* him?"

"Stabbed him to death, with a big old hunting knife he carried. Said he didn't even remember doing it. The whole world just went red, and next thing he knew he was in prison, with chains around his neck and his legs."

I shuddered. I knew what it felt like to have the whole world go red. It had happened to me when I attacked David Weismueller. So the spirit of the Celtic warrior had lived within my great-great-grandfather too. That was where he came from. He was an heirloom, like the nightmare of Mary Rory.

"Anyway," said Grandpa, "Willie spent the rest of the war in jail. They talked about hanging him, but I guess their hearts weren't in it. Willie got the chance to explain himself in court, and some other fellows spoke up about the kind of man Ferguson was, and how they were surprised nobody had killed him sooner, what with the way he treated everybody. But they couldn't very well let him go free either. So he spent the next four years in a jail cell. With a schoolteacher, as it turned out—that was how he learned to read and write."

"And what happened to Frederic?"

"Frederic," said my grandfather. His face grew dark. "Well, Frederic got killed."

"In battle?"

"Yeah. Antietam. Willie didn't know that, of course. In those days you rarely got notified of anything, and he wouldn't have heard anyway, because he was in jail. Back then, if you got killed, your family didn't get a letter from the government explaining everything. You just didn't come home after the war. By and by, when you didn't show up, your people just kind of figured it out. And that was what happened when Frederic didn't come home.

"Now there had always been this sort of unspoken bond between Willie and Frederic's parents. They trusted him with their boy, but they made it plain every time they went off hunting or fishing or swimming that they held Willie responsible for Frederic's well-being, him being the older of the two, and Willie took it to heart. He always did his best to keep the boy out of trouble. But war is a different thing altogether. Willie knew there was no way he could keep Frederic safe on a battlefield. And then, of course, while he was in prison, he didn't even know where Frederic was. Neither of them could write yet, so they couldn't send letters to each other. Willie got out of prison on the very day the treaty was signed, and he spent a few months hunting around for Frederic. Finally he managed to find some fellows from his old regiment, and they told him Frederic was dead. So Willie gave up and headed home without him.

"Willie hadn't been home in four years. In all that time, nobody back here had heard a word from either of the boys. So Willie's parents were overjoyed, of course, to see their son back safe and sound, if a mite silent. Of course, Willie didn't want to tell them where he'd really been, so he acted like he'd been through one battle too many and he didn't ever want to discuss it. His parents never knew that he'd never fought in any battles at all."

"What about his leg?" I interrupted. "His wounded leg?"

"Some farmer took a shot at him as Willie was stealing one of his chickens," Grandpa said. "Hit him in the thigh. That was the only time Willie ever came under fire in the whole war. And Frederic's parents never knew the boys hadn't been together either. They thought Willie and Frederic had been side by side the whole time, and they couldn't understand why Willie hadn't brought the boy back home. Well, Frederic's father kind of understood. And he knew also that there was nothing Willie could have done to save the boy in the middle of the fighting, even though there hadn't been any fighting for Willie. But Elspeth never forgave him. You know how parents are when it comes to their children. They just get crazy if they see them getting hurt or something, and if the child happens to be killed, why they can easily go around the bend altogether. I know. It happened to me.

"When Willie got home, the first thing he did was limp on up to his aunt's and uncle's place. He didn't want to do it, he said, but he knew if he didn't go right away he never would. When Elspeth saw Willie come walking up the road to their house alone, she was too worked up even to throw one of her fainting fits. She'd been steadily losing her mind ever since Frederic ran off, and when she understood that he was really dead, that he wasn't coming home, she lost it completely. She let loose with a curse on Willie and all the Manns. Not something simple like

'Damn you.' I mean a real old-fashioned curse, like people used to lay on each other around here when they believed in those kinds of things. She went on and on at him for about an hour, calling down all kinds of horrendous things on his head. Willie just stood by the gate and took it. When she was done, he turned around and went home. Soon after that, he found all that money, and he tried to give some to Frederic's parents, but Elspeth wouldn't take it. She forbade any further contact between the Manns and the Simpsons, and she poisoned the minds of all her relations against us. And soon after that, the Simpsons started to die off. It was like her curse had backfired on her. They died of the flu, mostly, which in those days still killed people. Measles too. Soon there were only a few left. And now they're all gone."

Grandpa heaved a deep sigh of relief.

"I thought for a while that we were done for too," he said. He looked at me. "But then you came along." He grinned. "Thank God for that."

"Thanks for telling me," I said.

"It's a hard story to tell," said Grandpa. "But I guess it doesn't seem that bad, now it's out. Willie never came out and told me this himself, you know. He put it all in the diary, and he gave me that, but I never got around to reading it until I was on that damn island. I never got the chance to talk to him about it. Every once in a while, after he gave it to me but before I left for the war, he'd say, 'You read that diary yet?' And I'd say, 'Not yet, Papa Willie.' And he'd say, real casual, 'Well, let me know when you get around to it.' Jesus. I wish—well, never mind what I wish. It's too late for me to be rewriting history. You help me upstairs and put me in my bed now," said Grandpa. "All this talking has worn me out."

Two more months passed, and the end of the school year grew tantalizingly closer. With it would come my graduation and my liberation from high school, and I would be free to search for my mother. But first I needed to know where to look, and I'd heard nothing further from the Air Force. I spent my days in a frenzy of restlessness.

I finally heard from Annie. She mailed me the picnic basket in

which I'd been delivered to Grandpa, and which I'd mistakenly left in
Montreal so long ago. Inside the basket were several copies of a French
magazine. The cover of it seemed familiar, and I looked at it for several moments, trying to place it. Then it hit me—it was *Le Journal des
Lettres*, the Montreal magazine for which I'd asked Annie to translate
my story.

"Dear Billy," she wrote:

> *I'm sorry I've been out of touch for so long. I don't think I need to
> explain. I never have, with you. You understand. Please keep trying to
> understand. Please never change that about you.*

> *I finally finished the translation, and guess what? They took it!
> They didn't offer any money, of course, but they did send me ten free
> copies. I kept two and sent you the rest. This is sort of a triumph for
> both of us, I guess. Congratulations!*

So I was finally published—in a language I couldn't read. It was a
triumph, all right. A bittersweet one, but a triumph nonetheless.

And my suspicions about where I stood with Annie were confirmed. "Please keep trying to understand," she'd written. In our secret
way of speaking to each other, that meant "Please keep leaving me
alone. Someday maybe things will be different, but not right now."

In the meantime, Grandpa grew paler. No, not paler—yellower.
His skin turned the shade of a maple leaf in autumn. His liver began to
wind down, refusing to process the toxins that his body naturally produced. He'd made it do too much work for too long, he said, and now
it was out of juice, or whatever it was that made it run. Grandpa's
understanding of the human body was intimately linked with his auto-
motive expertise. It was in these terms that he'd once explained to me
the mechanics of sex, in the parlance of crankshafts and piston wells,
oil and combustion, and he saw himself now as a machine that had
been driven too long without the proper maintenance; his body was
about to commit the human equivalent of throwing a rod, and there
was nothing anyone could do about it.

Mildred, who was about to lose the second man in her life—but as
she said, in many ways really her first—showed little or no emotion at
Grandpa's imminent passing. At least not in front of us, she didn't. But

passing by her room, through the closed door I could sometimes hear her sobbing out her secret pain. I would pause in the hallway, wondering what a life like hers must have been like. I was born already having lost everything, but Mildred . . . Mildred had built up an entire life and then watched it dwindle away through the bottom of a glass. Kind of like Grandpa, I guess.

Mildred was a practical woman, all business when necessary—she'd been raised in a time before women had the luxury of questioning their position, when they were expected to handle certain situations on their own. A man's death was one of those situations, something for which one rarely had the chance to prepare, so despite her emotion she couldn't pass up this opportunity to take advantage of the notice she'd been given and in this way feel that she was, perhaps, thumbing her nose at the specter of mortality. She cleaned the entire house again, scrubbing it from top to bottom with a vigor that shamed my previous efforts. She forced Grandpa to choose the suit he would wear in his coffin. When he fought her on this point, saying he didn't care what he wore and would just as soon go to the next life naked, she refused to accept his obstinacy.

"You can't just lay there in your birthday suit, now can you?" she said. When Mildred spoke to my grandfather, her eyes sparked in a way that said she loved him and that she would put up with no resistance. To look at her then, you wouldn't know she'd ever shed a tear in her life.

"I came into this world naked," said Grandpa, "didn't I? So I guess I can damn well go out of it naked."

"You mind your mouth. Nobody gets buried naked. What would people say?"

"Ha! They can't say anything about me they haven't said already."

"You'd be surprised," said Mildred.

"We're born naked, wet, and hungry," observed Grandpa to me. "And things just get worse from there. You like that? I read it on a bumper sticker."

"You pick a suit right now," she said, "or you're going to be leaving this world a lot sooner than you think."

"When you get married, Billy, pick a woman like this," said Grandpa, his eyes twinkling. "One with some life to her."

"And don't be afraid to die," said Mildred. "Not like your grandfather."

Grandpa's eyes grew wide in hurt amazement. He opened his mouth, and I thought he was going to yell. Instead, however, he laughed a long, loud laugh at himself, because of course Mildred was right. He didn't want to choose a burial suit because it forced him to imagine how he would look in his coffin.

When those words were out, words that only Mildred could get away with, all pretense was dropped. Grandpa meekly chose an old black tuxedo, which he had last worn as a young man eagerly awaiting the arrival of his ostriches from far-off Australia. He was unable to get out of bed now. I held up his tuxedo for him so he could examine it from his pillow.

"God, I feel like shit," he confided in me when we were alone. It was the only time I heard him complain. "I must look like shit too."

"You don't look too bad," I lied.

"Ha. I bet I look like I'm already dead."

I could say nothing to that, but the truth is he was right. He looked more like a corpse than a living man, and his room had already taken on the smell of death. The feeling in my chest was worsening by the day. I was afraid to go to school for fear he would slip off while I was gone and I would miss his departure; at the same time I was terrified of witnessing it. I had seen the death of Levi Miller's wife, and also the passing of Annie's father. They had been horrible, bloody, dramatic endings. I had no wish to see another.

"Listen, boy," he said. "Have you thought about what you're going to do after I'm gone?"

"You know what I'm going to do. I'm going to find my mother."

"I mean in general. Like a career."

"Writer."

"What else?"

"What do you mean, what else?"

"I mean suppose you don't get lucky right away. What are you going to do for money?"

"I can always get a job."

"Yeah. But there's jobs and then there's jobs."

"Like what?"

He sighed and decided to get to the point. "I want you to go to college," he said.

"I don't need to go to college."

"Wrong. This isn't the old days. Things are different now. A college degree is your only hope, unless you want to be poor all your life. You're smart. Don't make the same mistakes I made."

"I have some money saved up."

"You'll get some from me, too," he said. "But that won't be enough. I took out a policy on myself right before I got sick. You'll get most of it."

"What about Mildred?"

"I've talked it over with her. She doesn't need it like you will. She got some money from her husband, so she'll be all right."

"But what is she going to do?"

"Retire," said Grandpa. "Take it easy. Move into that new home they built over in Forestville, where they wait on you hand and foot and you play checkers all day."

"Will she like that?"

"Probably not," said Grandpa. "Not at first."

"After a while, though?"

"Well, she's an old lady."

"Meaning what?"

"Well, people get old," he said. "And then they die."

"She wants to die in a nursing home?"

"Nobody *wants* to die in a nursing home," said Grandpa. "But she doesn't have any people left."

"What about her children?"

"You've heard her talk about them. They don't write, they don't call. She doesn't even know where they are."

"Because of her husband, though. It's not her fault."

"They blame her, too, for putting up with him."

"What about the house?"

"This house? It's yours, of course," he said, shocked. "What did you think? It just disappears?"

"Mildred can stay here," I said.

"Well, it's your place to do with as you see fit," said Grandpa. He was trying to appear indifferent, but I could see tears welling up in his eyes. He turned away so I wouldn't see them. I pretended not to notice.

"I want her to," I said. "She belongs here just as much as you or I."

"That's mighty nice of you, boy."

I thought of Mildred wasting away little by little in an old folk's home. It would kill her as surely as a bullet in the brain, I thought. She needed activity to keep her going, things to occupy her mind, things to clean, things to worry about. She might be lonely in the big old house, but she wasn't a recluse, like Grandpa. She would make friends. She was that kind of woman.

"She's the closest thing to a mother I've ever had," I said. Hardly were those words out of my mouth when their full import struck me. I put my face in my hands.

"Aw, shoot," Grandpa said, and now it was his turn to pretend not to notice my tears. "Sometimes I hate the way things turned out for you, boy. It wasn't fair, none of it. You got the raw end of the stick. Especially with me around."

"Don't say that," I said. "You did fine."

"I shoulda quit drinking years ago. When I got you. When I think of all the time I wasted—"

"Stop it," I said. "I don't blame you."

"I'll never forget that day," he said. "Comin' out on the back porch like that, and that jet goin' over all of a sudden. Did I tell you about that jet?"

"You told me," I said, remembering how the F–4 had roared overhead just as Grandpa was about to step on me. He'd told me the story a hundred times.

"I never was so happy since the day I got back from the war. I knew you right away. It was like I recognized you. Like I'd known you before. I hated to think what would happen if I died and that was the last of us. Papa Willie and my mother had such high hopes for me. You know? Well, that all went to hell. Sometimes I think I shouldn't have let Eddie go to Vietnam, but there was really nothing I could have done about it. He was born to die young. I see it now. I see the whole picture. Anyway, boy, I'm glad you came along. That's why I want you to go to college. I don't care if you're rich, or famous, or anything like that. I just want you to live a good life. Full. Happy." He closed his eyes.

I was suddenly alarmed. "Hey," I said.

"I'm not dead yet," he said, his eyes still closed. "I'm just taking a nap."

I went into my room. Not knowing what else to do, I got out a fresh notebook and wrote down the words he'd just said to me as exactly as I could. Someday, I knew, I would reread them, and perhaps their meaning would change for me over time. But for now I was too full of everything to absorb them.

I went downstairs to the kitchen and put the kettle on the stove for some coffee. Mildred appeared from the yard, where she'd been looking over her garden.

She was short of breath, startled. Without a word she sat down opposite me at the kitchen table.

"What's the matter?" I asked.

"There's a man in the grotto," she said.

"A *what*?" I sprang to my feet.

The grotto was a small sunken area at the rear of the yard. Some long-gone Mann had dug it out. It was a sort of tiny amphitheater, no more than ten or twelve feet long, with a small bench in it facing a statue of the Virgin Mary. I ran to the kitchen window and peered out at the grotto. I could see a small form sitting hunched on the bench. It was a man, all right, albeit a very little one. For a moment I flashed back to my days of Munchkin-hunting, and a skein of the old panic was drawn through me, intertwined with a thread of fancy. Was it possible, I wondered, that the Munchkins were dying too, and that this was the last of their clan, come to make his peace with me before he passed on? It would make sense; for with Grandpa's departure imminent, other parts of the world would be folding in on themselves, disappearing forever, the Munchkins among them.

But I was no longer young enough to believe in such things. It was a human. He appeared to be either asleep or deep in thought.

"A man in the grotto," Mildred repeated, but I was already out the door and running across the yard.

He was smaller than I'd imagined, somehow. In the stories Grandpa had told me of him, he'd come to be larger than life, but now that he was here, he resumed his normal size. He couldn't have been more than five feet tall. I crossed the yard and stopped behind

him. After a lifetime of preparing for this moment, I was tongue-tied
and confused. I looked at the little man curiously from the back. He
wore a dark overcoat, with the collar turned up against the moist cool
air of spring, and he was staring at the plaster Virgin with great
curiosity. To him, I thought, Mary must appear like some foreign
god, and he would wonder about her powers, be entranced by her
strangeness. From behind he looked like a small boy wearing his
father's clothes. Suddenly he turned, alerted to my presence by my
breathing.

"Ahh," he said, his Oriental eyes folded in pleasure, his face dis-
solving into a thousand wrinkles. "And you are?"

"Billy," I said.

He stood up from the bench and approached me slowly. Standing,
he came only to the middle of my chest. My dream in Montreal had
been accurate: he was a very old man. He moved at a catlike rate, without a trace of arthritis in his knees, but carefully, as though he was
afraid of breaking himself. He stopped at a respectful distance and
bowed as far as his eighty-five-year-old spine would permit.

"Pleasure to meet you," he said. "Billy is short for William Amos
Mann, I presume. Named after your great-great-grandfather."

I bowed in return. It was the first time in my life I'd greeted someone in this fashion. Instinctively I knew that a man of this age, who had
come so far to fulfill an obligation that lesser men would have discarded, deserved my complete and unfettered respect. I bowed as low as I
could. When I straightened up, he was smiling even more broadly.

"For an American boy," he said, "you are very polite. How nice."

"Thank you," I said, at a loss for further words. We stood looking
at each other.

"Do you know who I am?" he inquired after a moment.

"Yes," I said. "I'm sorry. Won't you come in the house?"

"It's very chilly out here," he said. "I'm afraid I'm not as inured to
the elements as I once was."

We walked slowly toward the house. He held my elbow with one
hand. The yard was swimming before my eyes, and the chill of desperation in my chest had been for the moment replaced by wild joy.

Enzo Fujimora had come to Mannville.

* * *

The truth was, as Enzo explained to me later, there was no great mystery to determining in advance the date of Grandpa's death. Long ago, when he and Grandpa were living on the South Pacific island together, he had consulted a variety of signs to make his forecast, much as a farmer reads the wind to tell when the rain is coming. First, he read Grandpa's palm; the lifeline was long, but intersected before its natural termination by misfortune, or perhaps illness. Second, he asked him for the precise date and time of his birth, and then correlated the information with his vast knowledge of Eastern astrology, which he had memorized even as long ago as 1943. Finally, he improvised three coins of wood, upon which he made markings to distinguish heads from tails. Grandpa threw the coins, Enzo tallied up the markings, and then he consulted the other vast work he had memorized, the ancient and mystical Chinese work called the *I Ching*. His pronouncement: Grandpa was probably going to die sometime between 1987 and 1990.

Of course, said Enzo, he said nothing of this to Grandpa at the time. It wasn't right for a man to know in advance the date of his death.

"But how did you know it was now?" I asked in bewilderment. I was unwilling or unable to believe that he had made a lucky guess. The myth of my childhood had been that he would just know, and seeing him in the grotto had in a way not surprised me at all. I wouldn't have been surprised if he'd appeared from the sky riding a dragon.

But his final means relied not on fortune-telling or wizardry, but modern technology.

"I called the hospital in Mannville last month," Enzo said. "After I introduced myself as a healer, and told them I was hoping to encounter an old friend, who I thought might already be sick, they gave me information concerning your grandfather. They were not supposed to do that, of course, but I convinced them."

"How?"

Enzo winked and said nothing. Privately, I was encouraged. Perhaps he still had at least one trick up his sleeve, one that allowed him to control the minds of others at great distances, and so the magic of the myth was not completely destroyed.

I brought Enzo into the house. Mildred was cowering in the kitchen, but when she saw him chatting familiarly with me and noticed how small he was, she relaxed. She too had heard the story of

Grandpa's South Sea sojourn many a time, and when I introduced Enzo Fujimora himself, she was greatly impressed although still somewhat distrustful.

"Orientals are so *spooky*," she told me later, in almost a whisper. It was the only time I came close to losing my temper with her. I had to remember that Mildred came from a generation that had fought one war with Asians and sent its sons to fight a second. It wasn't her fault. She'd been taught to believe they weren't human.

Willie Mann addresses this issue:

> *It is much easier to kill someone when you don't allow yourself to think they are human like you. I was continually amazed, whenever I saw a Southerner, to see that he had two legs, two arms, ten fingers and toes, et cetera, just as I did. I had been told that Rebs looked more like dogs than people, and that killing one was about as significant.*

The first thing I did was take Enzo upstairs. I paused at the threshold of Grandpa's room and tapped lightly on the door.

"Grandpa," I said.

His eyelids flickered like two drunken butterflies. I could hear his breathing from across the room. "What is it," he sighed.

"Are you too sick for visitors?"

"Yes."

"Someone's here."

Grandpa was too weak to raise himself up on his pillow. He tried to see who was in the doorway behind me, but he wasn't wearing his glasses.

"Who?"

I led Enzo to the bed. He sat down next to Grandpa and put one tiny old hand on his. Grandpa's eyes grew wide and the ghost of a smile wreathed his cracked lips. "Enzo-san," he said.

"Thomas-san," said Enzo.

"You made it."

"Yes."

"I'm glad," said Grandpa. "You could have just mailed it."

"I made a promise," said Enzo. "Besides, I've always wanted to see beautiful Mannville. The house, and the garden, and everything."

Beautiful Mannville? I thought.

"I'm dying, Enzo," said Grandpa.

Enzo smiled. It was a smile of deep compassion.

"I know, Tom," he said.

The two old men stayed like that, one's hand resting on top of the other's. They said nothing further. They just rested.

I left them alone and went back downstairs to finish my coffee, which had grown cold. Mildred offered to heat it up for me.

"That's Enzo," I said.

Mildred said nothing. She poured my coffee into a saucepan and lit the burner.

"I ought to buy a microwave," I said.

Mildred shuddered. "I wouldn't have one of those things in *my* house," she said pointedly. "They give you cancer."

"You can heat up coffee in one minute with one of those," I said. "Just think of it." There were, in fact, a lot of things I wanted to buy. It had only been with the arrival of Mildred two years earlier that Grandpa had finally gotten rid of the old icebox and installed a modern electric refrigerator. "I want a *television*!" I said. "And a VCR. And video games. All the stuff that other people have."

"I guess you have been pretty sheltered," observed Mildred.

"Wouldn't you at least like a dishwasher?" I asked her. "Don't you get tired of doing the dishes by hand?"

Mildred said nothing, her eyes filling with tears, and she looked away. Then I remembered I hadn't yet asked her to stay.

"I was talking with Grandpa about you," I said.

"You were?"

"You know about his first wife, how she just left him one day?"

"I know."

"Grandpa never trusted anybody after that. No woman, or man, or anybody."

"I know," she said again.

"You've earned a place here as much as I have," I told her. "You're the one who made Grandpa happy again, as much as that sort of thing is possible. Even his wife was never this good for him. You have to stay. Please. Don't go to Forestville. Stay here."

Mildred sat at the table and put her face in her apron. I sipped my coffee and pretended once again that I didn't notice. There had been a lot of crying lately and I found it all very embarrassing. When her emotion subsided, she dried her eyes.

"Thank you," she said simply. We sat together, sipping coffee and saying little else.

After half an hour had gone by I went upstairs again. Enzo was seated in a chair by Grandpa's bedside. I waited outside the door for a minute. They remained silent, as though communing in some sort of secret way. When they became aware of my presence, Enzo turned and smiled again at me, and Grandpa beckoned with one long yellow finger. I entered timidly.

"He was just in time," said Grandpa with an effort. I looked at his eyes, his color, listened to his breathing. His skin was growing translucent even as I watched him. Grandpa closed his eyes and his breathing faded until it was nearly inaudible.

I noticed for the first time the book that lay on his chest, his free hand resting on it as though it was a source of strength. It was an old book, bound in plain leather, with no inscription on it. I could smell it from where I stood. It smelled of leather, and old paper, and of mildew; its odor suddenly seemed to permeate the room. How odd, I thought, that a book should have a smell. I inhaled deeply. There were other scents mixed into it: some strange sort of spice, or perhaps wood smoke, and another smell that hinted of someone else's house. It was a house far from Mannville, one that smelled nothing like any house around here.

Grandpa's eyes fluttered open once more. He grasped the book with both hands and pushed it up toward me with tremendous effort. I took it from him before he could falter. He tried to speak, but his mouth and throat were too dry. I gave him a sip of water. He moistened his lips and tried again.

"Read it," he said, after several tries. Then he closed his eyes for the last time.

Grandpa continued to breathe for three more hours. Enzo moved to one wall of the bedroom, out of the way, while I sat in his place and Mildred sat on the other side of the bed. We watched him until his breathing faded more and more into nothingness. At the last moment, Mildred and Enzo left the room and closed the door, and I was alone with him. I put his hand in mine and held it on the bed. At 3:43 P.M., his breathing finally stopped, the tiny pulse in his hand disappeared, and his skin began to grow cold.

I got up and opened the window. A flock of birds, disturbed by the noise, flew silently from their roosts and fluttered skyward. I leaned out of the window for several moments, looking out over the yard. Over the tops of the trees I could just see the roofs of the highest houses in the new subdivisions, sitting on what had once been Mann land. I meditated dully on them without really thinking.

After a time I turned from the window and leaned against the sill. As it happened, there was a mirror next to me on the wall, and another one on the wall opposite; it was an arrangement Grandpa had insisted on, saying that this confluence of reflections would allow his soul a clear path to escape. I looked into the far one and saw myself stretching away into an endless corridor of windowsills, curving off to the right into infinity. I saw myself repeated endlessly out of sight, like the line of generations that had created me. It was like my own history; I could only see so far before it disappeared, before I lost the trail.

When I was sure that enough time had passed, I got two pillowcases from Grandpa's closet and placed them over the mirrors. Then I opened the door and admitted Enzo and Mildred. In the time that had passed, the undertaker had arrived; there were two brawny young men bearing a wicker basket sitting in the parlor opposite Grandpa's room, wearing dark suits and looking somber. I greeted them with a flip of the hand. They nodded in return and stood up politely. I took another armful of pillowcases from the linen closet in the hall and went from room to room, covering all the mirrors, until the house was completely invisible to itself, and all the paths out, once taken, were closed. The old farmhouse had had enough of ghosts. Grandpa was on his way home.

Grandpa's Wake; the End of Some Things, and the Beginnings of Others

We Manns bury our own in the old-fashioned way. According to Grandpa's stories, there was once a time when there was no such thing as a funeral home. People were waked in their own homes and then carried up to the church on the shoulders of their family. That meant you had a dead body in the house for two or three or sometimes four days. I guess that was normal then; it's hard to imagine anybody doing that today. Except for us Manns, of course. But we've always done things a little bit differently than everyone else.

I did some figuring—I don't know why I was thinking about this, just trying to distract myself, I guess. I came to the conclusion that there had to have been at least twenty or so wakes in the old farmhouse even before I came along, and before that, God only knew how many in the tiny shack that had existed before Willie found the Rory money.

So once again, history saved me. If I'd sat there thinking I was the first of us to go through this, that it hadn't ever happened before, I might have lost my mind. But I thought of how many of us had gone before Grandpa, and how many Manns had sat around them in mourning, and that even *those* Manns had eventually passed on and lain right where Grandpa himself was now lying—well, it made it easier on me. And I knew that someday I too would be lying there, and people would be sitting around me having the same thoughts I was having now.

Concessions to the times had to be made, of course. Grandpa was embalmed at the funeral home—you're not allowed to have unembalmed bodies just lying around the house anymore—but then they brought him back and laid him out downstairs, right where he used to sit in his rocking chair.

No. Not Grandpa. Grandpa's *body*. I had to keep reminding myself of that.

So that was how it came to be that early the next afternoon Grandpa lay in his casket in the living room, his eyes covered with two heavy silver coins. The room had been cleared of furniture, and the walls were lined with rented folding chairs. A large brass candlestick stood at either end of the coffin, each holding a white candle, which in turn nourished a tiny yellow flame. Mildred had cleaned the house yet again, and every inch of it gleamed; one could nearly see one's reflection in the polished wood floor, and the old farmhouse smelled of lemon oil. I sat in one of the folding chairs, staring dully out the window. I'd been up all night reading the diary. My eyes burned with fatigue, and my head swam with confusion. A small voice in me kept repeating, *Grandpa is dead.*

Shut up, I would reply silently. And it would obey for a moment, but soon it would come back, more insistent, whispering, *Grandpa is dead. What will you do now?*

I don't know, I thought miserably. *I don't know.*

In death, Grandpa achieved a state of relaxation that life had never granted him. The lines of tension around his eyes and forehead had melted, and the yellow pallor of illness had disappeared and been replaced by waxy whiteness, which, though indisputably the color of death, nevertheless suited him much better than jaundice. And there was something else, something odd about him that I couldn't put my finger on. It wouldn't occur to me until later, when the house was full of people and I was drunk, that he was missing his fedora.

When I asked the undertakers about it later, they seemed confused.

They hadn't seen it, they claimed. I searched the entire house but it was never discovered. Finally I gave up. It seemed that Grandpa had, just maybe, been allowed to take *something* with him, in defiance of the rules. We Manns have never been much for rules anyway. We prefer to make our own. In any case, the hat was gone, and I never saw it again.

Mannville being the small town it was, word of death—anyone's death—spread quickly. It was almost unnecessary to print an obituary in the *Megaphone*. The news that Grandpa had departed, and that there would be an old-fashioned wake in the house, was across town within hours. To tell the truth, I was afraid nobody would come. Grandpa hadn't exactly gone out of his way to be friendly in the last forty-some years. Since he'd sobered up, he'd been getting out a little more, reestablishing some old acquaintanceships, but you can't erase four decades of isolation in just a couple of years. So at first it was just Mildred, Enzo, and I.

And Grandpa, of course.

No. *Not* Grandpa. Grandpa's *body*.

But around one o'clock, the first tentative knock came at the door, and Mr. and Mrs. Gruber entered. They spoke with Mildred in undertones, their voices flitting in and out of my fatigued mind like bats. Enzo was introduced. The Grubers came to me and I shook their hands, Emily's small and bony, Harold's large and warm, and their condolences echoed fuzzily in the bright room. In addition to the absence of flowers, which he hated, Grandpa had insisted on open windows and natural light. "I don't want a bunch of gloomy Gusses sitting around in the dark," he'd said. "Funerals are depressing enough already." And so the living room windows were unshuttered, and the sun, which shone uninterrupted, illuminated the proceedings with a warm, soft yellow glow.

An Irish wake means whiskey and food, and the old wooden table in the kitchen was laden with bottles, casserole dishes, silverware, and clean glasses. Mildred flitted about with a bottle of Bushmill's and a tray of glasses. She wouldn't touch it herself, she promised me, but she saw no reason why her broken love affair with alcohol should ruin everyone else's good time. Mrs. Gruber didn't drink either, but Harold cheerfully accepted a dram. Enzo joined him, wordlessly holding out his glass for Mildred to fill. Harold looked askance at Enzo for a moment; no doubt he was wondering where this tiny Oriental had appeared from and what he was doing there. But the two of them being old men, having the weight of years in common, they soon fell into conversation.

I ignored them. The voice had come back to me again. *Grandpa is dead*, it reminded me.

I considered screaming out loud to shut the voice up. Instead I forced myself to listen to Enzo and Harold.

"So this is Irish whiskey," Enzo was saying. He sniffed at his glass, tasted it. His eyebrows shot up. "My goodness," he said, and muttering in Japanese, he threw back his head and tossed the contents of the glass down his throat. Then he smiled broadly.

"My goodness," he said again.

"What was that you said just now?" asked Harold.

"It was something in my own language," said Enzo. "I think it means something like the English 'Here's mud in your eye.'"

"Now there's a phrase I haven't heard in a long time," said Harold.

"We used to say it to each other in college," said Enzo. "But we never drank anything like this."

"Well, you know, I'm not Irish," said Harold, "but I sure do appreciate what they've done for booze."

"It's very fine stuff," said Enzo. "And I'm certainly not Irish either."

"Say, Billy," said Harold, "how old are you now?"

I roused myself.

"Twenty-one," I said.

"Well, I know damn well you're not twenty-one," said Harold, "not that I care. This boy's been lying to me about his age ever since he was twelve," he said to Enzo, "except he never thought I knew it." To me he said, "Go and get yourself a glass, and drink a toast to your grandfather with us men."

"Now, Harold," said Emily, "I don't know about that."

"Emily, please," said Harold, "he's not a kid anymore. He can have a drink with us if he wants to."

"You be careful, Billy," said Emily, and from the look she shot her husband I knew he was in for it later.

"Okay," I said. I got a glass from the kitchen. Enzo poured the whiskey for me himself, his gnarled and spotted hands steady despite his great age.

"Here's mud in your eye," I said.

"Here's mud in *your* eye," said Harold.

"Here's mud in all of our eyes," said Enzo.

I drank the whiskey down, all of it. It was the first whiskey of my life. It burned as much as I remembered from my clandestine sip as a boy. I coughed.

"My goodness," I said.

"Exactly," said Enzo.

The doorbell clanged again and Mildred went to answer it. I poured myself another shot and offered the bottle to Enzo and Harold. Enzo declined a freshener, but Harold accepted a small one. Mrs. Gruber frowned at me, but I ignored her. The whiskey warmed me from the inside out.

"Man," I said to Harold, "this makes you feel all right. No wonder Grandpa liked it so much."

"Normally I never touch it," said Harold, "but at funerals . . . well, you know. Funerals were made for drinking. Or drinking was made for funerals. One or the other."

"Our condolences, Billy," said a voice. I turned to see the Greenes.

Mr. and Mrs. Greene were in their late sixties and wore twin crowns of silver hair. I delivered groceries to them once a week. They shook my hand, went to the catafalque, and knelt in front of the coffin, where they crossed themselves.

I observed this with curiosity—I'd never prayed in my life, but it seemed as if this would be a good occasion to learn. When they were done they crossed themselves again and stood. I made a mental note of the order of things, of how it was supposed to go: cross, kneel, pray, cross, get up. But what was praying?

I crossed the room and knelt where they had been. Awkwardly I made the sign of the cross on my chest. I rested my elbows on the velvet pad of the catafalque. Only then did I permit myself to look at what was left of my grandfather.

I'd glanced only briefly at the body after the undertakers had brought it back from the funeral home. Grandpa had died before my eyes, and so the sight of him in his coffin was not so terrible as it might have been. But I hadn't yet given myself time to take a long look. And I hadn't said anything to him. Or about him. Now, I felt, would be the right time for that. If I was going to pray, I ought to do it now.

But I couldn't. I just knelt there and looked at him. I thought of reaching out to touch his hand, but I knew it would be cold and lifeless. He wouldn't feel it.

Pray, already, I said to myself.

Right. Here we go.

Dear God, I prayed. *Here is the man who raised me from my infancy. He did the best he could, which I think was pretty good. He knew he had to die someday, and I knew it, and someday I will be dead too, so there's no point in going on about that part of it. The point is, I don't want him to linger. I want his spirit to go free. That's why I covered up all the mirrors. I want him to go on to whatever the next thing is, and I want him to tell every one of us Manns he sees over there, wherever he is, that I will be all right. They don't have anything to worry about. And I promise to tell all the old stories to my kids, when I have them. I promise to tell them about him, too. So if you would pass that message on for me, please, God, I would be very grateful. I would do it myself, but I don't quite know how.*

That was all I could think of.

Amen, I added, as an afterthought.

I wondered if I was supposed to wait for a response. After a moment, though, it appeared that none was forthcoming. Grandpa remained silent in his coffin, and God didn't reply—not that I was seriously expecting him to, but one never knows—so I crossed myself again and stood up.

The room had fallen silent and everyone was watching me. When I turned around they looked away; I heard sniffling. It was then that I had a moment much like the one Grandpa had experienced at the funeral of Jack Simpson. I don't mean I left my body, as he claimed he'd done. I mean I was able, just for an instant, to see myself as other people saw me. And I could tell it was a poignant moment for them— the young orphan boy saying good-bye to his only known relative. At that moment I understood how I'd always been seen by the people of this town, by the people who loved me. I was never just Eddie's bastard to them. I was the kid who'd made it mostly on his own, and I could see they respected me for that. And something changed in me at that moment, something impalpable and difficult to describe. But here is the best way to say it: Looking back on things now, if I had to pick a moment when my childhood was clearly and definitively over and I started looking at myself as an adult, I would have to say it was right then, standing next to the body of my grandfather.

The Greenes had joined the small knot of people in the corner and were holding paper plates of food. Mildred came in from the kitchen with another bottle of whiskey and a tray of clean glasses. Everybody took one except for Mr. Greene.

"Bushmill's, is it?" said Mr. Greene.

"It is."

"I mustn't, then," he said. "It's a Protestant whiskey."

"Oh, what does that have to do with it? This is America," said Mrs. Greene. To the room at large she explained, "He likes to pretend he's all wrapped up in the troubles in Northern Ireland. It makes him feel important." Thus shamed, Mr. Greene took a glass after all and nursed it silently, glowering at his wife.

Silence reigned for a time. It was my first wake, and I didn't know what to do next.

"He was a grand old man," said Harold.

"I alwuz did feel bad about them ostriches," said Mr. Greene.

"Hear hear."

Another toast was drunk by everyone, including me. It was my third. The doorbell rang again, and I went to get it myself. After ushering in Officer Madison and his wife, I hit upon the idea of propping open the front door with a chair. That way nobody would have to worry about answering the bell. I thought this a very intelligent plan and congratulated myself for having thought of it by pouring another drink. But Emily caught my eye and I set it off to the side, guiltily, to be consumed later.

"Great idea, having a home wake," said Madison. "They used to do this all the time."

Despite his complete ineptitude as a police officer, Madison had detected exactly what was needed to get people talking: nostalgia. There were memories abounding in those ancient gray heads. Madison had jogged them, and they came flying out.

"I remember when my own grandfather passed on," said Harold.

"That would have been when I was about seven. People didn't live as long then as they do today." He aimed that last comment at me because I was the youngest and therefore logically the most ignorant. Harold didn't know that I was more immersed in the past than any of them. I nodded, feigning interest. "It was in nineteen nineteen. Course everybody had home wakes then."

"What kind of customs do you have in Japan?" asked Mildred of Enzo.

"We cremate," he said. "Then we keep the ashes in a shrine."

"Now there's a hell of an idea," said Harold admiringly. "Save on space, right?"

"We worship our ancestors," said Enzo. "We like to have them close by us."

"How beautiful," said Mrs. Greene.

"Where exactly you from in Japan?" asked Mr. Greene.

"I am from Nagasaki," said Enzo.

There was another long and silent moment, during which I think everyone had the same image: a malevolent mushroom cloud glowing red and black in the Japanese sky. Someone coughed, and another person shuffled their feet.

"Friend of Tom Mann's, were you?" asked Harold finally.

"Oh yes," said Enzo. "We met during the war."

"Is that right," said Mr. Greene. "How'd that happen?"

"I shot down his plane," Enzo explained.

Mr. Greene began to choke on his whiskey. Mrs. Greene patted him on the back.

"You were the fella that shot down Tom's plane?" said Harold, his eyes wide.

"Yes," said Enzo. "That was I."

"My God," said Mr. Greene, recovering. "What the hell did you do that for?"

"It's all right," I said hastily. "This is the man Grandpa was marooned on that island with. They got to be good friends."

"I apologized to him afterward," Enzo assured Mr. Greene. "He understood. There was a war, after all. I had to do it."

"I remember when Tom come home after that," said Harold. "He was kind of a hero."

"Good American boys died on that plane, mister!" said Mr. Greene.

Enzo cleared his throat.

"My wife and children," he said, "were killed in Nagasaki by the atomic bomb."

The silence that ensued now was eons long. My face burned from whiskey and embarrassment.

"Well," said Mr. Greene finally, "I am sorry about that."

"It was a war," said Enzo, "and it was a long time ago. Things like that happen in wartime."

"Did you fly one of them Zeroes?" Harold asked.

This salvaged the situation, for the three elderly men, their wartime animosities dusty from disuse, immediately embarked on a discussion of the differences between the Japanese Zero and the American P–40. I listened. Soon the women began to talk to each other, their voices cutting through the rumble of their husbands' as though they weren't there, and the lilting of their voices gradually soothed my frayed nerves. Exhausted from being up all night, I had to jerk myself awake twice.

Then there were footsteps behind me, and I felt a hand on my shoulder. It was a familiar hand, large and heavy and hairy. For a moment, in my waking-dream state, I thought it was Doctor Connor returned from the grave. But an odor assailed my nostrils, rising above the smell of whiskey and candles and incense: manure. Manure and milk. And tobacco. Where had I smelled those before?

I stood and turned, still half asleep. It was not Doctor Connor, of course. It was Mr. Shumacher. And behind him, ranked in order of age as always, stood Mrs. Shumacher and seven Shumacher children, their round pudgy faces emitting a mixture of excitement and sadness.

I couldn't speak. Mr. Shumacher grabbed me by both shoulders and squeezed; he too was hard-pressed for words, it seemed. Mrs. Shumacher came to his rescue by flying past him and taking me to her massive bosom, which seemed, if possible, to have grown even larger. Neither appeared to have aged at all.

"Gruss Gott," gasped Mrs. Shumacher. "It's good to see you, boy."

"Yah," agreed Mr. Shumacher, as if those were exactly the words he'd been searching for. "Good to see you."

"Good to see you," murmured the man behind them. With a start I saw that the man was Amos Junior, now into his thirties and an exact replica of his father, right down to the handlebars depending lazily from his upper lip. He moved forward and pressed my hand in both of his. I watched my fingers disappear for a moment between his massive palms.

"Good to see you," said Amos Junior.

"Good to see you, Amos Junior," I said. Emotion was choking me and speech was difficult. I had to content myself with shaking his hand as firmly as I could, but the gesture was as absurd as an ant trying to lift a pancake.

Amos Junior was followed by Jan and Hans, Elsa, Hildy, and Marky, all of whom had turned into clones of their parents. They grabbed me to them as though I was a prodigal brother for whom they had grown tired of waiting. Without looking, I knew that in our driveway there would be parked a Shumacher convoy of two pickup trucks and a sedan. It was a regular family adventure.

The family filed past me and into the living room, where they went to the coffin and knelt to say prayers. Last in the line of Shumachers stood a kid near my age. He had a shock of fine blond hair cut in the shape of a soup bowl, and large limpid eyes an astonishing shade of blue. He looked uncomfortable in his suit, which was obviously new: someone had forgotten to snip the price tag off his pants. The kid looked down at the floor when he saw me staring at him and fidgeted with his fingers. Mr. Shumacher poked me in the back.

"He's shy, but he's been talking about you all the way here," he said. "Go say hi to him."

I sidled closer to the boy. He would be about sixteen by now, I calculated, but he still looked younger than he was; he probably always would. And by now, after eleven years, he would be a full-fledged Shumacher, if not in physical stature then at least in spirit.

"Hello, Adam," I said.

Adam looked me full in the eye for a long moment. I was transported back to the barn, feeling the crushed hay underfoot again as I played my airplane games while he looked on. His eyes had grown in concert with the rest of him. They were still too big for his body. The overall effect was of looking at someone whose soul was lurking just beneath the surface of his face waiting for the right moment to burst out and shine triumphantly.

"Hi," he said. "How you doing?"

I shrugged. "Okay. How you been?"

It was his turn to shrug.

"Pretty good," he said. His voice was still scratched and high, as though it hadn't been able to grow with the rest of him. The damage his father had done to his vocal cords was permanent.

"This is your house, huh?"

"Yah," I said. Unconsciously I was slipping back into the Shumacher mode of speech. Adam had adopted it as well.

"I remember you pretty good," he said.

I smiled. "I remember you too," I said.

"Yah. Good."

We stood there, awkwardly silent.

"You come by the house sometime," he said finally. "Visit."

"Yeah," I said. "I will."

"Really?"

"Sure."

"Good."

Abruptly Adam headed for Mrs. Shumacher. He sat down next to her and leaned his head on her shoulder. She reached up one hand and stroked his hair as she continued her conversation with Mrs. Greene. Adam looked at me once more, shyly, and finally smiled.

The house was slowly filling now with people. I recognized all of them, some more than others, from my jaunts around town as an agent of Gruber's Grocery. The men pressed my hand, the women pecked me on the cheek, all of them muttering words of commiseration and condolence under their breath. Some of them had brought bottles of their own, and deep dishes of food, and these they set on the counter in the kitchen.

I took advantage of the distraction to down my fourth whiskey. It had a smoky flavor, strong but not harsh, and I felt it racing down my throat like lava, sending a shudder through my body. I had often seen Grandpa give the same shudder when he drank. I'd wondered then why he drank at all if he hated it so much. Now I understood that it was only partly a shudder of distaste. The rest of it was pleasure, sheer delight at the perversion of deflowering oneself in such a manner, and also the convulsive struggle of the human organism against the intensity of the alcohol. Poison it was, surely, but delicious poison, sweet and welcoming, and I felt a certainty that I'd never felt before, a lightheadedness that quickly gave way to hilarious clarity. Suddenly many things I'd never understood were illuminated. Me, my life, growing up in the old farmhouse, Annie, Grandpa—everything made sense in a shrug-of-the-shoulder, what-the-hell kind of way. I was astonished at how easy it all seemed at that moment, how clear the whole matter of my existence was, how simple, how beautiful. I was drunk.

Willie Mann, in one of his lighter moods, writes of drinking:

Whiskey makes the old man young—
he feels his heart beat quickly.
But whiskey makes him old again
come morning, when he's sickly.

People had given up on ringing the doorbell and were just walki1ng in now. My fears that nobody would attend were diminishing by the moment. Already there were more people in the house than there had been at one time since I was born.

I noticed then a trio of men who were standing awkwardly off to one side of the gathering. They were all short and slightly built. One of them had flaming red hair. The redhead held a strange bundle of pipes under his arm, and the other two were clutching instrument cases—a fiddle, I surmised from the shape, and something else. I squinted carefully at the men. Their clothing was odd, foreign-looking yet somehow familiar. It reminded me of the old suits we kept in trunks up in the attic. They were the same old-fashioned cut, the same sort of style. The men were so out of place in this clothing that they almost looked to be in costume, and yet nobody else appeared to have noticed them, or if they had, they thought nothing of it.

The redheaded man saw me looking at them. He nudged his two companions. They approached me slowly, respectfully, with heads bowed.

"Our condolences to ye in yer time o' need," said the redheaded man. He had a thick Irish brogue, his words barely recognizable.

"Thanks," I said. I waited for them to introduce themselves, but instead they looked down shyly at the floor.

"'Tis an Irish wake here, they say," said the redheaded man presently.

"'Tis," said his companion who was holding the fiddle case.

"You guys Irish?" I asked. That's it, I thought; they're homesick Irishmen.

"Aye," said the third, who hadn't yet spoken. A smile lit his face for an instant and then disappeared as he appeared to remember where he was.

"You been over here long?"

"Here?"

"The States, I mean."

"Oh, the States," said the redheaded man. "Ahh . . . we've been over a good long time, yes."

I looked again at their clothes. Perhaps they were Irish clothes, I thought. That would explain it.

"Well," I said, feeling the whiskey surging through my blood, "whaddaya got in those cases? And what are all those pipes?"

"Ah," said the redheaded man, "we've a fiddle and a squeezebox, and these pipes are for makin' music."

"Music," I said. A flash of intuition lit my inebriated mind. "You guys are musicians!" I said brightly.

"We are," said the third man. "We—well . . . "

"All right," said the second man, "just come out and tell the man."

"Right, so. It's like this," said the redhead. "We heard of the passin' of yer grandfa'ar. We're all very sorry about it. And we heard too that t'was to be an Irish wake, the Manns bein' an old Irish clan. We're right sorry to just show up like this, y'see, but . . ." he appeared to lose confidence here, and he looked to his companions for encouragement.

"T'wouldn't be an Irish wake without Irish music," finished the second man. "So if ye'd like us to play fer ya, we can do it. And if not, why, we're sorry to just jump in like this, and we'll be on our way."

But he was speaking to empty space, for I had already begun clearing a spot for them against the wall. It was perfect, I thought. It was fate. How could I have forgotten to get Irish musicians for an Irish wake?

"You guys sit here," I said. "Play away. Play like maniacs. I don't know who told you to come up here, but I'm glad as hell you showed up."

The men sat down and two of them took out their instruments. The second one, the one who carried the fiddle case, bounced up again quickly from his chair and took me by the arm.

"If I might have a word with ye," he said. "In private, like."

We stepped into the kitchen, where it was slightly less crowded. The house had become full of people.

"I've been asked to deliver a message," said the man. All traces of shyness were gone now. He still clutched my arm, but his hand was almost weightless. I had to look to see if it was there at all.

"A message?" I said.

"Aye."

"From whom?"

"Someone who cares greatly about you," he said.

"What is it?"

The man cleared his throat and looked upward for a moment as though trying to refresh his memory.

"When God rejoices," he said, as if quoting, "you rejoice."

A chill went down my spine.

"What?" I said, though I'd heard him perfectly well.

"When God rejoices, you rejoice," said the man again.

We stood staring at each other for several moments. He looked directly into my eyes, and again I felt a surge of recognition, as if I had known this man at some time, somehow, somewhere. But I couldn't place his face. It didn't seem to matter, however. A sense of calm filtered through me as I thought about what he'd just told me. I thought I knew what this message meant. It was the equivalent of a telegram from one who has successfully completed a long voyage. It was the same sort of message immigrants from Ireland might have sent back home, years ago, when their journey across the ocean was completed and they were in the New World: arrived safely, all is well, please don't worry about me.

It was a message from Grandpa.

"Who the hell are you?" I asked.

"I'm a musician," said the man. "And an Irishman, like yourself."

"That doesn't tell me anything."

"Shhh," said the man. He patted me on the shoulder. "Listen to the music. Don't think so much. That's what music is for. It reminds you to dance once in a while."

Abruptly he went back into the living room. A moment later there was a heart-rending whine, and the piercing, poignant tones of a tune—a very old tune, from the sound of it—filled the living room. The redhead was playing his pipes. The houseful of mourners who'd come to see my grandfather off fell silent and listened. The sound was oddly familiar. The hair stood up on the back of my neck and another chill shot through me.

Grandpa had told me that in his youth the Manns had hosted endless parties, parties that featured exactly this kind of music. Ceili music, he called it. There had been more musicians around then, he said, and there were three in particular who used to show up every once in a while. When they did, the entire town turned out to listen to them—and to dance and drink and eat at the Manns' expense—because it was widely held that they were the best Irish musicians in America, and some said they played with an almost supernatural ability. They were itinerants, and it was not often folks in Mannville got a chance to hear them—only once or twice a year. Grandpa said he didn't know what had happened to the musicians. They looked a little thinner—a little more wan and haggard—every year, and then the last year before the war, they'd simply failed to show up. Nobody had ever seen them again. Grandpa spoke of them wistfully, as if still hoping they might reappear one day, grinning their shy grins and asking politely if they might be allowed to play, explaining their long absence by saying that they had temporarily lost their way, but that none of it mattered now—they were here again, and the music they offered commanded one to listen, and to forget.

The piper played a long time, I think. I remained standing where the little man had left me in the kitchen, my head against the wall. I knew what those pipes were now. They were called Uillean pipes. Grandpa had tried to describe them to me before, but there is no way to describe with words the sound that the Uillean pipes make, no way to explain the effect they have on a wounded heart. It was not just a tune the redheaded man was playing. It was as if he was telling something; a story, perhaps, or maybe just a bit of reassurance. The sound of the pipes is a plaintive lament, shrill, reedy, warm and bright with life and dark with deep despair at the same time; one listens not only with the ears but with the heart. I could feel it entering me, penetrating me right down to the hollow vibrating void that had been there since I had watched Grandpa close his eyes for the last time.

"You have begun reading the diary?"

The enquiry was made in a voice both small and powerful, and I turned to see Enzo. He seemed to have grown smaller in the company of so many burly Americans. His thick glasses gave him an owlish look.

"Yes," I said. "I hope you slept all right last night. Was the bed okay?"

Enzo dismissed this question with a flick of his hand as not worth answering. I have survived far worse catastrophes than uncomfortable beds, it seemed to say; do not insult me by asking how I slept.

"I wish to inform you of the arrival of the mail delivery," he said.

"What?"

"The mail. You have received letters."

"Thanks," I said. When he remained there staring at me, I said, "I'll get them later. I want to listen to the music."

"You do not think it important?"

"Not now," I said. "Probably a few bills or something. Always at least a few bills."

"Perhaps you ought to make sure," he said. Again his voice played that trick on my ears, barely audible yet impressing itself deeply on my mind. It must have been the same technique he used on the doctors at the hospital to find out Grandpa's condition. And suddenly his meaning became clear. I'd told him the story of my quest to discover who my mother was, right down to the detail of the Air Force having sent my father's personal effects to an address other than his home. And I'd said I was waiting to hear what that address might be. I'd been waiting so long to find out, I'd forgotten I was waiting at all. Enzo had seen the mailman arrive, and something had told him to go out and check the mailbox himself and then to come and get me.

"I'll go check it right now," I said.

Enzo smiled.

More cars pulled into the driveway as I walked out to the mailbox and opened it. The sounds of laughter were audible outside now, even where I was standing out by the mailbox, holding a thin blue envelope in my hand. Laughter. At Grandpa's wake. He would be delighted. It would have suited him just perfectly to have everyone forget his death and enjoy themselves one more time in their lives than they would have otherwise.

I held the envelope up to the sun. There was a single sheet of paper in it. Casually, feigning disinterest to myself, I opened the envelope and read the letter.

"Dear Mr. Mann," it read:

Pursuant to your request of March 1988, enclosed please find the information for which you have been looking.

Good luck.

Following was a street address in Santa Fe, New Mexico.

It was once my mother's address. And it might still be.

There was also a name above the address. A full name. *Her* name.

How easy it would be, I thought, to lose this piece of paper, which is almost lighter than air, and which would disappear if I tossed it up into the breeze. Or how easy to rip it up and toss it into a garbage can without anyone noticing, and my life would never have to change.

Occasionally our entire destiny hinges on something as insignificant as one thin piece of paper. It's at moments such as these that the machinations of fate are revealed to be as flimsy and pliable as a silk scarf. I could, I thought, stay here in Mannville forever and not know anything more than I already did. At least I wouldn't know any less, and the future itself would be certain. Grandpa had left me money. I could keep the house, get a job, get married, have more Manns, and tell them the stories of the ghosts who had once wandered through the dusty hallways. Nothing needed to change that.

But I knew that wasn't going to be the way it was. The future had always been blank to me, but it was not the obscurity of hopelessness; it was the darkness of what is unknown simply because it hasn't yet been explored. It was like looking down the corridor between the two mirrors in Grandpa's bedroom. I had to go into it. I had to explore. Otherwise I would never know what was around the bend, and I would live a miserable life, and die a disgruntled death.

I can always come back, I thought. There is no leaving so permanent that it cannot be undone by coming home again.

An image came to me then. It was the same image I'd had when I was seven years old, riding the lawnmower up the hill to the Simpson house to save Grandpa's life. It was an image of my father. He was tanned, as always, and shirtless, and grinning his bewitching grin. He flexed his arms, spit contemptuously on the ground, and slapped his palms together.

"Let's get to it," he said.

And he rubbed his hands in anticipation of the difficulty of the task ahead of us.

From where I was standing at the mailbox, I could just see Annie's house. The broken windows stared dumbly at the horizon. From the second-floor bedrooms, I knew, one could see far across the Lake, and on clear days Canada was visible, a thin black line on the horizon. For a moment I thought of going to her again; I had so much to tell her, and I wanted to take her in my arms and let her know that everything would be all right.

But the same small voice in my head spoke up again. *Just let her be*, it said. *If you really love her, let her be.*

I stuck the envelope in my shirt pocket and turned toward the house. I could hear the music clearly from where I stood out by the road. The musicians had shifted tempo now, after their initial lament. They were playing fast and hard, all three of them, with the peculiar pulsing tempo of genuine Irish music. The rhythm of Ceili music is irresistible, and to answer its call is instinctive. I could hear the entire house reverberating as dozens of feet stomped on the hardwood floor. I shuffled a few steps of an impromptu jig as I headed back.

My life has been made of stories from beginning to end, and just when it seems one is ending, a new one begins. The world itself is woven of stories, each man and woman and child of us threading our own brightly colored tale into the bigger story that was already being told as we were born, and that will continue to be woven by others long after our threads have run out. But I have no fear that the stories themselves will ever run out. Stories are what I was fed on as a baby, a young boy, a teenager. Grandpa was overjoyed that I'd come along, he'd said, because my arrival meant he'd finally have someone to talk to in the big old house, someone who would listen to his stories, to help breathe life and color back into them. And it meant also that he was not, as he'd feared, the last of the Manns, but that there would be more of us, and that perhaps things would be different from now on. I know he thought this in the same way I know everything else about who I am and the people I come from: Grandpa told me, in his deep, rumbling voice. He'd held me in his arms the day he found me on the steps, looked deep into my blue Mann eyes, and felt a great and unutterable sense of relief. And from that first moment, he'd begun telling stories.

Now that I was alone, the sole survivor of hundreds of years, the same thought began to occur to me, and I knew that I wouldn't be the last of the Manns. More would come along, someday. I would take them through the house as Grandpa had taken me, leading them through it by their tiny hands, room by room, telling them the stories of the Manns who'd once inhabited this place and were now long gone in body, but who lingered in spirit and would continue to do so for as long as their names were spoken aloud. I could see this happening already, sometime in the future. It was time to stop looking behind me, and to turn my attention instead to what lay ahead.

And I knew that when I looked into their baby-blue eyes, I would feel about them the same way Grandpa had felt about me. I would feel pride, joy, completion. We are daredevils, superpeople, heroes, we Manns. Small-town heroes, but heroes nonetheless. And I would think to myself as I looked at them what Grandpa had thought when he looked at me for the first time: *Perhaps our greatness has only just begun.*

By this form of story telling, the Blair Witch would be merely a misunderstood old woman with a penchant for rock collecting and making charming stick figures out of ~~wood~~ sticks and twine.

The narrator at times seems to have swallowed a case of happy pills. (47-48)   Needs a Nothingness

Poor Billy the Bastard.   West twist, a "A Cool
                                                        Million."
Robinson Crusoe, Tom Jones, David Copperfield
              Horatio Alger.   Harry Potter.
John Irving, Stephen Millhauser

He's like Opie.   The Summer of '42.

Mark Leyner he's not.   "Illegitimacy Never Had It So Good"

❽ Billy doesn't seem to realize the depth of
   his own narcissism, self-absorption and
   familial adoration when he blithely admits
   to keeping photocopies of his own letters,
   "[I'm] infatuated with my own way of expressing
   myself," nor ❊ in the novel's coda, "We
   are daredevils, superpeople, heroes, un Menns...."
   Acknowledging that he may be the last of the
   family line: "Perhaps our greatness has only
   just begun" (369).

              You half expect him to kiss a Polaroid
              of himself each morning as he
              wakes up, bright-eyed and bushy-tailed.

He's not the weirdo wearing his dead family's clothes.

(328) When ~~they start~~ they're fearful of incest with —cousins, it seems a bit dim.

- romanticization, rose-colored glasses
- easy to read, glib
- old-fashioned prose, a la Dickens, affected dictio
- too many opinions about the stories, lack of balance

(2)

(39) ref to Dickens (41) "lad" (42) greatness

(46) "time is a river" (48) the photo (49) unafraid

(53) Fried Baloney (55) 7 yrs old (61) cartoon villain

(65) Know Yourself (67) white trash (70) black guy sounds like Stepin Fetchit

(76) simple good & bad people (104) anachronistic slip

(111) phony confronting the bully scene (120) a man/Mann

(129) never able to keep mouth shut (140) odd in the Eighties

(140) incest (151) superpeople (156) "intellogst, friendly, good-lookg" VAIN AND SHALLOW

(160) a writer! (163) losing his virginity (187) embarrassing

(194) 50 years behind times (201) kills Simpson smug

(204) "perfect" (209) Camaro/Corvette (211) more compliments

(215) "My Hero" (228) the rejection letter (238) "writers"

(239) time sequence error 14-16 in 3 months.

(247) cliché (255) "This is horrible" about his fiction

(256) "a family historian" (269) awk thoughts in italics/lesbian fears

(287) "a wonderful little man" (310) Indian Ocean

(302) Hippies and war/Vietnam (319) his parents clothes

(330) telepathy? (331) greatness (356) clueless narcissist